PRAISE FOR CAME

D0404405

By the same author

THE AGE OF TYRANNY
The Traitor God
God of Broken Things

Cameron Johnston

THE MALEFICENT SEVEN

ANGRY ROBOT

ANGRY ROBOT
An imprint of Watkins Media Ltd

Unit 11, Shepperton House
89-93 Shepperton Road
London N1 3DF
UK

angryrobotbooks.com
twitter.com/angryrobotbooks
Can evil ever be good?

An Angry Robot paperback original, 2021

Cover by Mark Ecob
Edited by Simon Spanton and Gemma Creffield
Set in Meridien

ISBN 978 0 85766 908 7
Ebook ISBN 978 0 85766 909 4

Printed and bound in the United Kingdom by TJ Books Limited.

9 8 7 6 5 4 3 2 1

MIX
Paper from
responsible sources
FSC
www.fsc.org   FSC® C013056

To Mum and Dad,
who have always been there for me.

PROLOGUE

Fortress of Rakatoll, day twenty-three of the siege.
Seven hours before it all went to shit.

Fifty-one wooden posts were hammered into the ground, forming a line just out of bowshot from the fortress walls. Just before sunset, roaring braziers were placed before each one so both sides could witness the coming atrocity.

The captured nobles were stripped naked and dragged kicking and screaming from their pens, then bound to the posts as their men watched, helpless and cowering behind the crumbling walls of the fortress.

After five years of war, Black Herran had finally trapped most of the remaining royal families of Essoran and the remnants of their armies in Rakatoll, and she was eager to display the horrors she had in store for them. The disparate rebels, outcasts, bandits, mercenaries and monsters that made up her army were every bit as keen to watch their one-time oppressors suffer.

Black Herran, dread demonologist and supreme general, surveyed her army and smiled as any who met her gaze flinched and looked away. As dangerous as they were, it was good to remind them that she was far worse. They pushed and shoved and cursed one another, but did not dare draw steel. Only their bowel-loosening terror of her held this army together.

She stood with two of her captains, as thirty thousand bloodthirsty men and monsters scrutinised the captives struggling against their bonds. Coin changed hands as bets were placed on who would last the longest.

Black Herran ran a bejewelled hand through her short, red-tipped hair and looked to her fair-haired lover, who had refused all bets.

"Come now, Amadden," she said. "You are not usually this squeamish. Will you not choose one of their highnesses and make a wager with me?"

The warrior scowled and flicked a speck of dirt off his bright and shining breastplate. "Most might be corrupt, but some fought bravely for what they believed in."

"Do you always have to be such a prig?" Amadden's older sister Maeven said, her long dark hair wild and untamed in the wind. She was a powerful necromancer, and Black Herran's right hand – far more important to the general than a bed warmer like her brother, and she knew it. She shoved past him and flipped a gold coin into Black Herran's waiting hand. She pointed to a slender man in the middle of the line. "I choose that one. He is saving his strength instead of wailing and struggling. He will die well."

"I have the far left then," Black Herran replied, picking one at random.

With that, the night's festivities began.

As the sun sank below the horizon, the general's shadow demons slipped from cracks in the earth to pool at the feet of the captives. By flickering firelight, her army watched liquid darkness rise up the wooden posts and form razor-sharp teeth and claws. They cheered as the devouring began, jeering as their once-overlords screamed their throats red-raw. Her demons started with the toes and slowly ate their way upwards, stripping off skin and fat before gnawing on muscle and bone.

The little sister of her two captains, Grace, chose that moment to slip through the cheering throng towards her siblings. In one hand she carried a platter of cheese and cured meats, while the other clutched a much-patched brown sackcloth horse with one eye. She was golden-haired and beautiful despite the plain dress and sooty smears. None of the hardened killers in the army dared to even look at her in case Maeven's dark magic rotted the offending eyes right out of their sockets.

Grace tutted. "You forgot to eat, my sillies. You have to keep your strength up to fight the bad people."

Amadden hissed and moved to block her view of the fortress and the ongoing atrocity. "I told you to stay inside our tent."

Maeven rolled her eyes. "I asked her to fetch us food. Stop coddling her – this is the world Grace lives in, and she is capable of dealing with a little blood."

Her brother's face flushed an angry red and he reached out for his older sister's throat. Grace shoved the platter into his hand instead.

Maeven smirked, knowing he would never truly lay a finger on her in front of their sister. Losing Grace's affection would destroy him. As much as they disagreed on what was best for Grace, both would die before they let anything else hurt her – and they had ensured that everybody who tried had died.

The necromancer yelled encouragement to the screaming captives and grinned, her eyes unblinking as she took in the spectacle.

Amadden's face twisted in disgust as he watched his sister. His hand twitched around the hilt of the sword sheathed at his waist. "If Grace didn't love you..." he muttered through clenched teeth.

Grace's eyes were blank as they scanned across the horror of dying, devoured nobles, then flickered back into life as she met Black Herran's gaze. "Make sure you eat too. Keeping this army in line must be tiring."

Black Herran sighed. Grace always had a way of seeing the truth of things. She was so weary of their constant squabbling, requiring her constant intervention to keep them all from murdering one another. If it wasn't the bandits or rebels fighting over ideology and gold it was the ogres trying to eat the orcs, and her selfish captains were even worse – every one of them had their own agenda. Black Herran knew if she got up and walked away here and now, it would take less than an hour for them to be slitting each other's throats, Amadden and Maeven included.

In a similar way, only Grace kept her family together: she had taken it upon herself to look after her siblings by caring instead of killing. Amadden and Maeven only suffered each other's presence for their sister's benefit, and at Black Herran's command. The three siblings had never been the same after witnessing the murder of their parents and grandfather: Maeven had plunged into an obsessive study of death and necromancy, her brother into war and the search for some universal truth to reveal the purpose behind his pain, and their sweet and innocent sister had retreated almost wholly back into happier childhood memories. Grace's vulnerability had made her brother and sister easy to recruit, and their fierce protectiveness enabled Black Herran to mould them into deadly weapons.

The nobleman that held Black Herran's bet soiled himself, enraging the demon below him. It surged upwards and into his mouth, his screams muffled as it ripped its way down his throat.

"Alas, a poor selection on my part," she said. "Maeven, you have command. Ensure the attacks resume once the troops are done with their games. At first light, I intend to lead the final assault."

Black Herran headed for her command tent, and Amadden followed, his eyes filled half with adoration and half with fear. Just the way she liked her men, but not what she needed right then.

She slapped a hand on his breastplate. "No. Go and see to the army, and your sisters."

* * *

Back in the command tent, Black Herran slumped into her chair and savoured the relative peace and quiet. It didn't last. Atop the small table to her left, a silver hand mirror looted from a king's bedchamber, then enchanted using his blood and torment, trembled and spat sparks – the owner of her soul demanded her attention, and he was not forgiving of delay.

She took a deep calming breath, picked it up and held it at arm's length. Her reflection rippled and faded as another took its place, this one far from human.

Furnace-hot winds blew through the mirror, carrying the brimstone stench of Hellrath and the cries of tortured souls. Atop a throne of glistening bone and stretched, still-living human skin, lounged a bloated toad the size of a war horse, with eyes and tongue of flame: Duke Shemharai of Hellrath, the mighty demon lord who had granted Black Herran immense power in exchange for her soul. His sheer presence hit her like a hammer to the face, but she endured and hardened her expression – it was never wise to show weakness to a demon. Behind the throne loomed his fearsome general Malifer, a titanic armoured monster covered in red scales, something between man and crocodile that was ever ravenous.

"My precious mortal puppet," Shemharai said, purple lips smacking and spraying spittle. "Soon you will have all that you desire. You will finally uphold your end of the bargain and open the ways to Hellrath, and my conquest of your world. You may keep the continent of Essoran but all the other lands and seas of Crucible shall be mine – do not dare to disappoint me, wretch." His burning eyes dipped towards her belly and his misshapen nose twitched. "I smell you are with spawn." He licked his lips. "A delectable morsel. Should you wish to sell it..."

"You will get everything you are due, mighty Duke," she replied, eyes lowered. "That, I promise."

The Duke wheezed a laugh and waved a webbed hand. The image in the mirror rippled and reformed into her own sour expression. She sagged into a chair, relieved his overwhelming presence had departed.

Duke Shemharai was greedy for blood and souls to fuel his never-ending war with the other great powers of Hellrath, and that had made him easy to manipulate. Now that it was time to deliver what she had promised, she found she had other ideas in mind.

Being with child complicated many matters. Nobody but her had known, and while she had yet to discover any shred of maternal instinct, it had got her thinking about a future beyond this brutal war of hers. She had been blind, obsessed with revenge and conquest for so very long that she had not stopped to consider anything past her victory. What would she actually do after becoming Empress of Essoran? A mortal ruler in a world that would become a feeding ground for the demons of Hellrath...

She sat in the darkness of her command tent nursing a goblet of cooling blood, listening to the raucous music of the siege as it entered the final few hours. The distant screams of dying men did not hold the lustre they once had, and the prospect of imminent victory roused little joy in her heart. The entire continent of Essoran lay like glittering jewels in the palm of her hand... and she felt nothing. She was just going through the motions. This wicked world of Crucible had not seen might like hers in an age, and yet it all seemed so petty now.

Beyond flimsy walls of red canvas, her army's barrage continued through the night: the thunk of heavy catapult arms and the whoosh of burning balls of pitch sailing through the darkness. Magic crackled and boomed to the cheers of blood-mad warriors who lusted for a dawn that offered death and gold and glory.

She grimaced and upended her goblet. The blood didn't hit the ground; instead, it disappeared into a pool of deepest shadow that slicked out from beneath her seat. Invisible tongues lapped up the blood and the darkness vibrated with pleasure.

Black Herran looked to the living darkness pooled around her feet – her beloved shadow demons, summoned from their home by pit-born magic. Considered weak by the other inhabitants of Hellrath, they were her servants of choice, raised on her own blood and power. Unlike her mortal forces, they would never turn on her. They were all that she trusted, in this world or the other. The demons stroked and comforted her, relieved that the mighty Duke had turned his burning eyes from this place.

"What an arrogant prick," she growled. After a moment's thought she slammed the mirror down onto the table, shattering it.

"I want more than this," Black Herran said, rising to her feet. "Shemharai and his bargain be damned. I deserve more than the eternal servitude his path offers. As do you, my shadow sisters. Do not fear, for I have ways to ensure he never finds us."

The shadow demons stilled, shocked that their blood-sister would forsake her bargain and betray such a great and terrible power.

She whispered of futures yet to come, of plans already under way for a better life.

They understood. They feared. But they trusted too.

Black Herran took a moment to think of all her captains, including her lover Amadden, and his sister Maeven. "Fuck them," she said.

The shadow demons enveloped her. When they drained back into the cracks in the earth there was no sign of the dread demonologist.

Her captains, loyal veterans of five years of brutal battle, marshalled her squabbling army and continued the siege, unaware that their general had abandoned them on the eve of total victory.

BOOK ONE
The Gathering Storm

Forty years later…

CHAPTER 1

The imp kept its horned head low and crawled over the rocks, hissing as frozen spikes of granite stabbed its scales and numbed its feet. It found a vantage point overlooking the miserable human village of thatched roundhouses that squatted in the mouth of the winter-bound valley below. It hunkered down to keep watch, shivering and wrapping its leathery wings around itself to keep in what meagre warmth was left.

The chill slowly sapped its hellish heat. Concentration began to drift and drowsiness set in. Nictitating membranes flickered as its eyelids drooped. Then, the fear returned, a red claw twisting in its guts. It bit into its hand and the imp hissed with pain, blood steaming where it met icy rock.

It had been forty years since Black Herran last summoned it from the cosy fires of Hellrath, but the imp's terror was as fresh now as it had been then. Pretty words could never mask her ruthless ambition, worthy of the Dukes of Hellrath themselves – the imp was no fool; it knew beings far more powerful than itself had failed Black Herran and met fates far worse than death; were, in fact, still meeting it.

From its high perch, it waited and watched, invisible to feeble human eyesight. After hours of darkness the outer world's sun began to rise. The imp's keen eyes squinted as the first of the humans arrived, the ones it had been told to spy upon. At first it only felt contempt, but as they drew closer it tasted the power they carried. Horns trembled and claws dug gouges into stone. All thought of sleep fled. It kept very, very still.

The Falcon Prince and his men marched south past the snow-capped stone cairn he had erected so many years ago. He had almost forgotten this place. The pile of rocks marked the grave pit where he had tossed the bandits who had been the last ragged remnants of Black Herran's army. He had dug the pit and laid their stones with the same two hands that had cut them down. It lifted his spirits to remember a deed well done.

He arrived at the outskirts of Borrach with the coming of the dawn, riding his proud white warhorse through a foot of pristine snow. He wore shining silver battle plate and the gilded visor of his helmet was wrought into the fearsome image of his predatory namesake. His eyes were no longer human, but orbs of holy golden fire. He was the chosen of the Goddess, the bringer of light and the holy truth.

He topped a rise and studied the crude village below as the last snowfall of winter began to peter out. His breath misted the air as he ordered his followers to begin the purge.

Three holy knights, inquisitors bearing the Bright One's greatest blessing, moved up to flank him, riding white stallions that were the brothers of his own powerful beast. Grand Inquisitor Malleus, with his severe features and shaved head, marched a hundred footmen downhill in silence through the snow, the proud bannerman in the lead holding high the gold-on-white sunburst emblem of their Goddess. A dozen white-robed acolytes came with him, shaved and serene, murmuring prayers.

They advanced through the morning mist, silver armour and white fur tinted red by the sun rising over the hills. The footmen silently encircled the slumbering village, and in their twos moved to the door of each hovel, naked steel ready in their gloved fists. They looked to the inquisitors and their godly prince, waiting for the final command.

The Falcon Prince surveyed the thatched hovels of the heathens and shook his head sadly. His sword lifted and fell, shining blood-red as it cut the dawn-light. His men kicked in the doors. Where they found them soundly barred, they hacked through with axes.

Villagers screamed as they were dragged from their beds into the village square. They were stripped of furs and blankets and, at sword-point, forced to kneel on the frozen ground. One hovel resounded with the clang of steel and screams. Two footmen lurched out, one missing a hand and the other with a gaping ruin of a face. A burly farmer scarred by numerous fights roared and leapt through his doorway after them, hatchet swinging wildly.

The Falcon Prince scowled and levelled his blade at the peasant. "Oh, great and glorious Bright One," he cried. "Strike down this servant of evil."

The farmer looked up, mad-eyed and furious, eager to kill.

Golden fire lanced from the sword to burn a fist-sized tunnel right through the heathen's chest. He crumpled to the snow, a gaping hole where his heart had once been.

All of the Bright One's holy knights were able to channel a tiny fragment of Her burning power to smite Her enemies, but the Falcon Prince wielded vastly more than any mere inquisitor. He took great pride in being Her chosen, Her guardian, Her beloved.

After that unseemly display all resistance ceased. The prince and his entourage took up their reins and trotted down towards the square and the gathered villagers. Footmen bowed at their passing and kept their eyes lowered.

"What d'you want with us?" an old woman demanded, shivering in her nakedness in winter. She glowered her challenge at the armoured knights.

Grand Inquisitor Malleus lifted a finger and a footman

slammed the butt of his spear into her belly. She fell, gasping and curled up with pain. He glared down at her. "You speak to his holiness only when asked, filth."

The Falcon Prince slid from his mount and handed the reins to a waiting footman. "We are holy knights of the Lucent Empire," he said. "Which of you worships the Bright One?" None raised a hand. "A pity."

He paced up and down before them, scrutinising each villager in turn. "Dark tales have reached us of what occurs in this accursed village: witchcraft and sorcery. Perhaps worse things. Which of you practise such abominations? Who among you bargains with monsters and demons? Speak now and mercy shall be yours."

Silence.

He smiled coldly and moved to a young woman clutching a baby to her breast. She trembled with fear as he lifted his gauntlet. He slipped a cold steel finger under her chin and tilted her face up to meet his burning gaze. "Tell me, daughter, which of the others engage in such foul practices? Illuminate us and mercy will be yours, for you and your child. You will both be absolved of all sin."

She clutched her baby tight. "There's no dark magic or demon worship here. We follow the ways of the Elder Gods is all."

"Your Elder Gods, like the Skyfather, are vile demons in disguise," he said, regarding her child. "I do love children. So pure. So innocent. It would be a crime to allow their souls to fall from the path of righteousness into the corruption of your heathen ways. Tell me, has your child gone through the ritual dedication to your false gods?"

The woman swallowed and gave a shake of her head, then glanced to her right. A tear rolled down her cheek.

The Falcon Prince turned to face a wizened old man with a walking stick. "So, *you* are this village's sorcerer."

The old man's stick snapped up, the tip clanging against the

Falcon Prince's breastplate. He scowled, brown teeth behind scraggly white whiskers. The tang of burning tin filled the air as his sorcery manifested – talons of darkness that burst from his stick to attack the Falcon Prince.

While his robed acolytes gasped and prayed for his protection, the Falcon Prince merely made a mental note to flog whichever naive soldier had allowed the old man to keep his stick. The dark magic touched his breastplate and blew apart like dust hit by a stiff wind.

The old man's face fell, and the tip of his walking stick with it. He leaned on it heavily as blood drained from his face. "That's that then, I reckon."

"The Goddess protects the righteous," the Falcon Prince said.

The old man spat at his feet. "Righteous? You lot of murderers are every bit as depraved as that Black Herran ever was."

The Falcon Prince's armoured fist rammed into the old man's jaw. Bone snapped and teeth shattered as the man flew backwards.

"You dare compare *me* to the disgusting likes of *her*?" the Falcon Prince roared as he slammed the heel of his boot down on the man's skull. "Nothing but lies and wickedness escape your lips. I hunted the last of her followers down and buried them in a pit only a short distance north of here. Lies." He slammed his heel down again and again until bone crunched inwards and blood and brains turned the snow pink.

He stared at the mess for a moment, then took a deep, calming breath. "Deal with this," he ordered. Two footmen dragged the dead sorcerer to a hovel and flung him in, then tossed the heartless corpse of the farmer in on top. Another knelt before him to clean the mess off his boots.

Grand Inquisitor Malleus pointed an accusing finger as his gaze swept the crowd. "Who else among you practise the dark arts?"

This time fingers were quickly pointed and denials fervently screamed. The Falcon Prince left the task of winnowing truth from lies to his inquisitors and instead faced the sun and murmured a prayer to the Bright One, asking forgiveness for the necessary bloodshed.

Once all the children were taken aside it did not take his knights long to separate the handful of merely tainted adult souls – those who had recanted their heathen faith unprompted – from the dozens of irredeemably corrupt. His men shoved the vilest worshippers of evil and the dabblers in evil sorcery into their hovels and blocked the doors up with wood and stone.

"The wicked must burn," Malleus said, lifting his hands towards the red rising sun. The power of the Goddess flowed through him and the thatched roofs erupted into flames.

They watched and listened as the screams began, men and women clawing at wooden walls with splintered fingers, desperately trying to escape the smoke and fire while their children outside wailed in horror.

Some of his men turned away, sickened. "Do not dare avert your eyes," the Falcon Prince demanded. "If we must end their sinful lives to purge this land of evil then we must also suffer the unpleasantness of doing so."

They watched the houses burn until all the wicked were silenced.

The surviving adults huddled in a fearful clump, trying in vain to cover the eyes and ears of their children. Of the adults, only three women and two men of Borrach had proven worthy of the Bright One's mercy.

He signalled his men and they lifted the villagers to their feet. The Falcon Prince himself assisted the young woman with her child, both exhausted from terror. "Fear no more," he said softly. "Your pain is ended. Your tarnished souls now belong to the Bright One, and She will wash them clean of all bodily sin with Her own loving hands."

They began escorting the terrified villagers towards the

cliffs overlooking the shore, where they would kneel in prayer before Grand Inquisitor Malleus until just before sunset. The Falcon Prince prayed they would all pass their second test.

One way or another, the Bright One's light would cleanse their souls.

The imp remained motionless until the inquisitors were all at the cliff edge and fully occupied with the remaining villagers. Only when its own safety was assured did it launch itself into the air, wings flapping with the might of terror. Those humans wielded the powers of a god, and not even the wicked magic of its summoner, the legendary Black Herran, could stand against that.

At least, not alone.

CHAPTER 2

Days later, an aging woman stood in the trampled snow at the edge of Borrach, surveyeing the smouldering remnants of the once-prosperous village. Waves crashed against a nearby rocky shore and a frigid wind blew in off the sea to throw her white hair into disarray despite the lacquered wooden pins set to control it. She leaned heavily on her walking stick, as much from emotional fatigue as taking pressure off her grumbling hip.

The demonologist once known as Black Herran had ordered her shadow demons to carry her north through the secret places below the earth, to witness the fate of this village. To understand what would be coming for her when the snows retreated and the road south through the mountains reopened.

Footsteps behind her, soft sighs on the ashen earth, and an old, familiar sensation came with it: a shiver crawled up her spine as the chill of the grave seeped into her old bones.

She did not turn to greet the woman who had once served as her vicious right hand. "Maeven."

"Forty years without word," the necromancer said. "And now my old general sends a demon to summon me to this wretched ruin. Has age addled all your wits, Black Herran?"

"I abandoned both position and name long ago. I am known as Dalia now. Call me that or call me nothing at all."

The necromancer's dank breath caressed her cheek as

she leaned over Dalia's shoulder. "I would prefer to call you a corpse. Because of you I lost everything. So, you had best explain why I should not rip your soul from your withered flesh and keep it as my plaything."

Dalia turned and smiled. "I would wish you a hearty good luck with that. I fear the great Duke Shemharai of Hellrath would come to collect his property. Provisions have been made for such an eventuality."

After forty years apart they were finally stood face to face once more. They locked gazes, each trying to take the measure of the other.

"You always did have an answer for everything," Maeven snarled. The necromancer looked like a woman of thirty-odd summers instead of a natural age of over sixty. A closer look revealed she was well preserved rather than young, thanks to some trick of her magical arts. A puckered, ugly old scar cut across her face, only partially covered by a black tattoo that writhed up her neck and stretched across her cheek. The tendrils of inky black seemed to possess a life all of their own, moving through her skin like it was water.

"This is also your fault," Maeven said, running a finger down her cheek. "When you abandoned us, my brother went insane. He tried to murder me and abducted my sister, Grace. After I stitched my face back together I fled the ruin of your army and sought out my family. But I have found no sign these past decades. My brother boasts little magic of his own, but what little power of manipulation he does possess makes him almost impossible to find when he does not wish it."

Dalia shrugged. "He was unstable to begin with, and you were little better." She thought the necromancer might once have been considered pretty. It wasn't the scarring that made her ugly now: the callous look in her eyes and the twisted soul lurking behind them did that all on their own. The stink of death clung to Maeven like a lover's embrace, and every bit as obvious as the grey wolfskin cloaking her shoulders.

"Tell me," Dalia said. "Do you still carry that little box of bones with you? Some nights I heard you conversing with them, and occasionally I fancied something replied."

Maeven snorted and looked away. "You expect answers after everything you have done? You are the one that owes me answers, hag. Your demon told me that you know where Amadden and Grace are, and that is the only reason I am here. It is the only reason you still live."

Dalia nodded and turned her attention back to the village. "I know exactly where they are, and we will discuss that later. First we must discuss those who destroyed this village."

There was nothing left for crows and carrion eaters here; a village of five-and-fifty souls reduced to heaps of bone and charred timbers. Wind speckled her cloak and face with fine ash.

Dalia stirred the debris of a house with the toe of her boot, uncovering a blackened human skull. The old woman's expression didn't change – she'd done far worse to far more in the past.

The necromancer gave the human remains exactly as much notice as she would a dead fly. "Such a charming place," she said. "Explain why you called me here."

It was as callous a response as Dalia had expected. Both of them gained power from death, and they were well-used to it. Necromancers siphoned power from the act of dying, the energy released as a soul fled its corpse. As for demonologists, they were more concerned with the power born of pain and torment, and the blood that bore a creature's lifeforce throughout the body. The soul might be powerful, but only blood could open the secret ways to Hellrath. For demons, pain and torment were their finest of feasts. A demonologist's only use for souls was as currency, bartering them to others for favour and power.

Dalia cleared her throat. "I am reforming the army."

Maeven's laughter shrieked out across the dead village. "Are you mad? On the eve of victory you betrayed your captains. You betrayed me! And left without a single word. When they learned you had fled the field, the army turned upon itself. Rakatoll could barely believe its luck as we slaughtered each other outside its walls. Why would those of us who survived that day lift a hand to do anything other than slit your throat? Some thought you dead, but I knew better. Death would not come so easily to the likes of Black Herran."

Dalia shrugged. "Is it my fault none of you were up to the task? Were you little children needing your hands held every step of the way? I left you an army and an entire land ripe and ready to fall before you. And what did you do with that opportunity? You fell upon one another like hungry wolves. You could have been rulers, but you botched it."

Maeven ground her teeth. "Why. Am. I. Here?"

Dalia gazed at the ruined village. "Come the summer, the Lucent Empire will march south through the mountains. The town of Tarnbrooke occupies the southern mouth of this valley. Once the Lucent Empire crushes it, they will have free rein to expand through all the lands of the south. They will destroy the old ways, purge cities, and enforce worship of their new goddess. That must not come to pass."

"I am no damn hero," Maeven said. "Even if I could stand against an army, why in all the hells would I do it for you? Where has all this new-found concern for others come from? You are up to something I wager."

Dalia grinned, nothing pleasant. "Tarnbrooke is mine. It has been home to my family for forty years, and that is more than enough reason."

Maeven stared. "Family? You?" She laughed, almost driven to tears. Her mirth faded as fast as it had come.

"Yes, family," Dalia snapped.

"I pity your spawn."

Dalia ignored her. "I have lived and loved in Tarnbrooke all these years, and the years wrought a change in me. Time tempers the rage of the young and holds up a mirror to expose how selfish we used to be. I was so full of fire back then, so set on tearing it all down." She sighed and shook her head. "I can't say it has all gone, but my fire has dimmed and the sharp edges long since filed off my claws so that I may better comfort those that I love. I have been happy."

Maeven sneered at that. "You have changed beyond all recognition."

"You are in no position to judge me. On anything," Dalia replied. "To change is to live. Only the dead ever remain the same. And if you think I would not burn the world to save those I love, then you are badly mistaken – do not rekindle my old fire if you cannot handle its heat.

"I offer you a trade," Dalia swiftly added, tracing the necromancer's scars with her gaze. "Your service in exchange for the answers you yearn for. You searched all the lands for Amadden and Grace and never found a trace these past forty years. I pledge to bring your hated brother to you and tell you where your golden-haired sister Grace is. They both still live. What is your answer?"

Maeven rocked back on her heels, jaw muscles clenching, one eye twitching. "You will tell me now or else I walk away."

Dalia shook her head with exaggerated sadness. "No, my dear, you won't. Nobody else can tell you the secrets you desire. If you remember what I was then you know you cannot force these secrets from me. Death has no hold on me – other powers hold stronger sway over my old soul."

Maeven stretched a hand towards her, the black mist of death magic steaming from between her clawed fingers... then hesitated, a flicker of doubt in her eyes. "What proof do you possess?"

"None but my word. Never have I lied to you. I promise if you stand with me against these god-touched knights of the Lucent Empire then I will bring Amadden to you."

Maeven scowled. "You are mad – the Lucent Empire will

march right over us and whatever dung heap you call home."

Dalia scowled in derision. "I am not so weak as you imagine. I need you to gather my surviving captains. I made you my right hand for a reason – of them all you were the most vicious and the most manipulative. Will you do what I ask?"

They were both silent for some time, staring at the swirling, smouldering ashes of Borrach. Finally, Maeven spoke. "If you truly know the location of my siblings then I will do it."

Dalia handed over a scroll tube stuffed with pages of parchment. "This case contains the locations of my old captains. It also holds pages of purchase ledgers, accounts, reports of troop movements, and other things that detail the Lucent preparations for war and conquest over the last few years. Familiarise yourself with these and it may aid you in recruiting the others. I leave this task in your capable hands while I prepare the battlefield. Best be swift, we have little time remaining if you want your answers."

Maeven glanced at the first document: a list of names and locations. The familiar names made her grimace. "And how long is 'a little time' exactly?"

"Three months," Dalia replied.

Maeven's eyebrows climbed. "So be it. Before I leave, do you wish to know what the Lucent inquisitors did with the survivors? I imagine they will do the same to your little town without my help." Her lips quirked into a mocking smile. "The ghosts of this place whisper such horrors into my ears. And the Lucents dare to call such dreadful men 'holy knights'..."

"I suppose I should hear it," Dalia replied calmly. "I must know the hearts of the foe we face."

The necromancer led the way, squelching along a muddy trail following tracks heading up towards the sound of crashing waves. She stopped at a cliff edge and looked down to where gulls squawked and squabbled over red morsels. Salt and seaweed air couldn't disguise the sour stench of rotting meat.

"They marched their captives here," Maeven said. "The ones that renounced worship of the Elder Gods."

Broken bodies sprawled on the rocks below; men, women, even a couple of children... though it was hard to tell them apart now. Sad and bloated shapes floated in rock pools, picked over by scavengers.

"They made all but the very purest of souls fly," Maeven said. "After they were blessed, the Bright One was supposed to save them. Gather their tarnished souls to Her bosom, or some such nonsense. I suppose they failed some test or other. It was still a better death than being burned alive in their own homes like the heretics they consigned to Hellrath. The survivors were taken away for training and indoctrination by the acolytes."

"I wager the tortured souls of the dead tell you many such stories," Dalia said, studying the necromancer's cold eyes. "I suspect I would not care to hear them all."

Maeven smiled thinly, scarred lips whitening. "No, you would not. The scars you see are only flesh; I have many more, and have suffered much in the years since you abandoned me."

Twisted and foul a creature as the necromancer was, it was not all of her own making. Dalia took a long, lingering look at the heaped corpses and felt that old, familiar rage stir in her breast. It was not nearly as buried and forgotten as she had wished. She held her walking stick white-knuckled and turned her back on the dead.

She had searched far and wide for heroes, brave folk, stout of heart and strong of arm, willing to make a stand against the Lucent Empire. She'd found none. The Order of Oak, the Knights of Stone, the Sisterhood of Spears... all of the old orders were too afraid to face the behemoth grinding towards Tarnbrooke. They were all certain of the futility and the folly of even trying to fortify the town. No heroes were coming to their aid. So now, she was forced to turn to her old, dread monsters to save her world. But they were as likely to kill her as the enemy.

"Do you think you can control them?" Dalia asked. "Their fear of me and my authority will have dwindled over the years."

The necromancer smirked, a sordid mix of malevolence and pleasure. "Oh, I can't promise any sort of control over such wicked creatures as our old allies. The best I can do is bring them here and point them towards the enemy. Then they will do what they do best."

Dalia nodded. "So be it. After seeing the Empire's handiwork, I feel no compunction about using evil to fight evil. Bring my monsters home, summon your foul sorcery and use it to protect my town of Tarnbrooke. If my family survives, only then will I tell you what you wish to know."

The necromancer shook her head. "If in the middle of this mess it looks likely you will perish, you will tell me there and then. Otherwise, your family will not survive your fall."

"A fair amendment; agreed. When summer sun melts off the last of the snow and dries out the roads, the Lucent army will march. Be off with you now: bring me my vampire, the mad alchemist, the orcish warlord, the pirate queen and the once-god. Gather our creatures of darkness to stand against the army of the Bright One."

"As you wish, my *general*." The necromancer offered a low and mocking bow. "However, one answer will be mine here and now – why did you abandon our conquest forty years ago?"

Dalia looked south in the direction of her home. "I did it because of unexpected and unsought love, Maeven. Why else? Not for any man, of course, but for a child."

The necromancer's lip curled. "Love? For the fruit of your crotch? You must take me for a fool."

"And yet it is the truth," Dalia said.

Maeven studied her for a long moment. She sneered and then strode away, grey cloak flapping out behind her like a war-banner.

Dalia remained there on the cliff, thinking of past choices, of heartrending decisions made so very long ago. The wind tugged her towards the edge, urging her tired old bones to take one more step, to let go and leap.

How would the black-hearted Maeven react when she discovered that her own hated brother led the Lucent Empire? What would she do when Dalia told her what that deranged fanatic had done to her sister Grace on the day his goddess was born?

She took one last look at the bloated corpses broken on the rocks below. "What new evil have you wrought, my beloved Falcon? I should have seen the mad-eyed fanatic growing inside you. Perhaps I should have told you that you sired a daughter… But no. You would never have made a good father."

She snapped her fingers and a shadow demon detached from the cliff face and rose on legs of darkness. "Mistress?"

"Take your sisters and return to your lairs," she demanded. "Shake the hives and wake your slumbering spawn. I will have need of you in the coming months. Inform the others that my mortal life is ending. And that war is coming." She did not expect to survive the battle of Tarnbrooke, but she would make such an end as to make the gods tremble.

Maeven was more powerful than ever, and she had her own selfish goals, but Dalia was confident she could stay two steps ahead. The necromancer was arrogant, and had forgotten who she was dealing with. Just because Dalia had lived in peace and quiet did not mean she had grown feeble. "There is always another plan in play, my dear. Always."

CHAPTER 3

"Hurry, little man – stab me with your spear. Summon more of your god-touched magic and strike me down! Fight me! Fight!"

"You… you *monster*," the sole surviving Lucent soldier cried, stumbling back, spear slipping from his grip to clatter to the blood-slick flagstones of the ruined tower. "Bright One protect me!" Nearly blind in the moonless night, the soldier tripped and fell, laying wide-eyed and shaking amidst the dozen corpses of his unit, all shredded mail, flayed flesh and shattered bone. Even their holy acolyte's prayers of protection had proved useless before the monster they faced, and that man's shaved head now adorned a broken spear thrust into the earth. A pool of piss began spreading beneath the soldier.

The monster, Lorimer Felle, sighed and sagged, his unnatural flesh slipping out of war-form and back into human guise: claws retreated into fingers and toes, spiked tail retracted into a human spine, and his leathery hide smoothed back into soft dark skin. As always, he felt *lesser*, but the ever-present hunger also retreated to a dull roar, heightened only by the gaping wounds that marred his body. No matter. He would heal those as soon as he could be bothered to.

The vampire lord's once-fine scarlet tunic and fox-fur cloak hung in tatters around his broad black shoulders; the price paid for the change. The last of his finery was gone now that the Lucent Empire and their damnable inquisitors occupied his home of Fade's Reach. Mighty and enduring as he was, even he could not stand against such a host of men and magic. Not if he wanted to keep his remaining people alive.

"Pitiful mortal," he said. His voice was deep as humans reckoned, but after being in war-form it sounded weak and reedy. "Where are your god-touched knights with their golden fire? You think such a pathetic group can kill *me* with mere steel and petty magics? Fools." He picked up a fallen sword and separated the soldier's head from his body with a casual backswing.

He stepped over the corpse fountaining blood and returned to his makeshift camp in the shade of the crumbling south wall, to where his faithful old servant was pinned to the wall by a spear through the belly.

Only a month ago Lorimer had been at home in Fade's Reach, draped in fine furs and facing Estevan across a check board in the castle's library, each with a glass of ruinously expensive imported wine in hand as they advanced their playing pieces. It had been no surprise Estevan was winning again, but the vampire lord had learned a few new tricks from his books and was offering a good challenge. The fire had been roaring, the wine flowing, and it had been a most pleasant evening. Until the guards rang the warning bell.

Rushing to the window, they watched as over a thousand burning torches snaked up the hill – the Lucent army had invaded Fade's Reach. Their holy knights and fire drove Lorimer from his ancestral home. The last he had seen of it, they had been ripping his hunting trophies off the walls to build a bonfire of his belongings outside his own front door.

It had taken all of Estevan's calm logic to dissuade Lorimer from making a futile last stand. Instead, he had ordered all his people to flee, to hide and survive in the treacherous mountains of Mhorran's Spine where the Lucent soldiers would never find them. But Estevan, brave and loyal Estevan, had refused to leave with them and demanded to accompany him into exile. Come what may, he was determined to stand at his lord's side as they drew the enemy away from their people; the army followed in relentless pursuit of the vampire lord.

"Take your grace back, my Lord Felle," Estevan said, shivering in the freezing weather. His manservant's gaunt blood-spattered face twisted in agony, each breath a short sharp gasp of pain. His brown skin now held shades of deathly grey. "I shan't... have much need for it myself." He hissed as his legs threatened to buckle, body held upright only by the spear pinning him to the wall. Even his master's grace flowing through his veins could not heal such a wound, and the pool of blood beneath him was spreading with alarming speed.

"Very true," Lorimer said sadly. "You served me well, my old friend." The vampire's bloody wounds needled his ravening hunger, urging his jaw to distend and his teeth to grow into fangs that would rip and tear and swiftly devour. He would make it quick, a small mercy for a century of loyal service.

A familiar, loathsome voice pierced through the hunger. "Hold. He can yet be healed."

It took an act of enormous willpower to stop himself from tearing into the soft, succulent flesh of Estevan's neck, but his hate was stronger than his hunger. He spun to face the voice, hissing.

"Maeven." The last person he had ever expected to see.

She carefully stepped between the mangled corpses and sketched a brief bow. In one hand she clutched an obsidian knife with a silver hilt, and in the other a small glass vial, brandished like a weapon. "Well met, Lorimer Felle, Lord of Fade's Reach." She straightened, met and held his gaze. "Or you were, once."

He sensed the tingle of magic at work within both knife and vial and knew she had come prepared with deadly necrotic weapons. His body spasmed, jutting bone spines and razor claws. "Pray tell, why should I not feast on your withered heart?"

"For the very best of reasons," she replied. "Black Herran is alive, and she offers revenge on those same Lucent scum who have seized your home. Our previous personal entanglement has no bearing on current events. That, and I suspect you would find my withered heart somewhat tough and bitter."

He blinked and rocked back on his heels. "So, our old general has finally crawled back from whatever dank crypt she has been hiding in all these years? Most interesting." He chuckled, fangs causing it to emerge as a harsh hiss. He forced his flesh back into human guise; after all, he didn't need such might to slay a mere human woman. Her dark magic, of course, was another matter. The thrill of danger excited him.

"As for our personal business," he said, "heal Estevan and I vow to hear your words. Nothing more. Afterwards I will likely feast on your tainted blood."

His servant passed out from pain and blood loss and slumped onto the red spear, slowly sliding off the shaft. Lorimer held him in place, the spear being the only thing keeping his blood and guts from bursting out.

Lorimer's word had always been his bond, so Maeven shrugged, put the knife away in her backpack and slipped the vial into a pocket before approaching the dying servant. "Very well, but I think you will find your mind changed by what we have to offer you."

"I very much doubt it, creature. Black Herran's army is dust and my trust in her with it."

She examined Estevan's wound with a practiced eye. "You always did love this crusty old relic more than me."

"I value loyalty," he snapped, watching as she pressed her hands to the old man's chest. The flesh reddened at her touch and Lorimer smelled the sharp tang of sorcery on the air.

"Ease him off the shaft," she said. "Slow and steady."

Lorimer did as he was told and noted that no blood gushed from the closing wound. But the sight of that red and tempting flesh caused his teeth to itch.

They lowered Estevan to the floor and the necromancer straddled him, hands on his chest, nails piercing his skin. She muttered arcane words with too many syllables, ancient inhuman sounds that sent shivers rippling up even Lorimer's spine – an unsettling sensation for a vampire boasting innate mastery of his own flesh. This was the oldest of magics, the lore of blood and flesh and death.

Estevan's wounds closed, and for a moment Lorimer considered taking advantage of the distraction to rip the necromancer's head from her shoulders. Sadly, there were lines he wouldn't cross, and breaking his word was one of them. He refused to succumb to desire as others of his vampiric kin had in the past: he was entirely a monster, but who said monsters could not be civilised?

He left her to her work and began to feed while his fallen foe's meat was still warm, wolfing down the Lucent soldier in great glistening chunks, heedless of the blood and gore spattering his face and body. His gaze never left her. She was not to be trusted ever again. His own wounds began closing, the flesh replaced, mending without so much as a scar. Not that he paid it much attention – wounds and pain meant little to his kind. By the time he was cracking open bones to suck their marrow, Estevan was breathing easier. For the first time in weeks the old man's face was relaxed and peaceful. They had been through much hardship recently, and his servant was, after all, only human.

After an hour or so, Maeven groaned and clambered to her feet, stretching cramped muscles, her shoulders cracking. "Healing is really not my forte," she said. "It was close, but he will live. Though I cannot guarantee his future health. His organs were greatly damaged."

Lorimer flicked a gnawed human rib towards her feet. "Better than death. Now say your words before I kill you."

She wrinkled her nose at the ragged state of him and with the toe of her boot, flicked the rib off to one side. "You think to intimidate me?"

"Not intimidation," he replied. "I simply deny such a wretched creature as you the courtesy of table manners. Say your piece. Estevan is dear to me, but that only buys you a few more moments of survival."

She swallowed. "I don't expect your forgiveness for what I did in the years following the end of our war. I did what I felt necessary."

He said nothing and began cleaning his sharp teeth with a forked tongue.

"The Lucent Empire is growing stronger," she said. "Every year they expand their borders and spread the worship of their Bright One. The Alauna are scattered remnants. The Cahal'gilroy exterminated long ago. Vandaura, Fenoch Ford, Oakenholt and Fade's Reach have fallen. And now Borrach has been wiped off the map. The age of Elder Gods and old magic is ending and there is no place in their new world for the likes of us."

Lorimer dislodged a fragment of bone and spat it at her feet.

Unperturbed, she continued: "Tarnbrooke will be next. Black Herran and I intend on stopping the Lucent army there and slaughtering them before the people of that town suffer the same fate as Borrach and Fade's Reach."

He snorted. "Altruism is not in your nature, Maeven. What are you getting out of this?"

She shrugged. "Nor is it in yours. My personal reasons are my own affair. I am offering revenge, to face the inquisitors that drove you from your domain and rend them limb from limb."

He rose from his dinner and strode towards her, leaving a trail of bloody footprints. "Do not take me for a fool, harlot. I cannot defeat an entire army."

She held her ground. "You will not fight alone, Lorimer. Black Herran and I will fight with you, as will the others."

His hands twitched, eager to wrap around her throat and squeeze. "Black Herran is a betrayer and you fight for no one except yourself. You trust nothing except what you can kill and enslave."

She lifted a hand in warning, black mist writhing around her fingers. "Watch your tongue, vampire. You are undead, and I, a necromancer – this will not end well for you."

He smiled and flexed clawed fingers. "You think yourself the master of life and death, but I have trodden that knife's edge for centuries. If you think you can strip my soul from this house of flesh and bone, then you are very much mistaken."

Her eyes narrowed, and for a moment it seemed she might relish the challenge, but then she took a deep breath and lowered her hand. "We all stand to gain from crushing the Lucent Empire and we have much to lose if they sweep across all Essoran. Their faith holds no mercy for the likes of us, nor for any race other than human. Who now is left to oppose them? The southern city states and towns from shore to shore all squabble amongst themselves, and the barbarous tribes care more about warring with one another when not fighting the orcs."

He hissed in annoyance. "Cease cloaking your words in layers of deception. What do you stand to gain?"

She was silent for a long moment. "I made a deal with Black Herran. She knows where my brother and sister can be found. In exchange I am to help crush the army the Lucent Empire will send in the summer."

"Truth finally falls from your lips," he said. "Your obsession means nothing to me. What can you possibly offer to stop me tearing out your heart, never mind wage war on your behalf?"

She swallowed and looked into his eyes. "If you agree to protect Tarnbrooke for Black Herran then I will swear a blood oath that once we are victorious, I shall assist you and your remaining people to regain Fade's Reach."

That gave him pause. Her sorcery was undeniably formidable. "Assist? Pah! Once we are victorious you will swear to serve my people and I until Fade's Reach is free of the Lucent Empire."

There was no hesitation. "I agree to your terms."

He stared. This was... unlike her. Where was the bargaining and twisting of words, the wrestling for position and advantage?

Lorimer noticed Estevan's eyes twitch open. He had been awake and listening for some time. "My lord," he croaked, "I advise against it. This vile creature cannot be trusted."

Lorimer snorted. "I have not forgotten her nature. And yet I require her help to restore our people's home and freedom." He held up his hand and ran a claw down the palm to open up a long glistening wound, then extended it to her. "You will swear the blood oath here and now."

Maeven stared at it, then took a knife from her belt and nicked the back of her hand instead. "Wounds and healing are nothing to you – only idiots slit their palms open."

He grasped the back of her hand, their blood mingling. A frisson of binding magic ran through them both. The oath had been sealed. Estevan's eyes closed with a disappointed sigh.

"Well," she said, bending down to wipe her gory hand on the tattered gambeson of a Lucent soldier, "now that is resolved you had best take Estevan somewhere that he might recover. We need to make haste in recruiting all the others who still survive." She handed him the list of names Black Herran had given her.

Lorimer loosened a low and malevolent laugh. "Well now, this will prove interesting."

CHAPTER 4

From a shadowed doorway across the street, Lorimer and Maeven watched through the window as a fight broke out inside the decrepit shack the locals called a tavern. Years ago, some misguided devotee had carved the sunburst emblem of the Lucent's Bright One into the front door, and it was now overlaid with graphic sexual graffiti. The symbol split in two as a grizzled drunkard crashed through the tavern door.

The red-haired older man tumbled into the dark and muddy street in a shower of splinters, cursing and dragging two heavy-set farm boys down with him. He was tall with wide shoulders and battle-scarred arms, but his grey-shot tangled hair and bulging belly showed his best fighting days were long behind him. All three men's tunics and hose were ripped and stained with blood and beer.

Faces peered from the tavern's shattered doorway as the men exchanged a flurry of punches and kicks and then rolled through cart-churned mud and dung, cursing and grunting, limbs flailing. Drinkers exchanged coin as bets were placed.

Blood gushed from a fresh cut on the old warrior's forehead, staining his ginger beard. One of the farm boy's flailing elbows cracked into his face, causing blood and snot to dribble from an oft-broken nose.

The warrior grabbed the first farm boy by the throat and spat blood in his eyes. The boy yelped and rolled free, calloused

41

hands scrubbing at his eyes. It freed the warrior's hand to grab the other boy by the balls and squeeze. The second farm boy howled and then curled up cradling his crotch, sobbing.

The old warrior staggered upright, wobbling on unsteady feet. He closed one eye to focus on the prone form in front of him and then rammed a boot into the boy's belly. He swayed, peering at the two cloaked and hooded figures watching him from across the street. The man dismissed them from his clouded mind and began weaving back towards the tavern, slurring some kind of savage battle chant.

The first farm boy finished wiping the blood from his eyes and lurched after the old warrior. "Oi! We ain't done with you yet!" He swung a wide right hook.

The man swayed and the boy's clumsy punch sailed past his head. Maeven and Lorimer could not be certain if that was intentional or due to extreme inebriation. He spun, his own fist jabbing out to snap the farm boy's head back. It was a fine blow but then the drunken warrior continued spinning, arms flailing as he tried to regain his balance. The farm boy slowly fell to his knees and then pitched face-down in the mud. The older man finally managed to find his balance, then promptly doubled over and vomited a foamy stream of ale and bile over the back of the boy's head.

Disgruntled murmurs came from the tavern doorway as coin changed hands again. With the excitement over, the patrons slipped back into the warmth and their own ale cups.

Lorimer glared at Maeven. "Is this old and decrepit creature really Tiarnach, who was once a god of war? Are you certain?"

Maeven closed her eyes and sighed. "More of a demigod really, but he didn't take kindly to that. I am quite sure that is him. And you thought your position in life had fallen far, Lorimer."

Tiarnach yawned, then slowly toppled forward onto the farm boy's back and slid down to join him in the muddy pool of his own vomit, emitting rasping snores loud enough to wake the dead.

Maeven pinched between her eyes. "I can already feel the headache brewing. Damn him, he is going to be more of a nightmare than ever."

Lorimer chuckled nastily and approached their target. Tiarnach stank, not just of fresh vomit and alcohol, but the old sweat and sour piss scent of neglect. He grabbed a handful of greasy hair and lifted Tiarnach's face from the mud to examine him carefully.

"A face of barely healed scars with the stink of infection on them," Lorimer said. "He is no god or demigod. He is merely a mortal man long past his prime – nothing more than a drunken wretch."

"Tiarnach was the war god of the Cahal'gilroy," Maeven said. "A small god, granted, but still old and fearsome. Even as he is now, his knowledge of waging war is unsurpassed."

Lorimer's eyes held great doubt. "Never did any human display more ferocity than the Cahal. Those madmen fought against all odds, even against me." His voice held a touch of admiration, something Maeven had heard but rarely from his lips. "What happened to bring him to this sorry state?"

"Black Herran's documents say that after they failed to take the walls of Rakatoll the weakened remnants of the Cahal were hunted down and exterminated, oh, twenty years or so ago, by what eventually became the Lucent Empire," she said. "Not a man, woman or child of that bloodline survived. Tiarnach is a god without a people, and all their stories of his might are now whispers upon the wind."

"A shame to see how he honours the memory of his tribe," Lorimer replied.

Maeven scowled. "He lost everything. His family, his friends, his worshippers – his whole people."

"So touchy, Maeven. Did I hit a raw wound? How are your own family?"

"When was the last time you loved anything, you crusty old monster?"

Lorimer let Tiarnach's head drop back. He turned to face her, expressionless. "I love many things. Love was never *my* problem. You had best drag him on your own. I refuse to carry this stinking pig."

The farm boy with bruised balls struggled up to his feet and limped towards Lorimer. "You ain't taken this scum anywhere. He owes–"

Lorimer's clawed hand crunched through the man's ribcage. He ripped the heart free in a welter of blood. Maeven started – she hadn't even seen the vampire move. The farm boy gawped down at the hole in his chest for a split second, then collapsed to the mud.

"One for the road," Lorimer said, teeth elongating into fangs. He bit into the steaming organ with relish and ambled off into the darkness, leaving Maeven to try and figure out what to do with an unconscious man who was once a god.

Tiarnach was deep in the throes of the old nightmare. He was stuck reliving a moment of glory while knowing that the worst moment of his life was just around the corner, and yet unable to change a single thing.

The war god grinned and rammed his sword through the miller's chest, exulting as hot blood gushed over his hands. He roared in victory and lifted a bloody fist skyward, the cry taken up by his warriors. The old miller had been the last villager of Fenoch Mill to stand and fight the Cahal'gilroy. Tiarnach admired his bravery, and it was this man's honour to die by the hand of a god. Out of respect, he would take the man's skull home and keep it in his temple. The rest of the villagers were cowering curs who would die like vermin, drowned in the river instead of slain in honourable battle.

The Cahal'gilroy had never been dirt-grubbing farmers – they were a warrior people, reivers who came down from the hills to raid the towns and villages of soft southerners and slake their desires for women, men, meat and ale. Fenoch Ford had wisely paid them off in goods and livestock, but their neighbours at the water mill upstream had been defiant. An example had to be made before others dared to have the same idea.

His men whooped in delight at the discovery of barrels in the cellar of the mill, and on broaching them found them full of strong imported brandy rather than ale. The village's painted whores kept them entertained and the sounds of feasting, fucking and the screams of torment filled the air all night long. In the small hours somebody challenged their god to drain an entire barrel of brandy on his own. He accepted and he succeeded, naturally, being an immortal youth, but at the cost of all memory and consciousness.

It was the fire that woke him from his drunken stupor, boots smouldering as flames licked up the muddy leather. He groaned and staggered upright. His head hammered and rang. Smoke rose through the floorboards and the wooden stairs to the ground floor fell away into an inferno.

The entire mill was burning. Outside, men were screaming. He booted a window shutter open to witness the entire village enveloped in flames, every door blocked from the outside as his people within shouted for help, choking on the smoke. More warriors of the Cahal'gilroy lay dead in their blankets, throats slit while they slept off the strong alcohol. Mailed soldiers stalked the streets, felling more of his people before they were able to organise a proper defence.

A man armoured in silver appeared at the head of a force of archers, bearing the emblem of the Lucent Queendom on his white tabard. The visor of his helm was worked into the likeness of a falcon, and he was laughing. The village's painted whores laughed with him, cleaning the blood of Tiarnach's kin off their knives.

The war god snarled and climbed out onto the creaking water wheel, deftly making his way down towards the battle. "I'll gut you all like pigs!" he shouted.

"Your people die at the hands of the Falcon Prince," their leader shouted. "And so will you, heathen."

An arrow thudded into Tiarnach's chest, then another flew deep into his thigh. He ignored them and leapt from the wheel onto one of the soldiers, slamming the man's helmet into the ground so hard that steel and skull flattened. He picked up a fallen sword then staggered, nausea rising as a horrific emptiness filled him. All his power was draining away like a burst wineskin.

Somewhere, far to the north, the families of his warriors, his devout believers, were dying.

"Ignorant savages," the knight said. "It was pitifully simple to kill them while you slept. I hope you enjoyed my barrels of brandy, for it was your last. My second, Sir Malleus, is even now burning your hidden village and putting all within it to the sword. The murdering days of the Cahal'gilroy are finished."

Tiarnach roared and lifted his sword. An arrow took him in the throat. Such pain! Mortality was returning as his believers died. He stumbled backwards and fell into the river. Blood and water gushed into his mouth, choking him as the current sucked him under.

He came to, screaming, washed up many leagues downriver. He was alive and whole with wounds healed by the dregs of his godly power. But he was alone. Truly alone. The Cahal'gilroy were all gone: men, women, even the blessed little children...

It took him a week on foot to return to the ruin of his hidden village. The Lucent bastards had left the corpses where they fell to be gnawed on by wolves and scavengers. He built a pyre and watched them burn, wailing and sobbing until he ran dry. Finally, no longer a god but just a man, he set out for revenge.

He failed.

Time and time again he failed until it broke him. He gave up trying as the Lucent Queendom became a rising Empire with the Falcon Prince as its head.

Twenty years of failure – it couldn't help but change a man...

Tiarnach jerked awake from that old nightmare, sodden, freezing and face down on rough wood, splinters jabbing his cheek. The acidic burn of vomit lingered at the back of his parched throat and it felt like an army of blacksmiths were beating the shit out of his skull. He rolled onto his back and blinked away the sleep, staring up at a blanket of grey cloud. He opened his mouth to catch the drizzling rain but it didn't help.

He was lurching up and down, and the sounds of hooves and wheels sloshing through mud gave him some inkling that he'd been tossed into the back of a cart. He smelled blood, and it probably wasn't his. Slavers again most likely. They'd regret taking him.

He raised an aching, heavy head and peered at the two cloaked drivers with hoods up against the rain. His tongue felt like sandpaper as he tried to moisten cracked lips, wincing as he encountered a split.

A sodden family of five trudged through the mud at the side of the road, barefoot. Their few belongings were stuffed into sacks slung over their shoulders. More refugees from the Lucent purges in the north. Easy prey for bandits, or an old warrior in need of coin.

"Our passenger is awake," a deep male voice said, the one holding the reins to the shaggy and sorry-looking horse pulling them along.

The other hooded figure turned slightly towards him. Tiarnach started to grin when he noticed the shapely bulge of breasts under the cloak. Then he saw the black tendrils of tattoo swarming across her scarred face, reaching towards him hungrily.

"Fuck's up with your face?" he blurted out.

"This one is a natural born charmer," the man said. "Perhaps he likes his women soft and pretty."

The woman's eyes narrowed.

"Ach, no," Tiarnach said. "Scars tell a story. Why hide it behind that weird tattoo?"

"My personal business is not your concern," she hissed. "And you would do well to remember that, Tiarnach."

He grinned. "Fierce little thing, eh? Wait... how do you know my name?"

The man up front glanced back, revealing dark skin and a strip of black cloth tied across his eyes. Tiarnach blinked and sat up, regretting it instantly. He leaned over the side of the lurching cart and retched.

"You, big black lad up there," he gasped. "You're either blind or a blood drinker from Fade's Reach. Which is it, eh?"

The man grunted. "Seems the alcohol hasn't rotted all your instincts."

The woman up front chuckled.

He groaned and massaged his temples. "Don't know what you are, lass, other than bloody stupid – some sorceress most like – but him, well now... I'm older than you might think. Old enough to remember a tribe of folks with dark skin that make their home in the northern fells. Not many of them sort this side of the sea, save the ports o' course, and none of those smelled like blood."

"And just what do you remember of my people?" the man said.

Tiarnach grimaced as he sifted through dusty old memories. "Grand fighters they were. Good scholars, too, what with charting the stars and suchlike. The old magics ran strong and fierce in their veins: shapeshifters, shaman and blood magicians and the like. Wait, no, that voice... can it be? Lorimer Felle?"

"How interesting," the woman said, turning to the driver. "I spent two years with you and that one just told me more of your history than you ever did."

The man remained silent, staring straight at the road ahead.

Tiarnach groaned. "And that stink of death means that's a necromancer next to you. Is that your chattel then? Or... ah shit." He squinted through the rain. "It's fucking Maeven, isn't it? Fucking hells. I thought I'd seen the back of you bastards years ago."

Maeven turned and smiled coldly. "So good to see you again, Tiarnach."

His day was worsening by the second. He scowled and struggled up onto his knees, fumbling at his hip for the sword that he'd swapped for a barrel of ale in some dingy tavern years ago. "The fuck am I doing in the back of your cart?"

"Brash and brave and slightly stupid," she said. "He does make for a perfect war god. You, my dearest Tiarnach, have been conscripted. Black Herran is back and going into battle."

Tiarnach shuddered. He pulled a dagger from his boot, hangover forgotten. He roared and went for Maeven, blade plunging towards the back of her head.

Lorimer didn't bother to turn around, but his right hand shot out to block the blow. The dagger went deep and grated against the bones. "You are badly out of practice," he said, wrenching the dagger from Tiarnach's grip. "This harlot owes me a service, and I will make sure she lives to pay it." The vampire resumed steering their horse away from the deepest puddles and potholes, and left the dagger jutting from his flesh to make a point.

There was no chance of winning this fight. Tiarnach groaned and slumped back into the rear of the cart, trying not to throw up again. "What do you want from me?"

"What do *we* want?" the necromancer said. She chuckled. "You have the wrong idea. We are here to offer you something that *you* want. We offer you a glorious death in a battle against impossible odds. However, if you can pull yourself out of your ale cup long enough, then we offer you a chance to take down the Lucent Empire. They slaughtered the last of your people, did they not?"

She had his full attention now. All his physical pain was as nothing. He stared at her for a long moment. "Aye, before they called themselves an Empire. But I am not what I was. I am an old wastrel of a man. And you two are not enough to face the Lucents. As for Black Herran, she is a coward and a traitor."

"Who said we would be alone?" Maeven replied. "The others will soon be joining us."

"So," Tiarnach said, "Black Herran's surviving captains are gathering once more. Well, well. The leader of those so-called holy knights of the Lucent Empire, this Falcon Prince, is responsible for slaying my people." He balled his hands into fists. "I'll take a shit in his mouth and put his head on a stick for all to see!"

She shrugged. "If you can kill him, by all means. I can only promise you the opportunity to face him in battle."

"Aye, good enough for me," he said, eyeing the pitiful family of refugees struggling through muddy cart tracks behind them. "Wasn't doing much with my life anyway. Might as well throw it away on your suicidal scheme. I'll ram my sword right up that silver bastard's baby-soft arse until it bursts out of his cowardly throat."

He paused, pondering. "Eh, do either o' you happen to have a sword on you? It'll take a bit more work with that wee dagger."

CHAPTER 5

The Crow Tavern was as disreputable an establishment as you could find, even in a port town frequented by pirates. It was nestled in the cellar of a warehouse on the ramshackle docks of Sickle Bay, serving pirates, fences, mercenaries and thieves of all kinds. It was not the place for polite company, which of course made it exactly where Maeven, Lorimer and Tiarnach needed to be: it was a sorry, sodden trio that squelched through the slush and mud on foot, heading towards the bright red door that beckoned them in with thoughts of a roaring fire, hot food and drink.

Out in the bay, the sun was sinking below choppy waves, the white caps burned red and gold before swiftly fading as darkness descended. The Twins crested the horizon, their pale moonlight casting a silver cloak across the sea. Lorimer removed the strip of cloth protecting his sensitive eyes and sighed in appreciation of nature's beauty. Such a sight was entirely wasted on the other two.

"You didn't have to eat the horse," Tiarnach grumbled, using the doorstep to scrape mud from his caked boots. "One of us could have ridden the thing after the cart's wheel broke."

Lorimer shrugged. "It seemed only fair. Why should we walk while she rides?"

"Could have been me riding it," Tiarnach grumbled.

"Will you two bickering bastards please shut up?" Maeven snapped. "It's not like you get cold or tired, Lorimer. And

51

judging from the state of him when we found him, Tiarnach doesn't give a damn if he's covered head to toe in mud." She glared down at her own filth-crusted boots and cloak. "Burn you, Lorimer, I need to bargain with these people and you have me filthy as a beggar."

Lorimer chuckled. "My apologies. I did not realise pirates were such clean and fragrant people."

She scowled, shoved open the door and stomped down the steps to the cellar.

Warmth, light, and raucous chatter rolled over them as they opened the second red door leading to the inside of the Crow Tavern. Lorimer blinked, eyes adjusting to the dingy light. Men and women of all colours and creeds clustered around benches lit by smoky rushlights, their laughter and bawdy ballads filling the room. The rough wooden walls were adorned with wanted posters from towns and cities all across Essoran. Some were even from across the sea, written in strange flowing script. Every poster displayed a sketched depiction of sea-bitten bastardry and vile banditry with a list of their dark deeds noted below.

A stained Lucent Empire banner hung from the far wall. Three drunken sailors were using it as target practice for their throwing knives, betting on who could hit the centre of the sunburst emblem. People spat on it in passing – they bore no love for the fanatics here. In hushed, worried tones, some among them discussed the tales of armies said to be mustering in the Lucent heartlands. A holy war was coming, one said.

Tiarnach grinned and made straight for the ale barrels, and the greasy barkeep busy filling a jug with foamy nectar.

Lorimer grabbed his arm. "Keep your wits about you. We have no use for a drunken fool."

Tiarnach pulled his arm away – or he tried to. Lorimer was far stronger than any mere human. After a moment of tense deadlock they broke apart, Tiarnach cursing as he made his way to the bar. "Ale. Big black fella there is paying."

Lorimer tossed a coin to the barkeep for an ale and a cup of cheap wine for himself and sat on a rickety stool in the corner. A dark-skinned sailor with blue tattoos and gold studs in his nose and cheeks approached, thinking that perhaps here was a far-flung countryman of his. The vampire glowered until the man found somewhere safer to be. Lorimer's ancestors had fled across the sea because of their sort and he claimed no such thing as kin elsewhere.

Maeven scanned the crowded room until she found the sailor she sought, a loudmouthed bald man with bronze skin, gold hoops through his ears, and a long flowing moustache. He was sat at a table crowded with assorted scum, tossing bone dice from a cup.

"Your name is Craggan?" she said.

The man's gaze slid away from his dice to travel up and down her body, not even glancing at her face. "That would be me, wench." He shoved one of his companions down the bench to clear a space next to him, and when she sat, he rested a hand on her knee. His hand began creeping up.

"Come drink with old Craggan, darlin'. Then we can–" He finally looked up high enough to notice the tattoos writhing across her scarred face. His jaw dropped. A strangled choke broke off his leching. He snatched the hand back, staring at his grey and floppy fingers, pulsing black veins spreading down towards the wrist. He lurched to his feet and backed away. His companions exchanged worried glances, stood and drew daggers from their belts.

"Next time you take liberties you lose the hand," Maeven said. "If I feel merciful. I am here on business and I will not bandy pointless words with you."

He swallowed and nodded. The flush of life slowly crept back up to Craggan's fingertips.

Maeven's brow furrowed. "You will take me to meet with Verena Awildan. We are old friends, she and I."

Silence rippled outwards from her table as every head in the tavern turned to watch.

Leaning against the bar with a jack of ale in his hand and a foam moustache, Tiarnach laughed, harsh and mocking in the sudden silence. "Best listen to the bitch, little lads, or she'll have your balls for earrings."

His laughter got their backs up. Craggan flexed his fingers and drew a notched hatchet from his belt, glaring at Tiarnach before turning to Maeven. "Friends? Enemies more like. Who are you to come here and make demands of me? Maybe I'll just finish what somebody else started and split your skull right proper." Two of his men moved up beside him, one old and fat and the other young and cocky, both wielding keen-edged falchions.

Maeven glanced at her own allies, neither of whom showed any interest in helping – Tiarnach observed with malicious interest and Lorimer just looked bored.

She attempted a friendly smile. "I would prefer that you just agree to take us to Verena."

He snorted at that.

"Very well," she continued. "How many of your men do I need to kill to force your hand? A precise number would be most helpful."

He laughed. "This one doesn't have both her oars in the water."

Maeven held out a hand towards the older man on Craggan's right. His lifeforce was weak, heart struggling from years of over-indulgence. Her hand squeezed into a fist. The man stiffened and then dropped like a puppet with its strings cut. He convulsed and foamed at the mouth.

"One."

She pointed to the young man on the left and encouraged necrosis to bloom inside his neck. His face grew angry red and puffy, then purple and green as he clawed at his swollen throat and gaping mouth. Blood vessels burst across his face and he too, toppled.

"Two."

A man came from behind. One hand grabbed her backpack while the other readied to thrust a knife into her side. She didn't even bother to look. He screamed as the flesh and muscle of his hands and arms crumbled to ash, bones clattering to the floor.

"Three."

The entire tavern went for Maeven, knives out.

"Stop!" Craggan screamed. "For the love of the sea, get away from her." They froze, confused. He stared at her like she was a venomous serpent coiled around his waist – he might have seen magic before, but nothing like this. He knew just enough to be very afraid.

He licked his lips and cleared his throat. "No more. I'll do what you ask."

"That wasn't so hard, now, was it?" she said, patting his shoulder and making him flinch. "This makes everything easier." She leaned in close by his ear. "Maybe I'll take you to my bed later. Imagine the fun we can have."

She escorted a shivering Craggan and two of his crew towards the door, pausing to speak to Tiarnach. "Call me bitch one more time, drunkard, and I will rot your cock off."

He smirked as she marched out of the door.

Lorimer rose to his feet. "It is not wise for you to antagonise Maeven. She will make you pay for that interruption."

"Aye," he replied. "I expect so. But if you thought I would go into battle without taking the measure of my allies then you know sod-all about war. I'm no' that drunk. Seems she's still as nasty as ever." He downed the dregs of his ale, picked up a falchion belonging to one of the dead men, and tested the short sword's point with a finger. "Bit blunt. Guess I'll just need to ram it harder up that Falcon Prince's arse."

Lorimer considered that for a moment, then turned to face the murmuring crowd of drinkers. "And a good evening to all of you fine ladies and gentlemen. Please do feel free to come after us with your weapons drawn." He grinned, shark teeth glinting in the rush-light, and followed after his companions. He was sorely disappointed nobody took up his offer. Eating a horse had taken the edge off his ever-present hunger, but its coarse blood had lacked the rich and savoury complexity of a human meal, and, as Lord of Fade's Reach, he was accustomed to finer fare.

Aboard Craggan's caravel, *The Sly Griffin*, it did not take long for Maeven to cow his motley crew of freebooters and set them to work rigging the ship to set off. Their captain's grey and fearful expression did most of the convincing, but Lorimer's increasingly agitated flesh, rippling and forming claws and spines, would have done the job alone.

"What is wrong with you, big man?" Tiarnach asked.

Lorimer quietly seethed, glaring at Maeven. "You did not mention travel by sea."

She frowned, puzzled. "I had hoped to find her ashore in Sickle Bay, but Verena is queen of the Awildan pirates so surely it cannot come as a total shock."

"I will wait ashore," he said.

Maeven shook her head. "You swore an oath to protect Tarnbrooke. You can't do that sitting here being useless."

He growled and paced the deck, causing the sailors to scurry out of his way on each pass. Two refused to come down from the rigging and one leapt overboard into the rowboat tied to the side, just to avoid going near him.

Tiarnach climbed to the quarterdeck and slouched against the rail, glowering at the sailors while Maeven had a quiet discussion with their captain. They heaved the anchor aboard, the sails caught wind, and soon the sleek caravel was cutting out to sea. The crescent beach and the flickering lights of the docks and buildings of Sickle Bay gradually faded into darkness, leaving them alone on the slate-dark sea with only the light of the Twins and the spread of stars to guide their way.

Lorimer stared out to sea, clawed fingers gouging furrows into the wooden rail as the deck pitched and heaved beneath him.

Maeven approached, brow furrowed. "What is wrong with you? I have never seen you this unsettled."

"Surely the big bad blood drinker isn't seasick?" Tiarnach said.

Lorimer leaned over the rail and spewed a torrent of red over the side, making Tiarnach laugh. "I will rip your spleen out, you ginger bastard," he groaned.

Maeven quirked an eyebrow. "Really? Seasick? You?"

Lorimer's flesh sagged, and he held onto the rail for dear life. "My every sense is heightened. Your own may as well be smothered in blankets."

She grunted. "Makes sense. Well, you might not require sleep, but I do. Stand guard and wake me if anything interesting happens." With that she retired below decks.

"There, there, big man," Tiarnach said. "You still have me to look after you."

Lorimer snarled and tried to reply, but threw up again instead.

With Lorimer incapacitated, it didn't take long before one of the sailors dredged up the bravery to approach the more natural-seeming figure of Tiarnach.

A barefoot boy dressed in loose linens edged towards him and swallowed before speaking. "Er, excuse me, sir," he said. "Who are you people?" He aimed a fearful glance at Lorimer. "*What* are you people?"

"Ach, don't be afeart lad. Your fine captain is taking our sorceress to see Verena Awildan." The crew froze in place, listening intently. "We're all old friends, her and us." Tiarnach didn't see the need for subtlety, and as a rule he had always preferred the direct approach. All that dancing about the point just irritated him, and the slipperiest ones could drag that nonsense out for days.

The boy started sweating. "Our queen has no friends," he whispered. "She is a monster. She'll flay the skin off your backs for commandeering one of her ships. Best you steal the rowboat and take your chances elsewhere."

Tiarnach wiggled a finger in his ear, then examined the crust of wax. "That so? Our sorceress says she'll rot the cock off any man that steps out of line." It was a half-truth, but he reckoned she probably would. She certainly could. "Not sure I'd be up for risking that. As for the big angry man down there, well now, he'd be more likely to rip your heart out and eat it."

The boy swallowed. "And what about you?"

Tiarnach smiled sadly. "Me? I'm nobody now. Just a drunken old fool with a sword and a bad attitude."

The boy and the rest of the crew looked at him sceptically, thinking he was trying to hide an even worse secret. Tiarnach looked up at the Twins, shards of silver cutting through black clouds. He had once been so much more...

"Leave me be, boy. If you know what's healthy for you, be about your work." He settled down on the deck and rested his head against a coil of rope. Closing his eyes, he thought back to old battles, heard again the clash of steel and screams of the dying enemy, thousands of voices crying out in agony and pleading for mercy. Not one mortal had ever received that from the Cahal'gilroy. Those victories didn't fill him with the glee they once had. That fire inside him had burnt out, leaving only ashes. He was a hollow man, and with his tribe dead and gone, it all seemed so pointless.

He pulled from his filthy tunic a small clay jar of whisky – swiped from the Crow Tavern during the mayhem – and downed half in one long series of gulps. He barely felt the burn sliding down his gullet, but the hazy oblivion it offered was a welcome respite as he settled down to rest his eyes for a moment...

An outraged roar and screams woke Tiarnach just in time to see moonlight glint along the edge of a dagger plunging towards his eyeball. He rolled aside and kicked out. His boot caught the attacker in the ankle and something snapped. The boy howled and collapsed to the deck. Tiarnach staggered upright and scanned the ship, noting the broken segments of wooden rail, lack of Lorimer, and two sailors rolling in agony clutching shredded arms with white bone peeking through the mess. Of the rest of the crew, there was no sign.

Tiarnach drew his weapon and glanced overboard. Lorimer flailed in the sea, one arm desperately clutching the length of rail as he bobbed up and down while shouting for help. The big vampire floated like a boulder. He turned back to his attacker.

The boy held up an open hand. "Please, I'm only a–" The blade took his hand off at the wrist. He shrieked as blood spurted from the stump, then Tiarnach booted him in the face, breaking his jaw and shutting him up.

Tiarnach spat on his face as the boy bled out. "Old enough to kill, old enough to die." He raced towards the two men Lorimer had shredded on his way overboard. They didn't put up much of a fight as his sword rose and fell. He searched for the rest of the crew, and only then did he notice the rowboat on the far side was missing. He cursed at the sight of oars already churning away and a small sail rising up its mast.

"I'll gut the lot o' you," he shouted, swinging his falchion in the air.

Maeven burst through the door from the quarterdeck, blinking away the sleep, her hair in disarray. "What's all this shouting?"

"Scurvy bastards have abandoned ship," he said.

"Lorimer?" she asked.

"Looks like they tossed him overboard before bailing out."

"Throw him a rope before he sinks." She returned below decks to find Craggan still sitting where she had left him, calmly smoking a clay pipe.

"Something the matter?" he said.

"Order your men to return to their stations."

He sniffed. "Verena's orders are to abandon ship when faced with the likes of you lot. She will not allow enemies of power to set foot on Awildan shores."

"I just want to *talk* to the bloody woman," Maeven snarled.

He shrugged. "Then you should have sent a letter. In a few weeks—"

"I don't have weeks, and she has no time for this nonsense either! Everything you hold dear will perish unless you listen to me."

"Do as you will with me. I will not betray my queen."

"Loyalty, eh?" Tiarnach said from the doorway. "I admire that." He pointed a thumb over his shoulder. "The big lad though, I don't reckon he cares."

Lorimer blocked the doorway, a dripping mass of fang and ferocity.

Craggan's composure cracked and the pipe dropped from his lips. "Do whatever you want with me," he repeated, a little less convincingly, "but you can't do anything without a crew."

Maeven smiled. "Oh, I still have a crew." She concentrated and let her magic slip into the three corpses on the deck. They might be dead, but their flesh and muscles still remembered what to do.

Air wheezed from useless lungs. Feet dragged as the dead rose and approached. Blood drained from the captain's face as the boy with a missing hand and shattered face appeared behind Lorimer.

"I am no petty sorceress, Captain. I am something far worse." She waved the others away. "Let us go into your cabin and discuss matters in detail. I am sure you have something decent to drink in there, and torture gives me such a powerful thirst." Her animated corpses dragged him away kicking and screaming.

Lorimer and Tiarnach waited up on deck as shrieks rang out. The dead men returned and silently went about their tasks, manning the rudder and tweaking the rigging as best they could with body parts missing.

The silence between the two men finally got to Tiarnach. "Maeven's always been terrifying."

Lorimer glanced at him out of the corner of his eye. "So were you in your prime."

Tiarnach smiled sadly. "I was fucking glorious, wasn't I? Totally fearless."

Shrieks changed to sobs below decks. "So," Tiarnach said. "You can't swim, eh? I never knew that. How'd they manage to toss you overboard?"

"If you had stayed awake you might have noticed," Lorimer said. "I suggest you hold your tongue or I will remove it."

Tiarnach went to make a bad joke, then slowly closed his mouth. He offered Lorimer his small jar of whisky. The vampire took it and sipped. He nodded approval. They passed it back and forth in silence until it was finished. The screams and sobbing from below continued until dawn.

CHAPTER 6

On the deck of the mighty warship *Scourge of Malice*, the first mate of *The Sly Griffin* withered under Queen Verena Awildan's imperious glare. His surviving crewmen refused to meet her gaze. The old woman only stood as tall as his shoulder and yet her dark and angular eyes could break a man, and indeed had just done so. She paced up and down before him in dainty black shoes, a coiled, viciously barbed whip rhythmically slapping into her velvet glove.

Waves crashed against the hull, having less impact on the crew than their queen's whip against her palm.

Her grey hair was pinned up delicately above a warm, white slynx draped about her shoulders, the little animal acting like a living fur stole. Agitated by her ire, the rare animal opened its amber eyes and yawned, exposing needle-teeth. Irusen, she was told by scholars, was of the cat family, yet shaped much like a ferret and more elegant than both species. Verena spared a moment to rub its downy cheek with a finger, earning a soft purr of pleasure.

She wore a red silk dining dress with delicate thread-of-gold embroidery that exposed a generous portion of tanned cleavage. It was something a younger woman might wear to seduce a king; while Verena knew she was no longer smooth-skinned or as athletic as she once was, she didn't give a damn. Other than her own, only one person's opinion mattered, and he had been *well* on his way to showing his appreciation. She displayed her scars of age and battle proudly, even the ugly puckered scar across her left forearm that had been the parting gift of an old and vicious enemy.

She turned to face Craggan's men. "You interrupted my dinner to spout these lies?"

The sailor shuddered and sweat beaded his forehead. "It went just as we said, My Crown. The captain, 'e said the tattooed woman killed Fat Tom and Eck with sorcery, and another one of them weren't right at all – downright unnatural 'e was." Some of his men mumbled agreement. "Craggan always said to abandon ship and captain if we was boarded by magickers. Them as thought to retake the ship were slaughtered. We left them floating helpless with not a sailor among them."

She leaned in close and stared at him, searching for any hint of a lie. There was none, just honest panic. "On your feet and ready your steel. We will set sail to recover *The Sly Griffin*."

Dozens of pirates thumped fists against their chests and hurried to their stations. The lookout called down from the crow's nest, "Ship-ho! Sail to starboard."

Verena cursed and ran to the captain's quarters. Her husband stood up from the dinner table, his shirt half-unbuttoned. She paused to admire him for a moment. "No time for that, Henry. Keep the grandchildren below deck." She set down Irusen, carefully took off and folded her dress, and instead pulled on leather boots and armour.

Henry held out her sword belt and she buckled it on, sliding the sword around to rest comfortably at her hip. The slynx leapt back onto her shoulder and curled around her neck.

Her husband kissed her hard. "Stay safe out there, dear heart. I will take care of the little ones."

She kissed him back, laden with the promise of resuming where they had left off. "Let us hope it is a wallowing cog with a fat belly of gold and wine." In truth, a bad feeling was brewing in her guts.

She barked orders as she ascended the quarterdeck for a better view of the approaching ship. Her personal guards, armoured with heavy chain, helmets and shields, emerged from below decks to surround her with a wall of muscle and steel. Some strung war bows and laid out arrows the length of her arm, with heads wrapped in cloth and pitch, ready to set fire. One of them lit an enclosed charcoal brazier and made ready for battle. Her first mate Gormley, a huge and hairy beast of a man, joined her.

He handed over her spyglass and she peered through the sea haze. After some time, the sleek curves of a familiar caravel emerged, battling through the waves towards them.

"*The Sly Griffin* on approach!" she shouted.

Gormley drew his sword and tested its edge against his calloused thumb. A thin line of blood welled up and he grunted in satisfaction.

On deck, Craggan's ex-crew huddled together. "I thought you said there was not one sailor left alive among them?" she asked.

They looked at each other in confusion, then to their first mate.

She slammed a fist down on the wooden rail. "Speak up, sea-rats, or I'll have your tongues."

The Sly Griffin's first mate swallowed and wiped sweat from his brow with a dirty sleeve. "My Crown, I... there wasn't none, save Craggan who stayed behind. We all swear they was dirt-huggers, don't we mates?" His crew found their toes mutely fascinating.

She pointed to the sail in the distance. "Well, somebody is sailing that ship. You'd best hope there is a good explanation."

He swallowed and nodded.

"Draw your knives, you salty dogs!" she shouted. "If they board us, they will need to go through you first."

They blanched and shuffled their feet but did as they were told. As scared as these men were of whatever horrors were aboard *The Sly Griffin*, they knew Verena would flay them alive if they voiced any objection.

The *Scourge of Malice*'s crew fell silent as *The Sly Griffin* drew closer. The displaced crew of that ship lined up and steeled themselves to face their shame. Their first mate stiffened, staring out across the water at the distant figures manning the ship. His jaw dropped and blood drained from his face. He clutched a sea glass talisman of the Goddess of Storms tied around his neck and muttered prayers meant to ward off evil spirits.

"What do you see?" Verena demanded.

He turned to look up at her, his eyes wide and confused. "A ship crewed by dead men."

She studied the approaching ship through the spyglass, her eyes not being what they once were. An aging lunatic with flaming hair and bulging gut stood at the prow, stripped to the waist and waving a sword at them, but with the sea haze it was difficult to make out more detail. The wind whipped through his hair and beard and he was grinning as if eager for a fight. From the mass of scars covering his body, she had no doubt he had seen many. He seemed oddly familiar, a vague spark of recognition.

Lashed to the mast was a bigger man with dark skin, who would prove a more serious threat. Here was the unnatural creature that *The Sly Griffin*'s first mate had mentioned. His skin was covered in barbs and spines, and his fingers tipped with wicked claws. At a guess, Verena thought he might be a shapeshifter of some sort. Rare and dangerous as a wild beast, but nothing to be overly concerned about – an arrow through the skull could deal with those vicious creatures. She prayed he was nothing worse.

As she scanned across the oncoming ship and its handful of crew, something caught her eye, a hint of wrongness. She tracked back and stared at the two bloodied men tying lines to cleats and the boy with one hand and a smashed jaw manning the helm. Bone glinted through ragged wounds, and a black cloud of flies buzzed around them.

Verena lifted the glass from her eye, rubbed it, then took

another look. "Tits on a fish!" It was no mistake: the ship was crewed by dead men.

A hooded woman emerged from Craggan's cabin. She bore a strange tattoo with black tentacles across one side of her face that reminded Verena of her ruined dinner – it had to be that murdering sorceress *The Sly Griffin*'s crew had mentioned. A thrill of fear rippled up her spine as the woman turned and looked directly towards her.

Shit. Maeven. That explained the corpses crewing her ship.

It had been forty years since she last laid eyes on the cold-hearted necromancer, and she found it not nearly long enough. The old wound on her arm itched. Verena had been the commander of Black Herran's fleet, which thankfully limited her contact with the other land-bound captains. Sadly, that had mostly meant dealing with Black Herran's hand, Maeven.

Verena continued to watch them. The necromancer exchanged words with the shapeshifter, angry ones by their expressions. Then the red-haired warrior joined them and began running up a white flag of truce.

"My Crown?" Gormley said, nodding to her guards and their bows. "Want us to feather them?"

She pursed her lips, tapping the spyglass with her nails. It was tempting. So very tempting. But what would possess that wicked woman to approach her at sea, and why now? "Not just yet. I want to hear what they have to say first."

"And the sorceress?" he said, shifting his feet and clutching the amulet beneath his shirt. "I don't relish facing black witchery."

Verena scowled and rubbed Irusen's cheek. "Oh, we can deal with her sorcery well enough, can't we, my sweet little princess?" The slynx opened one eye and flicked a dismissive ear in *The Sly Griffin*'s direction before returning to sleep.

* * *

In the prow, Tiarnach leapt atop the weathered griffin figurehead, at ease with the lurching movements of the ship beneath him. For a moment he admired the inlaid bronze beak, eyes and claws, then peered through the sea spray. "Bloody big ship ahead, eh?" he shouted over the crash of waves and the wind. "I've never seen the like."

"Your tribe were savage hillfolk," Lorimer shouted back. "I doubt you have ever been on anything bigger than a log-boat." He was safely lashed to the mast, growling as the dead sailors shambled to and fro around him.

"A pox on what you think!" Tiarnach yelled. "You think yourself so old and experienced. You're a bloody stripling compared to me. I was taking the heads of your ancestors way before your da squirted you out."

"Please stop comparing the size of your manhoods," Maeven said, her voice cold as death. "Controlling these corpses is taxing enough without being distracted by your prattle."

She tried to block out their bickering as she focused inwards on her magic. There was something ominous ahead, a nothingness where her power could not enter. She had never encountered such a thing.

She chewed on her bottom lip, deep in thought as they drew closer to Verena's ship with every passing second. She had no idea what their reception would be, given that the last time she had seen the Awildan queen she had tried to rot the woman's arm off with magic. Unfortunate, but there was no escaping this now even if she wanted to.

"Fetch Craggan," she ordered. "It's time."

Tiarnach sauntered down below decks and returned dragging the ship's captain, sobbing and broken. There wasn't a mark on him, but he desperately clung to the warrior's arm and shied away from the necromancer's gaze.

Tiarnach raised an eyebrow and pondered asking Maeven for the details. For once though, he thought it wise to keep his mouth shut. Atrocity in the heat of battle when your blood was up was one thing, but this was cold and calculated torture, and he wanted nothing to do with it. He pried the man off his arm and dumped the quivering wretch in a heap at Maeven's feet.

She helped Craggan to stand. "Take command, Captain. We need your deft touch to bring us close to your queen. Corpses don't have the dexterity or judgement they had when they were alive. Once I have met with your queen, you are free to do whatever you wish. Take your place and relay your orders, Captain."

That seemed to bolster his spirits. He gripped the wheel white-knuckled and stared ahead at the *Scourge of Malice* with fevered longing. The corsair captain seemed to regain a measure of his old bravado as he barked orders and cursed the men, as if refusing to believe his current crew were animated corpses. Maeven relayed his orders to her minions, and their salt-scoured dead flesh remembered the correct physical responses. Where missing or shredded limbs and decaying minds proved inadequate – stumps and clumsy fingers pawed futilely at knots – Tiarnach had to step in.

Their course converged with the larger ship, its black bulk looming ever larger. The deck opposite and above them was packed by uneasy pirates bristling with bows and steel, staring down in horror at the living-dead crew. A few frightened and familiar faces filled out the front line.

Lorimer's mouth sprouted longer fangs. He growled at the sight of those who had pushed him overboard and rose to full hulking height, a monster of spite, spike and claw. He tore free of the bonds securing him to the mast.

Maeven placed a warning hand on the vampire's shoulder, stilling him for now. She kept her hood up and her face low in an attempt to hide it from the crowned queen of pirates until they were close enough to talk. As powerful as Maeven was, a flight of arrows might still kill her.

Craggan ordered the crew to strike sail and they coasted

closer until they were near enough for the *Scourge of Malice* to throw grappling ropes and secure their vessels.

"This was your stupid plan, Maeven," Lorimer said. "Try not to get us killed."

Verena was high up on the quarterdeck, but the former crew of *The Sly Griffin* cringed as she lifted her voice, a trembling line wavering between life and death, their lives slave to their queen's word. "Ho, *The Sly Griffin!*" she shouted. "Who is in charge? Which fool dared commandeer one of my ships, and kill my crew?"

"That," Maeven said, pulling back her hood, "would be me. It has been a long time, Verena."

The pirate queen's expression did not change. She looked to her archers.

Maeven hastily continued, "If you have no greeting for me then perhaps you do for Lorimer? No? Or perhaps Tiarnach – you two always did get along well."

Verena paused, hand half-raised to order the archers to fire. She stared down at the hulking mass of the vampire and the grizzled warrior. Trying to kill Maeven was one thing, and perhaps achievable, but an enraged Lorimer in a confined space? It was likely every human aboard would be torn to shreds.

"Tiarnach, you say?" Verena said, squinting down suspiciously at the grizzled, pot-bellied man that had once been a strapping eternal youth. There were indeed similarities there. She licked her lips. "Very well, necromancer, explain your actions or you die here and now."

CHAPTER 7

Aboard *The Sly Griffin*, Maeven bowed the precise depth as befitted meeting a queen. "Your Highness," she yelled over the creak of wood and slosh of waves. "We bring you tidings of urgent import and unfortunately your men offered only rape and violence instead of safe passage."

Verena was having none of it. "To Hellrath with you! You are a vile creature with death and disaster clinging to you like shit on a sheep."

Maeven rose from the bow to meet Verena's gaze. "We did not have time to play with cretins, not when your life and those of your children hang in the balance." Thanks to her interrogation of Craggan she knew a threat to Verena's family was the only way to safely get her attention. For a time. Trying to rot somebody's arm off was not the sort of thing people tended to forget or forgive.

The pirate queen ground her teeth and brandished her barbed whip. "Let us discuss your actions in depth." She turned to her sailors, who were uneasily eyeing the ship crewed by dead men.

Verena studied Lorimer and Tiarnach standing on the deck of *The Sly Griffin*. "Should those two move," she said to her crew, "cut every line and get them the fuck away from my ship. Fill them full of arrows if you have to."

* * *

"Charming," Tiarnach said as Craggan fled for the safety of the lowered rope.

"Indeed. As base as all of her piratical breed," Lorimer said, watching as Maeven clumsily climbed up the swaying rope. The crew gave her a wide berth, forcing her to clamber up and over without assistance.

"Ach, no, I wasn't being sarcastic," Tiarnach replied. "She's made of steel, that one. It gives me the horn."

Lorimer groaned. "You are attracted to withered crones with whips?" His hunger was rising and he could almost feel the crew's flesh ripping between his hands, and taste their blood on his lips.

"Don't knock it till ye try it," Tiarnach replied. "But this one is hardly that, you foul old leech. When I was a god, I often found that old crones spoke the most sense."

Lorimer shrugged, spines bristling. "How long do we give Maeven?"

Tiarnach squinted up at the sun and then studied the shadows cast on deck while scratching at his beard. "Until the mast's shadow reaches the wheel, I reckon. What do you plan to do if she doesn't return?"

Lorimer grinned his shark's smile. "Feed."

Verena enjoyed watching Maeven's laboured ascent of the rope: panting with the strain, feet and hands slipping. Had she felt so inclined, she could have ordered an actual rope ladder lowered to make it easier. But forty years ago this vile creature had tried to kill her, and had now murdered her men and taken her ship. No queen of the Awildan Isles could allow that to remain unavenged. All pirates bowed their heads to their Crown or they lost them – or a queen would inevitably lose her own.

As the wheezing necromancer clambered onto the deck, her crew clutched charms and in a dozen languages muttered folk-spells to ward off evil. The crew hailed from shores far and wide, and Verena hoped some of their protections were worth more than the breath wasted on them.

Verena descended from the quarterdeck to examine her old ally, her subsequent enemy, who had seemingly not aged at all. Irusen stirred around Verena's neck, the slynx's small body vibrating in agitation. Yes, things would turn out very differently this time, she decided. She would hear what Maeven had to say, and if there was any real threat to her family, she would force answers from her. Then the necromancer would die. Tiarnach she would try to save, if the mad savage could be persuaded to behave and have a drink with her. That land-pirate had always been the life of the party.

"Come this way," she said, turning her back and entering her cabin. She sat on a chair at the head of her table, waiting as Maeven – shadowed by the imposing bulk of Gormley – followed her in. Gormley closed and barred the door and then took station behind the sorceress, a knife ready in his fist.

Verena drummed her fingers on the table. "Begin."

Maeven cleared her throat. "Firstly, I should ap–"

"I have no time for apologies or excuses."

Maeven did not seem taken aback at her brusqueness. Instead, she leaned forward on her chair. "The Lucent Empire have built a fleet."

The drumming stopped. "Is that so?"

Maeven frowned, scouring her expression for any hint of what she was really thinking. She gave her nothing. "I had thought this information would have proven more disturbing. Have they not sworn to wipe your kind off the seas? To invade the Awildan Isles and put all pirate havens to the torch?"

"So I am told," Verena replied. "For centuries the Awildan queens have heard those very same boasts from the mouthpieces of kingdoms and city states all across Essoran. All have proved utterly incompetent at the task. Even Bridan Sere, called the greatest general in history, failed to conquer us. I reckon we have little to fear."

What she left unsaid was that Bridan Sere had been winning. Through numbers, magic and tactical genius, Bridan's fleet had forced her mother to resort to unleashing the Awildan bloodline's greatest secret – an ancient monster that slumbered in the deep darkness below the sea. Verena had accompanied her mother on a single small ship to face the massed fleet of five city states. There, her mother, great Queen of the Awildan Isles, sacrificed her life to the monster to save her people. When Verena returned home alone, not a single enemy remained alive. Verena had suffered nightmares ever since. Dread things lurked in the depths, with enormous eyes that stared deep into her soul, and hungered for it…

Verena suppressed a shudder and bent her mind back to the threat at hand. "The growing power of the Lucent Empire is hardly recent news to anybody with eyes and ears." She leaned back on her chair. "However, I have not received reports of warships being constructed anywhere along the coast, and you may trust that I certainly would have if they existed. I always pay attention to potential threats. So, then, necromancer, what now of your tale?"

Macven smirked. "Oh, I never said they were building them along the coast." She reached into her cloak and Gormley's blade was instantly at her throat. He flipped back the cloth to reveal a small scroll case on her belt. On removing the lid, he found it stuffed with papers. Verena waved him back. Maeven massaged her throat with one hand while the other pulled the papers free and pushed them across the table.

Verena glimpsed Black Herran's spidery handwriting and paled, shaken at last.

Maeven smiled coldly. "This warning does not come from me. She's back."

The pirate queen leaned forward, studying the papers.

"These pages of ledgers," Maeven said, "contain details of

seasoned timber, nails and steel fittings being delivered to Saroth Fort on the banks of the Caldar, along with orders for craftsmen to be sought out and brought there."

Verena rose and retrieved her silver-rimmed reading glass from a dresser fixed to the wall and peered at the papers. "The draft of a warship is too great for the Caldar," she said. On noticing Maeven's blank look she explained further, "The river is too shallow."

Maeven shrugged. "I bow to your knowledge, but Black Herran seems quite sure of it, and as you know she had – and apparently *still* has – demonic eyes everywhere. These documents clearly show they have spent years importing supplies, shipbuilders, blacksmiths and carpenters from across their empire. What else can it be?"

Verena studied the documents. They did indeed suggest that the Lucent Empire was building a great fleet – perhaps they had dredged the river to deepen it. They could be forgeries of course, but unless Maeven had also gained a master's knowledge of shipbuilding... "And what exactly do you want from me?"

"Oh, this is not for me," the necromancer said. "This is all Black Herran's idea. The Lucent army will march south come summer sun and drier paths, and she plans to crush them at Tarnbrooke."

Verena snorted. "Tarnbrooke has no army worthy of the name, nor walls high and thick enough to force a siege." She leaned forward. "And by all the hells, why would I ever help somebody who took one of my ships and tried to kill me? I should cut you down and tell my old general to go fuck herself with a hot poker."

Maeven grimaced and, for the first time in Verena's eyes, seemed ill at ease. "Black Herran's demons can go anywhere and get to anyone."

Verena stiffened. "I don't take kindly to threats."

Maeven sat there and said nothing.

"Where is the demon-fucking old bitch?" Verena demanded. "Where has she been all these years?"

Maeven gave her a knowing look.

"Tarnbrooke?" Verena laughed. "Rancid arse of a whoring sea-pig! She's spent her golden years in that run-down backwater? And she expects to bend me to her will?"

"Not just you," Maeven replied sourly. "I am gathering all of her surviving captains. Lorimer Felle, Tiarnach, you, and next I go for Amogg Hadakk. Lastly, I am tasked with retrieving Jerak Hyden."

Gormley hissed as the name Jerak Hyden was uttered. His face reddened and his hand and knife lifted, trembling with fury. Verena lifted a finger, chastising him with her gaze, promising a world of pain if he dared step out of line. He might be her first mate, but he was far from indispensable. Her chair scraped back as she rose to pace the room. "Madness, utter madness. Amogg was always a feral beast but she was useful, and honourable in her own way. Jerak is a true monster. I will have nothing to do with him." She looked to Gormley and his readied knife. Her lips pursed.

Maeven shook her head. "I would not recommend attacking me, oh righteous queen. As you are aware, I am no petty dabbler in the arcane arts."

"Is that so?" Verena said.

"My power runs deeper and darker than ever," Maeven replied. "Do not force me to defend myself."

"By all means – offer me a demonstration of your might."

Maeven pointed a finger at the queen's chest. Nothing happened. The necromancer's eyes widened in shock, staring not at Verena but Irusen's amber eyes glaring balefully from around her queen's neck.

Verena smirked as the little slynx hissed and bared its needle-like teeth. "Your power means nothing. Sorcery can no longer touch me. I should gut you and feed you to the sharks."

Maeven glanced at the wooden deck beneath her. "Can you

say the same for your ship? It was once living, after all. All that lives turns to dust, sooner or later. Would you like to wager which power would prevail, when not targeting you directly? In any case, if you did kill me your deaths are assured."

The pirate queen glanced at the deck, lips thinned. "By assured, I take it you mean the vampire lord? An arrow through his skull will leave him wallowing in the sea unable to reach us."

A smile slid back onto Maeven's lips. "Let your best shot try, if you are willing to lose your men."

Verena sat back down. "You are quite right. I should cut the lines between our ships and set *The Sly Griffin* adrift. Then I will set her alight with fire arrows."

Maeven hissed. "You would abandon one of your own ships?"

"Pride has been the downfall of many great and powerful people. Black Herran is a soulless creature, and you are selfish and slimy and as manipulative as always. She may have dug her claws back into your withered heart, but I refuse to do as she wishes. She is no longer my fierce general setting out to change the world."

Maeven grimaced. "When we face a common foe, it is madness to kill each other."

"Pray tell, why do I need you or your allies? The way I see it, Black Herran needs me."

"The Lucent Empire is expanding in all directions. Every marching season sees a new clutch of towns and tribes falling before them, to be absorbed into their armies and indoctrinated into the cult of the Bright One. If we don't band together to stop them now, it will be too late. You might be safe for the meantime across your sea and behind your walls of ships, but that will last only a few more years."

As much as Verena hated to admit it, the woman spoke some sense. Over the last few years she had received reports of armies of the Lucent faithful being trained, but until now she had heard nothing of a navy. She drummed her fingers on the tabletop again, thinking. "And what would Black Herran have me do?"

"Tarnbrooke straddles the Mhorran Valley; the only safe land route through the Mhorran's Spine mountain range. This makes it a natural choke point where the bastards can't bring their greater numbers to bear. We can hold them there, but if they are able to ship enough men behind us, they will crack us like a nut between hammer and anvil. She wants you to make sure that does not happen."

Verena pursed her lips. "Cargo ships full of soldiers would be slow and cumbersome. Easy pickings to our ship ballistae and catapults if we didn't try and board them. You are asking me to consign hundreds to a sea grave."

Maeven raised an eyebrow. "Is that a problem? Have you become squeamish in your old age?"

Verena tutted. "Most are likely blameless conscripts no different from any I might call my subject. Unlike you, I don't relish mass slaughter."

"But will you do it? In a few years the Lucent Empire will control the west coast from Vandaura in the north to Whiteport in the south. Where will your ships find berth on the mainland then? And of course, there is the fleet they are building..."

Verena ground her teeth, thinking. Storm clouds gathered across every possible future she could imagine. The survival of the Awildan Isles depended on Essoran's numerous cities, tribes and nations warring and bickering with each other. Their fleets were kept small and they were more concerned with their petty wars than low levels of piracy. She had taken great pains to spread her raids widely, so that no single ruler would see her pirates as a greater problem than their own neighbours.

The Lucent Empire was a new and growing threat, one that sought to swallow the entire continent. The agents of the Awildan Crown had always watched for would-be conquerors and the growing might of states; they would then snip off the bud before it could fully bloom. This time, however, their agents had fallen silent; assassinations and arson had failed, and the Lucents simply did not care about the economic impact of losing traders and ships. Their armies grew with each conquest, and their inquisitors had no equal on the field of battle... or did they? In the old days none could equal Black Herran and her captains...

"I can sink their ships easily enough," the queen said. "But if you fail that would only focus their attention on the Awildan Isles once they have seized Tarnbrooke."

"You deal with them on the sea and we shall deal with them on land," Maeven countered.

Verena narrowed her eyes. "And what do you get out of this?"

"None of your business," Maeven answered. "Black Herran gets her oh-so-precious town and children saved and you get your isles protected. That's all you need to know."

"She has *children*?" Verena marvelled. "Her? Poor bastards." She paced the creaking wood, thinking hard.

Behind Maeven, Gormley's hand trembled on the hilt of his knife, itching to cut the necromancer's throat. "They are monsters and dark-hearted sorcerers, My Crown," he said. "Their kind cannot be trusted. I always says so. It ain't right them being aboard."

Verena nodded, still pacing. Finally, she waved Gormley to stand down.

"I will let you live for now, Maeven. After this is done, we will have words. Do we have an–" Screams and cursing outside made her fling open the door to the deck.

One of her crew, a tall, pale-skinned northerner with a braided beard was leaning over the side of the ship, a war-bow larger than most of her crew in his hands. Helg, his name was – an arrogant barbarian who'd fled his village three years back. Supposedly the Lucents had made his home into a work camp now. The Awildan people were renowned for taking in every foreigner who washed up on their shores, accepting anybody who wanted a home and a trade, but sometimes that meant they had to deal with the dross too. And this fool had just loosed an arrow at *The Sly Griffin*, taking Lorimer Felle through the eye.

Helg grunted, nocked and loosed another arrow with a single swift movement. "I've taken harder shits. Now for the old ginger prick."

Lorimer blurred, contemptuously brushing aside the second arrow as it flew. Tiarnach leaned back against *The Sly Griffin's* mast, chuckling nastily, knowingly.

"Oh, Helg," the pirate queen said, shaking her head. "You were too dim-witted to live for much longer anyway."

Lorimer grasped the arrow lodged in his skull and shoved it all the way through, snapping off the point and then tearing the shaft out. His eye popped back into shape and he snarled and leapt clear across the water onto the side of the *Scourge of Malice*, clawed fingers burying into the wood, climbing in two great heaving pulls until he reached the northerner.

One second Helg's head was there, and the next it was bouncing across the deck with blood spraying across the shocked crew. Lorimer was a beast of twisted flesh and sharp bone that flowed up and onto the deck, fanged maw chewing.

"Hold, Lorimer!" Verena shouted. "You can see Maeven is unharmed. That idiot deserved to die for attacking you without orders."

Maeven placed herself between the vampire and the ship's crew before he slaughtered them all. "I trust that this demonstration was sufficient proof of our power?" she said. "He is only one of our companions, and not the worst. Your Majesty Verena Awildan, will you ally your forces to ours?"

Verena appreciated the deference shown in front of her crew. Maeven had always been sly. What choice did she now have with the vampire lord on board? Irusen baulked the necromancer's dark magic but the vampire could end them all with ease in such close quarters. "Agreed. We join forces against the Lucent Empire. May the sea swallow their wicked hearts."

Lorimer picked up Helg's corpse in one massive clawed hand and tore a leg free, biting a huge chunk of flesh from the thigh and moaning with pleasure like it was a cut of prime steak.

Men gagged and backed away, and Verena did not blame them. She looked to Maeven. "You are right. He is still far from the worst. Come back into my cabin. Gormley, with me."

The necromancer narrowed her eyes at Gormley's presence, but said nothing. She waited until the door was shut before choosing her words carefully. "Lorimer is a monster, that is true, but he is of old nobility with ethics and morals of a sort. Tiarnach and Amogg have slaughtered more men than live on your isles – they will be useful in the fight ahead. And then there is the one that worries even me; our skilled alchemist who must be rescued from his enslavement in Hive..." She paused, and shuddered. "We face a seasoned army, Verena. We need him."

"Jerak Hyden," Verena supplied, the name burning like venom on her tongue. "Not much scares me, but I am not ashamed to admit the mad alchemist does. I once took control of a small trading port he had been stationed in for a time, making weapons for Black Herran's war effort. What I found there gives me nightmares to this day. Children cut open and their organs stored in jars, some still living attached to mechanical contraptions of tubes and bladders filled with liquid. Men flayed, and the skin of animals grafted in place of their own. Women horrifically disfigured by chemical burns, coughing up their own teeth..."

Verena stopped her pacing. "And yet he would prove useful... so if I must, I will agree to help free him."

Gormley growled and stepped forward, looming over his

queen. "He is a monster, My Crown! You cannot possibly let him loose. I will–"

The pirate queen slapped him, the shock rocking him back on his heels. "You will still your tongue or I will have it removed. I deem this necessary, and I will hear no more about it."

She sat heavily into a chair, stroking an agitated Irusen. "If the Hivers really knew what they had imprisoned they should have ended his life long ago. That monster cannot be controlled, and any who try to use his alchemical arts for their own benefit are throwing their lives away. As for Hive itself, that alien place in the mountains is dangerous to all humans. Perhaps it is safer to leave him there, locked away from all human contact."

"No," Maeven admitted. "You are right that he cannot be controlled, but he is necessary. He can be aimed in the direction of the enemy. As for Hive, I have contacts even there."

"May the gods of the sea protect us," Verena said. "Our alliance stands as long as you keep that insane little man on land. What else does Black Herran require of me?"

"Set sail for the Orcish Highlands," Maeven replied. "I would have words with Amogg Hadakk. Once we have her, we head straight for Hive."

"Gormley, send your carrier pigeons to notify my captains. We sail to war." He opened his mouth to object but she stared him down. "Do as I say, man, or I'll flay the hide from your back."

Gormley scowled and went to spit on her deck.

Verena's raptor gaze fastened on him.

He thought better of it and swallowed, wiped a sudden sweat from his brow, and slunk out of the door to send the messages on behalf of his queen.

Unseen by his queen, however, her shaking, sweating first mate shook off his anger and fear and sent one additional pigeon winging its way north, this time on his own behalf.

This bird had been reared by others and given to him for just such a special occasion. He chose humans over monsters and magic, and that pigeon flew its way to Brightwater, capital city of the Lucent Empire.

CHAPTER 8

In Tarnbrooke, Dalia washed and dried her newly shortened hair and began to don her old and dreadful life. Her home for forty years seemed small and shabby as she embraced all that power and pride.

Her daughter Heline watched her grimly, arms crossed and lips pursed. "I knew your damned past would come back to haunt us one day, but I refuse to let it hurt Tristan and Edmond." She peered out of the door to check on her sons, busy squabbling over who first spotted a penny fallen in the street.

"Hoi!" Heline shouted. "Behave, you louts." They grumbled and shoved each other but quietened and their mother turned back to the conversation. "What do I tell my boys?" she demanded.

Dalia scowled, but Heline wasn't wrong. Her daughter was hard and ambitious, but she couldn't fathom why her loving mother had turned to the darkest powers of Hellrath to survive. But then Dalia had always kept the worst from her, and ensured her daughter grew up safe and happy. Even if that had meant feeding a number of undesirable suitors to her demons over the years.

"You tell your boys a mother does all she can to protect her children," she replied. "Tell them to stay alert and not to wander far. Are you almost ready to depart?"

Heline shook her head. "This is our home. Where are we

going that can possibly be any safer? The north is lost to us, the south is lawless and plagued by slavers, and the Awildan Isles are just as bad for outsiders."

Dalia opened a dusty old velvet-lined box, slipping her rings on one by one: the black onyx ripped from an earth elemental's eye, the ruby forged from a Duke of Hellrath's heart-blood, the diamond and dragonbone ring from the hoard of Alt Clua, the iron band forged from the heart of a fallen star. After a moment's hesitation, she added the simple gold band that Heline's father had given her so very long ago – that, too, might be a weapon in this coming war. She never had given Amadden an answer...

She reached for a bowl of chicken-blood and dipped her fingers into the congealing liquid. She ran the hand over her head and felt the tingle of small magic spiking her white hair and tipping it with red. It had made her aspect savage and fearsome, and those old habits helped her remember who she used to be. Though now that she was old and leaning on a stick, she wondered how effective it would prove.

Dalia took a deep breath, closed her eyes and unchained the doors inside her heart and mind that had been kept locked for decades. Dark power surged through her: delicious and potent enough to rip holes in the fabric of reality and create a bridge to the burning pits of Hellrath. It felt good to let go. Black Herran oozed out of her pores like a mix of blood and tar, until town elder Dalia of Tarnbrooke was submerged and sleeping. The shadows deepened around her.

Her eyes snapped open and Heline took a step back.

"Mother?"

"I am not your mother now, girl. Not until this is done. I am power and pride. I am Black Herran, and this town will bow to my will. Be quick in gathering what you need – you and the children will be leaving shortly. I have prepared a place of safety."

Heline studied her mother. "If that is what is best for my boys then so be it. Whatever else happens, it is nice to have somebody competent in charge. Do this right or we will be having words. Had I even a fraction of your power I would be out there knocking some sense into them myself."

Black Herran's daughter had inherited her steel, and that was something to be proud of. She nodded to Heline, then marched on the temple, where the other three town elders were gathered in council with notable townsfolk. It would be another evening of pointless discussion about the current crisis, spent arguing among themselves instead of getting work done. She would tolerate no more of their time wasting.

As she passed, the people on the streets of Tarnbrooke shot her confused and fearful looks. Even those that until today had thought they knew her best dared not stop and speak to her. They lowered their eyes, clutched their children tight and crossed the street.

Black Herran scowled on seeing the sunburst symbol of the Bright One, only recently painted onto that braggart Wimarc's window shutter. Their damned faith was spreading even here. She'd see to that shortly.

Raised voices snarled in fraught argument as she approached the temple door.

"We must flee," declared a voice from inside.

"Where to, you cretin? Only slavery awaits beggars like us. I refuse to fight in Herlot's slave armies or live chained to oars aboard a Damanion barge."

"Fight!"

"Flee!"

It would be a waste of time trying to get them to willingly submit to her rule. She would do what she always had: dominate through might and fear. She looked to the narrow passage between Tarnbrooke's temple and the storehouse next door, a gloomy place perfect for working her dark arts unseen… Then she decided it was also pointless to try and hide who and what she was. The people of Tarnbrooke would have to fight or all the Southlands would fall to the Lucent Empire. She needed to drown this valley in Lucent blood.

She pricked a finger on a sharp edge of her ruby ring and flicked her hand, scattering droplets of blood across the threshold of the temple. It soaked into thirsty cracks in the earth.

"The way is opened," she stated. "Come forth, my shadow sisters!" Her call stretched deep into the burning realms of Hellrath, and deeper still into the dark caverns below its Shadowlands.

The gloom deepened and thickened around her, devouring the light until it resembled late evening. Wisps of shadow trailed in her wake. It was perfect for making an effective entrance and for terrifying ignorant townsfolk. Black Herran fixed a glare in place and kicked open the door.

The council crowded the front of a table where the aged town elders were sat. They all turned and gaped at her uncouth entrance.

"You will all shut your mouths and listen to me," she said, calm and cold.

Her demons flooded from her shadow into the temple, hanging in corners like bloated black spiders, climbing the walls and ceiling to stare down with hateful hungry eyes. Noble-faced statues of a dozen Elder Gods looked down on her with disapproving expressions, the likes of the Skyfather, Forge Maiden and Lord of the Hunt all judging her for this desecration.

"Dalia?" Elder Cox said from the raised table at the back of the temple, staring at the darkness flooding the room. "What is this? What have you done?"

She struck him with a thought, a shadow demon acting as her fist. He sprawled to the stone floor, lip split and bleeding. The crowd panicked, huddling in a mass at the centre of the chamber as far from her horrors as possible.

"You know me as Dalia, but once I was known by another name, one you will have heard of: Black Herran."

Disbelief flitted across every face... until their eyes darted back to the demons. Then they began to fear.

"This town is now under my command, and you will all obey me if you want to live out the month. I am your only hope."

It had not taken much effort to cow the town council and the elders, nor to dissuade any runaways from fleeing south – her demons saw to that, visibly haunting paths and trackways to frighten rather than kill. Not that the townsfolk appreciated her restraint of course – she'd killed only that useless cretin Wimarc and had him eaten by her demons in the market square as a messy and instructive example for all the rest.

Heline and her boys were away and as safe as they could ever be, far from this coming mess and more protected than any other being on this world, perhaps only equalled by Maeven's sister Grace. If everything went to plan, in a few short months Dalia's – no, Black Herran's – family would be safe forevermore and living quiet, happy lives.

While Maeven carried out her orders elsewhere, Black Herran's days in Tarnbrooke passed in a bustle of industry, instructing the people to gather stone and erect wooden posts. She walked the growing ring of defences around the town, barking orders, and most of the townsfolk cringed and refused to meet her gaze. They would never look at her the same way again, but that was acceptable as long as they did what she ordered. What was necessary should never be regretted.

Behind her, a man cleared his throat. She turned to see an unfamiliar grey-bearded dark face and noted the war spear in his hands and the sword at his hip. A cart drawn by a hardy hill pony waited behind him, its contents covered with canvas. One of her newly formed town militia, a tile maker called Nicholas with a fine waxed moustache and short pointed beard, stood grinning at the stranger's side. The brainless lout's own spear was laying abandoned on the ground. He gave a wave. "Hello, Elder Dalia, this fine fellow says he happens to know you."

"Idiot," she snarled. "He could be anybody."

Nicholas cringed and fumbled on the ground for his spear.

"Forget it. It's too late now. Go keep watch from the wall and don't let anybody you don't know into our town. We are at war and you had best remember that or you will find your throat slit by a Lucent spy. Or eaten by my demons." Her eyes never left the stranger as Nicholas sprinted for his watch post.

The man doffed his hat with its fancy red feather and offered an elegant bow. "Estevan, my lady. I am the Lord Felle's manservant."

She blinked. He did look vaguely familiar. "You are fully human?"

"That is so, my lady. As long as my lord's blood flows in my veins I am perhaps a little stronger and hardier than the average man, and as you can see, I age very well indeed." He offered a wry smile at that last, entirely true comment.

He pulled back the canvas from the cart to reveal a small pile of spears, swords, daggers, dented but serviceable helms and mail hauberks in need of some repair. "With my Lord Felle's compliments. Alas, my lord's resources are not what they once were."

She noted the scraps of bloodstained white and gold cloth among the pile and offered a thin smile. "You are most welcome, Estevan. What other skills do you offer while we await Lorimer's return?"

"I am my noble lord's manservant, my lady. I see to all tasks that are beneath him." He raised a single eyebrow, which meant he organised most things. He was a household general in his own right, and that was exactly what Black Herran needed.

"Excellent," she said. "What do you make of our preparations?"

"Your ditches are shallow and your ramparts low and without a palisade. The wall you are constructing across the neck of the valley is little better than a mound of loose stone with no time available for mortar to set. Farmers and townsfolk will not hold the Lucent Empire for even an hour here, but I suspect you know this already. If I begin weapons training immediately then they may be able to hold for a time behind what defences we are able to erect in the weeks available." He looked over the wall again, over two hundred paces long. "Should the enemy take that then they will use it to fortify a camp – they will use it against you."

"Oh, I am counting on that," she replied. "See to the training. They must hold that wall for exactly a day before retreating behind what will become the ramparts of Tarnbrooke itself. Then I will have them exactly where I want them."

The wall was taking shape, and the ground immediately on either side was cleared of all rock to produce a smooth field perfect for an army to encamp. If they could stop the advance elements of the Lucent army from routing the townsfolk in a single charge then they stood a chance.

With Estevan drilling the townsfolk on bow, spear, axe and sword, it would allow her to devote more time to the careful construction of the drystone wall that throttled access to the valley. She did not want it to be too solid and well-packed, quite the reverse – it had to have certain weaknesses built in. She was beginning to think more like the old Black Herran, cunning and ruthless, and she found it not entirely unwelcome after forty years of learned restraint. Not that she had ever been accused of biting that sharp tongue of hers of course, but at least she hadn't removed those people who simply disagreed with her.

With Jerak Hyden's mad genius at her disposal, this defensive structure would be forged into a lethal weapon. Crafting explosive powders and poisonous gas was nothing to him. The only problem would be getting enough rare materials and reining in his more experimental tendencies. She was willing to accept a small number of civilian casualties at his hands if it allowed her to use the mass slaughter of the enemy to raise an abomination from the darkest pits of Hellrath.

Before the Lucent forces died, she would ensure they suffered every torment and terror she could devise. Her demons would feast on that heady mix of human emotion and it would make them strong. It would grant Black Herran as much power as she had ever possessed in her heyday.

CHAPTER 9

Laurant Daryn, the Landgrave of Allstane, heaved himself up onto his warhorse, mildly alarming the placid old beast as he settled his bulk. His lower back gave a twinge and he shifted in the saddle, new leather squeaking. He was not as young as he once was, or as accustomed to spending more than an afternoon hunting on horseback.

It was a fine but chilly day and his escort and servants were in no hurry as they assembled in the castle courtyard. None of them looked happy about it, but a summons from the Falcon Prince to attend him at his palace in Brightwater was not something that could be refused.

Sixteen years ago, Allstane had been a border region of the Lucent Queendom, before the Falcon Prince usurped the old ruler and began expanding the newly formed Lucent Empire's borders to envelop Fenoch Ford and Vandaura. It ruled most of the north now, but Daryn's land of Allstane was still an isolated backwater and that was exactly how a tired old general like Daryn preferred it.

He scowled at the Bright One's flag flapping from his towers but, yet again, bit his tongue. Brightwater was a very different place these days: fanatical and intolerant if reports were to be believed The nature of the priest they sent to convert his people, and to watch him, had convinced him the rumours were all true. He thanked the Elder Gods that he had chosen not to march against the Falcon Prince beside the rest of the old Lucent Queendom's indignant nobility. They had been mercilessly crushed, and the retaliatory purges of their lands had been brutal.

He turned in his saddle at a piercing scream from the keep. A few minutes later his cook Molly hurried out, wiping bloody hands on her apron.

"Deepest apologies, My Lord," she said. "It seems that Brother Orndan has, ahem, slipped and fallen down the stairs. Both legs badly broken I'm afraid. He will not be able to accompany you on your journey." She winked.

"Such a tragedy," Daryn replied, stifling a smile. Even here, he could not be sure what eyes were watching, but at least that particular spying priest would not be telling tales to the Empire's inquisitors anytime soon. It was such a shame that the local messengers were also unreliable when it came to delivering his letters containing details of the locals' transgressions. Thank you, Molly, and your goose fat, he thought.

"Set off, men," he shouted. "To Brightwater!"

They departed from the castle and wound down the hill through the main street of Allstane. People came out of their houses and down from their fields to wave them off. His wine merchant tossed him a skin for the road. He nodded in gratitude, put on a fake smile for his people and shouted greetings to them as he passed by. He hoped he would be allowed to return, but in his heart he feared that his old bones would be burning on a pyre before the season was out.

He stopped at the rusty gibbet on the outskirts of the village to look at the corpse swinging in the breeze. Brother Orndan had been busy rooting out heretics.

He turned to a nearby farmer who had ceased work to watch his lord ride out. "Brother Orndan seems to have fallen down the stairs and will be indisposed for quite some time. Cut this thing down and bury him."

The farmer's eyebrows lifted. "Such a shame about the good

Brother. Maybes he should have prayed harder. I'll see it done, my lord."

At this time of year it was seven days' hard ride to Brightwater, so he took ten at an easy pace, increasingly worried by what he saw as he approached the capital. Gibbets had sprouted like wildflowers in every village along the road and many of the condemned were still alive inside those iron cages, their blaspheming tongues burned from their mouths. The rest of the people not in gibbets were extremely vocal in their worship and their faith was on show for all to see.

Spring had arrived in the city of Brightwater and the streets had never looked so clean, not a speck of garbage or a single thieving, pox-ridden beggar in sight. Despite the drizzling rain, Daryn pulled the sodden hood of his cloak back to get a better look.

It had been many years since his last visit to the capital, and on the surface the city had never seemed so wealthy and prosperous, or so devout. The golden sunburst of the Bright One was proudly displayed on signs and doors everywhere, yet to a keen eye the smiles on the faces of shop workers and baker's boys, laundresses and bread sellers all seemed forced, and suspicious eyes followed his party's progress. The dark rumours he had heard back in Allstane had barely scratched the surface.

The sun finally peered through the blanket of grey cloud and set the waters of Ellsmere shimmering. The castle in the middle of the lake looked inviting, with white and gold flags atop its four lofty towers catching the sun. But Empire inquisitors, holy knights in full silver mail and plate, guarded the gates and bridges leading to the centre of the lake, and their presence made Daryn dab sweat from his brow with a kerchief. It wasn't like the old days of the queen, when a man might dine and dance and enjoy good company. This would be... something else entirely. He was one of the few members of the old court to keep his head on his shoulders after the coup, but that could change with but a click of this Falcon Prince's fingers.

As his party clopped across the bridge an inquisitor in white and gold emerged from the gate to greet them, arms clasped behind his back.

As they drew closer, Daryn recognised the dark bushy eyebrows, shaved scalp and severe features of Grand Inquisitor Malleus. He cursed under his breath and urged his mount on ahead of his party. "Well met, Grand Inquisitor," he said as he dismounted, with some difficulty thanks to a complaining back and sore arse. "I trust you are well?"

"May the Bright One's blessing fall upon you, Landgrave Daryn," Malleus said in rebuke. To his mind every meeting should start and end with Her blessing. The man's eyes dipped to Daryn's paunch and his bloodless lips tightened.

Daryn took the words for the veiled threat they were but kept his smile on. "Indeed, indeed. May it fall upon you as well." He thought it likely the odious creature asked for Her blessings before taking a shit.

Malleus's eyes flicked from face to face of Daryn's retinue. "Where is Brother Orndan? I had expected to see him by your side."

So he can inform on all my supposed sins? the landgrave mused. I think not. "Sadly Brother Orndan slipped on steps and broke his legs. He is recovering back in Allstane. Let us pray the Bright One hastens his healing."

The Grand Inquisitor narrowed his eyes but said nothing. "The Falcon Prince awaits you within the East Tower. Come, your men will be seen to."

Daryn took a deep shuddering breath, unclasped his sodden cloak and handed it to his squire. "Lead on, Grand Inquisitor. I would not want to keep His Highness waiting."

"No, you would not want that at all," Malleus agreed, ushering him through the gatehouse.

Daryn couldn't help but eye the murder holes in the ceiling as he passed beneath. The scent of blood and hot oil was acrid in his nostrils. No, things were very different from the old queen's day, when visitors were welcomed with wine, meat and song. But then she *had* grown lax and the entire queendom became decadent with its wealth. This new "holy" Lucent Empire was young and hungry for both land and believers. Wealth was only a secondary concern at best for them, a means to an end – it was minds and souls they were interested in.

After Black Herran and her monsters slaughtered their way across the continent, the Falcon Prince had arrived to offer the people all the safety and security they had prayed for. While the queen entertained her noble favourites at lavish balls, he had travelled the land killing the bandits and hunting down the monsters, rooting out traitors and criminals. He had become a hero. He gave the people everything they thought they wanted, and then he took everything from them – and they loved him for it. His priests inflamed the superstitious peasantry into a terrified, angry mob with tales of dark magic and monsters, ensuing he had their allegiance mind and soul. The people of the Lucent Queendom abandoned the old gods and old rulers that had failed to protect them and bought into this new goddess, the Bright One, setting themselves up as true patriots and holy warriors standing against evil.

Now? The inquisitors had total power over life and death in the empire and it was much too late for anybody to back out. To publicly criticise the Falcon Prince was to publicly side with evil, and that could only lead to rotting in the gibbet or roasting on a pyre.

Beyond the gate lay a courtyard filled with young men sparring in full gambeson, chain and helm, the clang of steel and gasps of pain oddly devoid of cursing. The silver forms of senior inquisitors passed among their lines, scrutinising their skills. Their presence explained the lack of cursing only too well. A new batch of armed fanatics in the making.

Daryn held in his groan as they entered the east tower and began climbing the three hundred and thirty-three steps spiralling up to the Falcon Prince's chambers. As a much younger man, he had deflowered a pretty young maid up there after one of the queen's legendarily debauched gatherings. This would not be nearly as much fun.

Malleus wore heavy armour but he didn't break a sweat as he ascended at a punishing pace. Daryn's calves began to burn halfway up. By the time he reached the top he was drenched in sweat and his legs were trembling.

The Grand Inquisitor awaited him by the door, a sneer on his face. "Indulgence in food and drink makes men weak in body and mind."

Daryn was too exhausted and out of breath to make any kind of answer to that and could only do his best to quickly straighten up and wipe the sweat from his face before Malleus had the door open and he was ushered into the presence of the Falcon Prince.

The ruler of the Lucent Empire was sat cross-legged before a pink marble statue of the Bright One in Her guise as the warrior: a beautiful woman in a simple homespun dress crouching to take up a fallen sword, Her face determined and defiant as She looks up to stare some unknown evil in the face. The Falcon Prince was dressed in a loose, flowing robe of pristine white, his blonde hair left loose around his shoulders, framing chiselled features worthy of a demigod. Two of his holy knights stood on either side of the room, swords raised and ready in their hands. The Prince stood, waved his guards to be at ease and then approached with his hands wide in welcome. "Landgrave Daryn," he said. "The Bright One's blessings be upon you in this most holy place."

His eyes... Daryn could not help but stare. The man's burning golden orbs drew him in, twisting something inside. He gasped and fell to one knee, the words flowing out unbidden as unaccustomed awe flushed through him: "Your Highness, I live to serve."

"Do you, Daryn? Do you serve the Bright One and Her holy Lucent Empire? Do you serve me?"

Daryn's throat turned to a desert and his legs trembled beneath him as his lord's power washed over him. "I... Pardon, my lord, but have I ever given you cause to doubt my allegiance? I was one of the few lords not to oppose your–" a choice of words flashed through his mind: coup, revolution, insurrection, "–ascension."

"That is not an answer, Landgrave," Grand Inquisitor Malleus said, eyes lit up with malicious glee. He was hoping to uncover another traitor to the faith.

Daryn cleared his throat. "I serve the Bright One, my lord, and I serve Her empire, Her people and Her sword, the Falcon Prince." He did not dare to even think the true name of the conscientious boy he had once known. Nor would he think of him as the bold knight at arms who rose to prominence exterminating the remnants of Black Herran's broken army, including those Cahal'gilroy savages. That was another man, a mere mortal. Now he was something more.

The marble statue of the Goddess turned Her face to Daryn. Her gaze evoked an exultation that lifted him to his feet, legs no longer sore and tired. He gasped as holy power burned through his body, the skin of his hands smoothing, age spots fading, grey hairs replaced with thick black. His paunch retreated into hard slabs of muscle, eyesight sharpening on the face of a god incarnate.

And then the statue returned to merely well-crafted marble, as if it had all been a fevered hallucination. He staggered back and Malleus caught his elbow, steadying him. The man's sneer had vanished, replaced with a look of religious fervour. "Blessed!" he cried. "You have been blessed."

Daryn stared at his hands, flexing strong supple fingers. His gaze rose to the Falcon Prince and he could see his own youthful features reflected in his lord's eyes. He took the knee once more, this time gladly. "Command me, Highness!" The need to prove himself worthy of Her blessing burned inside him, an insatiable desire to serve. He was no inquisitor, no holy knight, but She had still deemed him worthy of a sliver of Her power.

"Arise, Landgrave of Allstane."

Daryn rose, his muscles strong and smooth and seething with the power of youth. The two inquisitors stepped forward, one on either side of him and turned to face their leader.

The Falcon Prince laid a hand on Daryn's shoulder. "Our vigilant faithful among the heathens have uncovered a dreadful plot against our people. Evil gathers beyond our borders and we require your great skill as a general to cut out this disease before it spreads. Raise the Allstane levy and bring them here to join up with two hundred of my veterans. You will then make your way south to the corrupted land known as Hive. You will watch that town of unclean creatures and await the coming of the enemy. Sir Orwin, Sir Arral and a dozen acolytes will accompany you to behead this evil once it rears its loathsome head."

Daryn grinned, the joy of being able to serve his lord and his god pounding in his breast. *This feeling was not always so*, a small part of him whispered. *This is not natural.* It was quickly quashed.

"What is the nature of this evil, Highness, that it requires the presence of holy knights?"

Malleus stepped forward. "It is an abomination, Landgrave. A group of sorcerers and corrupt creatures empowered by blood sacrifice."

"The old magic lives on?" Daryn said.

"Dark sorcery," Malleus rebuked. "Evil itself."

Daryn ignored the foul man. At least those feelings had not changed... "We shall destroy this enemy, Highness," he vowed.

The Falcon Prince smiled, his pleasure suffusing the landgrave with righteous wrath.

CHAPTER 10

Near the town of Garsak, Orcish Highlands

Amogg Hadakk squinted into the night, spat, hefted her axe and threw. It spun through the air to crunch deep into the trunk of the distant pine, dislodging enough snow to bury several squealing grubbs.

The huge, battle-scarred orc laughed uproariously as the smiling green faces of young, unringed, would-be warriors fell and faded to grey, their ears drooping. As their fellow grubbs dug themselves free, those around her groaned in disappointment and sullenly heaved small jars of mead up onto her table. For the most part they took their loss well. A bet was a bet. To orcs, honour was all.

One of the younglings hissed and complained and held on tight to their prize, trying to slip back into the crowd. Amogg stormed over and cuffed them to the ground. They lay dazed and drooling as she took her jar from their limp fingers. A few of the other grubbs sneered at their broodmate. This one was now marked as dishonourable and likely wouldn't survive to grow into an adult. Orcs did not tolerate cheats and liars, but all grubbs were allowed one mistake. Only one.

Two of the clan's other elders, warleader Ragash and the aged shaman Wundak sat around the flickering embers of the burn, silhouetted big and black as they warmed their calloused hands. Gold rings through their ears and around their tusks glinted in the burnlight as they shook their heads knowingly at the impetuous younglings' groans and grumblings.

"Gardram's Tusks! Never bet against Amogg of the Hadakk," Ragash said. "Not even at fifty paces in the dark. If you grubbs learn anything, learn that."

Amogg nodded, pleased at her haul. A chieftain should live in such style, she thought, but food-gatherings and huntings had been weak this year and even the bees had produced less sweet than usual. One of the older and stronger grubbs tried in vain to prise her great axe from the tree, grunting with effort. She chuckled, strode over and wrenched it free in a shower of splinters.

The young grubb eyed the gold rings Amogg wore, each one denoting a hundred kills. "What's the secret, Chieftain? How does we get so good and strong?" Their eyes were bright and eager and the nubs of adult tusks were beginning to jut from their lips. Downy fuzz was spreading across their neck, lower chin and chest, indicating that this grubb had chosen to become a male.

She grunted and dropped her axe into his arms. The slender grubb staggered under the weight of steel. "You carry the axe of my ancestors and you get plenty strong soon enough. Good? Hah, that takes practice. Chopping logs comes first, heads come later. And see this scar–" she traced a line down her entire torso, "–most of all, you need brains to survive and grow strong."

The grubb sighed with relief as the chieftain took back her axe and leaned it against her shoulder, then he nodded earnestly and grinned at the dwindling fire. "Thank you, Chieftain. Burn needs more log so I start work on getting good now." The grubb scampered off into the wood-housing with the heaviest axe he could find.

Amogg smiled, grabbed two of her new jars of mead and squatted by the fire, wincing as she did so. She handed the drunk-makers to the elders and began wiping tree blood off her axe head with a rag. She wasn't fond of mead. Far too sweet for her tastes, and too easy to lose control. It was good for trading though.

Ragash noted her twinge of pain and glanced at her leg. "Pulled a muscle chucking that big axe, eh?" He stroked his white mane. "You're an old boot almost worn through."

Amogg winced again. "Nothing gets past you two, but the younglings don't need to know that. That's what the mead is for – to shut your yapping holes before I shut them for you."

The elders chuckled and exchanged glances, coming to an agreement. "Amogg is strong like steel and enduring as the mountain," Wundak said in the same tone she used when telling stories to gullible grubbs.

"And very generous," Ragash added, taking a sip and smacking his lips.

Amogg grunted and set her axe to one side. "Why do I suffer you two fools?"

Ragash grinned. "Who else would put up with your ugly face and stinking farts?"

Wundak laughed at that, adding: "Reeks like a human!"

Amogg growled and swiped for their mead, but a worried shout from the forest gave her pause.

"Chieftain! Chieftain!"

Amogg heaved herself up, axe in hand, as a ringed orc in green and brown leathers crashed through the treeline. It was one of her eyes 'n' ears out and about. He dashed over and stood panting before her.

"Three big ships have slipped past Gardram's Tusks," he gasped. "Lots of armed humans come ashore on smaller boats."

The grubbs clustered round, shoving and kicking to get closer, babbling about wanting to go see the bad humans.

Amogg'd had enough of them. She punched one and it went down, skull smashed. "Still your tongues or I'll rip them from your heads." It was no great loss. Only a handful of their number, the strongest and brainiest of their brood, would survive to grow into an orc. Food was scarce until summer and the grubbs were many, so the weak or wrong were fed to the pigs or went straight into the pot.

Three of the grubbs tried to shut the others up. Amogg was impressed and noted their faces – those ones might grow to be leaders. "Orcs listen and learn from their elders," she said. "Now, how many humans, and what drawing on the boat's flag?"

The panting orc thought about it, his lips twisting from the effort. He held up ten fingers. "Ten of tens, I reckon. Black flag with a red whip. Barbed it was too."

Amogg growled deep in her belly. "A hundred," she replied. "Ten of tens is a hundred." She licked the gold rings on her tusks as she tapped her axe against her shoulder. A hundred humans under the flag of the *Scourge of Malice*. That meant trouble. That meant the Chieftain of the Awildan Isles was on orcish shores.

"Grubbs!" she bellowed. "Get your shitty little arses back to the village and tell them to gather weapons and join us at the cliff. I'm off to cast an eye over Gardram's Tusks."

She didn't wait for an answer before taking to her heels and heading west. The orc that had brought the warning accompanied her, ears hard against his skull and lips peeled back into a feral snarl.

The carpet of pine needles was fragrant and springy underfoot as she pounded along the forest floor. Twigs and icicles scraped her face and hands, but she barely felt it as she crashed through every obstacle. There wasn't much that could stand in the way of a charging orc.

Ragash and Wundak quickly caught her up, bow staves slung over their shoulders and axes in their hands. A stag lifted its great antlered head as the four of them crashed through the undergrowth. It took one look and leapt a stream to escape.

The sound of surf crashing against rock grew louder and the soft dirt and pine needles underfoot were replaced by crumbling stone and a smattering of snow. Ahead of her the thick forest gave way to cloud and sky. Amogg slowed, settled down onto her belly and crawled forward to peer over the edge of the cliff.

Waves crashed against the jutting stone tusks of Gardram's Tusks, throwing up a spray of mist and foam that obscured the mouth of the bay. Spikes of jagged rock lurked just under the surface, eager to rip open the bellies of anything that didn't know the safe path through the Teeth. And yet three big human boats now sat at anchor in the bay with rowboats ferrying a small army onto orcish beaches. It was as her eyes 'n' ears had said; she recognised both flag and ship only too well.

Her ears clamped flat to her skull as she picked out a tiny grey-haired human coming ashore, feet sploshing through the surf. Humans all looked alike to her, but this woman was small and old and disgustingly feeble – it could only be Verena Awildan, Chieftain of the Awildan Isles. Even when Amogg had smashed heads in Black Herran's army, she had never trusted that human – a thief and a liar without honour. A few trade deals with her people in the many years since had not changed that opinion.

She turned to her eyes 'n' ears, and spoke quietly, though it was a struggle not to bellow and charge down, axe swinging. "Head up to Spear Point and look for more ships. I need to know if there are more than these three." He bared tusks in agreement and slipped away.

Amogg squinted at the other figures following Verena off the small boat. Their presence felt like a bubbling broth of acid in her gut. The ship's crew shied away from those three, and though it was hard to read human emotions she thought them afraid. Her gut told her they had every right to be. One was big and dark-skinned and there was something unnatural in his flesh – it shifted and moved. The tattooed corpse-white woman was unarmed but stank of sorcery, while the smaller pale man with burn-coloured hair and a sword tickled some old and almost forgotten memory. With it came a sharp sliver of fear. It was not an emotion she had experienced in decades, and she welcomed its return wholeheartedly. It meant a real challenge after years of dreary peace. She had always hated humans with burn-coloured hair. The problem with humans was that each and every one was clothed in lies. Their very skins lied: they remained the same colour instead of turning the grey of shame or the red of rage. Orcs were honest and better in every way.

She growled and gripped her axe tighter, unable to track the emotion to its source. Who was that human to make her feel such a thing? She could crush the little male's skull with a single hand.

Her unease did not go unnoticed by the two elders. "Is this an invasion?" Wundak said. "Want us to string our bows and start dropping them?"

Amogg grunted, "Not yet." What were any of them doing setting foot on orcish lands?

"You know this big boat, don't you?" Ragash said. "Dangerous humans, yes?"

She bared her tusks. "My gut's saying so." That caused the two elders to exchange worried glances. Amogg's gut was rarely wrong. "I knew their chieftain long ago. The word of humans is worthless. They lie and cheat to get what they want, and what they want is everything you have."

Ragash growled. "Truth."

"We wait," Amogg said. "There'll be no fighting until these trees are full of Hadakk orcs." There was much glory to be found in battle, but there was far more in winning.

Verena scanned the tree-line and cliff top, seeing nothing. She couldn't shake the feeling of being watched, and green and grey orcflesh made the vicious brutes especially hard to spot in forest.

"I appreciate their décor," Lorimer said, smiling at a grisly line of wooden stakes topped with human skulls that separated beach from forest. "Their celebration of life and death makes me feel most welcome."

"Aye, that's orcs fer you," Tiarnach replied. "Wonderfully savage big bastards, ain't they?"

The two men exchanged a puzzled look, aggrieved at finally finding something they could both agree on.

Maeven moved from post to post, examining the skulls. "Men, women, and even children," she said. "Orcs do not discriminate in who they slaughter. Certainly Amogg Hadakk never showed us they possess any concept of mercy."

"Mercy is weakness," Verena said. "And orcs cannot abide that. All orcs fight: male, female and even the sexless creatures that pass for their children take up arms as soon as they can hold them. Given they live in these barely fertile hills surrounded by fortified human towns I suppose they don't have much choice."

"Is that a hint of pity I hear on your tongue?" Maeven said.

Verena shrugged, causing the slynx around her shoulders to grumble. "There has never been any friendship between us. We had a common enemy a number of years back and I traded food and supplies in exchange for bars of orcish iron."

Tiarnach scratched matted red hair. "I doubt I could pick Amogg out from any other orc after all these years. Did she have an eyepatch?"

Lorimer snorted. "You are a drunkard and a fool."

He nodded. "Aye, what of it? I could be confusing her with some other orc with an eyepatch. Wait... or was that the big berserker from Vandaura? I've met or killed so many over the centuries that I've lost track, and their faces all blend together."

Verena again scanned the cliff tops surrounding the bay. "We had best tread carefully. I want no part of a war with orcs, and I doubt our trespass will go unnoticed for long."

"I have no fear of orcs." The necromancer glanced to Lorimer. "None of them can stand against a vampire, nor my sorcery."

Tiarnach chuckled. "Yon big vampire is scary, aye, but you've never been on the wrong side of an orc warhost, have you?"

She scowled at him. "Amogg was little bigger than Lorimer."

"In that case, no," he replied. "You haven't met a *real* orc. Amogg was a mere stripling warrior when she served under Black Herran." He didn't deign to elaborate further but his smirk seemed designed to annoy her.

As the necromancer and the once-god bickered, Lorimer ambled along the beach, sniffing the air. He turned to look east towards the forest. "I smell orc sweat, steel and oil. They are watching us."

Amogg pulled back from the edge as the dark-skinned human turned to face the paler ones. He was big for a human and definitely dangerous judging from how the lesser worker humans avoided him. He, too, seemed oddly familiar, but then she had killed more than a few humans that had foolishly chosen to raid orcish shores. She hoped this one might even pose a challenge in battle. His skull would guard the Hadakk's borders well against evil human spirits.

"Tell me Gardram's truth," she asked Wundak.

"The tattooed female has magic," the shaman replied. "Very bad. Death surrounds her. She should die first." Wundak was the closest thing orcs had to what humans called a sorcerer, but her power was good and pure – their god's will worked through her.

Amogg grunted, the feelings from her gut were always right. "What of the tall one and the burn-haired swordsman?"

"The tallest man-thing is not natural." Wundak growled and spat, as if he tasted of rotting food. "His spirit is not tied to his flesh as is right and proper. He wears a body like we would a cloak of animal skin."

"Humans!" Ragash said. "They corrupt all they touch."

"Truth," Amogg agreed, baring her tusks. This was a worrying group. This was sounding more and more like one of her old chieftain's other captains, who was also a darker skinned human. The vamp-ire they called him. Sword and spears and ogres had all failed to bring that man down.

"The burn-haired man," Wundak continued, "he sears my eyes. There is a speck of blinding light inside him. I think him not all human."

The sliver of fear Amogg had felt did not seem unwarranted now, but it only made her want to hack their heads off all the more. That was the orcish way.

She backed into the trees and stood stretching sore muscles. She gently ran a finger down the edge of her old axe, the metal slicing a neat line through the surface of her skin. A few beads of bright blood made her smile. Old and honoured it was, but still sharp, deadly and hard as always. She striped her cheeks with the blood, readying for battle.

Wundak and Ragash strung their bows and tested the pull to ensure the gut strings were good.

"We fight," Ragash said. "Take their heads and drive the rest back into the sea."

Wundak shook her head. "Something important is happening here. I feel power gathering. I am afraid."

Amogg laughed. "Afraid? You? A good joke."

Wundak's green face faded to grey and her ears pressed flat to her skull. "Do you not feel it? The world balances on the edge of a blade."

Amogg's mirth faded. "You think this little army so dangerous?"

Wundak scowled. "The normal humans are nothing, but the three you asked about are different. From their boat's chieftain I sense nothing at all. She is hidden from Gardram's sight."

That gave Amogg food for long thinking, and she was still chewing on it when her eyes 'n' ears re-emerged from the shadows.

"Chieftain," the orc said. "No more ships, and the Hadakk warriors are gathered."

She nodded and waved him off. "Well, Wundak. It is time. Is your advice fight or talk?"

Wundak shrugged.

Ragash nocked an arrow to his bow. "We talk and then fight, if they don't give us good reason."

"That is fair," Amogg said. "We shall do that."

The three of them slipped back through the forest and joined the warriors of the Hadakk who could be summoned at short notice: a hundred or so orcs gathered in an unruly mass in the hollow of the hill, armed with axes and spears. Some boasted steel chain and scraps of plate but most wore only leather, wool and wood. Only a dozen of them were elders, looming head and shoulders above their younger, smaller kin. Around orcish feet scurried a few dozen of the braver grubbs wielding sharpened sticks and jagged stones. If it came to a battle they'd likely be slaughtered, but any that survived would be well worth feeding up – Gardram made orcflesh so that when the battle-blood pounded through their veins, they grew straight and strong. That was why Amogg was the biggest and toughest of all.

A greeting rumbled through the warband at her approach. They knew better than to raise their voices too high before battle was joined. A few grubbs squawked loudly with excitement, but her orcs beat silence into them.

Amogg flung her hands wide. "Hadakk, my heart swells to see you come to fight. Armed humans walk our beach, and their big boats sit chained to Gardram's Tusks. This cannot go unchallenged."

The hulking forms of elder orcs shoved their way through the crowd towards her and began herding the others into groups. She bared her tusks at them and set her axe to her shoulder, watching them to ensure it was done right. The elders knew what do to though – every one of them bore numerous battle scars.

The orcs with bows had been shoved into one group, those

with spears into another, and those with the best axes and armour clumped around their elders. The poorest hill farmers, forced to make do with slingshot and clubs, were distributed among them to harry the enemy.

There was no shame in stones and arrows, but less risk meant less glory than meeting the enemy tusk-to-tusk. Every orc and grubb here had come hoping to earn themselves a story, and if they did something truly worthy, a title. Only a few orcs ever attained a title, and a handful of elders boasted two or three. Amogg had many.

She began the traditional orcish discussion about battle tactics with the other Hadakk elders. A single punch and a bloodied nose later they had all agreed to her plan. She sighed. There was little challenge left in them anymore. She missed her youth during the years of slaughter and war at Black Herran's side, yearned for a return to frantic ritual single combat over matters of honour. Nobody dared offer more than a token objection anymore. She stripped to the waist to show off all her scars, the fights she'd survived and won. Her orcs roared approval as she lifted her axe high, "Hadakk – to the beach!"

As she marched through the forest with the might of her clan at her back, she felt the stirrings of bloodlust again, the likes of which she had not felt in years. She hoped the talk would fail.

"Orcs are coming," Lorimer said, ambling back towards the beach. He sniffed the air again. "Lots." His fingernails cracked and spread, forming long claws at the tips of widening fingers. He grinned, jaw yawning wide to reveal an array of fangs. "I've never eaten orc before. I wonder if they taste anything like ogre."

Verena cursed and finalised arranging the men in a defensive line in front of her rowboats, a shield line at the front and bowmen at the back. If it came to a pitched battle, she was under no illusions how they would fare. As sailors, most wore little armour and with the cliffs circling most of the bay they would be incredibly vulnerable to archers. "Your vampire had best be up to this," she said to Maeven.

Lorimer shrugged, not terribly concerned.

Tiarnach drew his sword and tossed the makeshift scabbard aside, testing the balance with a few expert cuts. He shook his head at the vampire's indifferent attitude. "Seen you fight, big man, but a proper orc could easily lop that head from your shoulders. How quick would you heal then, eh?"

"He knows what he's doing," Maeven said. "Which is more than I can say for you."

Tiarnach tossed the sword up in the air, spinning, and snatched its hilt again on the way back down. "Oh, I know exactly what ah'm doin'. You just don't know what I do. You're underestimating the big green bastards. Amogg was cunning and vicious as any demon of Hellrath."

He stabbed his sword into the ground and then took a small case from his pocket. He snapped it open and dabbed a finger in, then began painting red lines and swirls across his face.

Verena rolled her eyes. "War paint? How barbaric."

He hawked up a blob of phlegm and spat it into the sand by the pirate queen's feet. "Guess I forgot that fighting was only for civilised folk like yourselves."

They didn't have to wait long for the orcs to show up. The greenskins were not known as a stealthy race and their arrival was heralded by widespread cracking of branches and a rustle of foliage not unlike a wave about to crash ashore. First to show their tusks were the orc archers atop the cliffs overlooking the bay, their bows bent and arrows nocked to strings.

Then a line of dark shapes appeared among the trunks of the forest, charging towards the beach. Tiarnach watched the others carefully as the largest orc he'd ever seen crashed through the undergrowth, lifted an axe and loosed a teeth-rattling, arse-clenching roar.

Lorimer and Maeven were wide-eyed and staring. Amogg had grown another head and shoulders taller and wider since any of them had seen her last.

Tiarnach gave an appreciative whistle. "Now *that's* a proper orc! It fair brings back memories." The others had been expecting to see the lesser breed, still larger and bulkier than the average human but not this half-giant looming over even Lorimer, and five times his bulk. Lorimer turned to Tiarnach and gave an admissive nod, making the warrior chuckle. "As I said, good luck w'thon big beastie."

A line of armed orcs crashed through behind Amogg to form a wall of green flesh and sharp steel. A handful were almost as big as the one at the front.

Verena cleared her throat and stepped forward, speaking first in the guttural language of the orcs and then in the trade tongue: "Amogg of the Hadakk, we are not here to make war. We come to bargain."

The biggest of the orcs held up a hand and her army stopped in a rough line waving axes and spears and growling angrily, champing at the bit to fling themselves into battle. She replied in a long, snarling sentence.

Verena paused, trying to understand and then translate orcish idioms to a human equivalent for the others to hear.

"Well? What did the ugly old beast say?" Lorimer asked.

Verena winced.

Amogg grinned, exposing her tusks. She slapped the haft of her axe into her palm. In an Awildan-accented human tongue she replied, "Ho. Ho. Ho. Amogg said we have no need to bargain with humans. Leave or we fight, vamp-ire."

Lorimer smiled. "Ah, you remember me, then? I am honoured."

Amogg snorted. "Lorimer Felle. Beside you stands Maeven Deathtouch and Tiarnach Burn-Hair. I know you now. Never friends with Amogg. You have insulted chieftain of the Hadakk, dung-for-brain humans. Now we fight. A long time since Amogg has had good fight."

"Wait!" Maeven said, moving forward. "I—"

One of the other big orcs leapt forward and snarled something, shaking a fist and bone bracelets. The metallic tang of magic rose up around Amogg, cloaking the chieftain. The line of orcs readied to charge.

Maeven instinctively seized hold of her own magic and felt the orc shaman's power swelling to try and match it. She drew in more, and yet more still until it hurt to contain it all.

Verena backed away among her men and they began to prepare an escape on their boats, if they could. There was nothing that could stop the orcs charging now.

"Shitty balls," Tiarnach muttered. "Up to me, is it?" He sighed and straightened his tunic, an insolent grin nailed to his face. "Oh, here, Amogg, there's something I never did tell you – the old memory ain't what it once was, but I remember that scar down the chest now I see it again. I killed your father, didn't I? Big lad w'steel tusks and no nose, wasn't he?"

Every human and orcish eye turned to stare at the warrior long past his prime.

"You drunken imbecile," Lorimer said. "Now you've really fucking done it." Bone spikes erupted all over his body as he prepared for battle.

CHAPTER 11

Wundak knew enough of the human tongue to be afraid. She wisely got out of Amogg's way a moment before the chieftain's axe slammed down to shatter the boulder in front of her.

"What is this?" Ragash said, seeing Amogg's ears press flat to her skull. Her skin flushed a furious red and she bared anger-froth covered tusks.

"The burn-haired human claims to have slain Vaggan Iron-tusk," Wundak said.

Ragash sneered and edged forward. "*That* puny human? Vaggan was strong as a god. His claim must be false."

Wundak clamped a hand around his arm and pulled him back as Amogg's axe came back up in one hand, sharp edge glinting. "I think it to be truth." Their chieftain was lusting to spill blood.

Amogg of the Hadakk traced the scar running the length of her broad chest, revisiting the memory of the sword that took her mighty sire's head and then casually slapped her younger self aside like vermin. The hideous war paint on the face of that monstrous enemy came into focus in her mind's eye and matched that of the human warrior before her.

She pointed her axe at him and spoke loud and slow in human trade tongue so even treacherous, dim-witted humans would understand. "You slew my sire and gave me this scar. I challenge you to single combat, as is my blood-right."

He snorted. "Nah, I've no' a smidgeon of interest in doin' that. Thanks for the offer though."

"What are they saying?" Ragash said.

"Amogg claimed blood-right to challenge him to ritual combat and he has refused. He shows his contempt."

Ragash snarled. "It is known that humans have no honour."

A group of three young hot-headed males overheard and flushed the deep red of orcish rage. Frothing at the tusks, they broke from the orcish line and charged, axes raised. Amogg bellowed in anger but was too far away to halt their attack.

The human warrior advanced to meet them, a feral grin on his painted face as he awaited their strikes. The first orcish axe came down. He side-stepped, the blow chopping only air. The point of his sword cut through the orc's braided mane to lick a green neck as his enemy stormed past. The orc's legs buckled and he went down spraying blood.

The second orc hefted his axe high, aiming to split the human in two. Amogg growled as the human darted forward into the blow before it could fall. Burn-hair's sword rammed up through the orc's exposed belly. The orc's own charge pushed the point through his heart and out his back. He went down, taking the sword with him. The human abandoned the weapon and spun to face the third orc bare-handed.

The line of Hadakk roared approval as the last orc bellowed and swung his axe in a mighty neck-chop. The human swayed back and allowed the weapon to sail past his chin, taking off only a few stray beard hairs. The fleet-footed human slipped behind the orc and leapt onto his back, wrapping arms and legs around the orc's torso.

Blunt human teeth sank into the orc's thick neck. The line of orcs ceased cheering. The muscles in the human's neck and jaw stood out as he tore out a mouthful of orcish throat. Burn-hair was stained deeper red as orcish blood gushed over him. The orc warrior snarled and punched back over his shoulder, but the blow was weak and unable to dislodge the feral human biting deeper, tearing free strings of muscle and severed arteries. The orc greyed, swaying. The human let go and landed on his feet as the orc buried his face in the sand.

The beach was silent save for the sounds of surf on stone and sand. The human spat out the orc flesh and then wrenched his sword free in a welter of guts. He rested the gory blade against his shoulder as he faced Amogg again. "Piss-poor. I expected better from orcs."

Amogg's skin had faded back to green as she studied him. "You dare anger me, human?"

He spat again, blood dribbling down his chin. "Course I do. I'm Tiarnach of the Cahal'gilroy, or did you forget?" He sneered his way down their entire line of battle, eyes full of casual contempt.

Amogg stared. She had forgotten his clan. All elders knew them, many bearing scars earned from vicious battles like no other since. Back when the orcs had inhabited parts of many lands, an army under her tyrant of a father had fought that clan of humans, the current elders mere grubbs at the time. She glanced to Wundak, shaman of Gardram and oldest living orc in the entire Orcish Highlands. Wundak was greyeing, deeply afraid, and not much could do that to Wundak. Here, finally, was the worthy challenge she had been craving for so long.

"We fight now," she said. "No butchering of young fools."

Tiarnach hocked up a blob of red-streaked phlegm and spat it towards her, then spoke in passable orcish, as well as any human could manage without tusks. "Oh aye? As chieftain o' the Hadakk your side have breached yer damnable honour. I fought your father in single combat – wielding that very same axe in your hand, so he was – and that means your claim to blood-right is fucked. Besides, I seem to recall that you, just a grubb at the time, interfered in that duel before it was finished. I let you off on account of being a young'un. And now you issue a challenge, and I'm attacked by your warriors before we're done yapping? That's right scummy and no mistake."

Amogg flinched and tinged grey. How did he know so much about orcish ways? And he recognised the axe of her ancestors. Had she really broken her own sire's ritual combat and tainted her honour? The memory was old and muddled.

"Is this true?" Wundak asked.

Amogg hesitated, then shrugged. "If it was single combat then it is likely."

"It was," Wundak said. "I remember this Tiarnach now, fallen so far from his days of glory. He is the war god of the Cahal'gilroy."

Tiarnach grinned and spread his hands wide. "How'd you like to fight a fucking god then? You must be so tired of all this bland peace and these–" he gestured to the corpses at his feet "–piss-poor weaklings. Come with us and I will show you a war beyond anything any orc has ever seen. If you are good enough to survive, only then will I agree to single combat. Come, let us talk this day."

Amogg grimaced. She wanted to fight right here and now. Her hands itched to spill human blood, to revel in a vicious struggle for survival. And yet she had to atone for a breach of honour in any way she could. Grubb or not, she owed him this.

"Today I talk," she said, grudgingly. "Tomorrow I decide if we fight then and there, or on a tomorrow yet to come."

As the threat of imminent slaughter dwindled, the Awildan sailors sighed and sagged with relief. The orcs growled and lashed out at trees and rocks, and occasionally each other in their frustration, but they obeyed their chieftain and kept to the tree line and cliffs.

"Well done," Lorimer said as Tiarnach turned and walked past him. "Didn't think you had that in you."

"Not so old and decrepit as you appear," Maeven added.

Verena offered only a relieved nod.

Tiarnach didn't reply and didn't stop, instead he increased his pace towards a rocky outcrop further along the beach out of sight of both orc and human. There he doubled over and emptied his churning guts.

"Fucking human emotions," he snarled, then heaved again. He'd been shitting himself at the thought of fighting Amogg. The previous night's two bottles of wine had done little to settle his stomach, or his nerves... He knew fine well Lorimer had judged the current state of him and assumed him useless. And he was, more or less. He was so dreadfully weak these days. Weak and old and so very foolish. It was all he could do to keep up the act of his younger days, when he'd been afraid of nothing – but he could still swing a sword as well as any mortal. He'd handled those three young orcs well enough...

"Ah'll not be able to take that bastard Falcon Prince's head like this," he said, spitting bile. He wiped his mouth and beard and took a deep breath before forcing the grin back on and sauntering over to the sailors on the beach. They clapped hands on his back and thrust a skin of wine into his hand. For a fleeting moment he felt like a war god again, basking in bright glory. Then he looked at Amogg Hadakk and felt the fear ooze back up his spine. Orcs were brutal bastards.

He drank and hoped it'd take the edge off. The old memories returned in the wake of his bloodshed: fire crackling, steel clanging, and his people screaming as they died, all while he lay useless in a drunken stupor. *Worthless piece of shit. You should have died there too.* He drank deeper and gripped the hilt of his sword tight. He should die, but not just yet. He'd do it fighting the damned Lucents. Maybe then he'd be able to rest easily in his grave.

"Did you see that?" Lorimer said. "Was that really the same drunken fool we dragged from a pool of mud and vomit?"

"He was once a great warrior," Maeven said. "If anybody

can understand the savage heart of an orc then it would be him. He has yet more to offer us, and if we can keep him sober enough, he'll be a huge boon to the militia of Tarnbrooke. He's seen more battles than any living human, and if anybody can give them a chance to survive, it's him."

"He's still fearsome," Verena said. "Slaying three orcs is most impressive. He even looks younger than I'd thought at first. I could have sworn his hair was greyer..."

Maeven watched the sailors clustered around their hero and her lips pursed in thought. "Perhaps this life agrees with him."

They had no more time for introspection as Amogg marched towards them. Humans scattered before her like a flock of startled pigeons.

The hulking orc came to a stop before Verena and bared her tusks, a terrifying sight for the two human guards bravely standing their ground between her and their queen.

"Verena Awildan," Amogg growled. "Pleasant to see you again. Your children; they are healthy and strong?"

Lorimer and Maeven stared, mouths gaping, but Verena merely blinked and then answered, "They are well, Amogg Hadakk, how are yours?"

She grunted at the three orc corpses staining the sand. "Some are stupid and dead. Others clever and strong. My oldest female is big and mighty, almost to my shoulder."

Verena looked to the others of her party. "To orcs, war and peace are entirely separate things. What happens during one does not affect their opinions in the other. In peace, Amogg and I have some little trade. I'm glad war didn't come between us."

Amogg scowled. "Sad we will not fight this day. Maybe kill you all tomorrow. Why do you land on my beach with an army?"

"Straight to the point," Lorimer said, a shark's smile on his face. "I respect that. We are here because of this damned necromancer."

Maeven stepped forward. "Well-met Amogg, chieftain of the Hadakk. It has been a long time. I apologise for setting foot on your land uninvited, but my mission is of the utmost urgency. Black Herran is back and she is gathering allies, the strongest and most deadly in all the land, for a great battle against the Lucent Empire. We invite you to fight beside us."

Amogg did not look impressed. "I no longer fight for humans."

"They have conquered almost everything north of Tarnbrooke," Verena said. "Come the summer their army will move south. My own Awildan Isles will soon be under threat from their ships."

"What of it?" Amogg said. "They come here and challenge us, we fight, some die. Maybe them, maybe Hadakk. The strong survive."

"They are purging every human who does not convert to follow their Bright One," Maeven said. "Sooner or later, they will come in their tens of thousands to exterminate you. They will not suffer the orcs to live. We must join forces to defeat them. How can you think of doing otherwise?"

Amogg shrugged.

Lorimer sighed. "I think we misunderstand the orcs, Maeven." He bowed to the orcish chieftain. "I–"

"Do you wish your head removed?" Amogg asked, lifting her axe. "I will be pleased to take it, unnatural creature."

He swiftly straightened. "Ah, I see. A bow is a sign of respect in many human cultures. As leader of my people of Fade's Reach I greet you as leader of the Hadakk."

She grunted and lowered her weapon. "Stupid to offer head to an axe. Humans are strange, but I understand."

He smiled mirthlessly. "The others are correct; this is an enemy none of us can survive on our own. We must fight together or fall before them. The orcs may be strong, but they are too few and the enemy have their god's power to aid them."

Amogg stuck a calloused thumb in the direction of a big,

aged orc covered with bone talismans and necklaces. "Wundak strong with Gardram's might. Our god stronger than any human god. Orcs stronger than humans. We have no fear."

"That may be so, Chieftain," Lorimer replied. "But why not stop them now, before they grow too powerful?"

The hulking orc just laughed, eyes tracking Tiarnach as he walked along the beach towards them.

"God of Cahal'gilroy," Amogg said, grinning. "I want to fight now. Your chattering worshippers bore me."

"Do you all have rocks fer brains?" Tiarnach said to his allies. "Amogg Hadakk, the enemy we fight are without honour. They torture and kill those already surrendered, and they enjoy it. They love to slaughter without challenge."

Her green skin flushed darker, shading towards red. An ominous rumble began in her belly. "The ways of humans are not those of orcs."

"Maybe so," he said, eyes twinkling, "but I say this as truth: their leader, the Falcon Prince, is the deadliest warrior in all the world. I include myself, you, and thon big vampire in that. He is probably unbeatable."

Amogg went still. "Unbeatable, you say?"

He grinned. "Probably. None who faced him in battle have survived. You orcs do not generally die o' old age and you must be bored o' all this piss-poor peace. Do you intend to die withered and weak or do you want to seize this opportunity to test your axe and skill against the mightiest warrior in the entire world? And if you kill him, then me and you can fight. Unless I kill him first, o' course – then I'll be the best in the world and refuse your challenge."

She roared with laughter. "This man knows the way of orcs." She glanced at her assembled Hadakk warriors and snorted. "I am bored. I will fight. I will win."

Wundak waited, silently seething, until Amogg returned. "Have

I knocked you around the head once too often, young Chieftain? You intend to go alone with these honourless creatures and fight in a battle that has nothing to do with any orc?"

Amogg shrugged. "Did your old ears not hear them say it would come to us sooner or later? It is the way of orcs to fight sooner."

Ragash began stowing his weapons away and gathering up his possessions. "When do we go?"

Amogg stilled. "What do you mean?"

He chuckled. "You are wrong if you think we will stay behind while you alone go to glorious battle."

"We go where you go," Wundak added, grudgingly. "My bones ache every morning and I will grow feeble in a few years. If our fool of a chieftain goes into battle, then we fight beside her."

"No," Amogg said. "You both must stay and lead the clan."

Ragash spat. "If they are strong, they will survive with the guidance of other elders. In truth, you have been too wise for their own good. They have become reliant on your leadership. It has made them weak in the mind. As for us, no orc should die weak and withered and in their blankets."

Amogg grunted, trying and failing to look annoyed. "We fight together. But ensure your rotten old bones do not slow me down."

CHAPTER 12

Three days via ship, then four more on foot along mountain paths found Amogg, Lorimer, Maeven and Tiarnach crouched atop a crag overlooking the isolated mining town known as Hive. Verena, who would not be upset if Jerak Hyden died horribly in a botched rescue attempt, had opted to stay behind on the *Scourge of Malice* and await their return.

The midday sun cast a vague suggestion of warmth onto their backs, but the rock was cold as ice. It was spring elsewhere but winter's grip on the mountains of Mhorran's Spine was only just loosening. A black torrent swollen by melt water roared through a split in the mountain and plunged over the cliff down to a small lake below. The river then continued down through the mountains heading towards the sea, the entire area rife with smugglers and slavers they couldn't afford the time to slaughter.

A sturdy barge was tied up at a stone dock further down the river. After offloading its latest cargo of human livestock, two men were busy scrubbing out the ingrained slave-stink with sea salt and sand.

At this distance from Hive, the miners and tradesmen looked like insects scurrying about the enormous conical stone fortress in the centre of the town. This had been built by the inhuman denizens that made up most of the population. Humans called this town's four-legged native inhabitants hivers, and as far as any could tell they were distantly related to the common ant, though much larger.

Around the base of the fortress was a ring of smaller conical buildings, and beyond those squatted the cruder square stone constructions that housed the town's outcasts: a small population of outcast hivers, humans and the odd orc. Mostly, the non-hivers worked as slavers in the south of Essoran, shipping their human cargo north and then upriver or through mountain passes to put them up for auction in Hive. Fully half of their stock was sold locally and put to work in the mines of Hive – a short and brutal life for most.

"What manner of demon are these hiver creatures?" Lorimer said, adjusting the cloth that protected his eyes from the sun's harsh glare.

Maeven shrugged. "I am not sure if they are. Certainly, they have been here as long as human memory. Fascinating creatures. So organised and industrious. We could learn much from them."

Amogg grunted. "Why have humans not tried to kill hivers? Not in your nature to let others be."

"They tried," Maeven answered. "Many times."

That earned a chuckle from Tiarnach. "There's a whole army o' the weird little fuckers burrowed into the earth beneath that there town, doing whatever bugs do. Men go in but they rarely come back out."

Amogg nodded thoughtfully. "Maybe I make hivers orc friends. Then we take back ancestral lands and get new lands for hivers too."

"One enemy at a time, Amogg," Maeven chided. "First we need to free Jerak Hyden and defeat the Lucent Empire."

"And where exactly is he to be found?" Lorimer asked.

"Therein lies the problem," she replied. "He's somewhere inside that hiver fortress. Inside, there is no light and no sense to the layout. It is a maze not meant for humans to navigate. Fortunately, I have a contact on the outside who has been looking into the matter. Lorimer and I will enter the town and obtain the information we need. Any more would cause people to take notice."

"Oh aye?" Tiarnach said. "And I'll just sit up here freezing my arse off keeping watch over this big lump o' orc, will I?"

"Not at all," Lorimer replied. "She's staying here to keep an eye on you."

Amogg laughed. "Unnatural thing or not, I grow to like you, human with claws and fangs. Not as arrogant now your lands have been taken from you. Maybe now you understand orcs a little better. In past you made me want to kiss your skull with my axe."

Lorimer scowled and stalked away, muttering vile obscenities he was too well-mannered to fully air.

Maeven checked the straps holding the pack on her back in place. "We need to go in quick and quiet. If we need help in a mass brawl, we will call for your aid."

"How will we know?" Amogg growled. "Cannot see you in there."

"Probably hear the screaming," Tiarnach said, thumping his arse down on a flat rock.

Maeven ignored him. "Any sorcerer worth the name can cast whispers over a short distance. My voice will reach your ears as soon as we are out. Should anything go wrong, meet us at that barge. It is the quickest escape to the sea and Verena."

Lorimer looked at her sharply. "And do any of us know how to sail a barge?"

Silence.

"I will sail," Amogg stated. "Cannot be hard. River goes to sea. Barge is made of wood. Wood floats. Barge goes to sea." She frowned and shook her head like the rest were all idiots.

"Maybe," Tiarnach said, laughing. "But do orcs float? This big lump of a vampire swims like a rock."

Lorimer's fangs lengthened as he glared at Tiarnach, a look

that suggested to all that the red-headed fool's throat was looking increasingly inviting, and that he was just another hot meal.

"Hopefully it will not come to that," Maeven snapped. With that she began descending to the streets of Hive and Lorimer happily went with her, glad not to suffer Tiarnach's presence any longer.

They entered the ramshackle outskirts of the town, a maze of stone and wood where only the barred doors and shutters seemed to be in a good state of repair. Stone was crumbling and wood riddled with rot, roof slates cracked and covered in moss. A ditch ran down the middle of the street, meltwaters carrying off the scum of sewage. A human corpse floated downstream, a dozen knife wounds in the back.

Lorimer scowled at the crust of horse and human manure that now coated his boots. "Where exactly are we heading?"

"To the edge of the fortress," Maeven said, picking her way through the filth that littered the street.

There were no old people in Hive, and the few grubby children stayed well clear of strangers. As they walked deeper into the town, outcast hivers became more frequent on the streets. They were the size of small humans, but with hard carapace, antennae, mandibles and compound eyes, and unlike their smaller kin, had sacrificed a pair of legs to gain arms and tool-using hands.

Some were chittering wrecks with missing eyes, legs or antennae, making them even more hideous to the human eye. Most appeared drunk on sweet-smelling mead, the dewy bladders of alcohol attached to their bodies with sticky balls of spit. Their antennae waved madly as they chirped away to themselves and tried to dig holes right in the middle of the street. Passing humans booted them off the road but the hardy ant-people barely noticed.

Maeven made her way to the empty doorway of one of the smaller conical buildings that circled the huge fortress. Instead of lime mortar, the stone blocks were stuck together with some sort of hardened glue, likely hiver-spit. She pulled a small vial of cloudy liquid from a pouch on her belt, dabbed it on her hand and then did the same to Lorimer.

His nostrils quivered. "What is that reek?"

Maeven sniffed but her human nose detected nothing. "Scent-marking," she said. "This is how hivers communicate with each other. Best not to ask where it comes from." With that she stepped through the doorway.

Lorimer was forced to stoop to pass through the low entrance. Inside was a single large chamber, the walls draped with human textiles in a variety of colours that were almost complementary. A dish of oil steamed over a lit candle, its too-pungent fragrance filling the room. A low table was set with dinner plates and fresh flowers arranged in a fine porcelain vase, all illuminated by an ornate silver candelabra in the centre. Cushions lay heaped either side of the table, unoccupied.

Lorimer nodded in appreciation. "Well, at least somebody in this town aspires to possess a measure of taste."

A scuffing from above drew their eyes to the black eyes and antennae that had been watching them from the ceiling. "Welcome, friends," it said in a clicking voice that somehow managed to imitate human tongue.

Lorimer resisted the urge to form his claws as a hiver twice the size of any other he'd seen scuttled down the wall to them. Its sharp mandibles were as long as Lorimer's forearm and clearly capable of tearing a human in two. A single diaphanous wing was folded across its back, the other side bearing a ragged, chewed stump.

It tilted its head, studying them, antennae quivering. Lorimer realised that even giant ants could look disappointed. "Maeven," it said. "This Queen in Waiting is not happy to see you. Please leave."

"Not even the bloody ants like you," Lorimer said, grinning.

Maeven glared at him and then took a deep breath, "Your Highness, I have not come to exchange pointless pleasantries; I am here for Jerak Hyden."

The hiver stilled. "You agree to my terms?"

She grimaced. "Is there nothing else you will accept?"

The hiver said nothing.

Maeven admitted defeat. "I accept your terms. We will kill the current queen of Hive for you."

Lorimer threw his hands up. "Oh, superb! I knew accompanying you would bring me only woe. Is this madness really the only solution?"

The tattoo writhed across her cheek. "What are a few bugs to the likes of the great Lorimer Felle? Besides, we won't stand any chance of finding him without her help."

He snarled and resisted ripping her heart out, as she had done to his all those years ago. "The sooner we return to retake Fade's Reach the better. Where is this bug queen? And do we require the aid of Amogg and Tiarnach?"

The necromancer shook her head. "Amogg won't fit in hiver tunnels, and as for Tiarnach... I think we can do without him messing it up."

The hiver chirped, almost like a laugh. "Come. Come. Follow. The way has been prepared. Slay the tainted queen and I will rule. Then the human designated Jerak Hyden will be yours." She shoved the table to one side and began to dig, legs spraying earth carelessly over fine cloth and cushions set out on show.

Eventually she uncovered a huge stone slab below the dwelling. Lorimer shoved it open with his foot – or at least he tried to. It shifted only slightly. He grunted and tried harder, grimacing as the stone slowly ground back to reveal a dark pit.

The Queen in Waiting hissed in annoyance, set her head down and flipped the huge stone slab upright with ease, and held it between her antennae. "Enter, enter."

Lorimer blinked, then nodded in admiration. Maeven removed a ring from a pouch and muttered over it until it glowed an eerie shade of emerald, then slipped it over a finger. She pulled the obsidian knife from her pack and steeled herself for a fight. They dropped into the crude tunnel beneath, the warm air stale and musty. The hiver dropped in after them and eased the slab back into place, cutting off any light from outside.

"I am impressed by your strength," Lorimer said. "It becomes obvious why the local humans were not successful in exterminating you."

The hiver squirted a sweet scent against the wall, then began leading them down the tunnel.

"I think she likes you," Maeven said.

"What is not to like?" he replied.

They clambered right, up, and then back down through a maze of featureless black chambers and identical narrow tunnels, already completely lost.

"You see now why I didn't fancy blindly wandering these tunnels alone," Maeven whispered. "Imagine fighting off an army of hivers without a guide through this place."

He nodded in agreement. "Were I mortal, I would be most worried."

Landgrave Daryn and the Allstane levy were encamped an hour's hike around the mountain from Hive, hundreds of tents sprawling across a rocky plateau hidden from prying eyes by sheer cliffs on three sides. Men sparred and drilled to hone their skills.

His estate gamekeeper approached the command tent where Daryn sat at a folding table, silver goblet of red wine in hand. The leather-faced outdoorsman and his subordinates made for fine scouts, though now they stalked human prey rather than deer. Many of his levy had been far less competent: armed farmers and bakers wanting to shiver around their fires, grumbling, cloaks pulled tight to keep out the wind. Their previous training amounted to only two weeks a year mandatory service, as stipulated in Empire law for all men over the age of thirteen. At least he had been able to procure them decent armour and weapons, and the Falcon Prince's personal interest in this mission had lit fires of faith and fear under them. The two hundred veterans, provided by his lord, kept to themselves and did not complain, and the acolytes were too absorbed in prayer to cause any trouble.

Daryn felt the cold not at all. He was a blessed being in his Goddess' sight and was now above such mortal weakness. Perhaps one day she would see fit to bestow the full power of a holy knight upon him.

"My lord," a grizzled scout said ,dropping to one knee before the landgrave. "Two of the enemy you asked us to keep an eye out for have entered a hiver hut and, uh, they didn't come back out. I went in myself an' found it deserted, 'cept for what looks like an entrance to a secret tunnel beneath. I couldn't shift the huge slab of stone though."

Daryn's hand dropped to the hilt of his arming sword. "Never mind the details, man, who did you see enter?" Sir Orwin and Sir Arral moved up to flank him, both already clad in full harness and helms, armoured in steel and faith. Their unblinking stares through lowered visors made the scout's forehead bead with sweat.

"The scarred sorceress and the vampire," he replied. "They was acting all stealthy like, with hoods up and such. Had a few of my lads loiter outside the taverns in town and one sent word they spotted the scum."

Daryn turned to his inquisitors. "Options?"

"It may be that they are in league with the monstrous denizens of this cesspit," Sir Orwin advised.

"Hmm, then do we wait? Or do we attack? With two holy knights at my side who could possibly resist us?" Daryn burned to eliminate the enemies of his faith.

Faith? You had none until recently, Laurant. He shuddered in horror at this inner voice. Filled with rage and self-recrimination he clenched his fist, crushing the metal goblet to a shapeless mass. Red stained his hand and dripped like blood to the muddied field. He savoured the enormous strength the Goddess had granted him.

The two inquisitors exchanged glances. "I would urge caution," Sir Arral said. "No human force has ever entered the hiver fortress and emerged intact. We have no personal experience of these creatures, but they are rumoured to be deadly foes."

"Then we surround the town," Daryn snarled. "Rouse the men. We unleash righteous fury on the vile practitioners of heathen sorcery the very moment they emerge from that den of monsters. Now, where are the rest of our scouts? They are late in returning."

CHAPTER 13

"So, the last time me an' a orc walked into a tavern this bad –" Tiarnach said as he sauntered into The Perky Pintle, apparently the finest drinking den in all of Hive, which really wasn't saying much, " flies were everywhere, right, an' one lands in the orc's drink. He curses, fishes it out and squashes it."

Human heads turned, horns of ale frozen mid-tilt to hairy lips as they goggled at the largest orc any of them had ever seen squeezing through the doorway. A pair of hivers supping on mead immediately picked up their wooden bowls in mandibles and scurried out the back door.

"One o' those flies lands itself in mine too," Tiarnach continued, "but me, I grab the fly, gives it a shake and start yelling 'Spit it back out, ye wee bastard!'" He laughed at his own joke while Amogg frowned and scratched her chin.

A bushy-bearded old man in grey robes and peaked hat sat in the corner by the fireplace, watching them while calmly puffing on a long-stemmed clay pipe. The two warriors glanced a warning to each other – they had both been around long enough to recognise the stink of wizard. Taverns were their favourite recruiting grounds when they had a scheme that required naive youngsters with bellies full of ale and heads filled with dreams of adventure and gold.

"Is this story of fly another attempt at joke?" Amogg replied. "Your humour is weak and manly." She bared her tusks at the

131

grimy locals, most of whom quickly found somewhere else to look; the old wizard in the corner didn't, and neither did two young moustachioed men loitering by the doorway – beneath their old cloaks both wore finer clothes than any inhabitant of Hive could ever afford.

Tiarnach pouted. "You are no fun at all." He sauntered up to the table nearest the ale barrels and tossed some coins to the tavernkeep. "Give us your best. The strong stuff."

The man quickly filled two of the largest drinking horns for them.

Amogg held the horn in two fingers, frowning at the dark and foamy liquid. "Why we wait here?"

Tiarnach went to clap a hand on her shoulder, then decided against it since he'd have to stretch way up to do it. "Why wait up there freezing our arses off when we can sit in the warmth with fine ale to wet our lips?" He glanced at his horn. "Well, some sort o' ale. Besides, we can see anybody making for the cargo barge from here, and we are closer to hand when those arrogant pricks need saving."

"Makes sense," she admitted. "I watch you here or there. No difference." Then she tossed the ale back in a single swallow, scowled at the empty horn and carefully placed it back on the counter. "Foul water, but better than sweet mead. Warm feels in my belly."

Tiarnach took a gulp and the bitterness at the back of his throat forced him to agree. If this was their best then he pitied anybody suffering their worst. At least it was strong, and that had a magic all of its own. Then he glanced at the two men by the doorway and rolled his eyes. Subtle they were not: the idiots thought themselves so fucking brave and were working up enough nerve to start a fight. The two of them wore near-identical rugged clothing – screaming military uniforms – and the steel hilts of the knives hanging from their belts didn't have a spot of rust. He had no patience to wait for these soldier-boys to get down to business, so he turned to face them instead. "Well? Are you two cunts going to have a go or not?"

They drew knives and advanced to stabbing range. "You are under arrest," one said. "Come quietly or we will kill you."

Amogg's arm snapped out, large green fingers enveloping the man's hand and hilt. Human finger bones cracked and popped as she yanked him howling off his feet and into the air. Her other hand grabbed his groin and she flung him head-first into the wall. He crumpled in a boneless heap while his friend gaped in mute horror.

She chuckled. "Kill Amogg with little knife? Now *that* is good joke."

The other man panicked and flailed his blade at Tiarnach's face, who ducked and rammed a fist into the man's belly. The soldier doubled over, and his face met Tiarnach's knee on its way up. He flew backwards, a stream of blood arcing into the air from his mashed nose. The next thing the poor fool knew, he was on his back and a wild-eyed savage was holding his own knife to his throat.

"Who do you work for?" Tiarnach snarled. Blood seeped from soft flesh as the keen edge of the knife pressed harder. "How many o' you are there?"

"Do your worst, heathen," the man snarled. "You cannot kill us all. My soul goes to the Bright One!"

"That so," Tiarnach said, a little disappointed. "Cheers, m' dears. I reckoned it would be harder to get you to spill your guts. Good to know more o' you Lucent fuckers are here." He plunged the knife into the man's neck and left it there, dragging the dying man out into the muddy street like a sack of mouldy grain.

Tiarnach dusted his hands off and scanned the silent folk in the tavern. "What? I didnae want to stain the floor o' the tavern. Makes a right mess when you cut a throat proper." He avoided the intensely interested gaze of the mad old wizard in the corner. He wasn't up for a second insane quest, and wizards were notoriously stingy bastards when it came to getting in the ales after you'd signed on – even more so if they were dredging the likes of Hive.

Amogg nodded. "Mush washing and scouring wish sand." She knocked back another horn of ale. Her green cheeks were flushed red and she swayed on her feet, leaning on a table to stabilise herself. It creaked alarmingly.

Tiarnach stared. "Surely you can't be drunk after only two ales? You're the size of a horse!"

"Amogg not had ale in forty yearsh." She growled at a local who came too close to the table on her way to the ale barrels. The poor man backpedalled, sat back down at his table and sighed at the empty horn he'd been hoping to get refilled.

"Wait… are you saying that orcs don't brew ale? You poor bastards."

"What of it?" she spat, glaring at him. "Want fight? Orcs prefer eat grain and boil leaves for tea. Mead is orcish drunk-maker."

Tiarnach grinned. The big orc was a bad drunk and things were about to get messy. This tavern brawl was going to be fucking legendary.

The warren of hiver tunnels was pitch black, save for the meagre circle of light shed by Maeven's ring. As they descended into the earth the air grew hot and moist and the walls glistened with hiver secretions. The silvery smears formed a map of scents to rival human language in complexity. Lorimer's head sprouted barbed horns as it turned this way and that, nostrils quivering at each new intersection as he tried to make sense of it all. To Maeven, it all smelled like a mix of sour milk and mouldy cheese.

As they proceeded down the tunnels they encountered a number of smaller hivers carrying goods and food on their backs, each of whom reared up ready to defend the hive. The Queen in Waiting took the lead and the fortress's residents calmed and then ignored the intruders.

Their hiver ally paused at a new passage, her antennae trembling, single remaining wing rustling in agitation. "Hive smells wrong. Sick. Few guards." She clicked and hissed, spitting what the humans could only imagine were the foulest of hiver curses. "You must kill the diseased queen."

"Just get us in there," Maeven replied. "We shall do the rest."

The tunnels twisted down through a maze of chambers hollowed out of the bedrock. The temperature swiftly increased until the necromancer's face was slick with sweat.

Lorimer abruptly stiffened, head bobbing as he sniffed the air. "Beware."

The tunnel walls exploded on either side of him. Two hivers snapped at Lorimer's throat with their wicked mandibles but found only air as he slipped between them. His claws ripped the eyes from one. It screeched, briefly, before the Queen in Waiting leapt on it, a savage bite crunching through its hard head into its brain.

Lorimer spun and grabbed a hold of the other's mandibles, pitting his vampiric might against hiver strength. He grunted and snarled as it thrashed in his grip. Its jaws inched towards his skull.

Maeven summoned her death magic, held her hand out and clenched. The hiver spasmed and dropped like a stone, reeking fluids gushing from its mouth.

Lorimer scowled at her. "I was not done with that."

"Yes, yes, I know you could have killed it whenever you wanted. We don't have time for contests of strength." She peered closely at the two dead guards, noting the fungus and filth crusting their carapaces.

"She is near," the Queen in Waiting said, limbs trembling and wing rustling. "Straight ahead. I can go no further. The diseased queen's commands are... difficult to resist. I will now spray confusion to mislead guards."

The two companions left her spitting on the walls and

moved on down the tunnel. Soon the rustling and chirping of hivers grew into a hiss of noise, and the darkness retreated before a faint septic-green glow. Maeven dimmed her ring as they crept forward.

The tunnel opened up high on the wall of a vast cavern. Phosphorescent fungus was growing on the mouldering bulk of the hiver queen at the heart of the chamber below, granting a horrific view of the writhing mass of her malformed spawn surrounding her. The bloated, fleshy body was barely even recognisable as a hiver queen. Rot and fleshy growths covered her spindly limbs and yellowish pus oozed from sores to coat the floor and her grotesque, scuttling brood.

Maeven doubled over as the stink wafted up to her. She was accustomed to the stench of death and decay but even she gagged and clapped a hand to her mouth, lest her retching alert the horde below.

The vampire cricked his neck. "That is truly disgusting. It's even worse than you. No wonder your odd friend wants to replace that rotting thing."

Maeven swallowed and straightened. "Let's get this done, retrieve Jerak Hyden and get out. When we kill that thing, I expect the rest will go quite mad." She considered the distance. "I don't suppose you could hit that thing with a glass vial?"

He shook his head. "It would be too light, and at this range I could not hit anything with enough accuracy. Judging from the fungal growth and slime below us, I'm not sure it would even break."

"So be it," she replied, and behind them came the clicking sound of two reanimated hiver corpses.

She shrugged at his inquiring look. "It would seem the best way to infiltrate the hive below and get close to their queen is with one of their own. Their familial scent should allow us to deliver death. Unless you wish to go down there yourself?"

"Oh no," he said. "I will happily bow out of this particular mess."

She slipped a vial from her pocket. "Perhaps you remember this little creation of mine?"

"Ah yes," he said. "You thought to threaten me with that toy."

"Only if you left me no other choice," she replied, settling it carefully into the oozing grip of a reanimated hiver. "Now you will witness the exquisite thing I created. I wonder if even you could survive it."

They watched from the lip of the tunnel as the two corpse-ants slowly made their way down the wall and began to cross the swarming, slimy floor of the queen's chamber. At first the living hivers paid them no heed, but as they moved closer to the diseased queen, a number of larger hivers armoured in steel plate rose to their feet. These elite guards were the same size as their own ally, the Queen in Waiting, and lacked the under-developed limbs and clouded eyes of the queen's newer spawn. Stubs of wings jutted from their backs, probably snipped off by the rotting queen's bite.

"An honour guard of sorts," Lorimer whispered. "They look to be fearsome foes."

"It won't matter how big they are," Maeven replied. "If they live and breathe, they will die here."

The larger hivers watched the zombie ants' plodding progress, and began chirping at them, growing agitated when they received no answer – Maeven didn't know how.

The queen's amorphous head turned towards the zombie ants. A bubbling hiss escaped from the ruin of her mouth. Every hiver in the room jerked upright as if their strings had all been pulled. They swarmed the reanimated corpses, tearing them apart with their mandibles.

As one of Maeven's puppets fell, its jaw parts clenched, crushing the glass vial. The liquid began to froth and boil, wisps of yellow smoke rising into the air.

A thick yolk-coloured fog rolled across the floor of the chamber below. Hivers began to die with shrieks of agony.

Hard carapaces softened and slumped, flesh rotting from the inside out and putrid liquids spurting. The swarm broke apart as hivers crawled atop each other, snapping and fighting to escape the necrotic fog that swiftly obscured the floor of the chamber from the two watchers.

Lorimer slowly turned to look at her. "Are you insane, woman? That would have killed you had you used it on me."

"Then I wouldn't have died alone," she said, shrugging.

"Perhaps..."

The screaming from below began dwindling into isolated bubbling squeals.

He eyed her pockets and pack. "Ah, do you have any more in there?"

She grimaced. "If you knew how much of my power was distilled into that one little vial you would not be asking that. And I have no time to make more."

"I hope Jerak Hyden is worth it," Lorimer said. "We could have used that weapon on the accursed Lucents instead. That would have been delightful."

"This is a child's toy compared to the wonders Jerak can concoct," she replied as the last of the hivers below ceased their screaming.

"Horrors, I think you mean."

She shrugged as they looked back down into the chamber. The fog was finally thinning and on the chamber floor nothing stirred. They stood and peered down. Maeven smiled and–

–Lorimer shoved her back down the tunnel, bouncing and skidding. Rock exploded beneath his feet. The entire entrance of the tunnel crumbled and fell away into the queen's chamber taking the vampire with it. He plummeted into the depths of the yellow fog, into the distilled death. The metallic tang of strange magic filled the air.

Spindly, rotting legs emerged from the chamber wall below the entrance, heaving the bulk of the hiver queen up into the tunnel. Her mouldering flesh sizzled and oozed but was far from dead. She hissed at Maeven, powerful mandibles clacking in eagerness to crack open her skull.

Maeven sensed power building inside the creature's ruined body. "Shit, the damn thing is a sorcerer!" Her magic reached for the queen's heart, but the necrotic power was blocked by the hiver's own magic before it could do more than dig shallow, blackening pits in its carapace.

The queen heaved her bulk towards Maeven, spindly limbs scrabbling in fury. Gouts of steaming fluid erupted from her mouth, just missing Maeven. The tunnel walls hissed as acid ate through earth and stone.

The necromancer grimaced and forced her magic through the hiver queen's protections, sucking life from the bloated creature's flesh. Fungal growth and rotten carapace sloughed off in sticky sheets. The queen screeched, setting her teeth on edge.

Just as Maeven prepared to deliver the death-stroke, the wall to her right crumbled and another maddened hiver guard crashed through to defend its queen. She fell back and lashed out with her obsidian knife. The moment it drew blood, the hiver died. It collapsed atop her knife-arm and legs, pinning her in place as the wounded queen dragged her bulk closer.

There was no time. Maeven drew breath and gathered power in one last desperate attack. Her magic burrowed through the queen's organs, blooming into rot and disease. The bloated body loomed above Maeven, mouth opening wide to snip her head off.

Blood gushed from its open mouth. Mandibles jerked and slackened as Maeven's necromantic sorcery killed the ant-queen from the inside. The diseased creature slumped atop her, flesh bursting and coating her with pus. Maeven gagged and tried to wipe gunk from her mouth, but found her arms trapped beneath the dead queen's bulk. Her ribs creaked as the weight began to slowly crush her.

The crushing weight vanished. She gasped for air as the hiver corpse was dragged back into the chamber it had come from.

Lorimer stood over her, his skull a melted ruin of flesh and bone. His clothes had rotted away, as had the skin beneath. His feet were molten nubs and his eyes were gone, blackened pits weeping blood. Without lips and much of a throat his grin was horrifying and his voice wheezing and bubbling. "It would not have ended well for you, had you used that weapon on me."

She wiped slime from her face and laughed. For a moment the two grinned at each other, before old memories and old grudges returned.

She climbed to her feet, wiping down her clothes as best she could while studying his ruined body. "Does it hurt? Will you heal?"

He chuckled and his jaw sprouted shark teeth. "Pain is nothing to me. This body is just flesh and blood and bone. It can be replaced. A decent meal and I will appear as I always do." He sniffed the air like a hunting beast and edged closer to her, fingers growing into claws as he fought back the urge to tear out her throat.

She swallowed and stepped back, keeping her knife between them as she examined the weapon of volcanic glass. "It is interesting to learn that hivers have souls of a sort." On death, the queen's soul had been devoured by her enchanted knife – a little more power that would now be at her disposal.

Maddened hiver shrieks echoed weirdly down their tunnel. The walls began to vibrate with the sound of hundreds of feet. The Queen in Waiting – the Queen now – scuttled towards them. "Come! Come! Before her diseased kin catch and kill you. To Jerak Hyden." She now had an entourage of older hivers, devoid of the deformities and disease that marked the previous queen's spawn. They carried barbed spears and seemed eager to use them.

"I hope he's worth it," Lorimer wheezed, a single bloodshot eyeball growing back into its socket.

"As do I," Maeven said. "Otherwise, we are likely fucked."

"Hah, by Lucent swords at that."

They were herded through the tunnels as civil war erupted. The new queen's scent took control of every healthy hiver she came across and set them to evict the spawn of the old, diseased queen.

A chamber ahead was being guarded by more deformed hivers. The guards were skewered by hiver spears and pinned thrashing to the wall until their heads were chewed off. Inside, human and hiver bodies lay in neat piles, dissected and needing to be disposed of. Living but twisted humans lay in cages, covered in maps of surgical stitching, their eyes blank and their minds gone. Amid a mess of glass tubes, bubbling pots and odd brass constructions leaking steam, a short and vicious fight erupted.

A small, wiry man with a straggly grey beard and long brown coat crawled from behind an overturned table. He groaned at the ruins of what appeared to be a human skeleton crafted from metal, then breathed on his crystal spectacles and gave them a wipe on his sleeve. He peered at the group of humans and hivers. "Goodness," Jerak Hyden said. "It is my old friends. Is this a rescue? I've never been rescued before."

"There is a first time for everything," Maeven said. "We need you to kill an army."

His eyebrows rose. "How marvellous! Such a challenge. Far more interesting than producing preservatives and food supplements. How quickly may I begin?"

"As soon as we get out," Lorimer said.

"Oh!" Jerak Hyden's eyes lit up as he studied the vampire's exposed muscle and organs. "Tell me, my good fellow, does that hurt? Describe every sensation in detail." He stretched a hand towards Lorimer's chest cavity and it was firmly slapped aside.

"Get us out," Lorimer demanded of Maeven, "before I am forced to eat this insane fool in order to shut him up."

CHAPTER 14

"Hive appears a little more, ah, interesting than I recalled," Jerak said as they exited a tunnel in the huge conical fortress and skidded to a stop before a crossroads.

Maeven stared at men laying broken and screaming in the middle of the intersection, their weapons discarded. Others sat dazed in the dirt, vainly trying to reattach severed limbs. A knot of leather-clad men sprinted across the intersection ahead, swords and axes raised. A few moments later some of them fled in a panic back the other way, splattered with blood.

"Cahal'gilroy!"

Tiarnach's face was bruised and his tunic torn away. Bare-chested, long red hair flying wild, he chased after them with a mad grin and a blooded sword. He lashed out and cut through an ankle. The man fell; Tiarnach stepped on his back and kept on going.

The huge form of Amogg rumbled unsteadily after him, trampling the fallen man into the dirt. Her axe swung down and came back up dripping bone and brains as she charged after her raging ally. "Face me, youse cowardsh!"

The necromancer turned to Lorimer, finding him crouched over a corpse eating the heart. His vampiric flesh was already regenerating, soft skin spreading over bone and glistening red muscle. Jerak Hyden watched rapt, fingers twitching.

The new hiver queen chirped happily and squirted her

sweet pleasure-scent. "Our deal is complete. Safest to leave Hive. Soon the rotten queen's spawn will be driven out into the streets." Her guards escorted her back into the warren of tunnels to continue the purge.

"Hurry," Maeven said, grabbing Jerak by the arm and forcing him to jog after their companions. "These are no mere town guards. I smell the stink of the Bright One upon them. Which can only mean one thing – inquisitors are near. We need to get out of here, and quickly."

Lorimer dropped to all fours, bone and muscle popping and cracking, reforming into a bestial, hairless wolf-shape. He caught up with her, loping by her side at an easy pace. "We shall not depart without a fight, I hope?" he growled. "These vermin owe me a debt of blood. I would feast on their flesh."

"You are never full," she panted, half-dragging a red-faced and flustered Jerak with her.

"True." Lorimer grinned and his wolf-fangs and claws grew, becoming truly monstrous.

They followed the sound of clashing steel and screams, turning the corner to see a pitched battle outside a grimy tavern. The locals cowered inside, peering through the shuttered windows as hands and heads flew through the air, shed by Amogg's huge axe.

The orc roared and swung at an armoured Lucent soldier. He tried to block the blow, but such was the force that his blade bent and rammed back into his face, denting his helmet and crushing his cheekbone. Her foot snapped up and thudded into his chest like a battering ram, cracking his sternum and launching him into a wall.

A soldier swung his sword at Tiarnach, a mighty but clumsy cut. He didn't deign to parry with the sword in his right or the knife in his left and instead slipped aside to let the sword cut only air. The soldier overbalanced and Tiarnach sighed as he rammed the knife up through the man's jaw into his brain.

"Where is the challenge in this?" he shouted. He left his

knife embedded in the dying soldier's skull, and as the corpse fell, Tiarnach deftly slipped the man's knife from his belt to replace his own. He scowled and looked around for another enemy, but his mirth evaporated as a small army marched into the street ahead. "Ah, shite."

These were no mere scouts or farm boys given weapons they didn't know how to use, but mailed veterans intent on killing, their shields raised. At their head were three knights in shining plate, wielding long and exquisitely crafted war swords – the air seemed to crackle and glow around two of the knights, and their swords burned with golden fire.

"Inquisitors," Lorimer growled as he leapt on the last soldier still fighting. His fangs tore out the man's throat, then he began to gulp the flesh down, consuming the unfortunate bastard to finish off the repairs of his own body.

Amogg grinned and started towards the knights, but looked down at the weight being dragged along with her arm. She seemed puzzled to find Maeven latched on to her, Jerak still gripped in the necromancer's other hand.

"We have to go. Now," the necromancer said.

"I not scared of humansh," Amogg said, swaying. "You break like twigsh."

Jerak gazed up with interest. "Goodness, you are quite large. Do you happen to know much about the internal organs of orcs? No? Would you like to?"

The big orc fiddled with her tusk-rings. "Mad alchemist is no fighter. Pathetic, even for human."

"He does not fight," Maeven said. "He kills. And you will see exactly why we need him once we are well away of here. A horde of diseased hivers are about to tear this entire town apart."

"You whit?" Tiarnach said, catching his breath. He glanced at the oncoming wall of steel and death filling the street ahead and his bloodlust abated, sword drooping as his mortal fear returned with a vengeance. He swallowed and backed towards Amogg. "Ach, there's no glory in dying here swarmed by bugs.

Come on, you big green bitch, let's retreat and kill more of these cocks another time."

Amogg scowled but started to run. "What word is bitch?"

"A female dog," Jerak said. "The word originated from the old Furmanicus word 'bicce', meaning–" Maeven shoved him hard and forced him to run.

Behind them the human army roared and charged. A few arrows feathered the street around them, too close for comfort.

The big orc swatted an arrow from the air with her axe and took off after the others. "Tiarnach has been hit in head? Amogg is orc not dog."

"It's an insult to women," Lorimer said, loping along beside her.

She chewed her lip in puzzlement. "Humans have separate insults for male and female?"

"You'll find they are mostly for women," Maeven said, wheezing for breath.

Amogg snorted. "Humans are strange."

"Aye," Tiarnach said. "Never underestimate the stupidity of folk and you'll never be disappointed."

A conical hiver home collapsed behind them, and the air filled with the maddened chittering of angry ant-people.

Maeven glanced back and then ran faster, panting with unaccustomed effort. "We can... talk about this... later. Run like your life... depends on it! It damn well does."

With the blessed strength and youth that his Goddess had bestowed upon him, Landgrave Daryn found running in full plate posed no more than a minor inconvenience. Heavy as it was in the hand, when worn his old battle armour fit like a glove. Yet only a few weeks previous he would not have been able to squeeze his flabby gut into it.

His scouts ranged ahead, pausing only to loose arrows at the backs of the fleeing enemy.

The dull-witted and savage orc was massive and imposing, but still swift as a charging bull, and the unnatural bestial creature beside it seemed swifter still. The grizzled madman beside the monsters undoubtedly had a similarly sordid provenance but he would die before Daryn needed to concern himself with his tale.

The enemy were being slowed by the scarred sorceress hauling a wiry little scholar of a man – surely that was the mass-murdering alchemist that the Falcon Prince's informant had written of? The orc reached over and picked the little man up by the scruff of the neck and tucked him under one arm. They began pulling away from his armoured host, and after seeing the orc in action he knew the sentinels he had left on that side of town to block off any escape would prove insufficient.

"The heretics cannot be allowed to leave," he shouted, his own voice muffled by arming cap and helm. "Drop shields and charge!" His footmen tossed their heavy shields aside and surged forward, eager for the kill.

Buildings to their left crumbled and collapsed, and through clouds of dust came a host of horrific monsters boiling up from below, their ant-like bodies twisted by some form of dark magic. The maddened beasts overwhelmed three surprised scouts before they knew what danger they were in. They went down flailing.

Daryn slowed, torn. The enemies of his Goddess were getting away – that could not be allowed! And yet the men of Allstane were now fighting for their lives against a horde of twisted hivers crawling through the streets. That moment of indecision cost one of his men an arm, torn free in a monster's mouth. The scream took away any other thought. Daryn leapt among them, forcing the beasts back. His sword split a hiver head, then took off another's antennae on the backswing. He booted a third in the face, pulping an eye. His most heavily armoured footmen followed his lead and formed a defensive line across the street while his scouts pulled the wounded back to safety.

He glanced left and right, finding no sign of the holy knights or their robed acolytes – their sole intent was slaying the enemy of the Goddess. The urge to obey her command slammed back into place, but as more and more hivers swarmed towards them his own survival was all he could manage. Those two inquisitors would have to look after themselves. He prayed they would succeed, but a traitorous part of him prayed harder for the lives of his men.

As the screams erupted behind them, Maeven smiled. This little rescue mission of hers had provided unexpected benefits. Not only did she have Jerak Hyden in her clutches, but they had also dragged the Lucent Empire into the middle of a hiver civil war. Every dead soldier was one less they had to face at Tarnbrooke.

"Where are you taking me?" Jerak wheezed from the crushing grip of Amogg's green arm as she casually butchered two Lucent soldiers that tried to block her path.

"To the river barge," Maeven replied, rotting another soldier's heart. "It's the quickest way out of here." Two other men left their friend to die and made a run for it down a side street; she let them go rather than slow down.

The party turned the corner and passed the outskirts of Hive, leaving them a straight run for the river. Two ragged slavers were leaning against the mooring platform smoking pipes and passing a green bottle back and forth. The men looked up. Pipes dropped from wine-dark lips. They scrambled to untie the barge and push off, which would eliminate the easiest escape from Hive.

Maeven summoned her power and struck, fingers of darkness stabbing into their hearts. The men pawed at their chests and fell, blood and wine gushing from their mouths.

Lorimer leapt aboard the barge, body shifting into a more human configuration. He dug his claws into the deck to anchor himself and waited for the others, a sick look stealing across his face. Tiarnach followed, helpfully catching a flailing Jerak as Amogg tossed him aboard. Then the big orc stiffened and spun to scan the town they had just come from, her axe raised.

Maeven, too, felt the oncoming storm. Her hair began to rise. Lightning flashed, once, twice. The first bolt struck Amogg's axe, flinging the big orc backwards into the river, arm and chest aflame. The second bolt struck within arm's reach of the necromancer's feet. The earth exploded, and from the smoke, two inquisitors charged, swords crackling and spitting shards of light. Three bald robed men arrived with them, hanging back and murmuring prayers of protection that sapped the necromancer's strength and made her feel queasy.

Maeven yelled and backpedalled, tripped and fell backwards. She flung a hand up and black talons struck at the nearest knight. Her magic shattered on his cuirass. The inquisitor's sword flashed towards her hand, intent on hacking it off.

A snarling mass of tooth and claw slammed into the knight, knocking him back, saving her hand and likely her life. Lorimer's flesh tore, spines and tentacles forming to pull the enemy into a deadly embrace.

Spikes and teeth squealed on steel as the vampire sought to penetrate the inquisitor's armour, claws digging at groin and armpit. The knight struggled to free himself, head-butting Lorimer's face repeatedly until his helm was stained red – not that it made much difference to the vampire.

Tiarnach leapt ashore, sword in hand, and helped Maeven to her feet. She winced and favoured her right ankle. He eyed the inquisitor's heavy harness. "A sword's not the weapon for this mess. Need a war-pick to pry open these steel crabs."

The second knight's burning sword cut deep into Lorimer's side, slicing through spines, tentacles and bone like a butcher's cleaver. Lorimer hissed and kicked out, sending the inquisitor lurching towards the river. The man teetered back and forth on the stony riverbank, arms windmilling, then caught his balance just before tumbling in.

The knight who had been struggling to free himself from Lorimer's grip stilled and began to glow. Golden flames burst from his armour. Vampiric flesh ignited and blackened, forcing Lorimer to let go, roll to put it out and then limp back to Maeven's side, hissing, "These wounds do not heal."

"Damned inquisitors," Maeven spat.

"All of you are the damned," the burning knight said. "You are vile heretics and creatures of dark magic. The Goddess demands your heads."

"Nah," Tiarnach said. "Unlike you lot, we are still using our brains." He clutched his crotch. "Your goddess can suck my big hairy cock tho'. Aye, an' I've seen her look at it and lick her lips too. Can't get enough cock, that one."

Next to the river, a strangled, furious choking emerged from the second inquisitor's helm. He was so enraged he didn't notice the scorched green hand burst from the water to wrap around his ankle and rip him from his feet, sending him spinning head over heels to smash visor-first into the stony riverbank. His sword slipped from his grip and was lost to the river with an angry bubbling hiss.

Amogg rose, a torrent of black water pouring off her broad back. "Magic is for weaklings. I would have enjoyed good fight." She wrapped a massive hand around his helm and began hammering it into a rock as he failed to free himself from her iron grip.

The burning knight went for Amogg.

"Oh no you don't, you big tin bucket," Tiarnach said, intercepting him. He took a risk and thrust at the man's visor slit.

His aim was true, and the holy knight was forced to parry or risk losing an eye, but he was in full harness and didn't much care if he was hit anywhere else by a mere sword. As their swords clashed again Tiarnach's blade was sheared in two, the edge of steel glowing white-hot and running. "Ah," he said, sensing the man's glee. But then, Tiarnach had only ever intended on delaying him for a few moments until help arrived.

Lorimer flashed forward, his foot ramming into an armoured knee with inhuman strength. Covered in steel the knight may have been, but the human knee wasn't meant to bend that way. He howled and fell, unable to come to his companion's aid in time.

The flames had left Lorimer's leg a lump of charred bone, but instead of attempting to heal the limb, he ripped it off and simply formed a new one.

Amogg smashed the second inquisitor face-first into the rock, again and again until his helm was flat and oozing pink mush. "Weak as grubb," she said, letting go of his armoured corpse. The icy river swallowed it without trace.

The burning knight rose on his one good leg, helm turning to take in each of them and his three unarmed acolytes, calculating the odds of victory and coming up on the wrong side of the equation. "We will purge you all," he said. "I swear it upon the Bright One's breast."

Tiarnach laughed. "Aye, and I'm betting that's not all you do with her big bright tits, eh lad?"

It did not get the result he was hoping for this time. The man did not attack; instead, he lifted his sword and sent a ball of light up into the air. Lucent soldiers began pouring from the streets of Hive to answer his call.

"That is our cue to depart this place," Maeven said, limping aboard the barge. She struck at the inquisitor with her dark magic as the rest boarded, cursing as her magic had no effect.

"You will not leave here alive," the knight said, levelling his sword at the barge. Flames lashed out towards them.

Maeven waved a hand and the fire was deflected to strike the water. Steam and dead fish rose as she smirked back at him. "Perhaps we cannot kill you here and now, but you cannot kill us either."

Tiarnach tossed the mooring rope aside and the swift current carried them downstream, picking up speed. The inquisitor launched gouts of golden fire at their backs. While Maeven fended off the enemy's magic, Tiarnach pulled up his ragged tunic and bared his arse at the gathered forces of the Lucent Empire. He gave it a hearty slap for good measure.

After a moment's puzzlement, Amogg joined him, waving her big green arse in their direction. "This is insult, yes?"

"Oh aye," Tiarnach said.

"Worse than calling Amogg bitch?"

"Er... yes?" he replied, straightening up.

She kneed him in the groin.

He lifted right off the ground and then went down with a whimper.

"I be gentle," she said. "Don't want you a ball-less bitch before I fight you proper."

"Fair," he wheezed.

The big orc clenched her blackened fist and licked the wounds. "What now?"

"We take Verena Awildan's ships to Tarnbrooke," Maeven said. "Then we prepare for a siege."

Landgrave Laurant Daryn was the last to retreat from the war-torn streets of Hive, his sword bent and bloodied from hard hiver heads. Despite the fierce combat his blessed sword-arm was still strong and swift, hacking limbs off the last of the ant-men to menace them. A second force of hivers wearing steel plate and carrying wicked barbed spears had marched from the central fortress and began a methodical slaughter of their diseased kin. This allowed the human force to disengage and drag their wounded towards the safety of the signal light cast by the holy knights.

When Daryn arrived at the riverside with the last of his men he immediately noticed that only Sir Orwin awaited him, the hands of his acolytes clamped to his knee and a soft golden light leaking from between their fingers. The barge was gone and their targets with it. He had saved his men instead of pursuing the creatures of dark magic he had sworn to stop. The holy knight's armour was muddied and dented from combat and his eyes were murderous.

The landgrave cursed and forced himself to meet the knight's gaze. "Tell me what you learned of their abilities. We will use it to crush these unholy beasts, I swear it."

"You have failed the Goddess and the Falcon Prince this day, Landgrave," Sir Orwin said. "I will not see you do so again. When we march on Tarnbrooke I will see to it that the people of Allstane form the vanguard of our army. You will attack first and redeem yourselves, or die like dogs to allow better men to finish the job."

BOOK TWO
The Calm Before The Storm

CHAPTER 15

From Hive, the party rode the sturdy slaver barge downriver to the coast. None of them had any experience in navigating anything larger than a puddle, never mind a river swollen with winter melt water, so it swiftly became a nerve-racking trip for all involved. Lorimer's claws nailed him to the deck as the barge heaved and dipped and battered into rocks and fallen branches.

Amogg and Tiarnach seized the long poles lashed to the side of the barge and attempted to push the boat away from the most dangerous of the rocks, while Maeven leaned on the tiller and tried her best to steer them in any direction at all as white water crashed across the dipping bow. Wood cracked and splintered, and water began gushing through the holes, with only Jerak Hyden and a small bucket to bail it back out.

Somehow, they managed to stay afloat until the river calmed and widened as it approached the coast.

From the deck of the *Scourge of Malice*, Verena Awildan and her sailors watched in horrified fascination as the party stumbled wet-footed from the wreckage. Her sailors gaped at the sheer incompetence of the barge's crew. Their queen ordered a rowboat to fetch them to her.

As Amogg lumbered onto dry land, the barge lurched and groaned, then settled down into a grave of silt. She dropped a bedraggled Jerak Hyden face-first onto the beach. The little man sat up, spat sand and adjusted his spectacles. Then he spotted Verena and gave her a joyous wave before running over and clambering into the rowboat, the others following at a more leisurely pace.

The sailors of the rowboat winced as the rest of the party climbed aboard, Amogg's weight causing the wood to groan and the boat to sink lower into the water. A short while later the soggy, bloodstained party clambered aboard the ship.

Jerak Hyden made a beeline for Verena Awildan. "Goodness! How marvellous to see you again. I require access to your stores, there is a certain experiment that I simply must–"

"Denied," Verena said. "Touch anything, you grotesque little monster, and I will run you through. You will remain in your room under guard at all times until I can get you off my ship. Then you are Black Herran's problem."

Her words did not upset him. People were no better than his mechanical automatons of brass cogs and copper wire – indeed, they were just a messier construction. The mention of Black Herran piqued his interest, however. "I do hope she wishes me to resume my old works. It has been so very long, and I do hate to leave a project unfinished. Would any of you happen to know the size of the army she wishes disposed of?"

Amogg laughed. "Scrawny human thinks too much of himself." Her eyes sought out Wundak and Ragash, perched beside netted barrels and sharpening their axes with whetstones. They lifted the weapons in brief salute. "Orc axes much stronger than little man."

Maeven exchanged an unsettled glance with Verena. "When we followed Black Herran you and Tiarnach were always on the front lines of battle. You never did see his creations at work."

"I did," Lorimer growled. "At Kal Thraka. He constructed a bronze-plated wagon that rolled towards the enemy and belched poison gas. They coughed up their own lungs and died without a single sword drawn on our side. There was no honour or glory to be found in battle that day."

Amogg and Tiarnach's faces twisted with disgust.

Jerak tutted. "What honour is there in death, or in sticking a pointy bit of metal through some fellow's skull before he can do the same to you? It is all very crude and pointless when you can win without a single loss on your own side, wouldn't you agree?"

"Enough," Verena shouted, as she studied her bloody allies. "You can discuss the finer points of martial honour later. Apart from that poor barge, what else did you kill in Hive?"

"Stinking Lucents were there waiting for us," Tiarnach said. "The bastards knew who we were and where we'd be."

"What? Gormley!" Verena shouted. The slynx around her neck lifted its little head and glared. Her first mate ran over and she grabbed him by the front of his shirt. He loomed over her but still cringed back in fear.

"You are my master of pigeons," she hissed. "Pray tell, did somebody send one of your little birds off carrying a message it shouldn't have?"

His face paled. "I swear, I had nothing to do with that. I will find out who is to blame."

From behind, Lorimer wrapped a clawed hand around Gormley's neck and leaned over his shoulder, fangs brushing his throat. "Your heart thunders in my ears, and a fresh sheen of sweat tells me that you lie. You reek of betrayal."

Verena drew a knife from her belt and set the tip to her first mate's stomach, pressing until a bead of blood ran down the steel. A belly wound was a slow and agonising way to die. "Is this true?" she asked, through gritted teeth.

Gormley grimaced. "Fuck the lot of you. I work for humans, not monsters. The Lucents have the right of it, and I hope they exterminate all of your kind."

"You were my first mate," Verena growled, her hand trembling as she struggled to resist gutting him like a fish. "I trusted you. You should have trusted me."

Lorimer's forked tongue trailed up Gormley's throat. "Do you wish me to dispose of this filth?"

She withdrew her knife and shook her head. "Goodness no, I can make better use of him. Gormley, for your many years of loyal service I offer you one last boon: if you cooperate then you may yet survive. Men, throw this scum in the brig for now."

After her former first mate had been dragged below decks, Maeven raised an eyebrow. "You are more forgiving than I remember. The old Verena would have nailed his balls to the mast and let him hang there howling."

"Oh, if he has no other use then he will die in agony," the pirate queen said. "But not until I have wrung every last piece of information from his sorry hide."

"Then your temper has cooled over the years," Maeven added.

"Oh no," Verena answered, smiling at the necromancer. "I have just learned to savour a full and hearty revenge more than a quick and messy murder."

Maeven eyed the old, puckered wound marring the pirate queen's arm, inflicted by her own necrotic magic long ago, and knew that debt would be repaid one way or another.

"It's time to set off for a heart-warming reunion with our old general," Verena said. She glared at the vampire. "If you even *think* of scarring my deck with those claws of yours, I will have you thrown overboard. If you prefer to swim there, then be my guest."

He scowled but retracted his claws and was once again in the full likeness of a man. He did, however, rip a length of rope from a sailor's hands and demand to be lashed to the mast.

Tiarnach took one last look across the sandy bay, knowing that the next time he stood on solid ground it would become a field of slaughter. Tarnbrooke would be his first true battle without his people by his side and their mad charge for glory or death. He had not expected those few Lucent knights at Hive to be so troublesome, and there'd be many more at Tarnbrooke. His godly power was truly dead, gone along with his family and friends, and his sober courage fled right along with it.

"We're a' fucking doomed," he said as he went off to search the ship for any kind of alcohol. All he had left to do was to kill the Falcon Prince or die trying. And dying was so much easier than living.

Days later, the *Scourge of Malice* anchored off the coast south-west of Tarnbrooke. The shore party found a hamlet of farmers able to provide carts and hardy hill ponies to carry them north to the mouth of the Mhorran Valley. The peasants didn't even complain, after Amogg tossed the first man through the wall of his own barn.

They set off in three carts, Black Herran's old captains in the lead, a pack of armed Awildan pirates behind, and then the hulking forms of Wundak and Ragash and a few frightened and silent sailors bringing up the rear.

It was a fine frosty day with clear skies, and Lorimer shook his head at the farmers and shepherds going about their daily business in the fields. "These ignorant peasants have no idea what is coming for them," he said, adjusting the cloth strip protecting his eyes. "They should run or stand and fight, not close their eyes and hope for the best."

"That is exactly it, Lord Felle," Verena replied. "These are but simple peasants, used to keeping their heads down and working the land of their ancestors. Most know little of war and the world beyond a few local villages."

Amogg grunted. "Ignorant orcs die young. Army always need food. Orcs keep some humans alive if we conquer."

"Aye, at least for a bit," Tiarnach added.

"If they hold it, they keep it," Amogg said. "If orcs stronger, orcs take. That is life."

"Savages," Lorimer said.

Amogg glanced back to exchange bewildered looks with

Wundak and Ragash, who were keeping a constant watch on their supposed allies. None of the orcs would ever understand humans.

"Are we there yet?" Jerak Hyden asked for the tenth time on their journey. "Your discourse is tedious, and I wish to begin my work."

Verena fought to keep her hand away from her knife, but the alchemist seemed oblivious to her agitation. Tiarnach elbowed her and leaned in close. "Laters, aye? Once he's done his damned work." She nodded grimly.

Tiarnach took off Jerak's spectacles and then punched him in the face. The little man slumped back, unconscious, and he carefully placed the lenses back on his nose. "Why don't we all shut the fuck up 'fore we kill each other?" Tiarnach said. "I'm trying to close my eyes back here." The others paid him no more heed as he settled in for a snooze.

The journey north was neither pleasant nor free of further bruises and bloodshed – Jerak woke up but swiftly quietened when Tiarnach punched him again.

By the time the steep craggy hills and the valley came into view over a rise, Tiarnach and Amogg both sported blooded lips and bruises, while Lorimer had teeth and claws out ready to kill. Verena and Maeven had knives in their hands but put them away as the cart crested the last rise, enabling them to glimpse their destination.

"What do you make of our little battlefield?" Maeven said.

Tarnbrooke sprawled across the mouth the valley, a middling sized town comprised of disorganised clumps of quaint old hamlets that subsequent generations had joined into a single entity, filling the gaps between with more modern construction. Low, mossy dry stone and turf cottages rubbed shoulders with two and three-storey modern buildings of dressed stone and tiled roofs, some even bearing decorative carvings and whitewashed walls. Plumes of smoke rose from myriad chimneys, and a great column billowed from the town's two forges, where smiths were hammering shovels and hoes into weapons. A spired tower reared above the town: the sole temple shared by the many Elder Gods. A watchman at the top balcony had already spotted them and was waving a red flag to alert the populace below.

"A decent enough little place," Verena said. "Rustic."

"A dung heap," Tiarnach countered.

The town was unremarkable, save for its location in the mouth of the fertile Mhorran Valley. It was by far the easiest and quickest route north and south by land, and the only one suitable for an army. Dozens of streams from the surrounding craggy and heavily forested hills joined together and bowed around the outskirts of the town. They provided plenty of fresh drinking water as they converged to form a river dashing towards the sea, not travelling any great distance but ideal for carrying logs and heavy goods downriver to trading vessels anchored in the wide sandy bay. The outskirts had been recently deforested, fresh stumps spreading up the foot of the nearby hills.

As the carts lurched closer, they were able to examine the defences with a more critical eye. A low dry-stone wall had once marked the boundary of the town proper, but now a log palisade enclosed the bulk of it. The northern side had been reinforced with boulders fallen from the high craggy cliff walls of the valley, dragged and rolled into place to form a more daunting barrier. Townsfolk crawled over the fortifications, hammering in sharpened wooden stakes, levering boulders into place, and using picks and shovels to deepen trenches. Despite the townsfolk's best efforts, Tarnbrooke had never been built with a siege in mind; it would take years to make the town truly defensible.

An older man in the hose and coat of a northern nobleman emerged from the iron-banded town gates as the cart pulled up. It was Estevan. He wore a wide brimmed hat with a distinctive red feather in the crown. A dozen spearmen in newly-sewn stiff linen and wool padded gambeson, with old mail and ill-fitting helmets, marched out behind him in two somewhat orderly ranks. He doffed his hat and bowed as the carts pulled up.

"My Lord Felle," Estevan said, straightening. "I am pleased to find you well. In your absence I have taken on the role of training the townsfolk in the arts of war as best I can in the time available." He nodded to the assembled party, shot Maeven a look of pure disgust, and then smiled at his lord. "It seems that your mission was a success."

Lorimer leapt down and clapped a hand on his servant's shoulder. "I am glad to see you well, my friend. We are gathered, and with Black Herran we will be seven. Enough to take on an army, or Maeven will die trying."

She pulled a face and rolled her eyes.

"Just as well we're all here," Tiarnach said, yawning and clambering out of the cart. "That lot of limp spears you have there will buckle at the first charge."

Amogg grunted assent as she followed him down. The cart lurched alarmingly as she stepped off and the sad-eyed ponies hitched to it looked greatly relieved.

Estevan noticed the wiry form of Jerak Hyden peering at him through broken slats in the cart, unblinking and intense. He shuddered and edged closer to his master. As Verena and her men pulled up, he offered her another bow full of flourish.

"Estevan?" Verena said, blinking with surprise, one hand petting the yawning slynx around her shoulders. "You look… remarkably young."

"I am pleased that one such as I am remembered by Your Majesty," he replied, donning his hat again. "It has indeed been many years."

"I always remember a man with a good eye for logistics and accounts," she replied, then she looked to Lorimer and back to Estevan comparing his apparent and real ages. "There are many mysteries I am not privy to, it seems. This passionless boor never deserved you. I don't suppose you would care to join my service?"

"I am afraid not, my lady."

Lorimer growled. "My man is not for stealing, pirate."

"Not while you live perhaps," she replied. "Come find me later, Estevan. The offer will remain open. Now, where is Black Herran?"

"At the northern wall," Estevan said. "The town is working hard to block the neck of the valley, to confront and contain the Lucent forces there. If you will all follow me? I have already taken the precaution of informing the townsfolk that Black Herran has requested a group of, ah, somewhat unconventional and fearsome allies."

As the humans followed the old male, Amogg and her elders were surrounded by the local warriors. One of them with fancy facial hair reached to take Amogg's great axe. She laughed. "Try take it, little male, and I take your head."

He snatched his hand back and nodded. "Was just going to carry it for you, uh, miss." He straightened his helmet, clutched his spear tight and then proceeded to escort the orcs through winding gravelled streets.

Ragash did not look impressed. "These feeble warriors are here to keep us prisoner?" The humans could not understand his orcish words but Amogg thought they understood his tone from the way they clutched their weapons tight.

Wundak shook her head, bone beads clacking. "Humans always afraid of us. They here to stop non-warriors running away with much wailing and waving of hands and loosening of bowels. Good. The wailing of human children is annoying. Useless things do not even make for good eating."

"We are far from orcish lands," Amogg said. "These humans lucky to have ever seen an orc, but never an elder. They know of the orc only by stories told of battle and our many chopping of heads."

As they approached the centre of town the road widened into a cobbled square occupied by market stalls and traders. As the three huge and heavily armed orcs entered, all the humans paused mid-conversation. Hammers stopped mid-strike, coins dropped from slack fingers to the earth, and sizzling meat began to burn on hot pans.

"Look at their fright," Ragash sneered. "Like startled rabbits." He reached for his axe as the humans began wailing, clutching one another and punching arms, strange flat faces twisted and weak jaws trembling. Their lips curved upwards in something that was definitely not fright. "Why do they not run from me?"

Amogg's belly rumbled with laughter as a swarm of unarmed human children enveloped Ragash, despite their mothers' attempts to herd them away. "Not fright. Surprise and then happy."

One of the children with a sticky dripping snout thrust a hot pie into Ragash's hand and bared its blunt teeth. Another with a long-braided mane slipped a bright yellow flower into his belt and then hid behind its brood-mate. It was no attack, but Ragash still gripped his axe tight, unsure of what to do. His eyes widened in mute appeal as he attempted to walk without crushing any of them.

"Endure it," Amogg commanded, tusks bared with glee. There was still fear there in the faces of some of the adult humans, but also desperate hope, or so she thought. It was so hard to tell with their liars' skin.

Their warriors managed to prod and cajole the children back to their mothers and the spearman with fancy facial hair turned to Amogg with what appeared to be embarrassment. Or perhaps he was experiencing shitting problems, she was not entirely certain.

"Apologies, my lady," he said. "They've been told help was coming, and, well, the bigger the better, I suppose."

"We are the help?" Amogg said. "Humans are happy to see orcs?"

"Yes, my lady," the man said, standing straight and sweating as she loomed over him.

"Never did I think such a day would come to pass," Wundak said, exchanging wondering glances with Amogg.

Ragash scowled and bared his tusks when she translated. "More like humans are happy to see orcs fighting for them."

Amogg ignored him and instead prodded the spearman's shoulder, causing him to stumble. "What is this word 'lady'?" she demanded.

The warrior's furry brows rose. "That's, ah, what we call dignitaries. Nobles and leaders and suchlike."

Amogg grinned. "An honour-word. I like. Not bitch. I hear Lorimer Felle called lord. Why is this?"

The spearman's eyes looked blank, even for a dull-witted human. "Uh, because he's a man. Lady is for women."

Amogg waited for more but that was all the answer he offered. "Humans are strange beasts. Always using too many words meaning same thing."

He had no answer to that, and instead hastened them across the square and through the newly-erected northern gates of the town. The wood was thick and bound with iron, but still green with the sharp tang of sap and resin. It would not last more than a season before warping beyond usability.

As Amogg left the town behind she joined Lorimer Felle, Maeven, Tiarnach, Verena and Jerak on the well-trodden path heading towards the Mhorran Valley and the wall under construction.

Five hundred and fifty paces north of the town at a natural narrow choke point, a black-clad figure with short white hair tipped with blood stood atop a section of fortified gatehouse. Her bejewelled hands were clasped behind her back as she supervised the ongoing construction.

The party stopped in their tracks as they saw their old general. Dark emotions and memories bubbled to the surface.

At the sight of her, Lorimer Felle's teeth grew into jagged fangs and his fingers into hooked rending claws. He hissed and shook with anger, barely holding himself back from ripping into her like a feral beast. "How I itch to rip her heart from her chest. It is no small thing for a lord to swear allegiance and she threw my oath away like trash."

Amogg snarled and exposed her ringed tusks. "I woke ready for final assault on Rakatoll. No general. Army fall apart. Black Herran cheated orcs of glorious victory."

Maeven stepped in front of them. "Calm yourselves. Until this war is over, set your old grudges aside. Or else we will once again fail." Despite her words, she too was visibly affected by the sight of her old general and mentor resplendent in all her arcane finery.

The pirate queen stood frowning, arms crossed. "We all stand to gain something from this madness," she said. "Lord Felle, we are both here to ensure a future for our people. Do not throw that precious thing away to slake a momentary impulse."

Tiarnach's grip on his sword hilt tightened, white knuckles trembling with blood lust. "Fuck her. If not for that bitch, the Lucent Empire wouldn't exist and my Cahal'gilroy might have survived."

"The true loss there," Jerak Hyden mused, "were the wonders I could have created with all that time and her resources."

Tiarnach turned to face the alchemist, slow and deliberate as he lifted his sword with murder in his eyes.

Verena grabbed his arm. "Now is not the time." She held his savage gaze until he lowered his sword. "The years have been harsh on me too," she continued, her eyes sweeping the rest of the group. "Many sought vengeance on the Awildan pirates for my support of Black Herran's army. While there is no love lost between Maeven and myself, if both of us advise restraint at this current time, then be assured it must be the wisest course of action."

Black Herran chose that moment to turn and notice them. Her eyes were cold and hard as she beckoned them to approach.

CHAPTER 16

Black Herran studied her old captains as they approached. These six monsters had managed to survive the others' rabid ambitions and all the hard years since their lives went to shit. It had been forty years since they had last assembled before their general. Now they were furious and on the knife-edge of murder, not unreasonably.

Only Jerak seemed pleased to see her, offering an energetic wave and manic grin. That bespectacled little devil never harboured grudges. Most people were lucky, or unlucky as the case may be, if he noticed them at all. The only thing he cared about was a chance to practise his alchemy and to perfect his macabre art of murder. Even so, he was not without a peculiar sort of charm when he wanted something.

"Leave us," she said to nearby townsfolk working on the wall.

They were more than happy to put down their picks and shovels; clearly more afraid of her than any of the legendary monsters standing in their path. These men and women had lived beside her all their lives without suspecting a thing, but now that they knew who and what she was, everything had changed. Old friends cringed under her gaze and fled her presence, and even youths she had once bounced on her knee wailed and hid. The dream of a peaceful life was now dust, and the stern but goodhearted figure of Elder Dalia had perished right along with it. Black Herran was back for one last atrocity, and being on the right side of the conflict was of little comfort.

"Welcome to my humble home," she said. "Shall we get this nonsense out of the way? Come and kill me if any of you black-hearted bastards think you are hard enough." She lifted a bejewelled hand and beckoned.

Forty years of festering betrayal bubbled over into rage. Amogg roared and charged, filled with the lust to prove her strength against the most powerful human she had ever known. Lorimer was not far behind, serrated bone jutting from his fingertips as the depths of her betrayal bit hard. Tiarnach followed, red hair streaming, steel glinting in his hand. His many misfortunes were all her fault.

Verena, though, stood still, hands clutching her hissing slynx. And Jerak, too, looked on with mild interest, hoping to see somebody's internal organs exposed. He didn't much care whose.

Black Herran made no move to stop them. She summoned no demons. She used no magic. Instead, she looked to the necromancer at the back and smiled knowingly.

"Sour-faced old hag," Maeven hissed. She was nobody's pawn, not anymore, but the information Black Herran held was what she desired above all else. And that cunning old creature knew it. Black Herran's smile was forcing Maeven to side with her and intervene.

So be it, Maeven thought. She had no qualms ripping the life from any of the others.

She let distilled death boil up from the depths of her soul, summoned through her connection to the void that waits beyond all life. A wall of life-devouring darkness erupted in front of the demonologist, hiding her from view.

Amogg and Lorimer skidded to a stop moments before plunging through. Tiarnach did not hesitate. That madman went straight ahead.

Maeven gasped in shock – not because of his stupidity, but

because she felt only a bare scraping of lifeforce ripped from him. The once-god did not boast life, at least not as she knew it.

As their rage drained, Maeven let her magic go. That prig of a vampire glowered at her as if she were filth to scrape off his boot, but that was nothing new.

The sorcery dissipated to reveal Tiarnach flat on his face and crawling with shadowy tentacles that seeped from the crevices in the makeshift wall Black Herran stood on. The shadow demons held him tight despite his struggles. They whispered their hunger into his ears and caressed his exposed flesh like long-lost lovers, each touch causing pinpricks of blood to well up.

Maeven glared at her old general. The hag always had a backup plan or two. Always. And now the others would think twice before trying to attack her again, curious if the necromancer would stab them in the back the moment it was turned. In one move Black Herran had crushed their united anger and replaced it with the old fear and divisive suspicion that had once kept them in line.

"You think we will fight for you?" Lorimer said. "You lost my allegiance when you left us without a word."

Black Herran shrugged. "I don't care what your reasons are, so long as you are here to slaughter the Lucent Empire."

"I fight," the big orc rumbled. "I kill Falcon Prince. Then kill Tiarnach and Black Herran. I strongest warrior."

Tiarnach winced as the shadows seeped back into the spaces between rocks, pinpricks of his blood taken as payment for daring to attack their master. He climbed to his feet, careful to keep his sword between himself and the defensive wall. "Oh aye, looking forward to it," he said to Amogg. "Just be sure you kill that strutting silver prick first."

Black Herran clapped her hands together in glee. "Excellent! I can work with lust for battle and revenge." Then she looked to Jerak Hyden. "And our ingenious alchemist – I have such plans for you. So much to build and so little time. I hope your skills have not diminished?"

His eyes lit up like a stoked furnace. "The talents of Jerak Hyden have increased beyond the dreams of your lesser minds. I have already thought up so many plans to–"

"Later, you pompous blowhard," Verena interrupted, eyes narrowing at Maeven, who stood silent and impassive. "We are all here for our own reasons and self-interest, but know this, Black Herran, we are no longer your captains and you are no longer our general. You trampled that right into the mud the night you abandoned us."

Black Herran shook her head with exaggerated sadness. "Oh, get over it. You fucked it all up after I left you everything you needed to win. You were all weak and I was your crutch."

Instant outrage.

Amogg growled, baring tusks.

Black Herran's gaze stabbed into her orcish eyes. "Are you not strong now? Independent? A renowned war-leader in your own right? When I was your general you obeyed my orders without a thought beyond swinging that axe. Would you be the great chieftain you are today if I still led you around by the nose?"

The big orc chewed on a tusk ring, thinking about the way she had just left her own clan to stand on their own. "Truth in what you say."

"She throws our oaths away like gnawed chicken legs and you agree with her?" Lorimer objected. "Tiarnach, your people would still be alive if we had prevailed – what of that?"

"The Cahal'gilroy," he answered, staring at the steel in his hand, "lived and died by the sword. Such was our way of life. But they shall be avenged."

The vampire threw his hands up in disgust. "So be it! I am here to save your miserable little town for a single reason: the necromancer has sworn to assist me in regaining my own lands once this is over. Do not get in my way."

Black Herran smiled. "So long as you fight. But if I catch you feeding off the townsfolk I will have demons drag you down to the deepest pits of Hellrath."

"I dare you to try," he sneered.

"Enough," Maeven said coldly. "I hate you all, and the feeling is mutual. I suggest we all accept it and work together one last time."

Lorimer said. "Not until she explains why she left us without a single word."

All eyes focused on Black Herran. She took a deep, slow breath and then looked each of them in the eye. There were levels of truth she did not wish them to know, and others they would not believe, so she decided a half-truth would best serve her cause.

"I left because there was no future to my old plan of conquest. I had already tortured and killed all who wronged me, and consigned their souls to the pits of Hellrath, where demons still gnaw on them to this day. I ripped their petty kingdoms apart and burned their ancestral homes. As my army swelled, I conquered their corrupt allies and brought low almost all the so-called noble houses of Essoran."

She looked at the bustling town she now called home. "The night before we were to crush the last remaining force of the old regimes, I found myself pondering what came next once I ruled unopposed. What was left for me to achieve?"

She shook her head at Maeven as the crawling tendrils of darkness writhed across the necromancer's face. "We have both made dark bargains that have scarred our souls. Using that power brings only death."

To Tiarnach and Amogg she said: "My temper is a fearsome thing. I was too vengeful to rule with mercy then. Time has now tempered my rage."

Next, she turned to Verena. "I was too dark-hearted to rule through love and admiration, and too dreadful to kindle true loyalty. I believe you know of what I speak."

Jerak Hyden met her gaze with a look of bored irritation, and Lorimer with suspicion. "I did not much care for the lives and problems of others," she continued. "And I would stop at nothing to achieve my goals. In short, I would have made for a terrible ruler. I would have been a bloody-handed tyrant chained to a throne, and that frustration could only ever go one way. I left before everything drowned in a tidal wave of blood."

Verena gaped. "You just upped and left, without even a thought of putting a chain of command in place. That is…"

"Callous?" Black Herran supplied. "Cruel? What part of not caring for the lives and problems of others did you fail to understand? I slaughtered a quarter of the rulers of Essoran for revenge, and another half on a whim. I didn't care then, and I certainly don't care now. What concerns me now is crushing the Lucent Empire before they destroy this pleasant little town I call home. The only question that remains is, will you help defend Tarnbrooke?"

For their own reasons, one by one, the six remaining captains of Black Herran's army gave their grudging assent.

"Excellent. Follow me and I shall introduce you to the townsfolk. It's best they realise the full extent of the might that is now on their side. And learn to avoid aggravating you." She led them back through the town and into the market square in front of the temple, yelling for her people to gather. Jerak Hyden seemed interested in the food stalls and had to be dragged away.

To Maeven's eyes the uneasy crowd were more afraid of Black Herran than they were obvious dangers like the orcs. Her general's lips were pressed tight and her eyes were cold and dead inside. The necromancer knew how much it hurt when those you loved turned on you and looked at you like you were a demon in human form. However, she couldn't find it in her heart to pity the old woman.

Black Herran had to stand on a box so all could see her. "You all know who I am and what I can do. Now I introduce my allies who will help you defeat the army sent by the Lucent Empire. You will have heard of them: Lorimer Felle, the vampire lord of Fade's Reach. Queen Verena Awildan of the Awildan Isles, grand admiral of its corsair fleets. The mighty war chief of the Hadakk orcs, Amogg. Tiarnach, war god of those legendary warriors, the Cahal'gilroy. Maeven, master of the deadly art of necromancy..." Each name was a wave of shock rippling through the crowd. Fear mixed with desperate hope. "And then there is Jerak Hyden, master of alchemy."

At this, the crowd flinched and began babbling, forcing her to shout to be heard: "The alchemist fights *with* us! Would you care to be on the other side of our walls facing his creations? Do you want to run away and end your days begging for mouldy scraps on strange southern streets, or as whipped slaves rowing oars on some gods-forsaken foreign sea?" She offered an evil grin. "Assuming you somehow survive the razor teeth of my ravenous demons that prowl the outskirts." Her expression changed into an angry glare. "Stand and fight with me to keep what is yours. Or else."

The sliver of hope she offered them dampened their fears, and the crowd eventually calmed and quietened. Though Black Herran did think a close eye would need to be kept on all food and drink until Jerak Hyden's presence here was a distant memory – he couldn't be trusted not to slip something hideous in as an experiment. His alchemy was every bit as magical to the townsfolk as demonology or necromancy, and the stories told about him were as dark as those of Black Herran herself.

"We will win," Black Herran said. "And then everything will be as it was. Tarnbrooke will again be a quiet and safe little town. In the meantime, you would all do well to obey our commands if you want to survive to see that day come to pass. Now be off with you! You all have your tasks."

The crowd slunk off, subdued and shrouded in whispers, leaving the seven of them in a rough circle, Amogg's orcs hanging back.

"And how can we face down such a huge army?" Black

Herran said. "I, of course, have a plan or two if you will hear me out?"

"Your pathetic wall will not hold them," Lorimer replied. "You cannot expect farmers and shepherds to hold such crude fortifications against a trained army. The magic wielded by those inquisitors we encountered in Hive will destroy them with ease. They have no counter to such might."

Black Herran held up a finger and smirked. "That is where we come in. You must ensure they are able to hold the wall for a single day until the sun sets. No more and no less." And then she looked to Jerak Hyden. "I will harvest the mass suffering and acute terror of the Lucent army, and use it to fuel my magic. Once that is done, he will see to the final disposal of the Lucent army with weapons he once crafted for me."

Even Lorimer was taken aback at the thought of so much indiscriminate carnage. He turned to the wiry alchemist and stared in disgust as the little man's smile grew wide.

Jerak clapped his hands together. "How very wonderful! I shall get to work immediately."

CHAPTER 17

Wheels turned, crucibles smoked and alembics bubbled over charcoal, distilling death. An orderly disorder that baffled the dim-witted, skittish minions assigned to fetch and carry whatever Jerak Hyden needed.

His general had anticipated his requirements and already gathered a goodly portion of the materials he required to produce certain minor works of art. She was now busy acquiring other items on his list of ingredients. He always found that working with Black Herran was a pleasure; she organised all the menial issues of supply, which left him able to focus on the delicate artistry of alchemy. Not that he was unable to do the task himself, but it was all so terribly tedious and took valuable time away from his studies.

While his brutish companions busied themselves with inspecting the town's defences and other low-brow labour, he got straight to work improving the crude workshop set up for him in the building adjoining the town's largest smithy.

The thick stone walls and packed clay floor were proof against fire. The workshop also contained wooden benches, braziers and two fireplaces; a collection of glassware and tools; sacks and crates of supplies, powders and bottles all meticulously labelled in Black Herran's scrawl.

"Adequate," he said, rubbing his shaking, eager hands

together. Two assistants exchanged glances – no doubt feeling some emotion or other.

Ideas flooded his mind, a veritable waterfall of inspiration that threatened to overwhelm him with the pleasure of choice. He took a deep shuddering breath to calm and reorder his mind to a state befitting a man of his supreme quality.

He had been captured, sold, and confined in Hive, forced to produce the same simple products for years. The boredom would have killed him had he not amused himself by undertaking a long-term experiment: adding certain chemical additives to the foodstuffs preferred by the hiver queens. The degenerative effects had made for a fascinating study, and now that he was free, he was resolved to document its effect on a human population once he had the time to assemble a workroom worthy of his skill.

Jerak hummed and hawed over the selection of crude tools he had to work with, and with the instructions he had been given. He quickly concluded that Black Herran's plans were but crude butchery and unworthy of his time. He would give her exactly what she asked for, but he would also concoct something far more imaginative. Something much more fun. If only he had been given the time to set up a proper workshop and gather more materials than he currently had access to...

"So, Black Herran requires the wall to hold against a trained army from dawn until dusk while she works her mumbo jumbo, does she? Using only this equipment and such limited supplies?" He had been meaning to try out a few promising ideas and this provided the perfect opportunity to experiment on a captive audience. It was an interesting conundrum, and not one he had faced before: if he was too efficient, he would kill every one of the enemy before they were ripe for use in her rituals. But, too little and the wall would be overrun and the enemy assault would envelop the town itself, which would not be ideal. The utmost precision was required.

The town militia marched as faceless numbers through his

head; he needed to factor how many of the enemy he had to kill or disable and how the peasants might compare to the numerical worth of a real soldier of the Lucent Empire. He needed more information gathered by the brutes bumbling around the town. The vampire, perhaps. Images of dissecting that creature's inhuman flesh flashed through his mind, ponderings of what fascinating new information he might find there. Perhaps this conflict could offer him such an opportunity.

He uncorked a few bottles and sniffed the contents, scowling at the sharp sinus-burn of distilled alcohol. "Mm, moderate purity." It was suitable for testing a weapon he had dearly wished to make and turn on those dreary hivers. All he needed now was a metal pipe, pigskin, bladders, a small tar-sealed cask and somebody to hold it and hope for the best.

His two assistants pressed themselves against the wall as he wandered past deep in thought. "Oh! Oh!" His head clamoured with a hundred ideas vying to push to the fore. "No – wait. Pigs! Yes, even better, I could use the pigs. What a fine jape that would be. Burn, burn little piggies. Furious food!" He laughed at his own joke, then turned to one of his assistants.

The young woman in a leather apron, a glassblower by trade, cringed away from his gaze, her feeble mind overawed by the glory of his unveiled genius. He had already forgotten her name, not that it mattered. He hazarded a guess that others might consider her attributes sexually attractive, but Jerak only had eyes for her hands: long-fingered, fine and nimble and clearly used to careful work judging from the lack of burn scars from molten glass or spitting wood. A fine pair of useful hands he would be loath to lose. He made a mental note to request leather gloves and a gag lest her screaming slow him down.

He snapped his fingers at the other female, a plodding creature. "You, peasant, fetch a pig and be quick about it." He did not see her leave, thoughts already consumed with schematics and equations. How much could a pig's stomach contain, and for how long before it was expelled? What if its anus was sewn or glued shut? What was the running speed of a panicked pig? Such things had to be carefully measured.

He began setting out the pans and powders he would use to create his initial assault on the Lucent Empire. It was a lower-order work of alchemy, but it would meet Black Herran's requirements. The testing and creation process would be swift, leaving him additional time to allocate to his more interesting and intricate creations.

He cackled to himself. It was so good to be busy once more. There was always so much to learn, and so many wonders to craft.

"Is it wise to leave that madman to his own devices?" Verena asked as Black Herran led them beyond the wall and deeper into the steep-sided valley, where the last dregs of winter stubbornly held on, blocking all passage between north and south. "Should he not be kept under armed guard?"

They tramped through slush and dwindling drifts of snow, crossing over a small, mossy stone bridge spanning the icy stream that wound down the centre of the valley. "He cannot cause us too much damage," Black Herran said. "At least, not yet. Every hand is needed to bolster the town's defences."

"That will not last," Verena replied. "He is a demon."

Black Herran snorted. "Oh no, he is far worse. The inhabitants of Hellrath are voracious and vicious, but he is an unfeeling monster."

"Enough of that man," Lorimer demanded. "Let him do his work while we do ours. What are your thoughts on defending this town?"

Black Herran gestured at the Mhorran Valley opening up ahead of them. A few farm buildings and fenced pasture studded the ground either side of the stream, tufts of grass poking through patches of melting snow. No smoke rose from

the thatch, and no goats or sheep grazed on hardy grasses –
most were already slaughtered, salted and in the storehouses.

Lorimer lifted the strip of cloth protecting his eyes and
squinted up at the surrounding hills. "I see glints of metal or
glass from the peaks. Yours or theirs?"

"Our watchers," Black Herran said. "Shepherds who know
the goat tracks and secret ways through the hills. They will light
signal fires when they see the enemy approaching. The rocks
are steep and treacherous, not suitable for an army to pass
through, but it is possible a handful of the enemy could slip
past into the southern plains, if they don't break their ankles
first. Those small numbers, if any, should not be a concern. I
have demons placed to deal with the likes of them."

Amogg grinned, baring tusks. "We will fight axe to axe and
tusk to tusk. As it should be."

"Then let us hope the Lucent army expect the same kind of
straightforward battle," Lorimer said. "These sheer walls and
rocky hills will prove no barrier to me. They will learn to fear
me."

"That too, is necessary," Black Herran said. "They must
advance through the valley fearing attack at every turn. I
want their soldiers pissing themselves in terror. Their torment
will fuel my demonic magic, allowing me to deliver the death
blow."

"It'll be a slaughter," Tiarnach said. "And I dinnae mean o'
them. What's to stop them merrily carrying on and overrunning
your wee town right after they take the wall?"

"By then they will have learned to dread the fall of night
over several sleepless ones," Black Herran said. "Between
my magic and Lorimer's fleet-footed night assaults, they will
quiver in terror at the very thought of venturing blind into the
darkness. They must be forced to march their troops through
the neck of the valley and then wait until dawn to attack the
town walls with overwhelming force."

"What then?" Verena asked. "If my fleet is to engage the

wallowing buckets they call ships in order to prevent an army landing to your rear, I need to know there will be a reason for it. Why should I put my crews at risk if this place falls to the next wave of troops pouring through the valley?"

"Once the Falcon Prince is slain," Maeven spat, "the empire will crumble. He is the power behind everything."

"If we kill enough men then he will be forced to come in person," Black Herran said. "I will see to that. There are monsters that only their inquisitors could hope to defeat, and he cannot possibly show his oh-so-righteous empire and glorious goddess succumbing to dark magic. Then he is all yours."

Amogg, Tiarnach, Maeven and Lorimer exchanged warning glances, each determined to be the one to slay him. Verena nodded thoughtfully, accepting the answer.

"What would ye have us do now?" Tiarnach said. "Sit on our arses and wait for the bastards to trot up ready for a fight?"

"Maeven and I have rituals to prepare," she replied. "I would like you and Amogg to take the militia in hand and forge them into warriors that will stand instead of run."

Tiarnach yawned. "I'll do my best. It would be grand to go into battle with true warriors again."

"I make them more afraid of me than little men," the big orc said.

"That will work," Black Herran said, smiling coldly. "If they can stand before you, they can stand against anything. And as for you, Lorimer, please learn the lay of the land and prepare to make the enemy huddle around their fires in abject fear."

She led them back towards the town and they studied the incomplete log palisade encircling it, and the townsfolk deepening ditches. A procession of people passed them, towing a log over rollers and then carefully sliding it into a post hole before packing it with stone and mud to keep it in place.

"We're buggered if they get this far, eh," Tiarnach said. "At least the logs are green and won't fire easily."

"Best get to work shoring up the defences then," Black Herran said.

"We have time yet," Verena responded. "My sailors know a thing or two about carpentry; I will order them to assist in the construction. The big orcs Amogg brought with her may also come in useful."

"Give Ragash and Wundak meat and mead," Amogg replied. "They carry big tree each. Easy."

The party lapsed into silence for a long moment, studying each other and remembering how easy it had felt back in simpler days when they had all hung on their general's every word, overawed by her presence and power. Now a white-haired old woman stood before them, physically old and weak but somehow still in charge.

Black Herran cleared her throat. "I have prepared lodgings at our finest inn. You can't miss it; it is the only one of any size. We will gather here again at dawn tomorrow to discuss a proper defence strategy. Amogg, Tiarnach, I have instructed the militia to gather in the market square for you to inspect. I would value your opinion on their current usefulness."

"I think we have all had enough of each other for one day," Lorimer said. He disrobed and fell to all fours like a beast, spine cracking and popping, hands and feet sprouting claws. He loped to the edge of the valley and scrambled up the sheer cliff-face, barely slowing as his claws and unnatural strength carried him up, up, over the edge and into the barren and icy hills beyond.

They went their separate ways without exchanging another word.

CHAPTER 18

Tiarnach spat on the cobbled square and looked up at the similarly unimpressed mountain of orc that was Amogg Hadakk. "What do you make o' this lot o' fools?"

The fifty most skilled members of the four hundred strong Tarnbrooke militia that Black Herran could spare stood in uneasy and uneven ranks, each dressed in a jumble of scavenged armour and weapons. Some wore old, dented helms and breastplates a century out of date, or badly rusted mail that left a dusting of orange behind with every step. But the majority had to make do with linen gambeson padded with wool, and their mother's best copper pot with a leather strap riveted on for a helmet. Most clutched working tools like axes and hammers or hunting spears, with a few of the poorer peasants holding wooden pitchforks and slings. A few proudly wielded old swords and shields passed down from more adventuresome parents and grandparents. If these farm boys were the best equipped and most experienced warriors Tarnbrooke had to offer, Tiarnach reckoned the rest must have been poor indeed.

Townsfolk paused in their tasks, baskets in hand, to cast an admiring eye over their defenders. To them, they were the largest and deadliest army any of them had ever seen. Children gawped at the shining spear heads and freshly sharpened axes, and picked up sticks and loaves of bread to masquerade as warriors themselves. The adults didn't know any better than their children how piss-poor this militia really was. Against common bandits they might do fine, but against a disciplined army, they would be frightened rabbits facing down hungry wolves.

Amogg looked down, sneering. "Lucky humans are so many. Only reason you took old orcish homeland."

"Hoi," Tiarnach said, standing straighter. "Don't you dare say the Cahal'gilroy were no' the match of any orc."

"These not your people," she replied.

He didn't have a witty answer for that, but he felt the need for hard drink rise up from the black and gnawing pit of guilt inside his belly.

Amogg searched the ranks of sweating, shifting men. "So few. Where are your females?"

"They don't tend to follow the path o' the warrior," Tiarnach replied. "Not in these baby-soft southern lands."

She stared at him incredulously. "I not understand. They have arms and hands. They have axes and knives. Why they not fight on wall if enemy come?"

"Damned if I know," he replied. "Humans are bloody weird."

She huffed and stomped over to the militia. Their lines bowed as they backed away from her looming presence. "Weak," she snarled, and hoisted one up by the front of his gambeson with a single hand. He squeaked and dropped his spear as his toes dangled in mid-air. She roared, spittle flecking his face, and shoved him back into his friends. Five went down in a tangled heap.

"Weak as grubbs," she said as she rejoined Tiarnach. "Best use as shield to slow down enemy while I chop heads."

"We need them to stand and fight," he protested.

"Make them," she suggested.

He eyed her slyly. "How do you feel about throwing a fight? I'll show them a mere human can beat even you."

Her belly rumbled with laughter. "Amogg fights or does

not fight." She patted her axe, then turned to leave. "I go find females to fight. Must be better than this."

Tiarnach sighed and scratched his beard, watching her broad back disappear into the town on a mission to harass every adult woman she happened across, give them a shake and demand they fight with her.

"Right, you lot o' pissy babies," he shouted. "What the fuck was that cringing cowardice? I can smell you shitting yourselves from here. May as well cut your balls off, ya eunuchs."

With the big orc gone the militia regained some of their bravado. One of the men who had been bowled over shoved forward to face him. He was a big lad with shoulders like a bull and a face only a drunken mother could love, and her a few cups downed at that.

"How do you expect us to fight that monster?" the lout demanded. "She picked up Bertrand here and tossed him away like a cored apple."

"Like anything else that lives an' breathes," Tiarnach said. "You poke the angry orc full of holes. She's no' a god."

"Love to see you try that then," the lad demanded, a mocking grin on his ugly face as he pushed right up into Tiarnach's space, nose to nose.

Tiarnach considered their respective heights. The lad had a few inches on him…

He cracked his forehead into the man's nose. It crunched and bent sideways spraying blood everywhere. His knee rammed up into the lad's crotch, lifting him off his feet just in time to receive Tiarnach's brutal right hook that sent him flying backwards into a crumpled and mewling heap.

Tiarnach grinned and spat, feeling the boy's blood staining his beard a deeper red. "Aye, Amogg's no' a god. Me, I was the fucking war god o' the Cahal'gilroy and I'll see you cringing curs fight or I'll kill you all myself, then I'll go make your women scream with pleasure. Which o' you bastards is next?

If you can make me bleed, I'll buy you a horn of ale. If you can't, then you're keeping me supplied all night long. It'll be sodding expensive when I drink your inn dry."

Nobody stepped forward, so he grabbed the nearest spear and ripped it from its owner's hand, then used the butt to brutalise the unfortunate man's balls. The militiaman sank to his knees and vomited.

"Ain't using those now, were you? Next!"

That got them motivated. They came for him, hesitantly at first. He contemptuously downed the next two and mocked their manhood. The rest charged with foolhardy arrogance emboldened by numbers.

He felt no fear as he rampaged among them, spear spinning and knocking heads until it got caught up in a tangle of straps and mail. He dropped it and fought hand to hand, never staying still so they could bring their overwhelming numbers to bear. Kicking. Punching. Biting like a feral beast.

It was refreshing to let go and fight as he used to, albeit less lethally. A shade of his old battle-joy returned, and he felt young and vital again as he bathed in their fear. At least, until three men joined forces to tackle him to the cobbles. Even then, two quick punches to two soft bellies and he rolled free and surged back to his feet.

The third man enveloped him in a bear hug from behind. "Got the mad bastard! Finish him off before he leaves us all bleeding in the dirt. He's just one man."

As a moustachioed militiaman's fist bounced off his hard skull with a yelp of pain, Tiarnach bellowed with laughter. "Yes! Yes! That's the spirit. Fight!" He sank his teeth into a hand holding him and he was free. They would learn to fight half as well as his weakest Cahal youth one way or another. He kicked the moustachioed man in the face and elbowed the one behind him in the belly, winding him.

"More!" The fun was only just beginning.

* * *

What is with these pathetic humans? Amogg thought, tossing yet another useless wailing creature to the dirt, disgusted by their weakness. How could any race survive if these were the strongest they could spawn? These humans seemed to prefer digging in dirt and growing crops to achieving glory. Perhaps she just needed to look harder. She had fought human warriors before and on occasion even been mildly impressed before she took their heads. Perhaps humans should embrace proper orcish ways and treat their spawn like grubbs – then only the strongest would survive to breed.

A female human emerged from an alley carrying a stack of firewood. It dropped its load and squeaked as she hoisted it off its feet. "You fight," she demanded. "I give weapon."

Urine dribbled down the human's leg and she spat out frantic "no"s. Her voice was deeper. Ah, Amogg was in error – this was a male without facial fur. "Females do not fight. Males do not fight. Even grubbs better than adult humans." She tossed the runt into the mud and forgot he ever existed.

She spotted another young human herding two boisterous, curious young away from the scene with a broom, a female for sure from the long skirts, curly hair and a ring through her nose. "You – come fight. I give weapon."

The human spun and pointed her broom like a spear aimed at Amogg's throat. "Stay back, beast. You leave my sisters alone or I'll set about you."

Amogg paused, eyeing the blunt length of wood held in small shaking hands. She wrapped a hand around the hilt of her big axe and leaned it on her broad shoulder, sharp steel glinting. The human female did not run or wail, despite Amogg being twice as tall, five times as heavy with muscle, and wielding a steel axe against her wooden broom.

"Finally," Amogg said, baring her tusks in pleasure. "What is name?"

The human blinked, as if surprised she spoke the trade tongue. In fact, Amogg spoke several languages to varying fluencies. To know your enemy, you had to be able to speak to them. Humans always thought orcs were too stupid to learn their language, and always said too much.

"Penny," the human said.

"I Amogg Hadakk. You are female?" Amogg wanted to be certain this time.

The human blinked, confused. "Er, yes."

"I too female. You would fight me, Penny?"

Penny stood straight and narrowed her eyes. "If I have to, darlin'."

"Good. I give you sharp weapon. You fight for me now. Your male warriors worse than grubbs."

Penny's mouth opened and closed but the broom remained where it was. "Uh, what's a grubb?"

Amogg frowned. Were humans so ignorant of orcish life? Of course, she did kill almost every human who encroached on their lands...

"Grubbs are small creature before they grow to become orc. Weak. Stupid."

"So... like human children?" Penny said, kicking one of her curious younger sisters back behind her.

"Yes, like human children. But intelligent and useful. Come, you fight. You know other females who need weapon?"

Penny shook her head, confused.

Amogg huffed and battled the broom to one side, deftly sweeping the human named Penny up under one arm. She stomped off carrying the squealing human like a side of pork until she returned to the market square where the militia were currently... where the militia *had* been drawn up to show off their shoddy armour and weapons to their new war chiefs. Now forty lay scattered across the blood-spattered cobbles in moaning heaps, clutching groins and broken noses.

The remaining ten bruised and bloodied men had Tiarnach surrounded. They held spears and swords and axes while he was barehanded and badly out of breath.

Amogg chuckled and dropped Penny to the cobbles. "There is male who fight good. Fierce. Warriors of Tarnbrooke weak like mindless runt of grubbs. You see?"

Penny winced as she climbed to her feet, rubbing her bruised elbows as she stared at the impossible scene before her. "How can one man have possibly defeated forty?"

"That not man," Amogg replied. "That a god. Or was. Amogg is unsure of current theological status."

Penny stared at her.

The huge orc shrugged, slabs of muscle rising and falling. "Amogg ate a human priest once. He talked lots while pot boiled."

The human shuddered, then looked to Tiarnach as the warrior caught his breath a moment, before charging between attackers who thought they had him at their mercy. He flung himself backwards to avoid a spear-thrust, and his charge carried him skidding across the bloody cobbles straight between the spearman's legs. A quick jab up as he passed, and another militiaman was out of the fight.

"Time's up, lads," Tiarnach said. "The big brute of an orc is back. Hoi, Amogg, fancy some fun?"

Amogg grinned at Penny. "Come, we fight. Fight good, or I punish." Then she ran at the militia like a battering ram, slamming two big, armoured men off their feet.

Penny thought hard for a few moments. She could make a run for it and hide at home with her sisters, but she had to come back out at some point. Orcs were notoriously brutal creatures, and this one also served Black Herran.

As Amogg casually backhanded a man unconscious with a huge fist that could easily have crushed his skull, Penny swallowed and decided that punching a human was preferable to whatever the orc would do to her.

She picked up a discarded shield and charged wildly into the melee, shield held up high in front of her face. She screamed as she slammed into somebody and fell atop him, her knee finding a soft target.

Amogg's laughter boomed across the square and a blindly flailing Penny found herself hoisted into the air by a big green hand. She dropped the shield and stared down at the man she had clobbered.

The battle-scarred warrior was down and foetal, cursing beneath her shield as the still-standing men of the militia stared at her like she had grown an extra head.

"Great help, Amogg," Tiarnach said.

"Better than fifty males, yes? Hurt you."

His blue eyes cut into Penny, chilling her blood with the promise of pain.

"Oh aye," he said. "This one is a natural talent. Best you train her real hard."

Penny winced. The fucker had stitched her up. There was no escaping this now.

CHAPTER 19

Black Herran and Maeven sat in awkward silence until the pot of water on the hearth began to boil. The demonologist groaned as she heaved her old bones up from the chair to take the pot off the heat and select herbs from small clay jars. The fragrant scents of peppermint, orange and ginger filled the air as she opened the lids, pondering which to choose. Finally, she made her choices, measured it out and popped it into the pot.

Maeven kept her backpack under the table, where she could keep a firm foot on it. She did not trust anybody with her secrets, especially Black Herran.

More silence followed as they waited until the leaves were steeped for a precise amount of time. Maeven looked around the modest and unremarkable home, trying and failing to imagine her dreadful old general spending the last forty years of her life living in such a hovel. It was all so earnestly everyday and boring: a bookcase containing only a handful of well-worn books, a single overstuffed armchair, wonky clay pots and wooden figures adorning a shelf that had itself been crafted by small and clumsy hands. Not a single ritual circle, far less a human heart atop a black altar.

Black Herran placed squares of muslin over two cups and poured the tea, then collected the leaves in the cloth and set them to one side for reuse. She set down the drinks and sat back at the table.

Maeven eyed her cup suspiciously and took a single scalding sip. The bitter liquid burned down her throat, causing her to cough.

"What is this vile potion?"

"Not a drinker of tea then," Black Herran said, nursing the cup in her aged hands, savouring the warmth. "I would wait until it cools a little." She smiled, eyes and mouth sprouting cracks and crevices rather than wrinkles. "It's peppermint tea with some turmeric from far across the seas – it's not available to most, but physical distance here means little to demons. It's good for joint pain, though it seems you are more preserved than I would have thought, given your true age."

"Being a master of life and death has its benefits," Maeven said.

"Since you were successful in gathering the others, what does our master of necromancy now think about the chances of us surviving this war?"

"Slim," Maeven replied. "If they have many more of those inquisitors then we will be in serious trouble. They would demolish any militia without breaking a sweat. We fought two in Hive and it could have gone very badly indeed. Lorimer's wounds refused to heal until a fair while after they were inflicted. He found it easier to remove and replace entire body parts. They throw fire and can use some sort of lightning to quickly move from place to place."

Black Herran cursed, more dangerous by far than anybody else using foul language. "Do you have any suggestions?"

Maeven chuckled. "More Amoggs. She bashed one's armoured brains out on a rock. Brute force seemed to work well, if you can get close enough without getting roasted. They may wield a fragment of the power of a god, but they are still mortal."

Black Herran took a sip of tea. "Then we must even the odds. Let us hope many of them gather around the wall once it has fallen."

A flicker of a smile played about Maeven's lips. "Yes, it

will prove interesting to see what Jerak Hyden concocts for you. But I suspect you have brought me here to discuss the aftermath rather than the event."

"Indeed. Come that night there will be many Lucent warriors embracing death. You can use that."

"As can you," Maeven replied. "So much blood seeping into soil, turning the streams red. Might as well be a massive human sacrifice." She shifted in her seat and stared down into the hot tea, shoulders tensed. "What manner of atrocity do you intend to summon?"

"I am... unsure."

Maeven's head jerked up to stare. "You? Unsure?"

Black Herran ran a hand through her red-tipped white hair. "I am old and tired. It is not a matter of will but one of being badly out of practice."

"You are not the primal force I once followed," Maeven said.

"So it would seem."

"I feared you might use the sacrifices to summon something truly fearful. A duke of Hellrath perhaps."

Black Herran laughed. "Oh, it would take many more than this coming slaughter to open a gate large enough to allow a duke through to this world. The only time I could possibly have..." She broke off and instead drank more tea.

Maeven leaned forward, studying her. "The day you left?" she said. "The allied armies trapped between the fortress of Rakatoll and the sea with no escape. It would have been a slaughter beyond all belief. You had been intending to summon a duke of Hellrath?"

"Bargains were struck long ago," Black Herran said, shrugging. "Once I ruled, Duke Shemharai would have stepped onto the soil of Crucible, free to do as he wished with all the other lands while we ruled the continent of Essoran without interference. At the time I had nothing, and it seemed like a good deal – something is always better than nothing."

Even Maeven was taken aback. "Monstrous. But not

unexpected, not of you. What I find surprising is that you stepped back from the precipice. Was dooming the world too rich for even your black blood?"

"With all my enemies dead or dying in agony, what did I care for ruling? My bargain was to summon the vile thing once I ruled, and he would get my soul when I died. Well, gods damn that disgusting creature for I never did rule Essoran, and I ensured he will never get his way."

"Hah, you stabbed the demon in the back? That will not earn you any favours when your soul finally writhes in its claws."

"Do you see me crying a river?" Black Herran said. "I knew what I was selling for power. And it was worth it. Are your own dark deals worth their cost? Do you think I never noticed you speaking to your grandfather's bones? That my demons did not report everything my captains were doing?"

Maeven hissed and flung her cup of tea to shatter on the hearth. She rose and leaned over the table. "That is none of your business, you withered old hag."

Black Herran pursed her lips at the mess of pottery and tea. "So very touchy, Maeven. You never did like exposing your weaknesses, which is why I so rarely mentioned them. Tell me whatever you wish, or nothing at all if you still fear this—" she waved a hand at herself, from short white hair down to knobbly ankles threaded with purple blood vessels. "You may never have another chance to unburden yourself to somebody who quite frankly does not give a shit, and will not be fussed by whatever dreadful thing it is. Of all people, who am I to judge? I am, as you say, monstrous."

"Enough," Maeven said as she thumped back into the chair. "My secrets are my own."

Black Herran shrugged. "As you wish. To get back to business, I intend to use the bloodshed to summon something large or many small, I have not yet decided how much I dare. As for you, how can you best use the power released by so much death? Can you raise their corpses as an army of the undead to fight for us?"

Maeven absently rubbed her cheek. "That is one possibility. To raise so many at once would mean they will be largely mindless and of limited capabilities, more use for causing infected wounds than for warfare. Our best use would be to raise one or two military minded, intact souls and give them the ability to direct the rest."

"Whatever you think best," Black Herran said.

Maeven frowned at her. "This is quite the reversal. Once you handed down the orders."

"Times change. I find it best to change with them."

"Even if we win," Maeven said, "do you expect to go on living here now that they know exactly who and what you are?"

Black Herran downed the last of her tea. "My life is burning to ash around my ears. I will not live here afterwards. It matters not at all as long as those I love survive. Oh, I see that expression. Yes, Maeven, love."

"It is unexpected to hear you admit to such a pointless emotion," the necromancer replied. "All it brings is weakness and pain."

"All true. And yet, it is well worth it. Not something your old general could ever contemplate, is it? Do you really not remember how happy you were when you had your sister at your side?"

Maeven shot to her feet and slung her pack over one shoulder. "Never speak of her again unless you are revealing her location. If you hold that against me one more time I will go out into your beloved little town and massacre everyone." She stormed to the door and kicked it open.

"It is good to see you again," Black Herran called after the necromancer. "Whatever else you might think, I have missed you from time to time."

"Liar," Maeven spat, though even she did not truly believe it. "As for me, I would much rather you were long-since rotted to bare bones in the dirt. If you were not of use to me, I would put you there myself." With that she left and slammed the door behind her.

Black Herran leaned back in her chair and smiled at the glistening eyes hidden in the shadowy corner of the room. "That went well, I think, my little ones. Maeven really seems to believe I abandoned my conquest because I feared to doom this world. She thinks me far less selfish than I really am, and she forgets how ambitious I was."

She looked up at the wonky pots and baked clay figures on the shelf, gifts crafted by her daughter and grandchildren. Small gifts, but so very wonderful and huge in import.

"I told you she would discount love as a motivation," she said to her demons watching from the shadows. "Nobody seems to consider that if I conquered Essoran for revenge, just how far I would go to protect my family. Tell our precious shadow sisters and all their spawn to get ready. You will soon feast."

Maeven marched along the path to the inn, barely noticing the fearful townsfolk giving her a wide berth. Her mind was rocked by old memories and emotions, but above all was her unutterable glee at fooling her old general into thinking she would go along with her plans.

The old woman had lost her edge. What was this talk of love? Pah! That creature had no idea what real love was. She had simply baulked at the massive cost of her rule, and it had all been downhill from there: from proud general to mother and bottom wiper, and then on to regretful decrepit crone. Maeven was not like her – to recover Grace, she would happily damn the rest of the world.

Black Herran would get everything she deserved as soon as Maeven had all the information and power she needed, and she already knew far more than the old woman suspected. She was playing right into Maeven's hands. Raising corpses? That was work for mere dabblers in necromancy. On the surface she would do as her general asked, but her real goal was to use the mass deaths of the Lucent soldiers to craft something far more potent. She couldn't care less about defeating the Lucent Empire itself – all she really wanted was to kill her brother and find her sister.

After having tried to murder her and scarring her face, Amadden needed to die in agony. He would suffer an age of torment for taking away her sister. His only use now was to locate Grace. Maeven had no idea how she had been these last forty years, only that she still lived – Maeven would certainly have felt Grace's soul passing into death, into her domain.

Maeven suspected she would burst into tears the moment she found her sister again. Her eyes were already wet just thinking about it.

"Damn that demon-whoring cow," Maeven snarled, causing a small child crossing the street to squeal and run for safety.

If Black Herran did not give her answers soon then Maeven would wring them from her scrawny old neck, even if she had to hold every last soul in Tarnbrooke hostage to do it. Including, and most especially, those she claimed to love. Maeven had made enquiries and discovered Black Herran's daughter was named Heline, and her grandsons were Tristan and Edmond, but as of yet, she'd had no luck in locating them. Sooner or later she would find them – there was nowhere on this world they could hide forever.

If she were able to find them, the balance of power would finally shift. Black Herran knew exactly what Maeven was capable of.

CHAPTER 20

While Verena Awildan's sailors helped with the construction of the town's defences, she sat down with her quartermaster and one of Tarnbrooke's elders to go over lists of goods in short supply. The old man seemed ill at ease in her company. Not that she could blame him – the rest of her party were all mass-murdering monsters, and she was queen of an entire fleet of pirates, likely little better in his eyes. This greybeard was merely an elder of a small backward town, more used to settling disputes about who owned a cow, who threw the first punch in a drunken brawl, or strong arming a fuzzy-cheeked lad into wedding the swollen-bellied farm girl he had tumbled in a barn.

The elder wiped his brow with a sleeve and finished detailing the contents of his list of necessary items: nails and carpentry tools, arrow shafts, salt meat and grain, bandages and medicine, and a number of other goods necessary to withstand a protracted siege. It was nothing she could not have devised on her own, but the man was being thorough and she did appreciate his dedication.

Poor ignorant bastard, Verena thought. A siege of this place would never last long enough to need so many supplies. She handed the list to her quartermaster. "Take a horse and return to the *Scourge of Malice*. See that the necessary items are delivered with haste." He nodded, tucked the paper into a pouch, bowed and departed.

"So, tell me," Verena said. "How are you taking the revelation that your town's elder is Black Herran?"

The man swallowed and his liver-spotted hands trembled. "I dare not speak of it, Your Majesty."

"That good is it? Well, I would have been most shocked to have shared meat and drink with the woman next door for years, only to discover that she dallies with demons and is the most infamous woman in history."

His face tinged green.

"Best to be on her side, I think, than to be her enemy," she admitted. "I find myself curious though – this Elder Dalia that you thought you knew, what was she like?"

He took a deep shuddering breath, and his eyes became distant and glazed. "Stern and unforgiving, a tyrant with a velvet glove. She was never shy about putting her opinion forward, but she was… kind. Yes, kind, if you can believe that of her. She believed that people could make good on their mistakes." He sniffed and gritted his teeth. "As if *she* could ever be forgiven for so much bloodshed and horror. Her poor, damned daughter…" He started, and clamped his lips shut in fear of revealing more of his thoughts.

Verena smiled, pointedly. He would do her favours and provide information if asked, now that she had obtained enough to have him eviscerated atop a black altar. Who knew if Black Herran would even care about casual insults these days, but the important thing was that he feared it, and feared Verena would pass his words on.

"Do keep me informed of her plans," Verena said. "I am reasonable, my friend, and not a monster like the rest. I will do my best to get you all out of this alive. I do what is best for my people, and for my allies. Do we understand each other?"

He nodded then scuttled away to safety, and no doubt a stiff drink.

She stood and stretched her sore muscles. At her age, long cart rides were bone-shaking affairs best avoided, and the pain and stiffness would last for days afterwards. She would be glad to get back to sea and leave these doomed people to their fate. If what the others encountered in Hive was any indication, then the holy knights of the Lucent Empire were more dangerous than she had feared. Could this group of villains even stand against an army? Black Herran was old, but Verena Awildan knew that only made her more dangerous.

The young might suggest that being old meant she had less time to lose, but Verena was old herself and quite happy to go on living, thank you very much. "Save the children!" people cried when their ships were going down – as if the young had any more right to go on living than the old. The young had years weighed on their side, but the old could lose children they had brought into the world and friends they had spent decades travelling through life with. Verena would say Black Herran had as much to lose as anyone, which made her desperate. And Verena found desperation in a demonologist of her power to be a blood-chilling prospect.

The necromancer and the demonologist were sequestered away to discuss their vile magical practices, and Verena was more than happy to let them get on with it without her. She rubbed her slynx's ears and it yawned and playfully nibbled on a finger. At least her lazy little pet provided her some protection against magic until this dreadful business was settled. The further away the better when they unleashed their unnatural powers. The naive townsfolk had no conception of what was about to overtake Tarnbrooke. It would scar them for life if they somehow managed to survive it. Necromancy and demonology married in mass death could only birth a new wave of horrors into this gods-forsaken valley.

Verena had no intention of being here when that happened. She would sleep much better if the Lucent Empire and Black Herran obliterated each other in the coming weeks. Speaking of sleep, dusk had fallen and her back ached for a good hammock beneath it.

* * *

Lorimer rather liked the Mhorran Valley. It was rugged and sparse, a maze of jagged rock and gushing streams, sheer stone cliffs and hidden dells populated with mountain ash and blackthorn. It reminded him of where his hill-top ancestral mansion sat, back in Fade's Reach.

"Damn those vermin that now infest it," he snarled. Anger throbbed through his veins at the thought of their muddy boots tramping through his halls and of the portraits and artefacts of his ancestors desecrated and looted.

It was his home. One way or another he would have it back and hunt all those despoilers down, even if it meant dealing with old betrayers instead of ripping out their withered hearts and eating it in front of them. For a moment he indulged in fantasies of doing just that to the necromancer, but it was a hollow feeling. Other than his loyal servant Estevan, his home and people were all he held dear in this world.

He loped along a rocky ridge on all fours, vaulted a crevice and scrabbled up a wide slope of snow and scree to achieve the peak of the hill. The white-wreathed valley spread out below him like a vast icy snake. It was ruggedly beautiful.

Wind and drizzle lashed his exposed flesh and he luxuriated in the emotional scouring that accompanied the physical. It was regrettable that he had lost control at the sight of his old general; indeed she had manipulated him into attempting to kill her before he was ready, just so she could stamp her authority on them once again. Maeven was already in thrall to Black Herran, it seemed. He should not have been surprised at that. Her blood oath would force her to aid him, but she would still play both sides to her own benefit whenever possible.

The machinations of magic users disgusted him, trying to twist others to serve their purposes as they did with their demons and their risen dead. He would not have it. Reluctant allies perhaps, but none would ever be master of Lorimer Felle again.

As the sun set over the Mhorran Valley, Lorimer removed the cloth from his eyes and bathed in the golden glory of a primal landscape. Serene, snow-capped mountains burned red and gold. The sight took his breath away.

His vampiric nature allowed him to go where mere mortals never could, and he exulted in witnessing such sights as no other eye ever had. That came at the price of his humanity. He enjoyed killing, though for a long time he had denied it. Part of him still believed he simply enjoyed a worthy challenge, and that killing for its own sake was beneath him. It was not entirely true, as he did derive great pleasure from exercising power. He was centuries old and, given time, even unpalatable truths become brutally obvious and must be accepted. Some of his kin had been unable to accept what they were, and fighting their nature broke their minds. Inflamed desires led to occasional loss of control, and on to black guilt and despair until they had become twisted monsters plaguing the mountains and forests near Fade's Reach. Lorimer had hunted most of them down, and after a great battle, devoured them. And he had enjoyed it. He was a monster in many ways, but he could accept that burden in order to protect his people.

He spotted movement on a lower rise overlooking the valley. He ran low and silent, using the contours of the hillside to mask his approach, feet widening to spread his weight across the snow and ice. A small stone and slate shepherd's hut lay ahead, with a stack of dry wood and peat outside intended to make a signal fire when the enemy was sighted. A fur-cloaked figure was busy removing the waxed canvas from the woodpile, allowing in snow and rain to ruin it.

The wind blew a very distinctive and mouth-watering scent towards him. Human blood. His jaw ached as his teeth grew longer, hunger rising. The figure kept its head down against the wind and re-entered the hut.

Lorimer sped across the snow and drew up outside the door. He shifted back into human form, ebony skin stark against the snow, and politely knocked.

There was no response for a moment, then a young man's voice came from the other side. "What do you want?"

He cleared his throat as the intoxicating scent of blood filled his nostrils. Saliva flooded his mouth. "It is hardly hospitable to let a man freeze to death in the dark of night on a snowy hillside."

"Should have thought about that 'fore you climbed up here all uninvited," the voice said. "Piss off."

Lorimer smiled. The man's accent was not local. The young man had the drawl of the hillfolk villages north of Fenoch Ford, one of the first and largest towns to fall to the Lucent Empire ten years before they had dared attack Fade's Reach.

The hardy hillfolk were said to make for excellent scouts. Which meant this young man had grown up under the Lucent Goddess and was here about her bloody business. He was no friend, merely food.

Lorimer kicked the door in. The man crashed into the back wall in a hail of splintered wreckage and slumped down, dazed and bleeding.

Inside was a cramped room with a single bed, smouldering fire pit and enough space for supplies to last a good few weeks of snowstorm. The bed was currently occupied by a weathered greybeard with his throat freshly cut.

"I believe you have made a terrible mistake this night," Lorimer said. "Enlighten me, how much does the Lucent Empire pay for your services?"

The man rose to his feet, a rivulet of blood winding down his cheek from a gash on his scalp. He drew a knife from his belt and lunged forward, burying it between Lorimer's ribs and into his heart.

Lorimer looked down at the mortal wound. Then back up to meet his supposed killer's gaze. "I do hope that was worth it." His jaw dropped and fangs erupted, razor-sharp forked tongue lashing out to pluck one of the man's eyes from his head.

The man shrieked and reeled back.

The eyeball popped pleasingly in Lorimer's mouth and filled it with the savoury taste of jelly. He drew the dagger from his chest and bent it in two before tossing it at his attacker's feet.

"When will your army attack?" he demanded. "How many others like you are currently in these hills?"

The man clamped a hand to his empty eye socket and snarled. "Whatever manner of beast you are, you'll have nothing from me. I go to the Bright One's bosom!"

"I am positive she will take great pleasure in having the likes of you suckling at her teats," Lorimer replied. "In any case, you will not be going anywhere for quite a while. I shall eat you one morsel at a time until you tell me everything I wish to know." He grinned and stepped forward, weathering futile kicks and flailing punches.

He started with an ear, then a finger, savouring the appetisers. Tears of pain rolled down the man's face but still he denied Lorimer. The vampire grabbed his arm and twisted the hand back to front with a crunch of bone and snap of tendons.

"Come, come, why prolong this?"

His words were met with a blob of phlegm dripping down his face.

"There is no need for rudeness." He pressed the Lucent scout to the floor with his left hand. Claws erupted from the fingers on his right and trailed down the sobbing man's chest, shearing through fur and cloth but leaving the skin beneath intact. Then it cut lower, freeing the man's cock and balls.

Lorimer grinned, forked tongue slowly licking jagged fangs. His claws pressed harder. A single claw, a delicate slit. A ball came away, soft and sticky in his hand, and he lifted it to his mouth as his prey writhed and screamed in horror. He paused. "Where have my manners gone? You must also be hungry." And he shoved the testicle into the man's mouth and clamped a hand over it until he choked it down. The man's single eye was wide and wild with terror.

"Now you are ready," the vampire said softly. "Tell me all I need to know, and I will make the rest of it quick."

The man broke, and as promised the unfortunate scout's end

was quick. Depending on weather, an advance force would arrive in around two or three weeks to secure Tarnbrooke. The man claimed a hundred thousand armoured soldiers and a hundred inquisitors, but Lorimer smelled the lie on him and pressed the issue, painfully. The man was good with a knife but really had no idea how to count beyond ten, twenty if he used his toes. What he was certain of was that the bulk of the army marched with the baggage train, conserving their strength as they trailed a handful of days behind the vanguard.

They had less time than Black Herran had hoped – only three weeks if the Elder Gods were feeling merciful enough to send bad weather to aid them. Lorimer doubted that Tarnbrooke could be made ready in time, but he would do his part until Maeven had what she wanted. Win or lose they would then leave, and he would take what he needed from her or they would both perish in the attempt.

There were other scouts abroad in the snowy hills, hunting for watchers and signal fires in order to blind Tarnbrooke to the Lucent attack. One of them would have more solid information on the enemy force. Lorimer was hungry, and tonight those men were his prey.

CHAPTER 21

The town's temple had been repurposed to act as the command centre for the Tarnbrooke defence forces. As grand as that sounded, all it meant was that tables had been procured from nearby houses and pushed together to form a square in the centre of the hall, with old maps of the town and surrounding area nailed to them. Small wooden warriors carved for children stood in for real military forces on the map. Pots of water and ale had been set off to one side, since arguing was thirsty work. Most importantly for Black Herran's purposes, the temple had its own privy. The town elders – herself included – were old and their bladders often proved unreliable.

As for the Elder Gods of Essoran whose statues looked down on them, well, Black Herran considered this their fight too. The Lucent Empire would slaughter all who followed the old ways, and if they proved victorious one of their first acts would be to reduce this temple to rubble. The least the Elder Gods could do was offer up their temple for her use – not that she much cared if they objected.

Black Herran had been up at the crow of dawn, washed, dressed and waiting as those she had ordered to attend arrived in dribs and drabs. Jerak Hyden arrived first with a scroll tucked under one arm, precise and punctual as the mechanical devices he crafted. The dark circles beneath his eyes suggested he had been so immersed in his work that he had forgotten to sleep again. He sat to her right, unfurled his scroll and with a charcoal stick, began amending diagrams, refusing to waste even a single moment of his valuable time on mindless pleasantries and small talk.

Lorimer's manservant Estevan was close on Jerak's heels. He doffed his feathered hat, offered her a respectful nod, and took a seat ready to take notes with quill and ink. Amogg and Tiarnach had usurped his role in training the militia, a position he was immensely grateful to be relieved of. It left him far more time to help organise the workers' tasks, oversee the construction of fortifications, and to make Black Herran's life easier in a hundred little ways she had no idea she had even needed. She suspected that this humble servant had far more to do with Lorimer's previous successes as her captain than she, or even Lorimer, ever realised.

Town elders Deem and Cox, beards combed and oiled, and Healy in her sombre grey dress, had arrived together as a united force, determined to protect their town from the evil tyrant in command as much as from the Lucent Empire. They sat to her left, as far away from Jerak Hyden as possible.

Black Herran smiled thinly. "Welcome. Best watch what you say here, elders. Not all are as forgiving as I am." They ignored her and sat stiff-backed in disapproving silence.

Verena and Maeven arrived next, closely followed by the bulk of Amogg squeezing through the merely human-sized doorway. The elders shivered at the realisation they were trapped indoors with her.

The big orc's eyes scanned the statues of the human gods. "Weaklings," she muttered. A sheepish young woman trailed after the orc chieftain.

"Penny?" Black Herran said. "What are you doing here?" She peered behind Amogg's broad back as the door swung shut. For her part Penny just gazed up at the huge orc with two parts fear and one part admiration.

Cox hissed as he noticed the skirt of Penny's dress was cut

scandalously short to just above the knees, and worse, slit halfway up the side as well. "Cover yourself, girl! That dress is
shameful."

Amogg snarled, making the elders flinch. "Penny wanted
fight me. She fight for me now. Make for good warrior. Silly
clothes no good to fight in so I make better."

Cox tutted at Penny. "You have allowed this mindless beast
to dress you like a brazen harlot."

Amogg strode forward and wrapped a hand around the
town elder's throat. She pulled the human to his feet, choking
and scrabbling at her iron grip. Her hand clenched and his
neck snapped like a wrung chicken.

Penny and the elders screamed as Amogg tossed the corpse
into the corner of the room and stared down at the other two
elders, a mountain of volcanic rage, her skin flushing angry
orcish red. "Weaklings insult Amogg and die. Insult Penny and
die."

Then her skin returned to a calmer green and she shoved a
pale-faced, shaking Penny towards the sturdiest bench in the
room, which creaked ominously under her bulk of muscle.
Penny looked sick from witnessing a murder and from the
realisation that orcish ways were brutally different from her
own. There would be no escape for her.

The Tarnbrooke residents looked at Black Herran in horror.

"You were warned," she said. The old Dalia would have been
upset, but the even older Black Herran had never liked that
self-righteous prick anyway. "Amogg Hadakk is of far more use
than a judgemental old idiot who cannot hold his tongue." She
turned to Amogg, "Are your orcish friends not joining us?"

Amogg shrugged. "They not speak human words so good.
They happy build bigger walls."

Black Herran nodded, then glowered at the door. "Lorimer
may not be back for some time but have any of you seen
Tiarnach?"

Amogg brightened. "Was good fight with burn-hair yesterday.

Many human males bled in the dirt. Then many of your ales were drunk. Amogg drink only one horn. Learned lesson at Hive. Head hurt very bad after. Cannot fight hangover."

Tiarnach chose that moment to stagger into the temple, his eyes bloodshot to match a swollen cheek and crusted nose. He shuddered as he crossed the threshold and refused to look up at the statues of the gods. Bruises bloomed across his neck and hands but were already fading from black and blue to green and yellows with preternatural speed. He noted and dismissed the fresh corpse in the corner like it was a potted plant or a discarded shoe.

"Male bonding" was his only explanation as he slumped into a chair and closed his eyes.

Black Herran scowled and then looked at the map. "We begin now. Lorimer can catch up later. What can you make of our militia?"

Tiarnach cracked an eyelid. "Your best are farmers and wee boys. The whole lot o' them will break at the first charge. Gimme a few weeks and we can do something with them, at least make a fight of it with those four hundred."

Amogg snorted. "They not warriors. Soft. Not brave like Penny who would fight me for sake of kin. Human females will fight better. I teach to fight like small orc."

"Interesting," Black Herran replied. "I am all in favour of arming any women willing to fight. The more the better. What say you, elders?"

Deem's lips tightened and the words were prised out like rotten teeth as he watched Amogg from the corner of his eyes. "If we must."

Healy looked more fearful and thoughtful as she studied Penny. "If they volunteer then I cannot object, given the circumstances. However, not all are as headstrong as Penny."

The young woman reddened under their stares.

"Who angers you?" Amogg said. "Kill them."

"She's embarrassed, you big green fool," Lorimer said from

the doorway. Dressed in little more than a strip of cloth around his eyes, his loins, and a fresh and dripping bear-hide cloak, his sweat-slick muscles glistened like those of a god.

He tossed a heavy sack across the room. It landed by Black Herran's feet and four heads rolled free. "You don't have many weeks left, Tiarnach. You have two. Three at most before their vanguard of three thousand men arrive. Their main force will only be days behind that, and if these men were correct, it is four times the size and contains both cavalry and siege engines."

Verena glanced at his gifts. "Lucent Empire spies?"

"Indeed. Some of your men set to watch the pass have been slain. The others have now been warned."

The elders moaned with loss. "Who did they kill?"

Lorimer described the dead, and how they died in graphic detail. Deem slumped in his chair, face buried in his hands to stifle the sobs.

"One of those men was his grandson," Healy explained.

"See the watchers are replaced," Black Herran said to the elders. "The enemy are fanatics. There is no bargaining or reasoning with them, and there will be no mercy for any of us if they succeed in taking the town. This is kill or be killed."

Deem rose, chair scraping across the floor. He staggered to Amogg and grabbed her huge shoulder with one hand, his other a fist pounding her chest. Such was her contempt for him that she did not even bother to defend herself.

"Destroy them," he snarled. "Kill them all. I don't care if you have to arm the children. Make them pay."

Amogg grunted and brushed him off. "That why we here."

"Sit down," Black Herran commanded. "Amogg – I will make it known among the women that you are willing to teach them to fight."

"They will fight," Amogg said. "Or else."

Penny nodded. "I... I know a few who might be willing."

"Just as well," Black Herran muttered, meeting Penny's

gaze. "I refuse to lose, and if they won't fight, I will use their blood to summon beings that will. You had best mention that too. Be a dear and go round them up in the market square. You have an hour."

Penny shuddered and half-ran for the door, almost stumbling as she caught sight of Cox's corpse again.

Black Herran turned her attention to Tiarnach and Amogg. "I leave the militia's training to you. Do the best you can. Now, Jerak, do you have all that you need?"

The alchemist looked up from his scroll, fingers charcoal-black. "That I need? Yes. That I want? No. I have a list somewhere." He began patting himself down and rummaging through pouches. "Bah. Those stupid assistants. I require a herd of pigs. And shovels. Yes, shovels too."

"For my plan for the wall?" Black Herran asked, one eyebrow raised.

"That nonsense?" he sneered. "Goodness no, that is child's play and already almost complete. I require pigs to stop the enemy from taking the wall too early. It will be ever so much fun. I never have had the chance to try out–"

"Fine!" Black Herran interrupted. "Whatever you require. I trust you to make their lives a nightmare. Now, elders, let us speak of the town's fortifications."

Healy cleared her throat. "We have done the best we can with what we have. With the help of Awildan carpenters and orc labour, in two weeks we may have a palisade in place all around the town, but we have little else. We have focused our efforts on the north side facing the valley, digging ditches and setting sharpened stakes. The south is still woefully open to attack."

Black Herran leaned over the map and drew on lines of defences with a charcoal stick. "Verena, I expect the Falcon Prince and most of his inquisitors to arrive from the north in the second wave. I will need your fleet to intercept any force they send south by sea with the intention of landing additional troops to our rear."

They discussed strategy and logistics for the better part of an hour, and the elders left with a large list of orders to hand down to their townsfolk. They dragged the corpse of Elder Cox with them as an example of the perils of disobedience.

Lorimer had been sitting quietly in the corner until the mortals had left. "Shall we now discuss the real battle? You did well not causing the peasants to flee in abject terror."

Black Herran smiled and leaned back on her chair. "Let's. The townsfolk must fight for the wall and retreat in an orderly fashion after holding until daylight fades. Then Jerak Hyden's little gifts will devastate the Lucent vanguard. Maeven and I have discussed the best use for that mass slaughter. We will summon demons and raise undead to blunt the advance of their main force. Lorimer, you and I shall sow terror as they advance. We will teach them to fear the vampire lord of Fade's Reach, and to vividly recall the legend of Black Herran. I need you to prowl the hills, to terrorise and slay all that you find. Be the death that comes with the darkness, but do leave some alive to spread tales of horrors yet to come."

He grinned, teeth sharp and deadly. "I could walk into their camp and kill hundreds with ease. Why should I not go and wreak bloody havoc?"

"They will have inquisitors and an unknown number of acolytes," she replied. "You are strong but still only one being. If their magic is able to weaken you even for a moment you may become trapped. Then all will be lost. They are too many, even for you."

His grin faded. "As you wish. I have a few suitably grisly gifts in mind. None of them will sleep well ever again, should they be lucky enough to survive that long."

"Excellent. I leave the valley beyond Tarnbrooke in your capable hands. If there is nothing else, then we will meet back here tomorrow morning. I must prepare my magic."

The rest of the party filtered from the hall and stood outside, pondering the meeting, all thinking the same thing: that it had felt like the old days, and marvelled at how easily they had slipped back into their captain roles.

Maeven snarled her goodbye and stormed off in search of a place to begin preparation for her rituals.

"Where might a gentleman procure some new clothing?" Lorimer asked his manservant as they watched her leave.

"The finest clothier in town is located two streets east of the temple," Estevan said. "I do of course mean 'fine' in a local, situational sense."

"You'll just rip them tae shreds again when you change shape," Tiarnach added. "Wear a sack."

The vampire turned and looked down his nose at the grubby warrior. "I am a lord, you buffoon. Go and train your screeching monkeys to wave their sticks."

Estevan doffed his hat to Tiarnach. "Once you are done with them, ask your militia to have their fellow archers meet me north of town for training." With that Estevan led his lord off in search of a brocaded tunic, coat and hose. Some of the town women stopped and stared at Lorimer's muscular naked chest as he swept past, their faces reddening.

"I'll do just that," Tiarnach said, pouting at the vampire's back. "Ooh, look at the big lord, all lah-de-dah and fancy pantaloons. What a prick. I'd cut his cock off but thon big vampire bastard would just grow it right back. At least Estevan is a decent sort. Come, Amogg. Let's see what goods we have to play with."

In the market square Penny waited with twenty other women of varying ages by the side of a cart filled with new spears wheeled down from the smithy. Off to the side the fifty bruised and bloodied "best" men of the militia waited with dread as the huge orc and their feral tormentor approached.

Ragash was sitting on the ground at the back, gnawing on a leg of roast pork while watching the humans with amused contempt. Wundak was deep in awkward conversation with the far slighter form of Penny.

"Fuck me," Tiarnach said to his men. "You're all here? I'd have bet Amogg's left nut some o' you lot would've run off with your tails between your legs. Fine, I admit you're all harder men than I thought. You've seen what I can do, so now I'll teach you to be a howling mad warrior like me. Those little Lucent laddies will piss themselves in terror when I'm done with you magnificent bastards." Their chests swelled with pride even while their eyes glowered hatred at him. He could work with that.

Amogg looked down on the women, who stared back with stubborn pride, their dresses already slit for better movement. She tossed each of them a spear. "You not female or male like silly human customs. You now just warrior who fight and kill like orc."

She grabbed Ragash, Wundak and the unfortunate Penny and used them to demonstrate the basics of spear use, the thrusts and guards, and beating with the butt. Amogg was far more proficient with her axe but the two other elder orcs still spat blood and nursed bruised flesh afterwards. She was only a little gentler with Penny.

Then it was the other humans' turn. Tiarnach's men howled in pain and anger as he taught them dirty tricks and techniques, but the women were pitted against the mighty war chief of the Hadakk. She went easy on them, like they were newborn grubbs. Only a few were knocked unconscious.

The number of women watching from the side of the square began to swell as her warriors caught on to the basics, their thrusts becoming quicker and more precise. By day's end, her force of twenty had grown to a hundred determined warriors in the making.

CHAPTER 22

The gloomy thatched hovel was barely suitable for Maeven's needs. Fragrant herbs and bags of grain hung by twine from hooks on the ceiling, and pots and pans from the rough stone walls to utilise every possible inch of the meagre space. How a family of six lived in this tiny, cramped room with its single table, central fire pit and bed of straw, the necromancer had no idea. Nor did she care where they had gone, after she sent them fleeing with a miniscule display of her magic.

She blocked off the entrances with barriers of churning death magic to stop anybody or anything from eavesdropping, then set down her pack and extracted the small box within. She set it down on the woven reed floor mats, dusted off the lid, opened it and removed her grandfather's finger bones from their velvet cushion. She carefully placed them on the hovel's table and took a seat as she called forth his ghost.

Then, safely hidden away from prying eyes and ears, she burst into great heaving sobs. Hot tears rolled down scarred, tattooed cheeks.

Cease your crocodile tears, the ghost whispered in her mind with a voice like dry parchment and old bone. *You have not cried truly for forty years and I believe it not. You will have no sympathy from me.*

Her sobs changed into mocking laughter. "One day I will fool you. Nevertheless, I am not a dusty old dead relic like you. I still hurt and I still feel – how you hate that you cannot..."

Save it for when you have the time, girl. We have work to do. Are you positive that this is the only option left? Even if he kidnapped your sister and tried to kill you, he is still your blood.

"My brother needs to die. My sister lives and I will step over his butchered corpse to free her from his grasp. Black Herran has promised me that he will appear on the field of battle. She thinks herself so very clever, when in truth I am the one manipulating her. When the time is right, Black Herran too, will die by my hand."

Have you readied the artefact?

She pulled the glossy black obsidian blade from her pack. It was set in a pure silver hilt, the grip bound in soft human leather skinned from a living wizard's left hand and forearm. He hadn't lived for long, of course, but long enough for her to complete the ritual of creation, bury the blade in his heart and seal his soul into it. The more lives it took, and the more souls sucked into it, the more power over death she could wield through it. At the current time it could kill any mortal with a single wound, though it could only empower her to raise and maintain a few dozen corpses. She needed more, much more to achieve her goals.

"The rituals of empowerment are complete and have been tested," she said. "It has absorbed a few souls already, including one from a hiver."

She felt the ghost of her grandfather reach out to it with interest, then hesitate and withdraw back into his bones. He had been a renowned enchanter in life, and a dabbler in the forbidden art of necromancy. This artefact was of his devising, though he had feared it too much to see it completed. Maeven had no such qualms, and saw to it that even in death his knowledge did not go to waste.

The arcane matrix is far from full, he said. *It must be filled with souls of uncommon strength.*

She thought of the inquisitors, and of Black Herran and the others. "The raw materials are converging here as we speak."

Excellent, my dear. Then you will have soon the power to cut away the life of anything this world or any other has to offer. You will be a one-woman army, capable of wielding the void itself as a weapon. His voice cracked like broken bone and broken promises. *Will you finally allow me to die? Please...*

"Soon," she promised. The nobles of Essoran had killed her mother and father, and would have tossed Maeven and her siblings into an unmarked grave as well if her mortally wounded grandfather had not taken them in hand and fled into the cursed forest. It had not been personal for those nobles, just another political game in the incessant inter-house squabbling of their kind. That time her family had paid the price.

"My encounter with the inquisitors of the Lucent Empire did not go as well as I had hoped. The power of their goddess seems to be antithetical to my own. Death magic could find no purchase on them."

Her grandfather sighed, morose, but pondered that for a while. He didn't have any choice. *Necromancy is commonly thought to deal with corpses by the rabble, but our true magic deals with life and the human soul. What if the power of gods is simply enormously powerful and processed soul essence? If so, you should be able to devise ways to bypass a measure of that protection.*

She sat back and absently rubbed her cheek. "Hmm. Tiarnach proved all but immune to my magic as well, which is interesting considering he is a god in name only, one without a single living worshipper. Perhaps some experimentation is in order."

The ghost agreed. *Yes. Poke and prod that drunken fool and learn what you may, then devour him. The strength of a god's soul, even a one such as him, would greatly empower our weapon. Assuming he has such a thing as a soul.*

The next two weeks passed in a blur of activity as the stubborn residents of Tarnbrooke prepared to face the vanguard of the

Lucent Empire army. Under Black Herran's leadership, and with Estevan's and the orcs' assistance, the defences grew higher, the ditches deeper and fully lined with sharpened wooden stakes. Food, bandages and supplies were stockpiled, and water barrels filled to face the threat of fire.

Jerak Hyden toiled away day and night in his workshop, the forges, kilns and crucibles belching oddly coloured stinking smoke at the cost of only two poisoned and quickly replaced assistants. He prowled the wall across the neck of the valley, muttering to himself as he took measurements and prepared his devious surprise for the invaders.

Dark magic rituals were wrought and readied for use by Maeven and Black Herran. Carved bone talismans were seeded in the ground all around the wall, ready to capture the power released by mass slaughter and safely channel it back to them.

With Estevan taking charge of training the archers among the town militia, it left the rest of the volunteers in the brutal but experienced hands of Amogg and Tiarnach, steadily growing more vicious in melee combat. Their initial fifty chosen men, and Penny, had swiftly become competent enough to help drill the rest in the basics. Of their five hundred total, perhaps half would make decent warriors. The rest would stand and fight, for a time, and would hopefully steady the armed civilians mucking in. During the training Tiarnach swatted and cursed at the constant fly bites, convinced nature had it in for him.

Those flies were not natural – Maeven was studying him from afar, examining the nature of gods and how to hurt them. From the knowledge she gleaned from his semi-divine flesh, her next encounter with a Lucent inquisitor would go very differently.

Verena coordinated logistics and oversaw goods and weapons shipped in from the Awildan Isles to bolster the town's defence and construction, while her pirate ships gathered from their hunting grounds across all the waters and isles of Essoran to form a mighty war fleet. Nobody knew how many sea-going vessels the Lucent Empire had managed to build, but it was better to attack their transports with too many ships than too few. With any luck she could seize any decent ships she found and add them to her own fleet.

Lorimer haunted the craggy hills and icy valleys, amusing himself by devouring choice cuts of hillfolk scouts and arranging the mangled remains in interesting ways for the next bunch to find. He was blinding the enemy while leaving some alive to carry back word of his handiwork. Every few days he returned to converse with Estevan, and spared little time for any other. He preferred his own company to that of the uncultured peasantry of Tarnbrooke.

On the thirteenth day the weather had taken a turn for the better. A southern wind brought warmer air into the Mhorran Valley, melting away the last frigid gasps of winter and heralding an early summer. A few days of warm and dry weather reopened the trackways to foot traffic. On the dawn of the fifteenth day, columns of black smoke rose from distant hilltops as Tarnbrooke's watchers lit their signal fires.

The Lucent army was on the march.

The townsfolk and militia raced to and fro to complete as much as they could before the enemy arrived. Verena gathered her sailors and readied to depart and take command of the Awildan fleet. Black Herran and Amogg were there to see her off, and the demonologist handed Verena a lacquered wooden box. "A tiny demon waits inside to carry your words to me if needed. Don't open it in direct sunlight – their little eyes are sensitive."

Verena scowled like she'd been handed a box of diseased rats and swiftly handed it off to one of her sailors. "I wish you luck," she said. "You will need it."

"May sea and sail be in your favour, Queen Verena Awildan," Black Herran said. "And thank you all for your efforts. You are all here for your own selfish reasons, but we will save thousands of innocents if we successfully crush the Lucent Empire. You are doing good, and that is to be celebrated."

A moment of sceptical silence passed. Then Amogg bellowed with laughter. "Yes, we have good fight. Much killing and much glory."

Other than Black Herran, none of them cared a whit about the lives of Tarnbrooke's people. "Ah well, fuck being polite then," she said. "Time to slaughter an army. Now is the time to unleash Lorimer and make an example of the enemy. When they reach that wall, I want their hands shaking and their boots filled with piss."

The war had begun.

CHAPTER 23

Robart of Allstane prayed to the Bright One to stop the rain, but, if anything, it came down all the harder. A spring deluge hissed through the night air, heavy drops tinging off his kettle helm with a relentless drumbeat. He propped his spear up against the tree trunk and huddled under the bare branches of one of the few trees that remained standing in this goddess-forsaken valley. The rest were now ragged stumps, hastily felled, offering neither shelter nor firewood. Goddess, how he missed his own bed back home in the civilised north.

He peered into the darkness and envied the bright fires in the distance, flickering along the rough and ready defences the doomed townsfolk had thrown up. At least those damned farmers would be warm and dry tonight, unlike him and his friend Tynolt stuck out in this shitty weather on picket duty.

Robart couldn't figure out what the point of them being out here was. Nobody would be out in this foul weather, especially not terrified peasants. They would be cowering behind their flimsy heap of wood and stone. Come the morrow three thousand proud Lucent soldiers would march right over it, and their hovels too. Their town... Carnbroke was it? Tarnbeck? Not that it mattered, it would soon have a new name and a new purpose as a fortified staging post for the Lucent Empire's expansion south. He thought the townsfolk's fate unfortunate, but on the positive side he could enjoy better weather and soft women with loose legs when they marched south. There would be plenty of widows to choose from. There would also be plunder to seize when they conquered the richer towns.

The Falcon Prince's inquisitors would purge those heathen towns, and only a handful of adults were ever judged pure enough to live. Him and Tynolt had been just young enough to escape the purge of their own village in the early days of the empire's expansion, before the inquisitors of the Goddess became quite so... thorough. Landgrave Daryn had claimed the boys, allowing them to dodge the indoctrination camps. He set them to work on his own lands with warm beds and honest work, and they would be forever grateful for that.

The fanatics of the Bright One terrified him, though. Which was why, being a loyal soldier and worshipper to anybody's eyes, he was now freezing his arse off in the soaking rain for the glory of the Goddess. And why he was happy enough to kill without complaint anybody the inquisitors deemed heretic. As nauseated as he was hearing the horror stories coming back from the few scouts who returned alive from the hills, he was far more scared of the Lucent force coming up from behind. If he fled back through the valley then he would meet the Falcon Prince himself, and he was not known for bestowing the Goddess's mercy. Supposedly, their lord had a special torture for deserters and traitors, one that lasted for weeks.

The Bright One was fine as gods went, but She did no more for Robart than the previous gods of earth, water, fire and air that his tribe had worshipped. He supposed he had got a fancy new cloak out of it at least.

He pulled the sodden, grubby white cloth tight around him – it had looked so very fine on the parade grounds of Brightwater before the Allstane levy marched out – and huddled lower in a vain attempt to stop the drip down the back of his neck. It worked: the drip became a torrent as sheets of rain hammered down. He lost sight of Tynolt, the other picket huddled in a similarly sorry heap beneath another tree only thirty paces away. They'd grown up together, survived together and enlisted together, and last night had seized the opportunity to get blind drunk together before the slaughter began. And now they were on half-rations and enjoying night watch together as punishment.

He waited in sodden, frozen misery for an age until his relief came to replace him, a tall shadow bent against driving rain. "You poor bastard," he shouted into the hiss. "What did you do to offend the Landgrave and get stuck out here?" The night had passed far swifter than he had expected if it was close to dawn already. This one was a big lad, and the bone-headed idiot had forgotten his spear. Instead, he was dragging a corpse.

Robart shot to his feet and fumbled for his own spear. He swung it round and thrust it deep into the man's chest.

The huge man's eyes crinkled with amusement. He cuffed Robart to the ground, the force of the blow tearing the spear from his hands.

Robart scrambled to his feet, back pressed against the tree trunk. The man carelessly yanked the spear free of his own flesh and hefted the body he had been dragging – sweet Goddess, Tynolt! – with inhuman strength, swinging it like a club. The blow knocked Robart back into the mud and his friend's body thumped down atop, pinning him. The man swung a leg over and straddled them both, grinning down into Robart's face.

Rain dripped from needle sharp fangs. Lots and lots of them so close to Robart's exposed throat. The stories that the heretic townsfolk were in league with creatures of dark magic were true! No wonder the streets of Hive had been overrun with monsters.

Tynolt groaned. Still alive, but dazed and bleeding. That gave Robart's panicked mind something to latch onto. He was alive. This man, this thing, wanted something from them. He might yet survive.

"What do you want from us?" he wheezed, blinking against the rain beating down onto his exposed face.

"One of you will live," the creature said in a deep and rumbling voice. "The other I will eat. Which of you wishes to live to carry my message to the leaders of the Lucent Empire?"

"Me!" Robart said. "I'll do it."

Tynolt gasped, finally having come to his senses. "No, we are friends. I–" His words choked off into a gurgle as the creature buried a taloned hand into his throat and ripped it out of his neck.

Robart vomited all over himself as his friend's blood gushed over him, hot on his rain-chilled skin.

The man popped Tynolt's flesh into his mouth and chewed as his prey writhed and bubbled wordless screams. "Delicious." Hard spines slid from his flesh and his fanged jaw distended in a grotesque melding of man and beast.

Robart soiled himself, shaking and sobbing as his childhood friend's struggles weakened and stilled.

I am alive. Alive! That's all that matters, he thought.

The feral creature, now more beast than man, grinned down at him, drooling Tynolt's blood across his face as the rain intensified. "You are willing to carry my message?"

"Yes," he screeched. "Anything! Just tell me what to say."

The monster grinned. "You should have bargained harder, betrayer of friends." Then it laughed. "Death would have been preferable to disloyalty."

Robart's screams of terror and agony were masked by the hissing rain.

While the vampire played with his food, shadows slipped from the cracks in the earth that the Lucent vanguard camped upon. Slicks of liquid night flowed unseen into the tents of sleeping soldiers. Another snuck into the supply wagons where the humans stored the bulk of their food and drink and began pouring small vials of cloudy green liquid into their ale barrels and food stores.

The human camp reeked of fear, and it caused Black

Herran's shadow demons to hunger. They itched to bury their teeth into soft sleeping throats and lap it up, but they were not here to kill now; they were to carry out acts of sabotage. The humans were not yet as ripe as they could be, and their dark master had promised them a greater and more filling feast. If they indulged here and now, then all restraint would flee. The Lucent holy knights would become aware of their presence, and the demons feared their fire.

The demons suppressed their desires and instead stealthily laid their hands on human steel. Their black claws ate into the metal like acid, hissing as they etched tiny demonic runes into the swords and spearheads. They winced as they briefly became conduits for Black Herran's power burning through them and into the runes.

With their work done, they escaped back into the shadowy cracks they had emerged from. All apart from two, one of whom paused to turn hungry eyes upon a pair of soldiers sleeping far from the protection of holy acolytes and powerful knights. It licked its needle-sharp teeth and sent a pulse of thought back along the link of power that tethered it to its master. It understood its human master's need for stealth, but hunger gnawed her and her sister's bellies.

Black Herran offered a suggestion that would please both: take only those two as a prize. Just make sure none of the other humans notice. No evidence of a struggle and no blood. Just two men gone missing from an armed camp in the middle of the night...

The demon burned with frustration and joy as it waited for its last sister to finish dripping the contents of its little vial into the stockpile of food and drink. It only had a vague understanding of what the purpose of that task was: their kind could gain power from the extremes of human emotion but they could and would devour anything that had ever lived, though the soul-rich flesh of intelligent creatures was always their food of choice. But as Black Herran commanded, so was it done.

Once the sister finished her task they crept over to the two sleeping human soldiers. Darkness flowed from the ground and filled the tent, clawed hands seized and stilled throats, jaws and tongues. No noise as their magic opened cracks in the earth wider and pulled the unfortunate humans down and down through mud and stone into their lair in the heart of Hellrath's Shadowlands, a warren of dark caves, vast caverns and magma flows where the shadow demons had made their home and raised their broods with help from Black Herran herself.

Under storm-lashed black clouds on a rocky outcrop above a burning lake, the demons prepared their excruciating feast by flaying meat and bone from screaming human souls. The old and tasteless souls that Black Herran had consigned here long ago during her previous war could finally be replaced with fresh food. Human souls were able to regrow some of what was lost, and the demons could make them last for decades if they were careful, but now was no time to be frugal – with what Black Herran had planned for them they needed all the strength they could muster. They consumed the captive soul's flesh as an appetiser, human terror adding a mouth-watering seasoning, and then the real feast began.

The dawn relief staggered back into the Lucent camp, pale-faced and pausing to vomit here and there as the soldier splashed through the mud leading to the command tent. The holy knight Sir Orwin took one look and summoned the Landgrave.

"What is it, man?" Daryn said. "What have you seen?"

The soldier gagged, shook his head and beckoned them onwards, retching all the way. The Landgrave buckled on a sword and followed with the inquisitor at his side, hands shielding their eyes from the wind-driven rain. They gathered men as they went until a fully armed host descended on the tree line where the pickets had been stationed.

Crows cawed and took flight at their approach, revealing the horror they had been feeding on. The remnants of a man hung impaled on tree branches, beast-gnawed bones and crow-pecked organs dangling, intestines twisting in the wind. The soldier's helmeted head had been stuck atop his own spear driven deep into the ground, and none could fail to recognise the look of utter terror frozen on the man's face.

"Tynolt," Daryn said.

"Sire!" one of his scouts said. "A survivor." He pointed to a cloaked form on the ground, still moving beneath blood-stained white. He ripped the cloak away.

Men hissed and stepped back behind the holy knight. Others gagged and turned away.

Robart writhed in the mud, arms and legs torn away, yet the stumps somehow already healed over. His eyes were gaping red pits. He opened his mouth to scream but only a wheezing moan and the blackened stump of a tongue emerged.

"How is he still alive?" the landgrave hissed.

A beam of ruddy dawn light washed the field, causing Robart to hiss and writhe. His skin swiftly reddened until it took on the hue of vibrant sunburn. His jaw yawned wide to scream and none could mistake the sharp fangs where human teeth had been only moments before. The soldiers gasped and the robed acolytes began praying for the Goddess's protection against evil.

"Step back, my lord," Sir Orwin said, hefting his burning blade. "This is a creature of darkest magic."

"Vampire," Daryn said. Then he realised his error in naming it. Such creatures were legendarily hard to kill: swift, vicious, and without mercy or human morals. They could also make their victims soulless abominations just like them. The whispers erupted through his men even as Sir Orwin beheaded the unfortunate picket's writhing remains and burned it to ash with purifying golden fire. The men were now wondering how many more of the monsters lurked behind the wall they were due to assault the next dawn.

"Fear not, men," Daryn said. "We attack in daylight and as you are witness to, the touch of the Bright One burns these vile things. Sir Orwin will take care of any of these creatures that dares to raise its filthy hand against us. Only one more night of vigilance before we set fire to their nest."

It did little to reassure the men, and even less so when they returned to the camp and discovered that two more men had gone missing in the night. Their bedrolls had been used, their clothes and equipment still present, and a wedge of cheese and bread left uneaten. There was no sign of any struggle – it appeared as if they had been plucked straight out of their tents right in the middle of an armed camp.

The worried whispers escalated to panicked talk. How many men had been taken now? And how many had been turned into unholy creatures like Robart, ready to attack them in the night? The only thing Daryn could do tonight was to have the acolytes cast their prayers of protection over the camp before turning in – it might not stop the most powerful creatures of the night, but it would at least weaken them.

After a hurried breakfast of porridge and morning ale, the vanguard formed ranks. Landgrave Laurant Daryn drew his sword. "Those damned monsters will pay for this. I vow that come the dawn we shall slaughter every heretic cowering behind that wall. Let none survive." He held his sword aloft. "March!"

Hours later, they stopped for food and ale rations, and it was only then that Daryn realised something was badly wrong with his men. The mountain streams became sewers as hundreds of his men's bowels erupted wherever they squatted or stood. They spewed from both ends, gasping for air as their bodies expelled all manner of eye-watering foulness.

Sir Orwin sniffed the ale and winced. "Thistleberry." His sword split the barrels in two. "The adverse effects will be temporary but severe. The enemy attempt to delay our arrival."

Daryn cursed. He had intended to camp near the wall and attack at first light, but with so many of his men weakened it seemed inadvisable to attempt that punishing pace. He would need to let his men rest and recover for a good few hours, then resume at a slower march, which meant the attack would have to take place in the late afternoon.

Pain stabbed into his skull. The urge to slay his Goddess's foes overflowed within him. Dawn. He had vowed to attack at dawn. The plan was in place and he could not deviate from it. He shook his head: there was good tactical sense in delaying the assault even further, until the next day when his men would be properly rested and recovered. The pain swelled inside him, the torment at even thinking of breaking his promise to carry out the will of the Goddess was overwhelming. The dark forces ahead of him needed to be exterminated. They could not be allowed to stain even one more day on Her world with their presence.

He decided to push his men harder than he knew he should. If they were as devout as they claimed, they would relish the opportunity to overcome their weakness to please Her. "We attack at noon tomorrow. Those who cannot walk will need to explain themselves to the Falcon Prince." The pain receded but did not depart entirely; it was a compromise that left him feeling like he had disappointed both his Goddess and himself. The guilt was almost overwhelming, but he endured it to protect his people.

His men pulled up their breeches and began to trudge down the valley: better to have shit running down their legs than to face the Prince's inquisitors.

CHAPTER 24

Night had fallen over the Mhorran Valley, and Penny and Nicholas the tile maker had drawn the short straw of the midnight watch along with ten other unfortunate bastards. Their watch on the wall began too early for more than a few hours' disturbed sleep and would end too late to catch any more. They were not overly upset – the assault by the Lucent Empire was imminent and a decent sleep would have escaped them anyway, and the rain was holding off for now.

Split into pairs, the watch guarded over two hundred paces of stone and timber fortifications, uneven and not entirely solid underfoot. It was all that protected them from the army of blood-crazed madmen coming from the north and they were glad to have it.

Nicholas unfastened his crude and chafing iron pot helmet and set it down next to a brazier, warming his hands over the glowing embers – actual flames would ruin their night vision and Tiarnach would have beaten them bloody for it. Underneath he wore a red cloth tied around his temples, and his short beard and moustache were dyed red in an attempt to ape Tiarnach.

"Very fierce, sir," Penny said, leaning on her spear. She wore mismatched scraps of chain and leather over a padded gambeson, and her curly hair was crammed into a proper steel helmet that Amogg had found somewhere.

"Thanking you," Nicholas said with a grin. Then his moustache quivered and his nose wrinkled in disgust. "What is that foul stench?"

Penny looked out across the wall towards the distant campfires twinkling in the night all up the valley floor, only a few hours' walk away. "They took one look at you and all shit themselves in terror?"

He smoothed out his moustache. "There's a darned good reason you are not married yet, wench."

"That's very true," Penny agreed. "All the men here are shit. Apart from Tom the smith. That one's a sexy beast."

Nicholas chuckled, but his mirth died as the distant screams of pain and terror began. Somewhere to the north, men were dying. He grabbed his crude helmet and stuffed it back onto his head and clutched his spear for dear life.

The two members of the Tarnbrooke militia kept watch as screams spread and campfires winked out one by one, and with it the clang of steel and shouts of anger.

"It seems nobody is getting much sleep tonight," Penny said. Earlier on that creep Jerak Hyden had been roaming the area in front of the wall digging random holes – they didn't dare get close enough to find out what he was up to – and now this.

Glowing red eyes flashed in the night, too close for comfort. Both stiffened and readied their spears in shaking hands.

"What do you reckon it is?" Nicholas whispered.

A soft whisper in his ear: "Vampires."

Nicholas and Penny yelped and stumbled back as Black Herran appeared at their side, her old bones wrapped in a thick woollen blanket.

"The vampire Lorimer Felle and some newborn spawn terrorise their prey," Black Herran said, squinting into the darkness. "I'm sure he is having fun out there tonight, but that is no reason to relax your guard. Keep an eye out for anything human getting too close to the wall."

They stood to attention and tried to look halfway competent

until she left, heading off to harass the next pair of guards further down the wall. They slumped back and wiped their suddenly sweaty brows.

"I almost soiled myself there," Nicholas said.

Penny took a deep shuddering breath. "That big brutal orc can chop a cow in two, but Elder Dalia turns my blood cold."

Nicholas shuddered. "She's not Dalia any more. It's Black Herran now. Best you remember that."

Penny swallowed and returned to her watch. Monsters roamed the night on both sides of the wall and she wasn't about to be caught napping. Amogg would have her head if she caught Penny slacking off. And Black Herran would do worse.

Hours passed as they listened to shrill screams and glimpsed torches running to and fro, firelight glinting off naked steel rising and falling. They near soiled themselves again when a blood-soaked monster of fang and claw pulled itself over the lip of the wall. Nicholas cried out and thrust his spear into the belly of the beast.

The bloody beast shifted back into the form of a man, and they both felt their stomachs drop at the sight of Lorimer Felle's naked body standing before them. With a spear buried right in his gut.

Nicholas swallowed and pulled it back with a slurp of flesh. "Er... sorry, your lordship." He quailed as the monster reached for him, his death certain.

"Quite alright, my good man," Lorimer said, patting him on the shoulder. The hole healed up without a scar. He wiped a smear of blood off with a scrap of white robe that had been hooked on one of his claws. "No harm done. Keep up the good work." He nodded to Penny and leapt down behind the wall, ambling off towards the town whistling a happy tune.

Nicholas stared at the bloody handprint on his shoulder. "Did you just see that?"

Penny's eyes were huge. "Aye. His cock is fucking massive."

Nicholas groaned and screwed up his eyes. "That is not what

I meant. I thought I was done for." They began to bicker, and both knew they were just using it as a distraction from just seeing a man get speared and then shrug it off.

The sky began to lighten, night giving way to a purple-tinged half-light that allowed them to see the first enemy scouts arriving from the north. They composed themselves and stood ready to fight, trying not to let their knees knock together and their hands shake with terror.

Penny lifted a horn to her lips and blew it three times, the warbling drone summoning the rest of the militia to the wall. War had arrived in Tarnbrooke, and death would not be far behind.

Black Herran, Maeven, Amogg, Lorimer and Tiarnach gathered atop the creaky wooden boards of the gate house to watch the Lucent Empire vanguard form up with military precision. A daunting wall of swords, spears, shields and steel as three thousand grim-faced men began their advance down the valley towards Tarnbrooke, murder on their minds. Their weapons thundered against shields in an ominous beat.

The rain and cloud had broken, and the noonday sun offered a weak warmth, but the valley was still muddy and treacherous, slowing the enemy's approach.

"The whoresons are finally here," Tiarnach said. "At least they gave us time to have breakfast, eh. Now, care to explain why that mad wee fucker o' an alchemist is herding a bunch o' pigs through the wall? Or why the fuck he has painted them black?"

Twenty-five squealing pigs were herded out of the sole gate in the wall into a makeshift pen fifty paces closer to the advancing Lucent army. Their bellies were grotesquely distended and their broad backs had been painted with thick and sticky black gunk that smelled of rotten eggs mixed with alcohol and sewage.

Jerak Hyden bent over the pen, peering at the animals through his round spectacles, nose wrinkled with distaste. His gloved assistant heaved a sack of grain down and stood holding a glass bottle in one hand and a flaming torch in the other.

"Trust in his skills," Black Herran said.

Tiarnach offered her a flat stare. Lorimer snorted.

"Trust in his madness then," she amended. "He loves to kill, and he takes pride in his work."

"That I can believe," Tiarnach said. Amogg rumbled her agreement.

Jerak Hyden's assistant handed him the bottle. He poured the contents into the sack of grain, tossed the bottle aside and then scattered the mix across the pen. The hungry pigs inhaled the food while he cackled.

Banners flapped and sun glinted on armour as lines of soldiers began advancing at a quick walk, a droning prayer to their goddess drifting across on the wind. Closer. Closer, until the defenders of Tarnbrooke could almost make out their foe's fierce scowls.

A few arrows soared from the wall, falling woefully short.

"Hold," Tiarnach screamed at the nervous archers. "The next lackwit who looses an arrow without my say-so gets my fist through their face!"

The pigs began to squeal in distress, snapping at each other and throwing themselves at the flimsy fence penning them in.

"Torch," Jerak Hyden demanded, holding his hand out, fingers clicking impatiently.

He lit a narrow trench filled with oil, straw and tinder. Flame and black smoke spread in a line across the valley between the pigs and the wall, leaving just a single patch for him to return safely. The pigs squealed and crowded the far side of the pen, terrified.

Jerak calmly moved to the north side of the pen, facing the army now advancing into bowshot and beginning to jog, their shields up. "Open the pen!" he demanded, waving the torch at the defenders on the wall to signal his readiness.

"Make some noise," Tiarnach ordered. "Rattle your shields and curse your enemies!"

A roar erupted all along the defences.

Jerak's assistant opened a hole in the pen just large enough for the struggling pigs to squeeze through one by one. His torch descended and the sticky substance on their backs burst into flames as they charged through and fled, squealing in pain, and panicked from the smoke and the din on the wall behind them. When the last pig had escaped the pen, both humans ran for the gatehouse and the doors were slammed shut behind them, thick bars thudding into place.

Jerak scrabbled up to the top of the gatehouse and stood beside Black Herran and the others, a mad grin on his face as he watched the screaming pigs leaping and bucking and rolling in the mud. The flames refused to die as they raced away from the smoke and shouting. The rolling only served to smear the burning substance all over their bodies.

"Does that not smell delicious?" the alchemist cried, gleefully rubbing his hands together. "I would happily feast on roast pork today."

The Lucent army broke into a run. They were slower than they should be, exhausted and ill as they were.

"Loose!" Tiarnach screamed. A black rain of arrows lashed into the enemy, bringing some down, but nowhere near enough. Another volley thudded into shields and flesh, and then the Lucent Empire soldiers roared and broke into the final charge.

The enemy dismissed the screaming, burning pigs as a distraction. Faced with crackling fire, smoke, and noise behind them and cliffs to either side, the terrified swine had nowhere to go but to run at the soldiers.

One of the burning pigs knocked a soldier from his feet and impaled itself on his sword. He cursed and stabbed it again, his sword opening up its belly.

The pig exploded. A fireball consumed five men and greasy black smoke rolled skywards.

Parts of men and swine rained red upon the Lucent army, fragments of burnt bone and hot steel rattling off shields and helmets, blood and guts in their eyes and mouths.

Another pig spitted itself on a spear. Flames licked at the wound.

The explosion tore open the battlefield, leaving another handful of men screaming, faces shredded and blinded.

The Lucent battle line broke apart as more explosions ripped through it. Men shoved past their fellows to avoid the screaming, burning pigs of death.

Jerak Hyden sighed in pleasure, eyes gleaming. "What a marvellous day."

"The fuck is that?" Tiarnach gasped.

"A special alchemical diet," the wiry little man replied. "Working with stomach acids to produce flammable gas and liquid inside the intestines of pigs." Then he leaned forward and scrutinised the warrior. "Do tell, how was your breakfast this morning?"

Amogg's big green arm wrapped around Tiarnach's waist and dragged him away before he could pound Jerak Hyden's face to mush. "Come, burn-hair. We go make ready to fight. Little coward makes funny joke. Amogg snap his neck if he tried."

Jerak removed his spectacles and polished them with a cloth. "Alas. True." All present knew that threat would not hold him forever if he really wanted to experiment on Tiarnach. He just couldn't help himself.

Enemy archers behind the front line managed to bring down the remaining pigs before they did any more damage. The Lucent army pulled itself together and resumed the advance.

"Looks like you failed, ya wee prick," Tiarnach shouted.

The alchemist smirked as he pulled a small brass device from his pocket. He watched the advance and waited for twelve more seconds, then pulled a lever.

On the battlefield, the clay pots he had buried earlier

exploded. Fragments of slate and scrap metal scythed across the Lucent forces, shredding exposed skin and cutting through leather boots. Hundreds reeled, clutching at bloodied faces and ruined eyes. The Lucent army limped back in disarray, dragging their wounded away under a hail of arrows. They fled towards their acolytes in the rear, desperate for them to lay hands and healing magic upon their torn flesh. The residents of Tarnbrooke raised a disbelieving cheer.

Jerak winked at Tiarnach. "The pigs were just to make things interesting. If I had been provided with more than these paltry supplies, I could have disposed of those savages all by myself."

"I can't believe we won," Nicholas shouted, hugging Penny and watching the retreating soldiers. "Soon, we will be back to our normal lives."

Amogg approached the militiaman with Tiarnach still squirming in her grip, still hurling crude threats in the wiry alchemist's direction. "Not be sad," the big orc said to Nicholas. "That was just first fight. Lots more chance for glory."

Nicholas's face fell. Amogg dropped Tiarnach and hefted her axe.

Tiarnach got to his feet and drew his sword, staring forlornly in the direction the alchemist had fled. He sighed, spun the sword in his hand and then laughed at Nicholas's expression. He grinned, trying and failing to be reassuring. "That was just one of that bastard's wee tricks. Wait until the real magic starts flying. There's more o' those ugly pricks than flies on a horse's arse so you'll have your fill o' killing today."

Nicholas shuddered, said nothing, shouldered his spear and rejoined the militia as horns began to blow to the north and the enemy lines slowly reformed.

With all eyes staring in the opposite direction, Tiarnach's false grin slipped. He took a deep shuddering breath, releasing some of the tension in his neck and ribs. The fear had him in its grip again. He was weak and mortal and facing a trained army with only a pack of grubby peasants. They were all fucking doomed. He only hoped he lasted long enough to gut that stinking Falcon Prince.

One of his men glanced back and he forced the mad grin back onto his face. "Should've been one o' those lying bards instead o' a warrior," he muttered as he leapt atop the wall to stand with his men.

He howled defiance at the enemy and bared his arse at them, a gesture quickly taken up by the men he had brutalised into something vaguely resembling warriors over the last few weeks. No other fucker here would be able to make paltry peasants stand and fight, so it was up to him to keep this rabble together. If that meant pretending he was the fearless warrior of old, then so be it. In any case, he was pretending more for himself than for them.

CHAPTER 25

Landgrave Laurant Daryn wiped gore from his face and surveyed the hundreds of wounded moaning in the mud, some dying or already dead at his feet. There were too many for so few acolytes to save. Some of his men were squatting right next to the dead, grunting and voiding their poisoned bowels, their faces red with disgust and shame.

Anger burned inside him, a raging torrent of the Goddess's wrath pounding through his veins demanding recompense.

"The filthy peasants mock us," he snarled to Sir Orwin. "They poison us and break our charge with swine! Swine! And now the degenerates expose themselves atop their wall."

The holy knight calmly drew his sword, the steel shedding rainbow light. "I am not concerned about the genitalia of peasants. It is the evil creatures lurking in the shadows pulling their strings that must be dealt with."

"Up!" Daryn bellowed. "Up, men. Form line. Archers to the rear." His men pulled up their breeches, tightened straps on armour and shuffled back into their lines.

"Advance! Make those peasants bleed."

"They come again," Amogg rumbled. She grinned at her squad, tusk rings glinting. "Good. I bored." Ragash and Wundak chuckled and hefted their weapons.

The orcs and her women warriors spread out among the other untrained townsfolk, the carpenters, hunters, masons and merchants that had been too busy building the defences to learn as much of the arts of war.

Amogg hefted her axe and pointed to the menacing bulk of Ragash and Wundak. "If humans run, orcs kill you."

Nobody doubted she meant it; not after she murdered the elder in the temple.

Tiarnach nodded to her and looked to his own men. "Those women will stand and fight. If any o' you runts don't do the same then don't you precious little babes worry, I won't kill you…"

He had trained the militia hard, and by now they knew him well enough to recognise the trap. They kept their expressions blank and their mouths shut.

"Aye, instead I'll hand you over to that mad wee fucker Jerak Hyden to make something useful out o' your sorry hides."

Their faces paled. Some fates were worse than death.

Tiarnach nodded in satisfaction. "That's what I thought. Get those spears and axes ready, my mad lads."

Lorimer's manservant Estevan assumed command of the archers and reserve units, leaving Tiarnach and Amogg free to inflict a dreadful slaughter on the first soldiers who dared try and climb their wall.

Through the strip of cloth protecting his eyes, Lorimer Felle watched the arrows raining down on the enemy. The sweet aroma of blood and sweat made him salivate and his jaw drop to accommodate lengthening fangs. He looked to Black Herran, her aged hands clasped behind her back as she calmly took in the battle beside Maeven, and a visibly bored and fidgeting Jerak Hyden at her side. "How would you have me fight this day?" he asked.

She didn't look away from the sight of men being skewered

by arrows. "You are the swiftest among us. Go wherever you are most needed."

He bowed, only half-mocking. "As you wish, oh great and powerful general."

She glared at him from the corner of her eyes. "If you act like a child, I will treat you as one. Now be a good little boy and go play with your food." Then her attention returned to the line of men charging her wall.

He hissed with laughter and loped off, fingers and toes lengthening into razor-tipped claws and bony plates of armour sliding across his skin.

"Such arrogance," Maeven said, shaking her head.

Black Herran snorted. "None of us have ever been short of that commodity. How are your magical preparations?"

Jerak Hyden yawned loudly and adjusted his spectacles. "I shall return to my work if you are discussing sorcerous flimflammery. Do try and keep the rabble from my wall until the sun is almost down. I will be most displeased if you do not." The little man scrabbled down the wall, rounded up his assistant and shepherded her towards his workshop.

Maeven ignored his exit, her lips twisted into a smile as a flight of arrows thudded into charging men. "My preparations are complete. Come the morning the dead outside Tarnbrooke will rise."

"Excellent," Black Herran said. "We must make the best use possible of this resource we have been given. Blood, death and corpses: the stuff of their lives shall not go to waste. We will need all of what they offer us when we face the Falcon Prince and his inquisitors."

Under a heavy rain of arrows and slingshot, the Lucent soldiers charged into a field of shallow foot-sized pits dug irregularly all across the valley floor. They were a simple but effective trap of Tiarnach's. With the recent heavy rains there was no way to tell which was a shallow puddle and which was a pit. Soldiers fell, twisting or breaking ankles, and all their armour couldn't save them. The rest slowed, the charge broken up as they tried to pick their way through the mess. At this range it made them easy targets for the archers and slingers of the Tarnbrooke militia. Men fell, but more pressed on behind their shields.

The Lucent vanguard finally reached the wall. Tiarnach and Amogg were there to meet them. The first line of heavy infantry crashed into the fortification, their shields held high as they attempted to climb up through a barrage of stones, arrows and spear points thrusting down at their faces. In the press, some impaled themselves on sharpened wooden stakes, howling in pain.

A squad of soldiers set their feet in the mud and hefted their shields to form steps up to the lip of the wall. Men charged up, only to be intercepted by the axe of Amogg Hadakk that reduced their shields to kindling and split their bodies. She roared with savage joy as the bloody pieces fell back into the press of men below.

Atop the wall, the Tarnbrooke militia frantically stabbed their spears down into the mass of flesh and steel, desperate to keep the soldiers away from them. There was little skill involved, just butchers operating a meat-grinder. The soldiers who managed to top the wall were run through by Tiarnach or slaughtered by Ragash and Wundak, their corpses thrown back down into the mud.

Archers following behind the Lucent battle line began feathering the engaged defenders of a single section of the wall. A dozen lightly armoured townsfolk fell, leaving a gap in the defences. Ragash grunted as a shaft thudded into his arm. He ripped it free and then plunged the arrow through the eyeball of a Lucent soldier.

A knot of climbing soldiers took advantage of the losses to force a breach. They cut through the remaining townsfolk and began helping up their comrades. The enemy began to pour through and assault the reeling militia on either side of them, forcing Ragash back with their superior numbers.

Lorimer was there in an instant, a storm of fang and claw that shredded everything around him. More armoured men climbed through the breach until he was surrounded. They stabbed him, slashed with swords and brutally battered with shields, but it was nothing to the vampire lord's flesh. His gaping wounds healed as if they were trying to cut the sea and he simply reattached the parts they cut off, then killed them for their affront. Horror stole over the Lucent soldiers as they realised that they could not bring him down with steel and guts alone.

"Where are your vaunted holy knights now?" Lorimer yelled as he ripped out a man's throat and tossed the gurgling wreck back over the wall. He held the breach alone with fang and ferocity until Estevan's archers were able to clear the wall allowing Ragash and the townsfolk to retake it.

Maeven stiffened as she spotted two men in heavy battle plate, one of whom was wreathed in golden fire. They both charged directly at the gatehouse.

"How much power can you spare?" Black Herran asked.

Maeven grimaced. "Not enough. The protection of their goddess will be difficult to breach without great effort."

"Then I shall deal with these pests. You concentrate on driving back the foot soldiers – do try not to kill too many before nightfall." She lifted a finger to her teeth and tore at the flesh by her nail, drawing blood.

From Maeven's vantage atop the gatehouse, she sought out wherever the Lucent soldiers fought the hardest and laid a touch of death on their bodies, not enough to kill, but enough to drop them screaming as nerves and muscles died and their flesh erupted in red and rotting sores. It was a weapon of terror rather than destruction, one that would leave their lives intact and ready to be harvested when darkness fell. Her magical plague began to spread from man to man.

The holy knight levelled his sword and golden fire lanced out towards the gate.

Black Herran casually lifted a bejewelled hand, the black onyx ring ripped from the eye of an earth elemental smeared with blood. She willed a wall of earth to burst from the ground in front of the gate.

Golden fire boomed into it, the blowback knocking soldiers from their feet and showering the inquisitor with mud. The battle paused for a moment. The wall of earth was damaged but still standing, and as they watched, the earth flowed up to fill in the smoking crater made by the impact. Swords and spears were all well and good, but magic turned the tide of battles.

She stood atop the gatehouse in full view of the enemy and their archers. "I am Black Herran!" she shouted across the battlefield, and as she spoke the sun darkened in a cloudless sky. A handful of opportunistic enemy archers loosed arrows at her, but she ignored them and none seemed able to hit their mark. "I am the slayer of kings and queens, the doom of armies and the master of demons. To fight me is to die. I will eat your souls."

The harrowing screams of souls damned to Hellrath wailed from the cracks in the earth, and with them came a sulphurous yellow fog that coalesced at the foot of the wall and crept up the legs of the Lucent soldiers. Men gagged and reeled back to safety. The assault floundered and failed beneath her imperious glare.

The inquisitor levelled his sword again, but the other knight laid a hand on his arm and pulled him back. They retreated in good order and waited out of bowshot for her fog and magic to dissipate. With the dark rituals she had to perform at nightfall she could not spare the power to keep it up for long, but it gave the defenders a chance to catch their breath.

The people of Tarnbrooke sat in the mud, breathing hard and bandaging wounds. Their hands shook and some sat staring at nothing, clutching weapons and trembling. Others dragged the corpses of their loved ones and friends into neat rows and said prayers to their gods.

Black Herran's captains gathered at the gatehouse and looked out over the field of dead and dying Lucent soldiers, the crows already descending to eat their fill. It was a horrendous slaughter to the townsfolk, but to old monsters like Black Herran it was barely worth calling a skirmish. They had all seen carpets of the dead stretching as far as the eye could see.

"That one with the inquisitor is the leader," Black Herran said, polishing her onyx ring and holding it up to a critical eye. They both stood out, dressed head to toe in fancy steel.

"I recognised those shiny pricks," Tiarnach said, using a scrap of a Lucent soldier's white tabard to wipe blood off his sword. "Here, Amogg, that's those bastards from Hive ain't they?"

The huge orc scratched her chin. "I not remember too good. Ale bad."

"It is them," Maeven replied. "That is one of the two inquisitors that sought to bar our escape. Lorimer broke his knee."

"Amogg remember that bit," the orc said, cheering. "Boring fight. Got hit by lightning. Had bath in river. Bashed little human's brains out on rock."

"How can that be boring to you?" Lorimer asked, wiping blood and gore from his body.

"Too quick," she said. "No fun without challenge."

The vampire looked up at her for a moment. "Ah. That I can understand. Not to worry, it looks like they are about ready for another assault."

Black Herran cast an eye over the defenders. "Our militia have not regained their senses as of yet. They may break, so I must buy you more time to reinvigorate them." She stretched out a hand towards the Lucent Empire army and called forth her pit-born magic.

She cackled as the runes etched into Lucent blades came to twisted life. Blades turned in their owner's hands and plunged into the throats of their friends and allies. The army turned on itself and men died in the confusion. With disappointing swiftness, the inquisitor was among them, blocking blows and ordering soldiers to disarm. Swords and shields dropped to the mud.

Had Black Herran possessed a competent army of her own, the battle would have been over then and there. As it was, she had to be content with the time it bought Tarnbrooke: every one of those weapons would need to be replaced or inspected and cleansed of Hellrath runes.

The holy knight knelt in the dirt and prodded a sword, tainted steel sparking as he touched it. His eyes turned towards the town. Black Herran offered a jaunty wave in return. Time was on her side, and the enemy had already enjoyed a taste of what nightfall would bring them.

CHAPTER 26

Three hours passed while the poisoned and sleep-deprived Lucent soldiers marshalled their strength. The inquisitor and his acolytes worked tirelessly to cleanse their weapons of demonic taint; his golden flames and their holy prayers burnt away the jagged sigils that carried Black Herran's malicious will.

Daryn paced back and forth, plagued by divine will to destroy but also not daring to risk an attack until he was sure his men would not unwittingly murder one another. "I know inquisitors can disappear and reappear in a flash of lightning," he asked Sir Orwin. "Could you bypass that wall of theirs?"

Sir Orwin nodded. "I could, but I will not. The distance I can safely travel is short, and it would leave me perilously weakened should those creatures of darkness join forces to assail me. This cleansing has already fatigued me."

Daryn resumed his pacing. Eventually he turned and studied the holy knight's fine and very distinctive heavy armour, finger tapping his chin. "How would you feel about attempting a little subterfuge?"

Finally, as the light began to fade and the weather worsened, the soldiers took up their righteous weapons again. They knelt to receive blessing of protection from their acolytes and then began another assault on the wall.

* * *

The sun had failed to struggle through the brooding clouds over the valley, and the rain and cold winds had returned – a beneficial situation for the defenders, who at least had warm fires and some cover from wind and rain. Black Herran sat on a comfy chair atop the gatehouse, shielded from drizzling rain by a canvas canopy. Her eyes never left the enemy. Her will was as indomitable as ever, but age was a relentless foe that had taken a heavy toll on her legs and back.

Somebody began climbing up to her. "Hello, Maeven," she said without looking back.

"You have eyes everywhere," the necromancer said as she pulled herself onto the creaky wooden platform. "One day they will fail you."

"My own aged eyes may," the demonologist admitted, "but those of my demons never will."

"You put too much trust in evil, inhuman creatures," Maeven replied.

Then Black Herran did turn to look at her. She smiled knowingly. "What do you know of inquisitors?"

"As much as any," the necromancer replied. "Which is precious little. Judging from the golden fire that has burned constantly these last few hours, it would seem that their supply of power is inexhaustible."

"That's gods for you," Black Herran said. "These mortal men wield borrowed power and I suspect it must hollow them out after a while. An unprepared soul must be weathered away by that torrent of magic, leaving only a slavish shell behind."

"More than likely," Maeven agreed. "Perhaps Tiarnach would prove more enlightening than I."

The demonologist shook her head. "Even at the height of his divine power he never boasted anywhere near as many worshippers and power as this Bright One. Nor, I think, would he ever want to. Not a bad idea though. By all means, ask him questions if you are quick about it. If you are lucky you might even get a straight answer out of the man."

Maeven took her leave, pulled her cloak hood up against the rain and went in search of the once-god. She was surprised not to find him at the wall with the Tarnbrooke militia, but one of the boys bringing supplies up from the town pointed to a hastily abandoned farmstead just south of the wall. She found him hidden in the barn, doubled over and retching, muttering, "Fuck fuck fuck," over and over.

"Drinking yourself senseless at a time like this?" she sneered. "They are beginning the next assault."

He jerked upright and wiped his red whiskers on his sleeve. "Fuck off, Maeven." His face was wet and sickly pale.

The necromancer stepped aside as he stormed off towards the wall. She kept pace with him. "What do you know of holy knights and their god-given power?"

He slowed, stopped and turned, wiping rainwater from his brow. "God-given? Those fuckers ain't holy and that power is taken."

Maeven blinked; she wasn't sure how to respond to that. Normally, getting a straight answer out of Tiarnach was like trying to get blood from a stone.

"See, the thing is," he continued, "that magic fire they spray about like a drunk taking a piss, it has a wee bit of their god's life in it. Like, if I cut a finger off and sprayed the blood in your face, 'cept that golden flame is not full of pain and anger. It's…" He thought about it for a long moment. "Suppose you might call it blank. Not a drop of ill-will in it. Almost innocent."

Blank? the necromancer thought. *How could a god's power used to kill possibly be innocent?* Dark thoughts about what the Falcon Prince was up to caused her blood to run cold.

Their discussion was cut short by the drone of war horns. Tiarnach cursed and jogged to the wall. Maeven followed, slow and full of worrisome thoughts. The look of relief on the sodden militiamen's faces as Tiarnach rejoined them piqued her interest and she pondered the lack of grey in the man's red hair. The deep lines around his eyes had softened too. She wondered if perhaps formal worship was not needed for a god to gain power. Was belief in them enough?

The top of the wall was crowded with trained militia and armed butchers, carpenters, hunters, shepherds and other townsfolk, all gritting their teeth and holding their weapons tight as the line of Lucent Empire soldiers advanced again at a steady walk. The enemy would not recklessly charge in again.

"You only need to hold this wall for an hour," Tiarnach shouted. "Just one more poxy hour! Then we can all bugger off back to Tarnbrooke, dry out and tap us some barrels o' ale."

The townsfolk shifted uneasily. They all knew some dark plan was afoot, but none knew the details, and none truly wanted to. They only knew that they did not want to be anywhere near the wall once the sun went down.

The Lucent army approached, and as the first rain of arrows fell, they broke into a jog. Arrows thudded into their upraised shields, pitifully few piercing mail and flesh. Two skewered boots and feet, pinning the men in place and leaving them howling.

Black Herran's brow furrowed as she studied the oncoming battle line, noting their leader in his heavy armour, shrugging off arrows like they were bugs. "Odd, I see only one knight. Where is that damned inquisitor?"

Maeven leaned forward and lifted her hand to shelter her eyes against the reddening sun sinking behind the hills. "I cannot see him on the field."

"Curse them," Black Herran snapped. "He must have taken off his armour – we cannot counter what we cannot see. Resume your necrotic plague to disable them. We have to lose, but not quite yet."

Maeven didn't deign to reply as she got to work, a black and flesh-devouring mist rising from the ground in the far left of the enemy line, climbing up their boots to... dissipate.

The necromancer blinked and tried again, this time on the centre. The men there began screaming as patches of exposed skin died and sloughed off to reveal the red and glistening layers of fat and muscle beneath. She opened her mouth to warn Black Herran but it was much too late.

Golden fire scythed across the top of the wall, reducing a dozen townsfolk and militia on the left flank to ash and smoking bones that clattered down across the rock. Lucent soldiers clambered up the charred fortification and attacked the other embattled defenders from the rear.

Amogg stood with Ragash and Wundak atop the wall shattering shields and skulls with their mighty axes. Amogg was covered in shallow wounds but they only seemed to enrage her. She spotted the breach, roared and charged along the wall to butcher the invaders, bellowing: "Fight well, little humans!"

What appeared to be a common footman in patched mail vaulted to the top and turned to face her. His sword burst into golden flames as he pointed it towards her. "I think not, brute. My name is Sir Orwin, and I will be your end."

Holy fire lanced towards her. Amogg grabbed hold of the nearest Lucent soldier and used him as a shield. She was blasted backwards and burned through the air to crash into the foot of the gate house on the Tarnbrooke side. She lay motionless, still clutching the charred corpse of the Lucent soldier, the front of his mail glowing cherry red.

Ragash and Wundak's skin turned the deeper red of orcish fury. The huge orcs loosed a roar that deafened the humans around them, spittle flying as they charged the inquisitor.

Lucent soldiers moved to stop them only to be brutally battered aside. It was as futile as trying to stop enraged bulls.

"God Gardram made us strong!" Wundak snarled. Her axe glimmered as their great god's power flowed through her. As the next blast of golden fire hit them she chopped down, splitting the stream of fire in two.

Sir Orwin was taken aback for only an instant, an instant too long to prevent Ragash from closing in on him.

The axe came down with the full fury of an elder orc behind it. The inquisitor wisely chose to leap from the wall, landing awkwardly on the Tarnbrooke side. He ignored a small boy with an armload of arrows, who fled screaming, and loosed his magic, not at the orcs, but at the gatehouse.

A pillar of golden flame engulfed the gatehouse and roared up into the darkening sky. The defenders gasped and faltered as Black Herran was attacked. When the flame abated, the structure was only missing a small chunk of wood and stone, the rest protected by a sphere of churning darkness. It swirled and retracted into a small ball in Maeven's hand. Her grey cloak was smoking and blackened and she was leaning on a post for support.

She scowled at the holy knight, then she lobbed the ball of darkness at him.

Sir Orwin chose to run rather than take the attack, sprinting straight back towards the segment of wall with the orcs atop it. There was no explosion of flashy magic on the ground behind him. The ball of darkness hit the earth and expanded to the size of a house. A moment later it was gone and where there had been stalks of grass and moss there was now only dust being washed away in the rain. He leapt unnaturally high and landed atop the wall in front of the orcs.

Ragash swung a huge fist at the knight's face, and to his astonishment, the human caught it with his free hand. He stopped it dead with only a grunt of effort. The human grinned and ran the big orc through with his fiery blade. It burned a hole right through Ragash's broad chest and burst out the back.

Wundak's foot slammed into the inquisitor's chest. Strong as the human was, he didn't have the weight to stop himself from bouncing along the wall to crash into a knot of his own men. Sir Orwin scrambled to his feet, dazed, as Ragash fell to all fours, gasping for air, bloody froth drooling from his tusks.

Wundak could see through the charred hole in his chest but she did not move to assist him. They both knew this was a fatal wound, and she refused to take this glorious death from him.

"Rise, warrior of Gardram," she said solemnly. "Rise and fight. Kill the enemy. Die well."

Ragash grimaced and levered himself upright. He limped towards the Lucent soldiers, his axe dragging along behind him, chest heaving in a futile attempt to catch breath.

"The brute is done for," a soldier cried, and seeing a chance for glory of his own, he hefted his sword overhead and charged.

Ragash lifted his free hand to block the downward cut. The sword sliced down through his fingers and palm before jarring to a stop against bone. The big orc grinned and swept his axe up, taking the human's arm off in a bloody spray.

Wundak did nothing but count as the knot of soldiers swarmed Ragash, stabbing and slicing into him as he swung his axe. One dead human. Two. Three. The axe slipped from clumsy blood-soaked fingers. A fourth human fell to a tusk through the eyeball. The elder orc faltered as an arrow thudded into his chest, and then finally died beneath their swords.

Only then did Wundak charge, bellowing red rage as her axe laid open an armoured chest and tore the head from another human.

The holy knight advanced to meet her, his burning sword flicking out like a deadly viper: darting at her eyes, her knee, at her throat – a feint – stabbing at her belly instead. She blocked with her glowing axe in a fountain of sparks. A human spearman took advantage to stab her in the thigh. Hot blood poured down her leg as she was forced backwards by the inquisitor's burning blade, hissing as it cut through the rain.

The Tarnbrooke militia streamed towards her, Tiarnach in the lead and intent on closing the breach in the defences. Wundak roared and swung her axe, but Sir Orwin ducked and loosed a blast of fire that washed over her and drove her to her knees, growling as she fought to resist their human god's might.

Sir Orwin grinned at her. "Burn, beast."

Golden fire blossomed all around, burning and eating away at her skin despite her god Gardram's protection. It only lasted a few agonizing seconds before Tiarnach's muddy boot burst through the fire to plant itself square in the inquisitor's face.

"Take that, ya fucking freak!" Tiarnach shouted as he kicked the shocked knight right off the wall to fall flailing and still burning back into the press of his own men scaling the defences. They screamed as their goddess's golden fire ate into them – that same fire that had left their mocking enemy untouched.

Tiarnach turned to glare at the Lucent soldiers atop the wall. They all stared back at him slack-jawed. "This is my wall, ya shitebags."

Amogg stirred, thrust the charred human shield aside and ran to rejoin the fight. The militia joined her, streaming past Tiarnach, spears levelled in a charge. The Lucent soldiers glanced down at the smoking, screaming mess of their reinforcements below, then back to the militia, Tiarnach and the hulking form of Amogg bearing down on them. They panicked and leapt from the wall.

Their attack had failed with the defeat of their holy knight. The Lucent leader withdrew his men, and the inquisitor and his burned soldiers limped back to join them. Tarnbrooke had survived again, but there was just enough time for one more attack before nightfall.

CHAPTER 27

The militia and armed townsfolk caught their breath, sipping water and shaking. They were a fit and hardy practical people but unused to extreme fear and battle stress, which drained them more than any physical exertion. The old and young of Tarnbrooke began dragging the dead and dying from the blood-drenched wall to clear a space for the next fight, and for the next to fall. With the fire and fury of combat over with for now, the cold of the wind and rain caused them to huddle close to their braziers and pray to their gods.

"How did Tiarnach survive their golden fire?" Penny asked, blood dripping down her face. Some of it was hers, most of it some other poor bastard's. "We all saw it turn people to bone and ash."

Amogg scowled at the Lucent corpses and swung her axe in annoyance. She hated missing a good fight. "Tiarnach is war god. Gods resist power of gods. Make sense to Amogg." She might not have been entirely familiar with humans, but she knew enough to recognise their shock and confusion.

Penny stared. "We thought calling him a god of war was just a grand nickname."

Tiarnach wasn't paying them any notice. He leaned out over the wall and shouted at the retreating inquisitor. "Hoi! Orwin, was it? That all you got, ya wee prick? That tickled!" He chuckled and noisily hawked a blob of phlegm over the wall.

Then turned to see the militia staring at him with undisguised awe. "Aw fuck. What now?"

Penny swallowed and wiped her bloody face with a sleeve, succeeding only in staining the fabric red. "Are... are you really a god?"

Tiarnach ran a hand through his long hair – the grey strands had now entirely disappeared from his head and chin. "Oh, that? Aye. Once, anyway." He squinted at the enemy as they began to reform. It would take a little time to reorganise and ready their units for a new assault. "Looks like we have time for a drink, eh, young Red Penny? How's about me and you head back for a bit and..."

Amogg loomed over him, a flat stare on a viciously unimpressed face.

"Er, maybe not," Tiarnach said. He winked at her and mimicked drinking a horn of ale as he beat a hasty retreat. "Laters, aye?"

"Red Penny," Amogg rumbled, eyeing the blood-soaked human. "Good name. Tiarnach is bad choice of mate. Your grubbs would be strong but very stupid and smelly."

"Grubbs?" Penny said, frowning.

"Do humans not teach their young?" Amogg said. "I explain mating later." She left the militia to get themselves ready and moved to Wundak, who stood over Ragash's corpse, favouring her wounded leg.

"It was a good fight," Wundak said, flakes of her crisped skin cracking and falling away. "Had a hole in his chest and still killed four. Would have killed many more if that human had not used a god's strength to defeat him. There was no shame in falling to that enemy."

Amogg lifted her head and howled, a long and mournful cry fit to draw Gardram's eye to one of his mightiest fallen. "He fought with honour. Died a glorious death. Orcs ask for nothing more."

"This place will be the death of us all," Wundak said. Then

she grinned. "But what a death! We will not fade away to tuskless husks unable to even lift an axe. Our deaths will be remembered."

Amogg stiffened. *Come to me*, a voice whispered in her ear. *Black Herran calls you.* She spun and lashed out behind her, but caught only shadows. "I must go and talk war. Take Ragash's body into town and prepare his meat for the honour feast later."

Amogg joined Tiarnach and Black Herran at the charred gatehouse. Tiarnach kicked a wooden post and cursed. "It sticks in my craw to run away."

Black Herran nodded to Amogg. "When the next attack reaches the wall, you both must lose, and make it appear convincing. They have to believe that our retreat back into the town is genuine."

Tiarnach spat over the wall. "An' what's to stop them rolling right over our militia and smashing through that wee palisade around town? That pile of twigs is not going to hold them long."

"The sun is going down," the aged demonologist replied. "They will not have time. Lorimer Felle will stop them. He has been busy sharing his vampiric blood with some unfortunate soldiers he acquired earlier. Let us see how eager the enemy are for a night assault when their own blood-starved friends crawl from their graves looking to open human throats."

Amogg grunted in agreement, picked her nose and examined the results before flicking it away. "Apart from god-men, human warriors are not worth the effort of fighting. I will kill the Falcon Prince instead."

"Oh, he is coming," Black Herran said. "Have no doubt of that. And when he does, we will need every advantage we can get."

Wundak winced as she kicked open the door to a hovel and set Ragash's body down on a table, ready for the ritual butchering and feast to partake of his strength. His soul was with Gardram now, and only his flesh remained to give strength to the Hadakk. It was tradition for the elders to take the choice cuts and leave the rest for the grubbs, but Amogg and herself would feast well tonight instead. Her mind and body were exhausted from resisting the human god's power and Ragash would grant her his might to fight on.

She groaned and sat at the table, the fragile human-sized chair under her creaking alarmingly. Fresh blood seeped through the rags she had tied around her leg.

The tattooed necromancer sauntered through the doorway and nodded at her leg. "I think you need stitches for that."

Wundak grunted, pulled a knife from her belt and began cutting the clothing from the corpse.

"Unless you would like me to quickly seal the wound for you and be on my way?"

The orc was too tired to argue. "Be quick and be away, human. This is no place for you tonight."

The necromancer nodded and moved to examine the spear wound, tutting at the filthy rags. She removed her backpack and pulled out a roll of tools and fresh linen strips. She selected an obsidian knife and slit through gory cloth, pale fingers peeling it back to reveal the gaping flesh and muscle beneath.

The necromancer paused. "I don't suppose you would happen to know where Black Herran's daughter and grandchildren are? What do you orcs call them? Her grubbs?"

Wundak snorted. "I care nothing for human grubbs."

"A shame." The necromancer thrust her knife into Wundak's wound.

Cold... so cold... a whirlpool of death sucking in Wundak's soul.

The orc's head thudded into the table top, stone-cold dead. Maeven smiled and wiped down her obsidian knife with clean linen. The knife felt warm in her hand, pulsing with life granted by the strong old soul it had just devoured. The orc's essence felt like an ancient mossy stone, hard and immovable. That additional power would allow her to raise a small army of the living dead to obey her every whim. It was a shame the other big brute died before she'd had the chance to kill him directly and steal his soul too. She had leeched the impressive power loosed by his death, but regrettably the soul itself had escaped her clutches.

The expended lives of peasants and soldiers she had already gathered were as nothing to the power of this single soul taken directly from the source, and this was only the beginning. Black Herran, Tiarnach, Amogg Hadakk, the deluded Lucent inquisitors... their souls would all serve to further her necromantic goals. The question was in what order she could kill them all and get away with it. If she could find a way to break the blood oath she had sworn, she would also be more than happy to kill Lorimer Felle.

The dry voice of her grandfather whispered in the back of her mind, urging her to hurry, eager for her to complete the weapon. His ghost was desperate to finally be allowed to rest. She gathered her gear and slipped out the door, closing it behind her.

A young girl carrying a big basket of fresh-baked bread from the bakery to the storehouse spotted her as she left the hovel, and had a heart attack and died before the necromancer turned the corner. The girl's soul was a feeble, flitting thing barely worth collecting, but when Jerak Hyden's little surprise went off there would be soul essence and power a-plenty. It would prove most useful to quicken her knife.

War horns sounded to the north and she hurried back to the wall to witness the rest of the evening's festivities.

Laurant Daryn's linen gambeson was soaked through and heavy, and a stream of icy rainwater ran down his back and buttocks. The mud sucked hungrily at his steel sabatons and oozed between the foot plates with every step, as if the whole accursed valley had turned against him. An arrow tinged off his helmet, another off his chest. Encased in ruinously expensive steel, he had little to fear from arrows save for a very lucky shot. His men were not so perfectly armoured and had to rely on their shields.

Two fell screaming with arrows in their legs, but Daryn lowered his head and charged on, weathering the storm of arrows that thudded against him like hail on a tiled roof. Glimpsed through the rain clouds, the sun was now a burning crescent sinking below the hills, and they had no more time to spare. He would do the Bright One's bidding. He was wrath.

The wall was right ahead, well-lit by braziers and torches. It was a sorry heap of stone around wooden posts that was already crumbling, rocks falling away beneath the boots of the righteous and hastily piled back up by the heathens. These demon worshippers could not hold it for long against him, even with their dark magic.

Sir Orwin was taking care of the wrinkled old witch atop the gatehouse – it was laughable that she boasted to be the legendary Black Herran, not seen these past forty years. As if those chosen by the Goddess would be afraid of a decrepit old woman with a dark name. The holy knight's golden fire was slowly burning away their gatehouse, inadequately protected by earth and sorcery. He left the witch no opportunity to deal with the holy army scaling their pathetic wall.

The huge orc took a spear from a brave soldier thrusting from below and reeled away, bellowing and clutching her belly. The mad, red-haired warrior who had defied Sir Orwin fell back with an arrow in the chest – whatever dark magic had protected him against holy fire had no power over a shaft of honest wood and steel.

Daryn reached the foot of the wall. His men were ascending through a forest of stabbing spears. He did not climb, he leapt, his blessed strength propelling him to land amidst the enemy, an armoured bringer of justice ripping through the poorly trained heretics. His sword sang as it severed limbs and laid open chests and throats.

All around him in the fading light, Lucent soldiers were engaging in brutal melee. The defenders were few, most already having fled. He savoured the enemy's despair. The wall was quickly breached in four places, his men swarming over it.

A bell tolled from the town's temple, summoning the wicked creatures back to their nest. The entire defence broke apart and fled towards the open gates in the palisade hastily erected around their town. They abandoned weapons to the mud in absolute panic.

Daryn gave chase, intent on ensuring those gates did not close. Many of those fleeing were women, young and old wielding butcher's cleavers and hunting spears. This was barely a militia, and certainly not an army. This could well have been the peasantry of his home of Allstane.

Fight for me!

The impulse was irresistible, his Goddess's fury searing through his veins. Arrows tinged off him still as he charged, cutting down a portly limping woman with a pot on her head. He ran an old man through the back and trampled him into the dirt.

His men weathered defensive arrow fire and raced ahead, every sword burning gold by the light of the setting sun. The edge of the disc sank behind the hill.

The earth erupted ahead of Daryn's charge. Men that had gone missing over the previous days crawled from muddy graves, eyes burning an unholy red. One leapt through the air to land on Daryn, his jaw yawning unnaturally wide and full of jagged fangs. He rammed his steel-clad knee into the belly of the beast but it barely noticed, teeth screeching along the steel gorget protecting his neck.

He grabbed the monster by the neck and heaved it off of him. Vampire. No doubt about it. The creature struggled in his grip, unable to break the strength granted to him by his Goddess. He rammed the point of his blade through its eye, then dropped the still-squirming thing and severed its head from its shoulders with a single blow.

His men were falling back under an onslaught of similar creatures, their cuts and stabs having little effect on unnatural flesh. Over to his right, golden fire bloomed, incinerating two of the creatures. Up ahead the enemy stragglers had reached the town gates. He could still get there in time, as could Sir Orwin. But his men...

Fight for me!

His feet took two steps forward.

A grizzled gamekeeper he had known all his life screamed as a vampire tore off half his face.

Kill for me!

He screamed, fighting against the fire in his veins. His men... his Goddess... his duty as liege lord... He turned and flung himself at the nearest vampire, saving the life of a boy he'd watched grow to manhood.

The sun set. The gates of Tarnbrooke slammed shut. He had lost an easy victory over the townsfolk this night, but there was always a new dawn.

From atop the temple spire, Black Herran and her six captains listened to the screams and clash of steel as the Lucent Empire army retreated back to the wall, using the light of its plentiful braziers and torches to see and dismember the remaining vampire spawn.

Jerak Hyden giggled and wrung trembling hands. "Is it time? Is it? Is it?"

"As soon as they are settled into their camp," Black Herran replied.

Jerak Hyden reached into a pouch on his belt and pulled out a little box of brass and glass, small sparks of lightning crackling around his fingers. "It has many siblings built into the wall."

"We do not care how it works," Lorimer snapped. "Only that it does."

The bulk of the Lucent force withdrew behind the wall, using it as a makeshift fortification of their own. Men swarmed over it setting up guard posts, watching for more unnatural creatures.

Jerak giggled and shook his head at the futility of it all.

The army pitched their tents on the flat space directly behind the wall, laid out their wounded and began treating them.

The mad alchemist ran his fingers lovingly over the box in his hand. He licked his lips and waited, enjoying the anticipation.

As camp fires sprang up and exhausted men finally settled down to eat their rations, thinking themselves safe behind their new defences, Black Herran gave him the nod. Jerak twisted a brass knob and pulled a tiny lever.

The world lurched beneath them.

The temple spire shivered and leaned dangerously as the alchemist's shrill laughter filled the air. To the north, the defensive wall ceased to exist. Violent blue flame exploded all along its length, shattering wood and stone and sending body parts flying.

"You fucking wee monster," Tiarnach said, part disgust, part awe.

"There no glory in this," Amogg growled.

Jerak Hyden didn't care or show any evidence he heard at all; he was absorbed by the results of his careful crafting and application of knowledge.

Maeven and Black Herran gasped and clutched onto the stonework. They glanced at each other's ecstasy filled eyes. The obscene power released by mass bloodshed and death flooded into them through the ritual bone talismans they had placed around the area.

To the necromancer, the human soul was a powerful thing,

a magical focus point created by the universe that overflowed with life and suffused every part of the human body. Even if a limb should be removed, the soul-limb remembered and remained, resulting in ghostly pains and impossible itches. By the same token, recently cut hair or nails could be used to inflict all manner of sorcerous plagues upon the owner, however far away they were from the practitioner. The remaining soul essence linked back to the rest of the soul.

Natural death through old age or illness was a slow ebbing of life: the human soul slowly withdrawing from the flesh. Murder and sudden death were very different – the link between body and soul was untimely severed, and all that soul essence left behind in the flesh was a great resource. The obsidian blade at the necromancer's hip grew warm as that cast off essence was sucked into it.

Maeven shuddered and bit her lip. Had she tried to contain so much power within her own flesh she would have immediately exploded and painted the walls with her body parts. The knife vibrated, growing closer to awakening. The released power could not compare to that of a strong soul, and she needed something greater to awaken the weapon to its true potential.

As for the demonologist, her demons had acted quickly, snatching away some confused souls to the depths of Hellrath before the necromancer's deathly touch could fall upon them. Let Maeven take the bulk of the soul essence, for Black Herran was more concerned with blood flavoured with pain. Her demons drank up all that terror and torment she had carefully built up inside the enemy and turned it into raw power.

She reached out with her arts and triggered the demonic glyphs she had spent weeks preparing before the battle. Her magic wrenched all lifeforce from the gory mess of the battlefield and bound it to her service. The glyphs throbbed in her mind, blinding with power as they revolved around the field of the slain, visible only to the eye of a demonologist.

Faster and faster until they were a screaming blur of power. Thunder boomed as it lanced down through the earth, shattering a hundred doors between Essoran and Hellrath, opening the path for something vast and powerful to come through. She called out to Duke Shemharai and informed him of old bargains finally being honoured. She offered her world to the demon who owned her soul. In the deep and burning darkness, Duke Shemharai raged at her tardiness, but accepted her plea and sent his mighty general on ahead to widen the ways between the worlds.

Black Herran shuddered. "Now we are ready to fight the Falcon Prince."

"Perhaps," Lorimer said. "But once he is dealt with, who will fight what you two have wrought? My skin crawls with your sorcery, and all here know nothing good will come from this."

Black Herran ran a trembling hand through her short, red-tipped white hair. "You are correct, Lord of Fade's Reach, something very bad indeed is coming from this. One step away from the end of the world, in fact. I have broken open the gates to Hellrath and Duke Shemharai's great general Malifer approaches. I have just unleashed one of the mightiest of all demons upon the Lucent Empire."

BOOK THREE
Darkness Devouring Light

CHAPTER 28

The noonday sun burned away banks of thick sea fog, enabling the spotter up in the *Scourge of Malice*'s crow's nest to catch sight of a half-dozen Lucent Empire ships lumbering south, hugging the rocky coast as if their lives depended on it. It looked as if they had become separated from the rest of their fleet in the fog. Poor little calves, straying so far from the safety of the herd…

Queen Verena Awildan gave the order for her flotilla to give chase. Her five swift and heavily armed warships forced the inexperienced Lucent captains and their over-laden cargo hulks to head further out to sea in a vain attempt to escape – there was no safe port for them until they neared Tarnbrooke and she would ensure they never reached it.

Her warships quickly caught up to the enemy and their catapults and ballistae rained incendiary shot down. Columns of black smoke writhed up into the sky from flaming, sinking ships. The air tasted of burning tar, salted with the tears of the dead and dying. The crash of white-peaked waves did not quite drown out the screams.

Verena stood on her deck chewing blackroot as the *Scourge of Malice* closed on the last of the enemy vessels, the potent taste chasing away the stench of burnt flesh and the loss of ships and gold. She spat black overboard and screamed: "Loose!"

The catapult arm thunked forward and a fiery ball of pitch

sizzled through the air. It arced out over the water towards the wallowing Lucent ship. It was no valuable supply ship bearing trade goods, but instead packed with soldiers about to die.

The missile struck the mast and broke apart, showering the human cargo with sticky burning pitch. The men took light before the ship, their linen and wool gambesons bursting into flame. Some leapt overboard, preferring to drown than be burned alive. Many wore their armour, heads and hands bobbing up and down for only moments before the weight of steel and leather dragged them down into the silent depths.

Verena waited until the sails and mast came down in a burning mass atop the hulk's remaining crew. Then she waved her archers to lower their bows. There was no need to waste arrows on this lot of doomed landsmen. Her crew did not cheer as they left the enemy behind – for fire was a terror to all sailors. This was not respectable piracy where a captured crew might have a chance to be ransomed back to their loved ones and lords, this was a slaughter. She was glad that her family were safely back home in her fortified manor in the Awildan Isles, as far away from danger as she could get them.

The *Scourge of Malice* and her flotilla left the flotsam behind, heedless of the cries from survivors grimly clutching onto debris as waves crashed over them. Some might survive long enough to wash ashore somewhere, but Verena doubted it. These waters were cold and shark-infested at this time of year, and there were things worse than sharks – things that swallowed those predators whole.

An hour later, on a northerly heading, they sighted a forest of sails and masts flying the emblem of the barbed whip – the main Awildan fleet. Signal flags were run up the *Scourge of Malice*'s mainmast and shuttered lanterns flashed orders to follow their queen north and regroup with the two flotillas she had sent on ahead to track enemy movements.

She didn't expect to face much of a challenge from the enemy. Only ten years ago the Lucent Empire had been completely land-locked, their experience of sailing limited to navigating the calm waters of a single large lake, the Ellsmere. Their best sailors had been conscripted from recent conquests, the empire subsuming city states and petty kingdoms all along the northern coast. They lacked dedicated captains and skilled crews trained for naval combat.

Spoiling to vent some stress, Verena toured the deck with her whip in hand examining every rope, knot and plank to ensure the ship was battle-ready. Her crew were the best, but nobody is perfect all the time; she bent to examine droplets of solidified pitch below the cup of the catapult. A treated cow hide had been stretched across the deck, now spotted with scorch marks. Its operator, Krevan, paled and backed away, only to be seized and held by her armoured guards.

"Unacceptable," she snapped. "This could have caught light. Your carelessness endangers this ship and our lives." Her vicious barbed whip uncoiled across the deck like an angry sea snake.

Her guards stripped the trembling crewman of his shirt before lashing him to the mast, his back exposed to receive the whip.

Verena looked out across the sea to the north. More enemy ships would be on the way, and nobody knew just how many the bastards had managed to cobble together; with them she expected to see at least a few actual warships rather than crude cargo transports and repurposed fishing boats. She sighed in disappointment and sent a guard off to fetch her a less lethal bull-hide whip. As much as she wanted to strip all the flesh from Krevan's bones, at the moment she needed him able to work. She tested the hide whip, sturdy leather creaking in her hands, and then looked to her sweating sailor.

"Krevan," she said, "take care of my ship and her crew or I will no longer take care of you. This is for your own good." Her whip snapped out, tearing a narrow strip of skin from his back. Krevan bit his lip to stifle a scream. She licked her lips and struck again, his back bearing a bloody X. This time Verena smiled as he howled and strained at his bonds. She worked out her stress on his bloody flesh, a dozen lashes that left her panting and satisfied, and her damned hip throbbing.

She tossed the dripping whip aside and waved her sailors to take care of the mess. "Do better, Krevan." They leapt to carry out her will, scrambling to demonstrate fervent obedience to their beloved queen.

She returned to the quarterdeck and her new first mate, Aleeva, a bald black woman with arms thicker than Verena's thighs who had transferred over from the *Moon Queen*. The extensively tattooed foreigner was an improvement on the traitorous Gormley, still lingering in her brig, and could be relied upon to keep her mouth shut when it was none of her business. Verena rewarded loyalty, competence, and the ability of not pissing her off – except when she truly needed a talking to. It was a fine line, and crossing it had shredded many a back, but it was also the quickest route to a captaincy in her fleet.

"Easy pickings, My Crown," Aleeva said. "Even for land-pigs."

Verena sat on a barrel to rest her aching hip and pursed her lips. "We can hope they are all as incompetent."

Aleeva quirked an eyebrow. "How many ships and soldiers can the vermin have left? Six sunken ships and over two hundred men now walking the briny depths."

"It's not the number of ships and soldiers that concern me," Verena replied. "It's what might come with them. Storm and fire are a sailor's greatest fear... under normal circumstances. Where magic is involved, nothing is ever certain."

A cry from the crow's nest: "Ship, ho! Caravel approaching at speed. One of ours."

Aleeva and Verena exchanged glances. *Dark Spear* and *Morning Mist* were far swifter and more manoeuvrable than dedicated warships like the *Scourge of Malice* and had been sent on ahead to scout for the bulk of the enemy fleet. For only one to return meant they had found trouble.

The *Dark Spear* ran a sequence of flags up its mast: enemy fleet sighted to the north-west. Prey. Predator. A mix of cargo ships and warships. Then the flag that every Awildan most dreaded was run up the line – a black skull on bright red with lightning bolts to either side, the warning of magic users.

Verena cursed. Something had gone badly wrong. They should never have got close enough to the enemy to find out if they had magic or not. She started as something warm and soft leapt onto her shoulders. Irusen settled down around her neck, the slynx's quiet cat-like growling and needling claws doing far more to worry her than sighting any number of warships on the horizon. Beyond being late feeding her, only strong magic ever irritated the lazy little creature.

As the *Dark Spear* drew closer every eye was fixated on a black scar running down her entire starboard side. The slynx hissed and glared as the ship drew up alongside and shortened her sail to match speeds with the *Scourge of Malice*. Her captain, Sly Maldane, caught the knotted rope flung from the flagship and squirreled up it in no time.

"My Crown," he said, fist pressed over his heart. His eyes were red and his face, braids and beard were grey with ash.

"Report."

Her crew stilled, ears straining.

"*Morning Mist* is lost with all hands. Golden fire burned her up from bow to stern. The Lucent warships have magickers on board."

Groans and curses rippled through her crew. Verena glared at them and they hurried about their tasks. "What's the point in having scout ships if you get too close to the enemy?"

The captain scrubbed a hand through his beard, dislodging a shower of ash. "Two of their warships took on unnatural speed running against the wind. *Morning Mist* was ahead of us and the only reason *Dark Spear* escaped is the land-pigs ripped their sails and rigging apart in the attempt."

"How many?" Verena asked.

"I counted twelve heavy warships heading south along the coast, leading eighty-odd low-riding cargo hulks."

Verena's eyebrows climbed. Such a number was beyond all expectations. The Lucent Empire was not a sea power, and this misadventure had been sold to her as a skirmish at most, a simple task to prevent a small force from landing soldiers to threaten the rear of Tarnbrooke. Instead, they faced a full-blown invasion fleet.

"Two magickers tossed fire at the *Mist* from separate ships," Sly Maldane added. He wasn't a man to waste words on maybes and what ifs, he was a slippery but solid smuggler who dealt in hard fact and assumed nothing; he left the hard thinking and speculating up to his betters.

"Current distance?" she demanded.

He glanced up at the flags, flapping in a rising wind from the south. "In this weather? We can reach them in an hour."

Verena's nails dug into her palms and she fought to keep her expression calm. Did twelve warships mean a full twelve of those shitty inquisitors able to strike at a distance comparable to her catapults? More of them could be on the cargo ships... but Black Herran had sounded so very certain that the main force would be coming via land. It might only be the two of them there to shepherd their flock through unfamiliar seas, but lack of information had sunk many a ship in the past. The only way to know for sure was to dip a hooked line into the water and see what manner of monster took a bite.

She looked to the captain of the *Dark Spear*. "The warships were at the head of the fleet, you say? The hulks – were they clustered together?"

Sly Maldane nodded, a malevolent twinkle in his eyes. "Aye and aye."

Verena Awildan chuckled. "The fools are trying to fight a land war at sea. Magic or not, we will have them."

She called her signal-master to attend her and laid out the master plan for the fleet. A series of flags were hoisted and lanterns flashed their messages from ship to ship until all understood their role. Flammable cargo was shifted to six older, smaller ships in need of repair. Those crews transferred to her largest warships leaving only a skeleton crew behind to steer their fire ships towards the massed enemy, tie off the rudder and then leap into rowboats. It was a wildly dangerous job to crew a fire ship, but great rewards were paid in Verena Awildan's favour, in gold, and in glory. Only the hardest and bravest of pirates were up to the task – an opinion that generations of Awildan queens had encouraged. It was arguable as to which reward proved the greatest incentive to them, but Verena was inclined to go with glory – pirates did love their bragging rights.

The fleet split in two, the bulk of her smaller and swifter vessels and the six readied fire ships under Sly Maldane's command heading west until they had sailed out of sight. Soon they would curve round to the north and return to smash the enemy cargo ships in the rear. The rest of the fleet would lure the lead warships and their damnable magickers forward into an engagement.

The holy knights would be the greatest threat to her fleet, but she did wonder how well they would swim when their ships broke apart beneath them. All those bleeding men she intended to ditch into the water would likely whip the sharks up into a feeding frenzy.

Verena embraced the edge afforded by fear and gave the signal to set off. The *Scourge of Malice*'s sails bloomed out to catch the wind and the heavy warships of the Awildan Isles cut through the waves heading north. An armada of shark fins trailed in their wake, the dread beasts knowing that a feast of human flesh would soon be coming their way. All those legs and feet dangling down like juicy worms…

She eyed the dark waters the sharks swam through and licked her lips nervously. Far hungrier beasts dwelled in the deeps that only the line of Awildan queens knew how to summon as a last resort. She prayed to the many gods of the sea that she would never have to see the Kraken again. Once had been enough to give her a lifetime of nightmares. Humans, who thought of themselves as the rulers of the world, couldn't abide the idea of being no more than snacks to vast and ancient beings beyond their comprehension.

After perhaps half an hour, a cry from the crow's nest announced that the Lucent fleet had been sighted. Verena peered through the spyglass at the distant ships with sunburst white flags flying from their masts. The flag atop the largest and heaviest warship was different from the others, gold trim and a crown above the sun of their Goddess. As they closed the distance, Verena eventually made out a figure in shining silver standing at the prow, the visor of his helmet worked into the golden visage of a falcon.

The queen froze, staring. A shiver rippled up her spine. The Falcon Prince was here in person and not heading south with his main army. The man lifted his visor and peered towards her fleet.

Even after all these years she instantly recognised another of Black Herran's one-time captains: Maeven's deranged little brother, Amadden, the judgemental brat that had trailed after his necromancer sister like shit clinging to a fish. No wonder the Lucent Empire was so vicious if he was the one leading it.

The wind began to shift, filling Awildan sails while slowing the Lucent fleet. It seemed that the gods of wind and water were with her.

She smiled thinly. He had been the one who cut open his sister's face – and who could blame him for that! If only he had finished the job instead of leaving her with a hideous scar. Verena could not kill the necromancer for the moment, but she would happily try to murder her brother. With any luck she would see this Falcon Prince drowned within the hour.

In the view of her spyglass, Maeven's brother looked directly towards her and sneered. He looked so like his sister that it roused her ire. She would have his head.

"Ready catapults!"

CHAPTER 29

Dawn arrived in Tarnbrooke, clear skies and harsh sunlight burning away the comforting morning mist that had hidden Jerak Hyden's horrors from the sight of the exhausted townsfolk.

Not a soul had ventured past the town's palisade since the wall had ceased to exist in a conflagration of alchemical fire, and none wanted to. The victory celebrations, such as they were, consisted of hard drinking and huddling under blankets, numb to the world as the townsfolk tried to ignore the cloying stench of burning human flesh. The night had been filled with the crackle and hiss of unnatural flame and the harrowing screams had continued for hours, until one by one those voices fell silent. Most of the town took no pleasure in such things.

Lorimer and Amogg shoved open the crude town gates and a cackling Jerak Hyden squeezed past, his hands and eyes twitching in undisguised glee as he raced out to examine his handiwork. Black Herran, Maeven and Tiarnach followed through and the rising sun revealed the bloody ruin they had wrought upon the Mhorran Valley.

The townsfolk clustered around the gate to stare in silent horror. A few doubled over and emptied their guts. More followed suit as one of their hunting dogs darted out, returning with a severed arm in its mouth which it deposited at its owner's feet, tail wagging proudly.

A new chasm split the valley in two along the line of the wall, and on either side great gouges had been taken out of the cliff walls.

Limbs jutted from the mud like a macabre forest of bone and muscle. Blackened corpses lay all around, blue flames still licking them here and there. Many more had been torn apart by stones flung by the detonation. Scraps of armour, broken swords and helmets – with and without heads – littered the area.

Jerak Hyden scampered over to a smoking corpse and bent over to examine its brittle, deformed armour and blackened bones. "Goodness. Experiments are all well and good, but nothing surpasses a large-scale practical application. The heat damage to the steel is beyond what I had expected." He flitted from corpses to half-melted stones and broken weapons, muttering, swatting at flies and laughing shrilly as he examined each with the same intense but fleeting interest.

Tiarnach and Amogg regarded the wiry little man's antics with disgust. They turned their backs on him and returned to the village with the goal of finding a decent breakfast to fill their bellies.

The mad alchemist gave a cry of joy as he lifted a shield to find somebody still living beneath it: a man lay moaning, his body broken and bent, half his skull missing to expose glistening pink brain beneath. He hissed as sunlight played over his flesh – which turned red and began to sizzle.

"A newborn vampire!" Jerak screeched. He dropped the heavy shield back in place and spun to face Lorimer. "I want it."

"Be my guest," Lorimer said. "I have no more use for the thing." He picked up a stray human leg, wrenched it off at the knee and wandered back into town, gnawing on it.

The alchemist crouched, deep in thought as he examined the sunburned skin of the creature.

The ground trembled. Maeven cast a worried look at Black Herran as the old woman winced and stumbled. "I assume that is your work?"

The demonologist groaned and lifted a hand to her forehead. "Malifer comes. There is no stopping Hellrath's greatest general now; he's a huge demon, always angry, and really cannot take a joke. It will be a struggle to delay his arrival until the time is right, so best leave me to it and get on with your own work."

Maeven grunted and wandered towards where the wall had stood. Blood and mud and unidentifiable other things squelched with every step. It reeked like a cut-price butcher shop on a hot day, but she didn't mind; she was long since used to the stench of death and decay, and she always appreciated the silence.

She had told Black Herran her intention was to raise corpses to fight the enemy, but that was not Maeven's main goal here. That was petty magic, mostly practiced by corpse-botherers and sexual deviants. No, she was in this place of death to siphon off the remnants of life force to finish forging her necromantic weapon. She prowled the brutalised valley, and while her blade devoured any remaining shreds of soul essence, she catalogued the new materials she had to work with.

Precious few corpses were in one piece, but many remained usable. The risen dead would damage the enemy's morale more than their bodies, at least at first. Any wound from the teeth and nails of a rotting corpse would turn into rampaging infection in a matter of hours.

Not all of the bodies lying in the mud were dead: she could sense a few resilient souls still stuck in dying flesh. They were good material. She killed them and fed their stubborn souls to her knife. Two more were god-touched; one was far greater than the other and she sought it out like a cat on a mouse.

She paused and held her breath, listening. A groan of pain from underneath a pile of corpses. She stalked closer, eyeing the reeking heap of flesh. A man with a gaping hole right through his armoured chest. Another with head and helmet badly dented along one side. One had been shredded, reduced to gory tatters of flesh and mail links. There – a twitching hand encased in gauntlets of fine steel.

She knelt in the mud, heedless of the filth coating her legs, and yanked stiff dead arms out of the way to reveal the face of the inquisitor that called himself Sir Orwin. His visor was a mangled ruin crusted with blood. Breath still wheezed in and out of the air holes. His soul burned with hidden power, and he was healing.

She looked left and right, and with nobody watching she set the obsidian blade to a rent in the visor, then knifed him right through the eye. The obsidian blade burned hot in her hand as it plunged into his skull and ate his soul – too hot. She gritted her teeth as her palm and fingers reddened and blistered, but she refused to let go until it had drunk up all that was left of him.

She rolled back and sat in the mud staring at her blackened and blistered skin. The knife throbbed in her hand, almost alive and eager to be used – or was it just echoing her own desires? The weapon was already powerful, and yet something had left the holy knight's body along with the soul, but whatever it was had escaped being absorbed. The presence and power of his goddess? Poking and prodding Tiarnach had provided some interesting paths of research, but the exact nature of gods and their peculiar powers was still beyond her knowledge, for the moment. One soul down, one to go…

Laurant Daryn yearned to die, but his Goddess refused to let him go. He lay face down in filth, and the corpses of his friends and servants, those he had been supposed to protect, piled on top of his broken body and pressed him down like the vindictive boot of his elder brother. Each gasping bubbling breath was an excruciating ordeal, but the Goddess's relentless will pushed him ever onward and burned away any hope of succumbing to a painless final slumber.

Fight! Fight!

His men were all dead. All dead because of her and her fucking Falcon Prince.

Fight!

What was the point now?

From his corpse-prison he heard the splash of feet approaching.

"Hello there," a woman said. "And what do we have here?"

Arms and legs, stones and broken shields were slid free from over his head and he lifted his mouth from the muck to take a blessed breath without drinking the blood and bile of his own dead men. A pale grey-clad woman with dark hair looked down on him, head cocked curiously. A black tattoo writhed angrily across her scarred face – the sorceress that had fought them on the wall. Her lips were pursed, and she absently tapped a black stone blade onto her palm.

"Kill me," he rasped, closing his eyes.

"Why should I do that?" she said, sitting down on an upturned shield beside him, her face inhuman and expressionless amid so much slaughter. "Not when I'm having such a productive day already."

Kill her! Kill her! his Goddess urged.

He snarled back at the voice inside his head: *Fuck off, bitch!*

A moment of appalled silence left him free to be himself for the first time since meeting the Falcon Prince. "What more do you want?" he rasped. "You have done your worst already."

"Not even remotely true," the woman replied. "I feel your goddess within you, but you do not seem as fanatical as those holy knights. Yet you were the one leading them; so tell me, why is that?"

He laughed, hysterical and hoarse. "Fuck them. Fuck their Goddess. Fuck their Falco–" His throat seized up.

KILL HER!

He snarled and tried to rise, to rip her apart with his bare hands. The stiff limbs of corpses grabbed him and pushed him back down into the muck, eyes stinging, mouth filling.

"I am a necromancer," the woman said. "You won't have any luck at all trying to lay a hand on me in the middle of a battlefield. Tell me, who are you and what do you really know of your goddess?"

He spat at her. He tried to rise and failed yet again. His Goddess demanded her death, but his broken body was inadequate to the task. Her disappointment was his keenest pain.

The woman sighed, looked at the knife and then slid it into her belt. Then she picked up a broken sword and examined the jagged point. "I suppose this will serve." She crouched down and pressed the blade to his neck.

He felt a small nick, and then his blood spurted out across her boots. She had opened an artery and he would be dead in moments. A surge of relief overwhelmed his Goddess's fading fury. His men were all dead and he was glad to be joining them.

He felt the Goddess withdraw as death took him...

When he woke up, his heart was still and cold in his breast.

"Hello, lover," the necromancer said, a cold smile playing across scarred lips. "Now we can talk without any meddling god getting in our way."

The hovel had been destroyed in a rage, every chair and shelf broken and a sturdy wooden table torn apart. The entire building listed badly due to broken support beams and a fist-shaped hole through one wall. Amogg's chest heaved as she caught her breath, staring down at the corpses of her old friends.

Wundak had disappeared after going off to prepare Ragash's corpse for the honour-feast. Only with the coming of daylight had their bodies been found.

Amogg's skin burned red and her fists shook. Ragash's body lay unprepared, spoiling and covered in flies. Wundak was face-down on the table, a small pool of dried blood staining the floor beneath her wounded leg. While Amogg fought and killed, Wundak had died alone devoid of all glory.

How could their god Gardram have ever allowed this travesty? Especially to one who acted as his ears and tongue in this world. It was not right. As she calmed, Amogg grew suspicious. A little spear wound to the leg wound not have killed an elder orc, but the inquisitor's holy power had also touched her, and that Amogg had no knowledge of. But she knew someone who did.

It did not take long to find Tiarnach, his face buried in yet another cup of ale. The creases clustered around his eyes had smoothed out and his limp greyeing hair had become red and thick as a callow youth's. He looked far younger than he had before the battle, but his hands also trembled and vomit stained his beard. It was a conundrum Amogg noted but did not care enough to query, she simply grabbed him and dragged him to the hovel.

Amogg scowled, tusks exposed. "Wundak is dead," she snarled. "Little spear wound not kill elder orc. Tell how this happen. Tell about powers of human gods."

Tiarnach did not mock and jeer, as was his wont. Instead he looked up into the orc's eyes. "I'm sorry for your loss," he said. "I know how this feels only too bloody well."

He examined Wundak's corpse, prodding the areas of crisped flesh on the arms and face, the gift of the Lucent goddess and her flaming knights. He shook his head. "All o' this is pish, just wee burns." Then he turned his attention to the spear wound and stuck a finger in, then withdrew it, the digit covered in yellow-green pus that he sniffed and then wiped on her clothing. "This fucker is different though. See here, it's already run to rot. That ain't right, it's far too fucking quick."

"I fetch Maeven," Amogg said, turning to leave. "She knows death better."

Tiarnach grabbed her thick wrist, more of a suggestion than to physically stop her. "That there might be the problem.

Sure you can trust her? Those magic types are only out for themselves. Maeven, Black Herran, and Jerak Hyden, they're all as mad and bad as each other. At least the alchemist doesn't try to hide it."

Amogg stared down at him. "You say one of them kill Wundak? Why?"

He shrugged. "We both know that pissy little spear didn't kill her. I reckon their holy knights and acolytes didn't either. Who else is there? I didn't see any other magic users on their side. I say speak to the vampire and ask him your questions. He's a right weird cunt but he knows his flesh, and he'd be as likely to know the real cause as the necromancer. At least he has some honour left."

"And you?" Amogg said. "You have honour?"

He snorted and shook his head. "Nah, I left all that shit behind when my people died because I was blind drunk. I'm only here for revenge, and don't forget I used your honour against you to get you here. I don't give a fuck if you all die so long as I can take that Falcon Prince's head. Me, I'm dead simple to understand."

She grunted and looked to Wundak's corpse. "Yes, vengeance easy to understand. We will both have it even if means we gut the others."

CHAPTER 30

Twelve crudely-made warships of the Lucent Empire lumbered forward in a broad battle line to engage the Awildan fleet, outpacing their more vulnerable cargo hulks packed with men and war materiel – many more ships than she had been expecting. Verena watched through her spyglass as her vanguard moved forward to meet theirs. Her blood was up and she was eager for the battle to begin – her sleek warships and seasoned crews would make them pay for daring to sail a fleet across her seas.

A glint of silver caught her eye as she swept the scene. She moved back and focused on an armoured form stepping up to the prow of the lead Lucent warship. Maeven's brother. He lifted his sword and the hair on the back of her neck rose as the blade caught fire. He slashed the air and golden fire scythed across the front of her fleet, a torrent of power eating through wood and men, leaving behind burning debris and human ash to darken the churning waves. None of her crews even had time to scream. The magic-nullifying slynx curled around her neck, hissed and dug needle claws through leather and cloth into her collar bones. She had never felt Irusen's little heart race so much.

Verena's own nails dug furrows into the carefully polished rail of her quarterdeck. The Awildan fleet was burning. Five ships lost in a single heartbeat and more aflame, listing and

285

holed, their surviving crews leaping into shark-infested waves. Amadden had grown powerful indeed. Fortune favoured the bold – and a stiff wind at their backs blowing from land to sea allowed the Awildan fleet to close the distance quickly. Her ships continued to brave the attack as they readied catapults and ballistae. Silver-armoured inquisitors stepped up to the prows of other Lucent warships, and they struck as the Awildan fleet entered catapult range – luckily the range of their damned fire was far less than their lord's. Golden fire washed over another two ships, incinerating anybody above deck and setting ship and sails ablaze. In return, burning shots from catapults set a Lucent warship on fire, roasting an inquisitor in his heavy armour. Black smoke billowed into the air from drifting wrecks, creating a haze that stung the eyes.

Verena blinked as a thought struck her. If those holy knights were far less powerful than Maeven's brother, then he truly was a man to be feared, and his reputation well deserved. It also meant that if they could outmanoeuvre Amadden's ship and keep it at a distance, then her fleet stood a slim chance of survival.

Verena cursed Black Herran, fumbling in her belt pouch for the small lacquered wooden box her old general had given her for communication. She wrenched the lid off and a tiny demon as small as a bat uncurled, yawned and stretched papery wings, tiny eyes like chips of ice blinking up into sudden daylight.

"You will listen to my message and carry it to Black Herran," Verena said.

The creature's head whipped round to face the direction of the Falcon Prince as he burned another ship from stem to stern, its crew becoming ash drifting on the wind. "Hell no," it squeaked, taking frantic flight in the other direction.

From around Verena's neck, Irusen's paw swiped out, claws only just missing the tiny demon.

"Tell Black Herran the Falcon Prince is coming by sea," Verena shouted after it.

Black Herran must have known Maeven's brother was the Falcon Prince – he was only the most powerful mortal in the entire bloody world. Interesting she didn't think to tell the rest of them that little fact. Perhaps their old general still had a soft spot for her previous bed warmer.

The bulk of her fleet had been committed before she knew the full extent of his power. She ordered retreat flags run up the lines but only the gods knew how many of her ships would see it through the smoke, never mind survive this debacle.

None of her captains were fools; the ships at the rear began to turn into the wind and fill their sails, intent on putting distance between them and the Falcon Prince's golden fire. Those at the front had no such luxury; if they turned now, their ships would lose speed and present the enemy with a tempting broadside to burn to ash. Instead, their only chance was to point their bows at the line of enemy warships and put on even more speed, hoping to punch through and get out the other side in one piece. Then, on to sea and safety, perhaps to get a lucky catapult shot off as they passed, or failing any other options, to ram the enemy into oblivion. Behind her lead ships, others filtered into single file to use those in the van as sacrificial shields.

The Lucent warships were lumbering things, and the wind was against them. Their manoeuvrability was low and their turning circles hopelessly wide, allowing several Awildan ships to evade them and slip past, speeding on a heading leading away from the coast.

Some few Awildan survivors splashed in the sea, but there was no time to pick them all up. Only a very lucky few were able to grab hold of thrown ropes and get hauled on board. Some of the men and women waving and screaming for help abruptly disappeared, dragged under by things unseen. They did not resurface.

Black smoke was starting to obscure the entire area, sowing confusion but offering the Awildans some small respite from the unerring aim of the inquisitors' deadly fire. The catapult operators on the ships ahead of the *Scourge of Malice* saw the futility of attacking the knights and switched to targeting the warships themselves. There were more Awildan ships than Lucent warships, and the knights couldn't defend against them all. One of the crude Lucent vessels was struck twice, the second shot crashing right through the deck, flames leaping up as it consumed the ship from within.

The *Scourge of Malice* was the largest of the Awildan warships and dead centre of the fleet with precious little room to safely manoeuvre. The inquisitors would be unable to resist turning their power on her as soon as she came into range. Verena clutched Irusen tight and moved to the bow of her ship. Her only hope was that her furry little friend's strange power could help protect the ship long enough to allow her ships to escape. Or to give the Awildans a chance to kill them – one could always hope.

"Crowd sail!" she shouted. Her crew set every last one of the *Scourge of Malice*'s sails and the ship groaned as she caught wind, building up a fearsome speed cutting through the waves.

The lead ships of Verena's fleet erupted into flames, gutted and falling apart, but behind them more Awildan ships ploughed through the debris and bodies. Catapults sent balls of fiery pitch soaring towards the enemy, only to be met in mid-air with bolts of golden fire. The catapult shots exploded harmlessly in the air, producing only a pall of thick black smoke and a few quickly extinguished droplets spattering the enemy's decks. The swifter ballista bolts proved more effective, piercing men and hulls and fouling the rigging.

"Punch through, then come about and lure these Lucent warships away to the south," she shouted to her first mate. The *Scourge*'s square sails and cunning rigging would allow her to easily outpace the Lucent ships, especially sailing into the wind. It seemed their inexperienced captains had little idea of how to manage anything at a decent speed.

"Keep us as far from their lead warship as we can manage." Her crew moved lively under First Mate Aleeva's whip and were about their work even before Verena had finished giving the order.

Two more Awildan ships were gutted by inquisitors' golden fire, their crews incinerated. The Falcon Prince's power consumed another three, his greater range taking a dreadful toll.

The smoke thickened around the *Scourge of Malice*, making Verena's eyes water and catching the back of her throat. She stood at the prow of her ship surrounded by her armoured guards holding heavy shields. Stomach sinking, breath held, she prayed the little slynx around her neck would be strong enough to ward off this god-fire. Irusen hissed and swiped a paw at the air. A bolt of holy fire was batted aside and hissed into the sea. Verena breathed again as several sharks surfaced and rolled belly-up.

The Awildan ships ahead of the *Scourge of Malice* sped between the Lucent warships, exchanging arrows. The smoke was so thick it muffled the screams and the crackle of flames. Catapults and ballistae aimed and loosed with hope more than skill. Holy fire cut through the air like a knife. Burning shot arced dimly through the smoke.

Arrows thudded into a shield guarding Verena and she exchanged a grateful glance with her guard. More arrows – one taking a pirate in the shoulder. Her crew bent their own heavy bows and loosed arrows at any shadow they could see. Men screamed. Ships shattered and came apart, gifting sailors to the swarming sharks. Somewhere far to her right in the smoke and gloom, the clash of steel on steel announced a boarding action.

Minutes ground past, every moment fearing another flash of golden fire. As they pulled ahead, the smoke began to thin, and the Lucent invasion fleet came back into view. The sea to the north was now filled with burning cargo vessels –

deprived of their guardian warships, the heavily laden hulks had been easy prey for Sly Maldane's force. His fleet had come in from the west, unseen and unexpected by the Lucent forces fixated on the battle raging ahead of them. Before the enemy could react, Maldane had lit his fire ships and cast them adrift among the tightly packed enemy fleet. The inexperienced fools had never considered "safety in numbers" to be a fallacy at sea. Flames eagerly leapt from ship to ship, sails and rigging quickly catching light, and there was no room for their ships to escape without colliding. Soldiers leapt overboard, clusters of men thrashing wildly and churning the sea to froth as they fought to stay afloat, their ships abandoned to drift into others. Many men couldn't swim at all, or were pushed under by the desperate flailing and grabbing hands of others.

Verena laughed grimly. "Take that, you fatherfucking land-pigs."

A heavy impact to port toppled her to the deck, timbers grinding and splitting. She wasn't sure who was more shocked: her crew or the smaller Lucent cargo ship that had unwittingly crushed its shoddy prow against her hull. The *Scourge of Malice* groaned as the Lucent warship listed and began taking on water.

Her own crew reacted first, arrows raining down on the human cargo packed into the enemy ship like a sinking bucket full of rats. The Lucent soldiers scrabbled for shields and weapons. They tried to climb to the higher deck of the mighty Awildan ship, but it was a disorganised assault and nobody came close to reaching her deck.

Golden fire bloomed, eating through part of the *Scourge*'s hull and ashing some of her crew who had sailed with her for ten years. A shining silver blur leapt through the smoke to thump onto her deck. The inquisitor's sword burst into flame and sheared through Krevan and his catapult with a single swing. Arrows tinged uselessly off heavy plate as he stormed towards Verena, butchering a pirate with every step.

Two of her guards stayed to defend her as the others rushed forward, shields slamming into the holy knight, who did not give ground.

The knight's boot thundered into a shield and blasted the man backwards to crash senseless into the rail beside Verena, his shield in ruins. The burning sword carved through steel and wood and the hands behind them like they were soft cheese.

Verena's two remaining guards swore and thought about diving overboard, quite rightly surmising they had better chances swimming with the sharks.

"Fuck it," Verena said, lifting a protesting Irusen from around her neck and carefully setting the little slynx down to one side where she would be safe. She drew a knife from her belt and pushed past the dumbfounded guards, hissing under her breath: "Get ready to shove him up and over." She spat and raised her voice, addressing her attacker. "Come on then, fanatic! Let's see how you handle an old woman."

Aleeva had rallied the crew and she was coming to aid Verena with a cutlass in each meaty hand, but she would arrive too late.

The holy knight charged, metal-shod feet pounding the swaying deck, eyes behind his visor mad and red from smoke. An arrow deflected off his helmet and another embedded itself in the mail rings and gambeson protecting his armpit but drew no blood. His charge was unstoppable.

The inquisitor lifted his sword high to cut her in two, but she had no thought of trying to parry. She flung her knife at his eyes and dropped to the deck like a sack of grain. He flinched, a moment of distraction, and found a new obstacle tripping him up.

She grimaced as his feet thudded into her side, but his unstoppable charge carried him forward, flailing for balance, to be met by the shields of her guards ramming up into his face and body. They shoved him up and out over the rails. The heavily armoured knight's screams were abruptly cut off by a splash of water.

Her guards helped her up and Aleeva arrived, wiping sweat off her bald scalp as they all peered over the side. Light flashed somewhere below, illuminating the shapes of sharks underwater. Steam and a torrent of bubbles erupted as the light dimmed, sinking deeper as his armour dragged him into the depths.

Aleeva's eyebrows were raised as she turned to her queen. "That was…" she paused, carefully considering her next words.

Verena grunted. "As elegant and skilled as a sack of shit. But it worked. That lot have no sea legs."

No other Lucent warship was close enough to pose a threat, offering them a few moments of respite. Aleeva nodded her head towards the massed Lucent invasion fleet. "We have more problems. Sly Maldane is burned to ash and his ships are retreating in disarray. Even more of those fire-spitting pricks are on board the cargo ships."

"Tits on a fish," Verena said, peering through smoke at the embattled remnants of her fleet as her crew brought the *Scourge of Malice* about. Awildan warships and fire ships were inflicting heavy casualties as they tried to disengage and flee, but that holy flame the inquisitors tossed about was taking a hideous and unsustainable toll. She was losing badly, and right when she thought the tide had turned! She was tempted to back off and let them land their army at Tarnbrooke to plague Black Herran, who deserved to die. But after seeing what the enemy could do, she was under no illusion that they would leave her precious islands alone once they were done with Tarnbrooke. Her only option was one that she had never imagined she would ever have any cause to resort to, and she had to strike while they were all gathered in one place. With any luck, she would take care of the Falcon Prince and end the Lucent threat forever.

Fleeing had taken a terrible toll on the Awildan fleet, but it had to be done or they would all have been doomed. "Keep the *Scourge of Malice* just ahead and out of range of their fire. Taunt them to give chase."

The Lucent warships recognised her flag and took the bait, abandoning the chase of her fleet to focus on running down their queen. Her crew set to it while Aleeva waited in silence, knowing yet more horror was coming.

Verena's stomach churned as she paced the deck. She felt a cold sweat slicking her forehead and underarms. It was the only way to take down the invasion fleet without risking every man and woman sailing under her flag. She was an Awildan queen, and that came with grave responsibilities her line had honoured for generations. She would kill herself before she stood aside and watched her people burned alive at the whim of some cruel foreign god.

She stopped and spun to face her first mate. "Bring me that traitor Gormley and a sharp axe."

Aleeva gave the orders, offering no judgement as the prisoner was dragged out and she handed a hand axe to her captain and queen.

Verena nicked her thumb on the edge of the axe, and drew an undulating eldritch sigil on Gormley's forehead, marking him as a sacrifice for the Kraken. Then she waited for the right time to strike. She bore witness to the remnants of her fleet disengaging where they could, or attempting to smash through the Lucent line and keep on going if they could not. Those who survived fled out to sea with their sails full.

When the last of her ships fled the area, shedding barrels and bodies, it was time. Her crew pinned Gormley to the deck and Verena unceremoniously beheaded the traitor with two swings. She kicked the corpse overboard and spat after him for good measure. Then she laid her left hand flat on the wooden rail and raised the axe in her right. She shuddered, swallowed, then brought the axe down on her wrist, screaming as steel bit through flesh and bone.

The axe and severed hand dropped to the deck and she lurched back clutching the spurting stump.

Aleeva grabbed her arm and squeezed it tight in both hands

to stem the flow. "What have you done, you madwoman?"

Verena forgave the insult. It was indeed utterly mad. No madder than her severed hand moving of its own volition, using fingers as legs as it scuttled across the deck and leapt overboard, sacrificing Verena's royal flesh and blood to something far older than the gods of the sea.

Many sailors claimed to have the sea in their blood, but only the Awildan queens could prove the truth of it.

Waves stilled and the wind died, becalming every ship still in the area. Verena's slynx crawled up her leg and curled back around her neck, cowering.

Something was coming, a looming dread building in human blood and bone telling them to flee for their lives. Nobody now alive had ever seen it, nobody that was, save Verena Awildan.

She trembled, more from fear than pain. "The Kraken is coming."

CHAPTER 31

Tiarnach leaned against the wall and watched with interest as Lorimer Felle removed his fingers from the suppurating hole in Wundak's cold thigh, if those malleable appendages of his could still be called fingers. Being a shapechanger had its advantages.

"This wound is not deep," the vampire said. "Despite the strangely advanced decay, she did not die from this. Her heart appears to have simply stopped, from what I can determine."

Amogg pounded a wall in denial, her tusks sheathed in anger-froth. "Bad heart not kill elder orc."

Tiarnach cleaned dirt from his nails with the point of a knife. "If it wasn't the wound, a bad heart or holy fire, then which was it: poison or sorcery?"

The vampire paused and then turned away from Amogg to face Tiarnach, his eyes pleading for assistance. "The powers of gods are unknown to me. Other than their damnable fire, could these god-touched Lucent knights have other magical weapons at their disposal?"

Tiarnach paused for a moment, then nodded. "Even at my best I was never as strong as their bloody big goddess. So many devout believers and deluded fanatics... If you are asking me if her power could cause a wee wound to kill or cause a stout heart to give out later... aye, those bastard inquisitors could likely do that with her power."

Amogg howled and rammed her fist through the wall of the hovel. The building groaned and shifted, then settled back down. "I kill them all," the huge orc snarled. "I train Tarnbrooke warriors hard. We butcher the rest of Lucent army." She stormed out and the two men watched her leave, then turned wary eyes upon one another.

"Was a good lie," Tiarnach said. "A raging orc is a right useful thing to have on your side."

The vampire's skin shifted, hints of spines and ridges moving below the surface. "I do not lie."

"And you don't thank a man either, eh?" Tiarnach wagged his knife at him. "Maybe no' a lie, but don't think I didn't notice you avoided a straight answer. You might not have said the words, but you were asking me to aim Amogg Hadakk at our enemies instead o' our own so-called allies."

Lorimer loomed over the warrior, exposing razor-teeth in a shark-smile. "And what exactly are you suggesting? You provided no alternative explanation."

Tiarnach snorted. "Which one was it then, the corpse-botherer or the batshit alchemist? Makes no difference to me. Whatever best gets me revenge on the Falcon Prince."

Lorimer's skin and teeth settled down and he appeared wholly human again. "Jerak Hyden would not have wasted the chance to skin an elder orc and poke about its insides. Which leaves one."

Tiarnach nodded. "It's no skin off my nose normally, but Maeven just cost us a huge orc. That's…" his brow furrowed, deep in thought, "…what, worth twenty militia? Probably more. If the bitch fucks us over again, I'll shove a knife through her eyeball."

Lorimer looked away. "Until she assists me in retaking my home of Fade's Reach, touch her and die. After that you may do whatever you like with my enthusiastic blessing."

Tiarnach studied the vampire lord. "Why make deals with the likes o' her to retake your home in the first place? Amogg or Verena could help just as much, no?"

"I need her magic," Lorimer replied. "It will counter the holy fire of their inquisitors, and every corpse she raises to fight for me means one of my people does not need to."

"You'd be better off making deals with demons," Tiarnach replied. He shook his head and put his knife away. "You'll regret this and no mistake."

"I already do," the vampire replied as he walked out the doorway.

Tiarnach didn't linger much longer in the ruined hovel, just enough for the cold and stinking corpses of two great warriors and the ghost of Amogg's pain to thoroughly remind him of the Cahal'gilroy. What was the point of a god when you were all alone and weak as any other mortal man? He had been human once, in another age – or so his dim recollection suggested – before his prowess and mad bravery gathered a mighty warband and made him something greater. His life had been filled with fighting, fucking and feasting, and what was he now but a pathetic ghoul still clutching onto mouldering bones. The wheel had turned full circle and had ground his life into dust beneath it.

He left the hovel and stared into the distance, walking the streets unseeing, dwelling on his many failures for what seemed like hours. His feet, inevitably, found their way to an ale house, that familiar old thirst upon him.

It was a seedy sort of barn on the outskirts of town, pressed right up against the makeshift palisade. The floorboards were caked in mud, and the owner had given up trying to sweep it all out. It was packed with unwashed townsfolk but quiet as a tomb. People were not here to carouse but to silently drink themselves into oblivion in an attempt to wash away the sight of friends and family slit open by spears and swords, or burnt away to drifting ash. And they knew the enemy would soon be back for more. If all roads south hadn't been infested with Black Herran's demons most of them would have fled; here, all they had to face were mortal men.

He silently wished them good luck as he shouldered his way through the throng and signalled for ale. He had tried to forget his own woes for a mortal lifetime, and all it had brought him was more misery. He. Could. Not. Forget.

He downed warm, bitter ale like it was water and fell into black brooding. He didn't get the blessing of a numbing stupor, but fell into maudlin introspection. Despite his sadness, a spark of hope niggled at the brooding. For a little while there atop the wall, he had felt like his old self. He had a sword in his hand and the thrill of the fight had temporarily burned away all his fear. Now though, his hands shook and his belly churned.

Somebody nudged his elbow and spilled his ale. His hand clenched into a fist and he turned, a cruel smile on his lips.

"Sorry, chief," a young woman with wild curly hair said, a mug of ale clutched tight in her own trembling hands. Her eyes were red and dark-circled, but she was putting on a brave face.

Drunk as he was, he still remembered her name. His fist unclenched with reluctance. He would have welcomed the pain, but she had fought beside him and she didn't deserve it. "Red Penny, eh. Come to Tiarnach for a good time, have you?" His heart wasn't in it. She knew it and ignored the comment.

Penny looked back to the moustachioed militiaman accompanying her. Nicholas's hat was carelessly askew and his face scoured to get off every trace of blood and grime. "Don't think any of us will be having a good time for a while," she said.

Tiarnach sighed, deep and slow. He couldn't remember when or where or even against who, but the feeling of his own first battle had stuck with him all these years: the bowel-loosening terror, the mad panic, the pounding of his heart and the thrill of victory, of survival...

"You both did well," he said, then took a deep swallow of ale.

Penny downed her drink. "I think I killed four men."

"I stabbed one in the eye," Nicholas added. "It came out

stuck to my spear." He shuddered and his eyes glazed over as he stared down into his ale.

"They'd have done the same to you," Tiarnach said. "And they'd be boasting of it right now instead of sitting here shaking, so don't feel sorry for those pricks."

"How do you do it?" Penny asked, staring up into his eyes, searching.

"Do what?" He slurped more ale.

"Atop the wall. You charged right in, killing and kicking in faces. You showed no fear at all."

He choked and thumped his chest to loosen it up – he'd been shitting himself for most of it. He was disgustingly mortal these days.

Penny leaned closer. "Is it because you are a war god?"

Nicholas stirred and his gaze sharpened as he listened for the reply. Some of the others in the deathly quiet ale house paused their drinking and turned to look.

Tiarnach almost laughed at the absurdity of it all. He'd been terrified, but he couldn't break their morale by saying so. He was a waste of skin now, but he still remembered being a leader.

"Nah, nothing to do with that," he said. "I was too furious to be afraid. Those bastards killed my people and I'll be damned if I'll let them do the same to yours." He drew his belt knife and stabbed it into a table top. "They are just men, not gods. How dare the bastards come to your home an' kill your people. Fuck no! Get bloody angry, not scared. Do what old Tiarnach does an' gut those murdering pricks with cold steel."

Heads nodded and cups were raised.

"Fuck them," somebody said, breaking the silence from the other drinkers. "They killed my brother."

"Aye, I'll fuck them – with my spear up their arses!" somebody else added.

Soon the ale house was rowdy and buzzing with noise, filled with people roused from despair and emboldened into anger.

Many looked towards Tiarnach, talking about the fight on the wall and the enemy's fire having no effect, and of him kicking the Lucent inquisitor off it to land on his arse in the mud, right where the murdering bastard belonged.

Tiarnach sat blinking in confusion as men and women called him brave and slapped him on the shoulder as they passed. Penny and Nicholas stood by his side, their black moods blown away by the call to action.

"Is this the power of a war god?" Nicholas asked, his eyes wide. "Granting courage?"

"Oh, aye, that it is." He took a big gulp of ale and felt more than just alcohol warming his belly. Faith was a funny old thing, and after all these years of decrepitude, the burn of their belief going down felt damned good.

You fucking fraud... But if it enabled him to kill the Falcon Prince then he'd happily milk this cow for all it was worth. He'd be sick outside later, crippled by fear and hypocrisy, but here and now, this was a moment for them, not him.

North of the bustling town of Tarnbrooke was a literal ghost town. Not a living soul moved among the broken outbuildings, fragments of wall, and the shuffling silent corpses and drifting shades trailing mist and mournful whispers.

Lorimer made his way through the blasted, rotting and lifeless landscape. He knew Maeven was there of course, but he didn't count that soulless, vile creature.

Through a thick fog of buzzing flies, he caught sight of her. She was defiling more corpses, up to her elbows in guts, stitching two or three together to make something resembling a whole human form. On her face was a sick smile of satisfaction, and Lorimer thought she had far more in common with Jerak Hyden than she would ever admit. A gore-caked man in the buckled plate harness of a Lucent knight stood beside her, his eyes haunted and his heart stopped. The vampire could smell the rot inside despite the acrid stench of necromantic magic worming through him.

The corpse-knight stepped out to block Lorimer's path, limbs jerking against its will like a puppet on strings. The vampire cuffed it aside into a pile of the dead.

Maeven didn't look up as his shadow fell over her work. "Please don't destroy that one. He was the leader of their army and I intend on having him lead this one for me."

Lorimer reached down, grasped her by the neck and lifted her kicking into the air. "Are you insane?" he yelled. "I knew you were selfish and cruel but now you have enraged Amogg Hadakk!"

Filthy fingers scrabbled at his hand. He squeezed until her face began to purple. Her feet drummed a futile beat against his chest and groin. He loosened his grip, just a little.

"Whatever do you mean?" she wheezed.

Instead of heeding the impulse to crush her neck to pulp, he let go. She sprawled in the muck, rubbing her bruised throat. "I have misled Amogg for you," he hissed. "What did you do to the other orc?"

The smile returned to the necromancer's face, scar and tattoo twisting. "What's the problem? She was old, wounded, and entirely expendable. I promised you that I would aid your quest to retake your home from the mortal filth that infest it, and that was a necessary step along the path."

He ground his teeth, hand flexing, nails lengthening into claws. "You disgust me," he said slowly. "But my people must be free."

Her armoured slave helped her stand and brushed mud and bits of bone off her grey cloak. "Do you have more posturing to do?" she asked. "Or can I get on with my work? You do *want* an army of the dead to march sometime soon, yes?"

Shuffling corpses began to crowd around them, silent stinking soulless forms staring at Lorimer with witch-fire eyes. That one corpse-knight still had his own mind and soul though, there was no mistaking the man's horrified gaze. No doubt the necromancer had some reason to shackle the man's soul to his rotting corpse. "Who were you?" Lorimer asked him.

The man's voice was dry and croaking: "Laurant Daryn, once the Landgrave of Allstane and all its people."

"Another fanatic knight," the vampire replied, smirking. "How it must pain you to fight your own god."

"I..." his face twisted in confusion, "am not a believer."

Lorimer blinked. "What pathetic ruse is this? I saw your face during the battle and heard your shouted prayers."

The corpse shook his head. "I do not deny it. However, I am... was, a noble of the old queen's court at Brightwater. I was no fanatic until I met the Falcon Prince and felt the touch of his goddess burning inside me, changing me. I became younger, stronger, and was forced to carry out her will. When I died her divine presence departed."

Daryn surveyed the corpse-strewn battlefield and the ranks of risen dead. "My own mind and will were returned to me. That usurper enslaved my mind and my people."

"Interesting," Lorimer said. "That power would explain the virulent spread of their goddess's creed and the suicidal fanaticism of her inquisitors. And what of your people all around us now, serving at the whims of this wicked necromancer?"

"I confess that I feel little at all about the matter," the corpse-knight replied. "I recognise the horror but do not feel it."

"Death has many benefits," Maeven answered. "The flesh is to blame for many extremes of emotion and desire. As I am sure you know, Lorimer."

"What can you tell us of their goddess and their forces?" Lorimer asked.

The corpse-knight's steel-clad fists clenched. "I am not sure there even is a true goddess – everything seemed to be by the Falcon Prince's will alone and serves to further his personal goals. The power burning inside me did not feel of independent will. The approaching army is ten thousand strong, with at least a dozen holy knights, five hundred cavalry and two dozen siege engines. Two more such armies are mustering in the north. You will not survive this."

"Enough prattle," Maeven demanded. "Lorimer, do let me get on with raising an army of my own. The work might be tedious but it must be done correctly if you don't want them wandering off to devour the townsfolk instead of the enemy."

"Be cautious, necromancer," he snapped. "It would be a terrible shame if Amogg learned the truth of your murderous ways and stamped your skull to paste."

He left her to her grisly work and pondered going off to find a kind woman and a warm bed for the night. As a vampire lord, sex was exquisite for all involved, but sometimes pleasant and wholesome company was what he truly craved, especially after enduring Maeven's corrupting presence.

Others thought him a monster, but he still had a basic human need for companionship and he could not always use his loyal servant Estevan as a crutch – the man was far too busy helping to organise the town and its defences to bother with Lorimer's petty personal issues. Gods knew he wouldn't get anything other than a headache from associating with Black Herran and her other captains.

He found a newly widowed young woman on the palisade, her husband's old hunting spear clutched in her bloodstained hands. He could smell the grief on her, sharp and raw. She was too deep in despair to fear him, making her unique in this place. He would work his charms on her. There would be no sex tonight, but both could offer a measure of comfort simply by sharing a warm bed for a single night. On the eve of battle, both yearned to feel human, for a time, before they mercilessly butchered men.

Tomorrow, Lorimer Felle would again embrace the monster in his blood. He feared that one day he would lose himself to it.

CHAPTER 32

Jerak Hyden oohed and ahhed as he applied the hot poker to the vampire spawn's belly again, studying the blistering, crawling inhuman flesh with feverish interest. The limbless torso on the table bucked against its chains, and its fanged, de-tongued mouth snapped as close to the alchemist as it could get.

He straightened up and pushed his spectacles back up his nose. "Note: increased resistance to heat confirmed. Healing rate is vastly decreased when compared to blunt trauma or... ah..."

The scroll and quill and ink lay unattended on his workbench. He'd forgotten his latest assistant had run away hours earlier during one or other of his procedures – probably the removal of the subject's tongue with tongs and a hot knife had been too much for them. He'd had another assistant as well, but he wasn't entirely sure if that plodding creature had died while making the quicklime. What had happened to the glass blower with the good fingers? He couldn't quite recall. He was far too busy to monitor the movements of other people, who invariably proved inept or unreliable.

He sighed, dropped the hot poker onto the anvil to cool down and wiped grimy hands on his apron. "The youth of today have no curiosity." One day he hoped to replace human assistants with mechanical golems boasting the manual dexterity required for alchemic experimentation. Sadly, his original experiments in that field had run amok and his workshop had been burned to the ground by a mob of idiot villagers. He had only abducted and used two of their farmers which was, to his mind, a small price to pay for advancements in knowledge. The families of the farmers evidently lacked any appreciation of the alchemic arts.

He surveyed the workshop and catalogued his preparations for the coming war. Given the meagre forces defending Tarnbrooke the numbers came up wanting. He had created jars of quicklime to blind and burn, exploding iron spheres, acids, vomiting gas, and a particular old favourite: the seeing gas that gave subjects visions of other worlds and drove them mad. All were heavily weather and wind dependant, and nature was a fickle thing that managed to defy his best predictions half the time. Those creations were all somewhat uninspired, which proved irksome to a genius like himself. He had enjoyed the explosive pigs but that had created an acute shortage of the beasts, and he was loathe to repeat an experiment knowing the result would be identical. It was drudgery best duplicated by lesser minds. He pursed his lips at the canvas-covered figure in the corner, cloth draped over sharp metal edges. It would be a cruel surprise for anybody that decided to menace him, be they Lucent soldier, filthy farmer or dim-witted brute of a colleague.

For a moment he considered abandoning the whole idea of killing the Lucent army and embracing the gift of vampirism that lay upon his table. Age would prove the ultimate enemy to his vast intellect, and he was well aware of the possibility of fading faculties as his mortal body aged. His eyesight was already an issue, though nothing that glass lenses and decent lanterns could not counteract. For now. The only problem was that the spawn of Lorimer Felle had all proven to be feral beasts. He would need to do more research on the matter before making an irrevocable choice. The entire world would weep to lose a mind like his.

He glimpsed the white-haired form of Black Herran

306	THE MALEFICENT SEVEN

watching him from the doorway of his workshop, and given his immensely deep and important thoughts, she had perhaps been observing him for quite some time.

"How are you getting on?" she asked, gazing dispassionately at the dismembered torso of the vampire.

He studied her for a second, noting the sagging skin, dark circles beneath the eyes, the furrowed brow and lips tight from pain. Magic took its toll on the user, he thought. Perhaps that was because they were mere users whereas he was learning the intricate inner workings of the world and applying that beautiful knowledge. They were powerful, granted, but they lacked true understanding of the forces they claimed to control.

She cleared her throat.

He blinked and dragged his attention outward instead of in. "Adequately," he replied, "given the time and material available. I have prepared alchemic substances in those jars at the far wall, but it will not prove sufficient to stop a concerted attack by superior forces of the size you are expecting."

"Every little helps," she said. "And I am sure your contribution will prove far from little. What do you have under that canvas?"

"A work in progress," he said, and offered no further detail. He certainly wasn't about to divulge information on the lovely little death machine he intended to use to escape this backwater. Nobody truly understood his genius. They called him mad when in truth he was an enlightened being. His medical research alone would usher in a new age of treatments and procedures for three hundred and eighty-nine ailments once he organised it into set texts and had scribes produce copies. Not that he cared about human life – it was the knowledge that was important, and it offended him that even the so-called scholars of Essoran knew so little about their own bodies. He would show them all how limited their thinking was, and perhaps one or two might recognise his genius and follow his example to lift themselves from the morass of morons.

Black Herran took his obfuscation in her stride. "What else can you produce over the next few days?"

He retrieved a square of soft white cloth from his pocket and proceeded to give his spectacle lenses a thorough clean. "That would depend entirely on how squeamish you have become. I can create wonders if you are willing to pay the price. Or, should I say, if you are willing to have others pay that price to achieve your goals. My work with the hivers might have involved interminable drudgery but in the fields of chemical and mineral research it proved most illuminating. I could create a most useful potion for you."

Black Herran closed her eyes and took a deep breath. "And just what price must the people of Tarnbrooke pay?"

He replaced the spectacles on his nose. "Using a high dosage, those who survive may experience a range of permanent side effects including joint and muscle degradation, intestinal erosion, difficulty breathing, insanity and death."

"What if you gave them less of this substance of yours?"

He pouted. "Utilising a lower dosage would merely grant fever and loose bowels. A high dose will grant them increased strength, speed and ferocity, which is what you need, I think."

She opened her eyes again. "I will ask for volunteers."

He frowned. "Excuse me?"

"I have no doubt there are some who will take your trade, those who have already lost loved ones to the initial Lucent attack with no great and abiding desire to endure the future without them."

Jerak Hyden thought back to the many, many times he had forced his procedures and experiments upon unwilling subjects on her behalf. Not a one of them had appreciated his pursuit of knowledge, and lacking that, to him it had indeed seemed illogical for any living being to willingly throw away their lives and health without being forced. It occurred to him that in his dismissal of humanity's base nature he had overlooked other, less onerous methods of acquiring subjects:

such as offering gold to starving families, or enabling revenge. It was a stunning, game-changing revelation.

"I thank you for your insight," he replied earnestly.

"I will spread the word," she said. "Prepare your potions."

At that moment a tiny winged creature with horns dived through the doorway and fluttered around her head.

"Shoo," the alchemist said, flapping his hands at the thing. "Away, you vile creature! You will not befoul my work with your droppings."

It settled on Black Herran's shoulder and its beady eyes glared hatred at the man. "Piss off," it said. Then it leaned in close to her ear and whispered.

Her face became stony. "It would seem that the Falcon Prince is on his way. Not on foot but by ship. A whole fleet of them."

"So?" he asked.

"It means that we have badly underestimated how many ships they built. An entire Lucent army might soon be landing to our nigh-undefended rear. Verena Awildan has few ways to counter inquisitors, never mind that bloody-handed Falcon Prince himself."

"Ah," he said. "In that case I should best head south to safety immediately."

"I think not," she countered. "You will stay here and do whatever I command." The shadows in the workshop deepened, lengthened and hungry red eyes stared out at him. "I asked you to kill an army for me, and you will do that or die trying. Are we clear?"

He nodded. Everything was very clear indeed.

As she hurried off to spread the bad news and begin preparations, he looked at the twitching vampire torso. To ensure his survival, it seemed he would need to take some risks. He so hated to conduct blind experiments upon himself.

* * *

Aleeva endured the panicked slynx's shredding claws to thrust her queen's bleeding stump of a wrist into the brazier of hot coals used to light catapult-shot. In a war zone there was no time for surgery or to heat metal and cauterise wounds cleanly, so needs must. Even as Verena screamed and writhed in her first mate's iron grip, she too recognised the necessity.

Her stump emerged still sizzling, a charred mess of flesh and coal dust. She slumped to her knees, teeth clenched hard to stifle more screams. It did not befit a queen to scream in front of her crew. Irusen curled tight around her neck, worried and purring solace, licking bloodied paws.

The *Scourge of Malice*'s sails and flags hung limp. The sea was eerily calm. The Lucent fleet floated aimlessly to the north, confused and impotent. To the west and south the remaining Awildan ships had already scattered to safety, far enough away from the unnatural stillness to catch the wind and survive what was coming. Or so she hoped.

Aleeva backed away, dabbing at blood oozing from her many scratches as the slynx glared its venomous hatred.

"It's alright, my darling," Verena said, her good hand stroking soft white fur. "Mother is fine."

The glassy sea bulged beneath a dozen becalmed Lucent ships, and some slid sideways down the slope, listing and swirling. Sharks fled the area, fins cutting through the water in every direction.

The sea opened up beneath a Lucent warship and a torrent of water carried its crew howling in terror down into an enormous yellow beak that snapped shut with a crunch of wood and bone. Another swallowed a cargo hulk filled with screaming horses and their riders.

Vast octopus arms encased in a crab-like shell rose from the sea and wrapped around three more cargo hulks, squeezing and dragging their screaming prey down to hungry snapping beaks. More arms rose from the depths, snatching up anything living they could find, be they human or shark. Verena's crew moaned with fear and kept away from the edge of the deck – as if a little wood would make any difference if it came for them. One or two even pissed themselves in terror.

"Behold the Kraken," Verena gasped, voice bitter with regret. "Pray you never see its like again." The vast and ancient creature was not a single entity, but a god-like being composed of many bodies, all working with one mind and one implacable will.

Her ship bucked beneath her and listed to port. The water churned as armoured limbs large as trees rose from the depths, spiked suckers contracting like mouths all along its underside. An enormous, bulbous head rose from the sea, water gushing off its carapace. Pulsing sacs expanded and contracted from between hard plates. Two vibrant metallic green eyes with black u-shaped pupils rose from the depths to gaze at Verena Awildan with inhuman interest.

Some of her crew threw themselves into the sea to starboard. They were fools but Verena did not have it in her to judge them for it. She waved her stump towards the floundering Lucent fleet. "I bid you let this ship go, then devour my enemies on the ships over there? I offer you my life to do this."

The soft flesh visible between plates of shell shimmered a series of violet and pink, then deepened to flashes of dark blue, a visual language only the queens of the Awildan Isles had ever deciphered.

Verena bowed her head. Tears fell freely. Her heart ached as if she had been stabbed, an agony far worse than any severed hand. It didn't want her – it demanded the life of another far more precious. "It is agreed." The words felt like ashes in her mouth.

The Kraken flushed bright green and yellow, then plunged back into the sea like a falling mountain. As the *Scourge of Malice* lurched in the waves, Aleeva licked her lips and stared at her. "What dark bargain did you make with that monster?" she demanded.

Verena ignored the disrespect; her own heart and soul were far too wounded to care. "My next grandchild will be taken by the sea. For what purpose I do not know. In the face of the overwhelming Lucent threat, it is the only way to ensure the rest of my family will be safe."

Aleeva said nothing but her eyes brimmed; Verena appreciated both responses.

Of the becalmed Lucent fleet, only the Falcon Prince's ship was able to move, a sorcerous wind propelling it directly towards the monsters devouring the rest of his fleet.

The Kraken came up from below to smash open wooden shells of transport ships and feast on the humans inside, picking men up like sweetmeats and dropping them into snapping beaks.

Verena's crew did not cheer, but instead were filled with relief that they would survive this battle. The *Scourge of Malice's* sails billowed with a sudden strong wind – a gift from the Kraken – and she picked up speed. Her timbers shuddered and groaned, telling a story of damage deep inside.

Verena stamped her grief and pain down, not allowing herself to grieve until she was alone. "Send men below!"

Aleeva jerked into action, rounded up two crewmen and dragged them below. Verena could hear her sudden cursing right through the deck. She returned in a hurry, her legs soaked. "That blasted golden fire has holed us just above the water line, and the timbers below it are blackened and cracked. I expect they will give way sooner rather than later."

"Can you patch it?"

"Already on it, My Crown. It won't hold long."

Which meant they would not have enough time to reach the Awildan Isles. They had to head south through calmer seas to the nearest safe landing and beach the *Scourge of Malice* while they made repairs. Verena thought the sandy bay downriver from Tarnbrooke was their best bet, but with luck the *Scourge* would hold together long enough for them to bypass that accursed place and reach one a few leagues further south. All they would need to do was take it slow and stead–

An unearthly shriek set hairs rising on the back of Verena's neck. Golden fire bloomed to the north. "Spyglass," she snapped, and Aleeva handed it to her. With her single hand, the pirate queen fumbled it to her eye.

Part of the Kraken burned, cored like an apple. The great armoured corpse slid off the Falcon Prince's ship and down into boiling water.

The sea thrashed in agony, tossing ships to and fro. The Falcon Prince did not care; he stepped off his ship and floated there unconcerned as his fleet spun like leaves in a flood, shedding men and war materiels.

In the eye of her glass, the Falcon Prince turned to face the *Scourge of Malice*, and his hand lifted to point directly at Verena. His message was clear as day: "I am coming for you." Then he lifted his hands sunwards and soared into the air.

He began to glow, to burn hot and bright. He grew large, encased in a mountainous form of holy fire as his Goddess manifested around him – golden armour around a soft and rounded female figure. A huge golden hand plunged into the boiling sea and ripped one of the Kraken's bodies out, its armoured limbs smoking and blackening in his Goddess' grip.

Verena felt her knees go weak and went to grab hold of the rail, but Aleeva was there to steady her and keep her from tumbling to the deck, for that arm ended in a stump now. Some of her crew fell to their knees, shaking, staring, praying to their gods.

The shrieking set Verena's teeth on edge but it drove the rest of the Kraken into a fury, smashing ships and men as it fought to reach the being inflicting such pain upon it. Verena had little hope now that even the great sea monster could stop a fucking flying goddess made of holy fire.

She lowered her spyglass. "Head for Tarnbrooke at all speed, and to Hellrath with the damage we take."

She had no idea how much of the Lucent fleet would survive, but she had no doubt its leader would be coming for her after the hundreds of his men she had consigned to the depths. To survive she needed to hide behind another monster. If anybody could deal with that godly avatar then it would be Black Herran. She needed to be informed of the Falcon Prince's capabilities so she could counter them – Verena's general always had plans within plans, contingencies and extra cards hidden up her sleeves. This time she might need a whole set up her sleeve.

Verena turned her back on the screaming Kraken and drowning men, and focused on holding her crew, her ship and her sanity together.

CHAPTER 33

The last time Verena rode a horse she had been young and flexible and riding her husband's placid prize mare. Now her hips ached and this dishevelled, ungainly farm beast could only charitably be classed as a horse; it was more donkey than anything, stubborn and depressed. After beaching the *Scourge of Malice* she had half-killed the poor beast by racing to Tarnbrooke. At least it was a sunny day, and that was likely all that was going to go right for her anytime soon.

She arrived on the rise above the fortified town with only half her crew marching behind her – the fiercely loyal half that had defied a direct order to run south and board ships heading back home to the Isles and safety. She also arrived with the beginnings of a fever. Her stump oozed yellowish fluids and was agony beyond anything but childbirth. Her missing fingers burned and ached, despite being at the bottom of the sea inside the Kraken's belly. She endured it stoically, relying on willpower and copious amounts of alcohol to see her through.

The smell of the town hit them first: an overpowering reek of rotten meat. Her crew stumbled to a stop atop the rise, staring with dumb shock at the army of the dead forming just north of town: hundreds, all glistening bone, empty-eyed skulls and putrefying human flesh. A black storm-cloud of carrion crows boiled above them.

"Fucking necromancers," Verena growled. Irusen curled

tighter around her neck and hissed towards the undead army. She checked her barbed whip and knife were secured to her belt and then dug her heels into her lumbering mount, urging it onwards.

People were swarming over the walls, digging pits and setting wooden stakes in a last-ditch attempt to bolster the town's defences. The gates swung wide and wizened old Black Herran herself was there to greet the pirate queen, gaudy rings glinting on every finger.

Verena had to be helped off the beast, and she wobbled over on cramping legs. She would have slapped Black Herran if she could – the fear of losing her remaining hand was all that stopped her. The slynx's claws dug deep into her shoulder in warning, drawing blood. The little animal trembled as badly as it had when faced with the Falcon Prince.

Black Herran appeared pale and drawn, her skin papery with a hint of jaundice. She trembled, not with any kind of frailty but with barely-restrained energy. She glanced at Verena's stump and dismissed it with a sour twitch of the lips.

Verena swayed on sore legs as the ground moved beneath her. Somewhere in town an old building cracked and collapsed. She wanted nothing to do with the sort of magic that could make earth move like water.

"I received your message, such as it was," Black Herran said. "Set your crew to shoring up these southern defences and come with me, we have much to discuss."

Verena walked behind her and in graphic detail imagined plunging her knife into that hunched back. As they passed a smithy, a sooty and sweaty man with arms like tree trunks stood at his anvil pounding glowing steel strips. Verena flinched as golden sparks died in the mud by her boots, thoughts of holy fire filling her mind. She'd had enough of biting her tongue and stewing in her own anger, and now didn't care who heard what. "So Maeven's hated brother is the Falcon Prince, is he? That would have been good to know."

Black Herran misstepped and almost stumbled before she caught her balance using her walking stick.

Verena cradled her butchered stump of an arm and spat a yellow glob of phlegm onto the demonologist's boots.

As hammer blows rang out and sparks rained down around them both, Black Herran turned and sighed. "All reports had him leading the land army to the north. I had no way to know he would choose to lead a handful of ships south."

Verena spluttered in outrage. "A handful? He had over a hundred! And at least a dozen inquisitors with him."

The demonologist's eyebrows rose. "So many? Hiding so much construction must have been quite the task, but that just means more men drowning. From your presence here, I assume that you failed?" She held her hand up to forestall Verena's rage. "I don't mean that as a criticism. My little demon informed me of how powerful the Falcon Prince has become. I doubt any mortal could have stopped him."

"Or immortal," Verena snapped. "I savaged those bilge scum but many more survived and they will soon be at your walls."

The demonologist's eyebrow quirked, but she didn't ask for further details. "This is no time for idle chatter. Your encounter may prove fortuitous if we can glean details of his powers. Come, let us discuss your revenge in detail. If you can, please bite your tongue about Amadden being the Falcon Prince."

Verena's eyes narrowed shrewdly. "You will owe me a large favour."

Black Herran nodded in acceptance of the debt, then hurried her to the temple where the others were waiting. Under the hard eyes of stone gods, they sat in war council with Lorimer Felle and Estevan, Jerak Hyden, Amogg Hadakk, Tiarnach and Maeven.

Black Herran waved a hand to one corner where her other guests sat: the locals of Tarnbrooke huddled in a nervous mass. "Deem and Healy, you will not speak unless spoken to. You are here only to carry out my orders." They shot worried looks at the hulking form of Amogg Hadakk, who had recently crushed the skull of their fellow town elder.

Her eyes next fell upon the sweaty, fidgeting forms of two of the Tarnbrooke militia dressed in muddy chain and stained leather. "Hmm. *Red* Penny, is it now?" The girl nodded. "So be it, Red Penny and Nicholas Tiler, you are here to represent the military forces of this town. Speak your minds or lose your tongue later. Are we clear?" Two heads bobbed in unison.

"Estevan," the demonologist said. "Your assessment of supplies and defence preparations?"

The old man stroked his neat beard. "We are low on medicines and properly trained healers, but we do have an adequate supply of bandages, needle and thread. We have plenty of arrows and spears but little in the way of serviceable mail or shields. Tom the smith has been set to produce steel bands to reinforce crude shields and wooden armour. It is little more than greenwood planks lashed together, but it may turn a few blows. The reinforcement of the southern palisade is nearing completion, and I have diverted men away from the north to dig defensive ditches there."

Tiarnach snorted. "Aye, for all the good that will do. In the north, the Lucents rolled over stone walls and proper keeps without breaking a sweat – yon little wooden wall will only slow them down."

"Time is all we need," Black Herran said. "Red Penny, Nicholas, how fare the militia?"

They exchanged glances. As the silence deepened, Penny swallowed, looked to Tiarnach for courage, and then spoke up. "Training has been... hellish, but we'll put up a good fight and kill as many of those Lucent scum as we can. We don't have anywhere else to go, what with demons and slavers to the south of us."

Black Herran nodded in appreciation. "I'm glad to see some townsfolk with sensible heads and stiff backbones."

Nicholas mumbled something into his moustache, then

spoke up when he realised it had been noticed. "Not enough of us though. They have better weapons, armour and training. They have an army of trained killers and we're just simple country folk. How can we hope to win?"

Black Herran shivered and dabbed sweat from her brow with a handkerchief. "We don't need to kill the whole army, just their holy knights and leaders. We will take care of that. The militia are to keep the rest of the rabble away from us."

Amogg slammed a fist onto the table, cracking the wood. "I kill Falcon Prince. Cowardly human bowels will loosen. I take a hundred heads, build mighty cairn for Wundak and Ragash."

Verena cleared her throat. "I wish you good luck with that endeavour. After my experience of fighting him at sea I am not so eager. The Lucent inquisitors are bad enough, but him…" She glanced at Maeven, whose brow furrowed. "He is something else entirely. I would rather fight a dozen of them at once over facing the Falcon Prince in the flesh."

Maeven shrugged. "That man will die like all the rest."

Verena pursed her lips. It didn't seem to her that Maeven knew they were talking about her own brother. Black Herran's eyes pleaded with the pirate queen to hold her tongue.

Verena winked and Black Herran relaxed. A debt from her would be well worth collecting; besides, anything that aided Maeven was not something Verena cared to facilitate.

Amogg rose to her feet. "I tired of talk. Talk, talk. Nothing but talk. I want to fight."

"Mindless beast," Lorimer muttered. Tiarnach overheard and his eyes narrowed as he reached for his sword.

"All of you settle down," Black Herran said. "This route of invasion changes nothing. If anything, it means he should arrive with less men beside him. Queen Verena Awildan, please tell us of your sea battle."

The pirate queen cradled her scorched stump as she related what her fleet had encountered, and the observed capabilities of the Lucent forces. "So, how do you plan to deal with the champion of the Bright One?" she asked.

Jerak Hyden decided at that moment to pipe up. "I could create a most wondrous—"

"Shut your yapping pie-hole," Tiarnach said. "Aye, aye, you have your fancy dancy alchemy, wee man. All very impressive, so it is. You are a godless, soulless piece o' shit and your presence stains this room. I want nothing more to do with you unless you can help me gut the Falcon Prince. Can you do that?"

"Well, no, but—"

"That's what I thought," Tiarnach spat. "You can kill normal folk but when it comes to real power it's all flimflammery." He turned to Maeven. "And as for you, you corpse-botherer—"

Amogg's fist smashed another table into kindling. She rose, looming over the riven war council. "Enough! I will take many heads for Wundak and Ragash. What is plan?"

Black Herran seemed to age before their eyes, lines deepening to shadowy chasms in her face. "Maeven, the Lucent force to the north is only two days away. It is time to send your army of the dead to slow them down and give us time to face the deadlier threat disembarking onto our shores even as we speak. If they attack us from both directions at the same time, then we are all done for."

Maeven smiled and drummed her fingers on the table. "You will tell me where my brother and sister are first."

Lorimer sneered. "Is this what all your scheming is for, some petty sibling rivalry?"

The necromancer scowled back at him. "Some things cannot be forgiven. And my sister will be freed from his clutches."

The vampire's sneer faded, replaced with something worse to her mind – pity. "So, you *do* have some kind of soul after all."

"Your brother arrives with the ships," Black Herran said, exchanging a glance with Verena. "I will reveal your sister's whereabouts once the Lucent army has been defeated. Now please send your corpse army north."

"You might have mentioned he was fighting with the Lucent forces," Maeven snapped. "You said you would bring him to me but you did not say he would come with an entire army around him." The necromancer tilted her head for a moment, concentrating. "It is done. They are on the march." She proceeded to glare at her general and imagine all the different ways to kill her.

Black Herran stood and ran a calming hand through her hair. "I will deal with this Bright One the Lucents worship. The great demon general Malifer knocks on the door to this world and only my iron will delays his entrance. When the time is right, I will throw open that door. It is my hope that godly avatar and demon will destroy each other."

They chewed over the details and plans for hours, almost coming to blows several times. Under the stone eyes of the Elder Gods, they finalised their battle strategy and handed down orders to Estevan and the town elders.

In the end it would all come down to luck, timing, and blind hope. All present knew how likely it was that none of them would survive the coming conflict, and only Amogg seemed pleased at the prospect of a brutal death in battle.

CHAPTER 34

Johann of Allstane scouted south through the valley, keeping to the main drover's track revealed by the recent thaw. Off the track there were still sinkholes and snow-covered hollows that could easily turn a man's ankle. There was no sign of men or monsters, praise the gods – no, he corrected himself, praise the Bright One!

He was alone and hadn't spoken aloud, but the fear was upon him all the same, heart pounding, eyes scouring the darkness around him for sign of inquisitors who might have overheard. His home had been spared the worst of the purges thanks to Lord Daryn, but the priests and acolytes had still torn people from their beds and taken them away, never to be seen again. Now that Grand Inquisitor Malleus was in charge of the whole northern army, Johann's paranoia had climbed to new heights.

He took a deep and calming breath. To the south, monsters; to the north, another sort of monster; and Johann was alone in a quiet place somewhere between the two. He took another breath and felt his heartbeat slowing as he passed abandoned hovels and farmsteads.

It was a dreary sort of place, barren and sparse compared to the deep woods and wide rivers of Allstane. What he wouldn't give to be back home, sat in the sun with his rod and line in the lazy river and a skin of cheap wine beside him. It wounded his

heart to think so many of his friends' and family's graves were
here on this cold heathen land – not that Johann was any great
believer in sentimentality, but it didn't sit right with him that
they were buried so far from home. If buried they in fact were
and not left in a heap for the crows to pick over.

Guilt and anger mixed in his belly, a heady brew that had
gifted him sleepless nights. He had been carrying messages
and reports back and forth, and had been with the main army
when the vanguard under Lord Daryn had been annihilated in
a tremendous explosion of unknown magic. Grand Inquisitor
Malleus had now tasked him to range ahead, take note of
enemy positions, and try to find out what had happened to the
rest of the Allstane levy.

He was ranging a day's march ahead of the army when
darkness fell. It was an overcast night, dark clouds blocking out
most of the moonlight from the Twins above, and the terrain
was too treacherous to stumble about blindly. He found a
secluded hollow under a tree by a dry stone wall that protected
him from the worst of the wind, and curled up in his blanket
in an attempt to catch a few hours' sleep. He tossed and turned
on the cold hard earth. Sleep proved an elusive foe, the faces
of the slain trooping through his mind.

A distant clink of metal to the south caused him to lie still,
hold his breath and listen hard. It came again, near the main
track through the valley, accompanied this time by the clack
of pebbles kicked across rock. He swallowed and prayed it
was something innocuous: a wild goat or a fox caught in a
hunter's trap perhaps, and not one of those vicious vampire
creatures that had attacked them a few days ago. As the
sound came closer he realised it was being followed by many
more. A shuffling and scuffing of hundreds of feet and the
clinking of steel on steel approached and passed by his hiding
place, heading north away from Tarnbrooke. Those were not
animals.

He cracked an eyelid and peered through gaps in the old

stone wall. The darker-than-night outlines of men were on the move under the cover of darkness, slow and steady as if bone-weary. Hundreds marched past. He couldn't make out much detail from this distance.

Johann slowly peeled back his blanket and kept low, crawling along the earth until he could get a better view. His eyes widened at the sight of men in armour from the Lucent Empire. Some bore the sunburst emblem of the Goddess on their battered breastplates and stained tabards. The men of Allstane were coming home.

He almost rose to shout out, but some dark thought whispered a warning that something was not right. The way they moved, those lurching steps... and then he realised that they marched without lanterns to light their way. Then there was the fetid stench.

A man walked into view, his armour rent all along one side of his caved-in torso. Broken ribs pierced through flesh and torn mail, white bone visible even on a cloudy night.

Johann gasped and hastily clamped a hand over his mouth. A dozen heads turned as one towards his direction, searching. Not all had eyes in their skulls, their hollow sockets flickering with a dull green flame. He lay very, very still. Six shambling dead men broke away from the army and fanned out, walking in his direction and searching through grass, trees and over walls. Cold sweat exploded across his body and ice rippled up his spine. He was doomed.

Johann swallowed and struggled to keep his breathing slow and quiet. He would die here, but the choice of how was up to him. He could curl up into a ball and cower, hoping the Goddess's mercy would fall upon him – a likely story! – or he could stand, draw his sword and go down fighting the forces of evil like his lord had.

He wasn't sure about any supposed afterlife but he didn't much feel like dying like a snivelling weakling in this one. Many of his friends and family had already perished in this accursed place and he didn't want to shame their memory. He stood and drew his sword.

"Come on then, you stinking corpses!" he shouted, backing up to the tree so they couldn't attack him from the rear. He took a fighting stance with his sword held high and tried to ignore the wavering point.

Three dead men in blackened and twisted mail came for him, hands of shredded leather gloves and bare bone outstretched. Bile seared the back of his throat at the stench. All six abruptly stopped. They turned as one and marched right back the way they had come to rejoin the army of the dead.

He stood mouth agape, heart thundering in his ears.

"Hello, Johann," a familiar voice said from behind.

Johann spun, sword up, keeping the tree between the owner of that voice and himself. "Landgrave? It… it can't be."

Daryn approached slowly, his helmet held under one arm. His plate armour was bent and blackened, the enamelled golden sunburst of the Bright One ripped away, but his face – what was left of it – was unmistakable.

"What are you, creature?" Johann said, hand shaking, bladder complaining.

The corpse-knight's lips curved, juddering back over dry teeth to reveal a broken smile. "Why, I'm a dead man walking, Johann."

The scout swallowed and kept his sword up between them. "Whatever dark magic controls you, monster, it shall not have me."

The corpse-knight's smile faded. "Not if I can help it, no."

Johann frowned. "Eh?"

"I have no intention of killing you. It was I who stopped those nigh-mindless dead men from gnawing on your flesh."

The sword point dipped lower. "I… Landgrave, is it really you?"

He nodded. "Alas, I am no longer your lord. As you can see, I am quite dead. In fact, it would seem that you are the only one of the brave men of Allstane to survive this accursed conflict. I would see at least one of us return home to a warm bed and a cold cup of ale. Return as one of the living, I mean." He cricked his head to one side, as if listening to some invisible voice. "What she doesn't know won't hurt her."

"The Bright One?"

The corpse-knight winced. "That accursed god of the Falcon Prince? I think not. I speak of the necromancer who has me in thrall."

Johann's sword point fell to rest upon the earth. He licked his lips and glanced around. "Recently you prayed to the Bright One every morning and night, and Her name was a blessing from your lips every time you spoke."

"Not by choice, my good man, curse her name. The Falcon Prince did something to me. He infected me with a most unholy magic that altered my thoughts and turned me into a fanatic. It is his manipulation that led to the massacre of our people."

Johann stifled a sob and fell to one knee. "You are truly back, my lord."

Daryn grimaced and shook his head. "I have exchanged one accursed existence for another, and my will is now enslaved to that of a vile necromancer. On this occasion our desires, what I have left of those, run in the same direction. She has made of me a weapon packed with dark magic, a dread gift for the Lucent Empire. The men of Allstane will not stand to see the Bright One's cruelty spread to all other lands as it has ours. We march to war one last time."

Johann eyed the marching dead. "I will join you."

"Denied," Daryn countered. "There is a small goat track east of here by a split boulder that will lead you north past the Lucent camp. Take it, return home and live long and well. I pray to the Elder Gods that the Lucent Empire will be broken by this small town and its dark denizens, allowing freedom to return to our land. Let us hope some good comes from this massacre."

Tears wet Johann's cheeks. "I will tell of your sacrifice, my lord. I should inform you that Grand Inquisitor Malleus and ten thousand men are encamped only a day's march from here."

The corpse-knight nodded. "I am aware. We will be on him before the dawn. The dead do not tire." He cocked his head again. "I suggest you gather your belongings and run. The necromancer sleeps for now, but she will soon wake. When that happens, I imagine the ice-hearted witch will compel me to kill you."

Johann grabbed his belongings and fled the valley and the war. The corpse-knight watched his old friend leave and felt nothing. He rejoined the army of animated corpses, back where he belonged, and resumed his march.

Two hours before dawn Daryn sighted the enemy camp. Back in Tarnbrooke, the necromancer woke and her remorseless will pushed into him. She looked through his eyes at the orderly lines of campfires ahead, red and gold stars flickering in the night. He gasped, his dead body burning as she crammed in yet more dark magic – he could apparently still feel pain, though not as keen as it had been in life. She bottled it all up inside him until he felt ready to burst at the seams. Only then was she satisfied with her magical working, her deadly gift for the Lucent army's leaders.

Daryn knew exactly how the Lucent army worked – he'd had a hand in writing some of the treatises on warfare for the old queen of Brightwater. Grand Inquisitor Malleus was one to follow the letter of the rule, unless it benefitted him personally to do otherwise. Lookouts would be placed every fifty paces, two staggered lines across the valley with twenty paces between them. A force of heavy infantry would act as night-guard closer to the camp and would spend their lives buying time for the rest of the army to rouse from their beds and repel attackers. Malleus and his command staff would be in the very centre of that camp and ringed with veteran warriors.

Ten thousand men waited ahead, and the corpse-knight only had hundreds of the walking dead.

"Some have been gifted with greater necromantic power," Maeven advised, her voice a cold deluge across his soul. Shades and ghosts drifted here and there among the ranks of corpses, their translucent forms immune to most mortal weapons and their touch deadly to all living flesh. "The inquisitors and acolytes will have to use all their god-given powers to deal with those," she added.

"You are not here to win the day through force of arms, my little corpse-knight," she said. "Their numbers make that impossible. You are here to kill Malleus and as many of his inquisitors as you can take by surprise. The dead are not as swift as in life, but they are relentless. Every wound from your rotting hands and teeth will putrefy, causing fever and perhaps even death. Spread your death and disease among them."

"I understand," he replied. She retreated into the back of his mind and watched as he willed the bulk of her army to form up in a pincer formation and advance. The remainder would charge straight ahead in what might otherwise be called a suicidal frontal assault. With any luck Lucent soldiers awakened by screams and clashing steel would rush forward to the front while the greater part of the dead cut in from both flanks to meet in the centre and bury their rotting teeth in Malleus' throat.

The first line of lookouts peered into the darkness as the sounds of feet and creaking steel, leather and bone approached. Then they screamed as the silent tide of dead men washed over them, heedless of sword and spear. The second line of lookouts ran for it, blowing horns to alert the night-guard to an attack.

The corpse-knight went left with his most heavily armoured and intact dead soldiers, taking the few incorporeal shades and ghosts with him. The other side of the pincer attack was out of sight but not out of mind – the necromancer could see everything the dead could; she was inside them all, and she made them his to command.

The army of the dead hit the centre of the enemy lines, thundering into the raised shields of the night-guard in a clash of steel and breaking bone. Shouts and screams tore the night as bone fingers and broken teeth tore human flesh, heedless of all wounds other than blows that caused total destruction. Mortal men rallied and counter-attacked, only to fall back in disbelieving terror when they discovered they faced an army of the dead in all their grotesque glory. Some fell to their knees praying for supernatural aid – and their goddess did not protect them from cold steel.

A total rout was stopped only by several acolytes of the Bright One who lifted their hands and cast a golden light down on groups of soldiers, stiffening their resolve while weakening the necromantic power animating the undead. Those soldiers charged back into the fray shouting hymns and fighting with unmatched fanaticism. The defenders wavered and then steadied, forming up into organised units and battle lines around the acolytes. They aimed for the heads of the undead, but the mindless ones did not need brains or even skulls. Bone and jellied blood sprayed the night to little effect – their bodies were only puppets dancing on the necromancer's strings.

The right pincer struck and began chewing its way through the night-guard and the panicked, still-rising men behind them. The entire camp roused, firelight glinting from naked steel.

The corpse-knight and his troops smashed into the left flank, the shades and ghosts passing right through shields and armour, stopping hearts or freezing flesh with their touch. They opened the way and the dead burst through, overrunning everything in relentless advance towards the command tents. Resistance quickly stiffened as more soldiers rose from sleep, but it was not easy to kill the already-dead and fear caused many hands to hesitate. The necromancer squatting in what was left of Daryn's mind gloated at her use of terror as a weapon.

A flare of golden light and a shade to his left burned out of existence. To his right, a knot of corpses in mail and shield exploded in holy fire. But the dead kept coming, an unstoppable tide engulfing the two isolated inquisitors guarding the command tents. They pulled the knights down, stabbing and clawing. Then they were among the tents fighting half-dressed men. As the minutes passed, hundreds of Lucent soldiers awoke and began to swarm them, a meat grinder even the mindless dead could not long endure.

Daryn's sword rose and fell, wreaking bloody ruin as he cut his way into the centre of the enemy camp. Grand Inquisitor Malleus stepped from a tent right in his path, dressed only in loose night clothes. The man's cruel eyes blazed with holy fire and fanatic belief, hand outstretched to burn all the monsters from his camp. Daryn cut it off at the wrist, then reversed the blow and slit the bastard's belly open. As Malleus' intestines slopped to the earth, Daryn realised he had been wrong earlier – he *could* still feel joy.

Arrows clanged off his armour. A spear penetrated his bent and buckled plate and gouged his thigh. He ignored it and lifted his sword high to finish the filth off.

Malleus pawed at his gaping belly and looked up into the eyes of the corpse-knight. "You!"

"I piss on the Bright One," Daryn said as he split that shaved pate into two. "May demons forever gnaw on that withered husk you call a soul."

Five soldiers slammed into him, blades bouncing off his armour before finding holes in harness and mail. More arrived to drag him down and they wrenched off his helmet. A few gasped, recognising his ravaged features.

He felt the necromancer's power welling up inside him, a boiling mass of distilled death. "I pity you all," he said. It was the last words he would ever utter. As the first beautiful burning rays of dawn appeared behind the cliff face of the valley, an axe crushed Daryn's skull and extinguished his sight. The last thing he felt was her dark power exploding from within, emptying him like a burst bladder.

A gangrenous mist billowed from his flesh to fill the valley two hundred paces all around, bringing all manner of death and disease.

The golden fire that consumed the corpse-knight's body came far too late to save the Lucent leaders. They died choking, faces purpling and blood gushing from their decaying lungs.

CHAPTER 35

Black Herran sweated and shivered, her wrinkled old hide sallow and waxy as she stood on the rise just south of Tarnbrooke. Her breath misted the morning air as she triple-checked her work for flaws. By the light of the twin moons, she had carved a complex demonic sigil into the earth with the point of her walking stick, the lines dark and glistening with her blood. The fluid shivered and crawled with its own will, the demonic magic within her fighting for release.

She nodded at a job well done, then leaned heavily on her stick and watched the line of armoured men in the distance snaking their way from the coast towards her home: a white and gold viper that spat deadly fire. She wondered if the Lucent army wore those colours in an attempt to depict a goodness that none of the Lucent leaders actually possessed. Two thousand elite soldiers, and an unknown number of inquisitors, here to raze Tarnbrooke and slaughter all inside its walls. Unless she was able to stop them.

She was on the flip side of the coin from her days besieging the fortress of Rakatoll, and she decided she much preferred attacking over defending. Defending meant you had something to protect, something you cared about at risk. It irked her.

"You look ready to bite the dirt," Maeven said. "Holding that demon in will be the end of you. My power has already sent their northern army into disarray. Grand Inquisitor Malleus is dead, and by now thousands of soldiers will be burning up with infection and disease. I have bought you time and my work here is done. Be reasonable, it is time for you to tell me where my brother and sister are."

Black Herran snorted and glanced up. "When have I ever been reasonable? I give you my word that your brother marches with the approaching Lucent army; seek him out and kill him if you wish. Save my town, only then will I tell you of your sister."

The necromancer hissed and fought down the deadly magic building between her clawed fingers. "I will find your family and rip their souls out if you don't tell me here and now."

"I'm tired and sore and not in the mood for posturing," the demonologist said. "You won't find my family. I know you have already made many enquiries. They have been sent somewhere beyond even your reach."

Maeven shook her head in disbelief. "If your family aren't even here, why are we? What is this game of yours truly all about?"

"Saving souls," Black Herran replied. "Nowhere will be safe if the Falcon Prince is allowed to run rampant like a stupid farm boy given a magic sword and a prophecy. As for your brother and sister, I was always fond of Grace and would see her free at the end of this, and that can never happen while Amadden lives."

Maeven was silent for a long moment. "Many were fond of her and many took advantage of her goodness."

Wizened lips curved upwards. "Until you found out."

"Until I killed them." Many corpses and not a shred of regret. "I should kill you now, too."

Black Herran nodded, no trace of judgement in her eyes. "Grace has not ventured out into the light of day in twenty years. She is in a place guarded day and night by elite inquisitors and fanatical priests, kept safe from all harm and from any kind of independent life." She studied Maeven. "Killing me before I reveal her location would avail you nothing. In any case, if you killed me now the demon general Malifer would break free right beneath your feet. You would not enjoy that, I think."

Maeven searched Black Herran's eyes for any hint of a lie and found none. "By all the gods, I loathe you."

Black Herran patted her hand. "I know, dear. Now please cover up my workings with grass and leaves and then help an old woman hobble back to town."

When the demonic sigil was disguised Maeven took her arm and led her downhill. As they passed over the stake-lined muddy trench around the town, the militia dragged the crude plank bridge back behind them and destroyed it with an axe. Lorimer Felle was at the gate waiting for them, dressed in a fine white linen shirt, opened just enough to tease impressive muscles straining beneath.

"We are as ready as we can be," he said. "I have just returned from the north and a third of that army is now on the move, albeit slowly and without their cavalry and siege engines. Were I a betting man, I would wager good money they will reach our walls around noon tomorrow. What decrepit state they will be in by then I cannot say, but those numbers alone will be enough to end this town."

Black Herran coughed, and wiped specks of blood away with a handkerchief. "Maeven, we need to end this thing today before his northern army arrives on the morrow. The Falcon Prince and your brother will be here in an hour and they cannot be allowed to wait us out."

"Good," Maeven answered, taking the old woman's arm, nails digging in hard. "I imagine that, much like my brother, the Falcon Prince is self-righteous and swollen with pride. The correct words should set him off like an enraged bull. We will force their hand and destroy them."

Black Herran's eyes narrowed, but Maeven showed no outwards sign she knew both men were one and the same. She would have expected anger and accusations if so, but there was nothing.

"Good," Lorimer said. "As soon as their leader is dead, the Lucent grip on Fade's Reach will crumble. I will have my home back."

Red specks appeared on Black Herran's sleeve as another coughing fit racked her. "Locate Jerak Hyden and tell him to liaise with Tiarnach and the militia volunteers. It is time to distribute his potions."

Tiarnach and Red Penny waited with the dozen crazed fools of the militia who had volunteered to take part in the mad alchemist's schemes. Most had already lost loved ones in the battle for the wall or had nobody in the first place. Tiarnach was applying his war paint and daydreaming of better times when a small child grabbed hold of the end of his scabbard.

Tug tug.

He didn't bother looking down and instead swatted a lazy hand at her. She backed away for a moment before creeping back.

Tug tug.

He pulled the scabbard from her grip and snarled down at her, the war paint gifting him a savage visage. "What is it, brat?"

Red Penny turned and glared at him, a warning on her lips.

It was a plump dark-haired girl of six or seven heavily layered against the cold, and she had tied sticks and part of a broken chair to her dress aping the cobbled-together armour of the militia. She swallowed and held up an eating knife in one hand and a fork with the other. "I fight too, Mr God."

His snarl faltered. "Whit?"

A little boy shuffled up behind her, similarly armed with a wooden spoon and a bowl precariously balanced atop his head. The girl prodded him and both lifted their weapons, a gesture he assumed was meant to appear fierce. "Rarr!" she said. "We brave warriors. Da says the gods protect Tarnbrooke and not to worry, but we come help you, Mr God."

His snarl died. He was of the opinion that most people were selfish shits, but these children didn't deserve to suffer what was happening to their home, and he didn't want the likes of Jerak Hyden anywhere near them either. "Here now, are you two not a mite small to be on the walls?"

They pouted and their eyes turned watery. Red Penny poked him in the ribs, frowning.

"Ahaha, right," he said. "Nah, I see now you're brave wee bastards."

Red Penny crouched down. "Can we trust you two to guard the town elders? That's a very important job."

The boy silently nodded, bowl wobbling. The girl frowned, far from convinced.

"See this lot," Tiarnach said, nodding at the militia members. "Bunch of stinking lackwits. Can't even pee without my help. You two though, you are this here god's own guards, and I can't trust any o' these cunts to guard a cup of ale."

Red Penny winced at his language and ushered the children away towards the town's temple, the strongest building in Tarnbrooke where many of the non-combatants would lock themselves away until the battle was over.

"The war god entrusts you with guarding the old folks and the babies inside here," Red Penny explained. "Don't let Tiarnach down now."

"We promise," the children said in unison, pudgy hands grimly clutching their weapons as the town's older inhabitants dragged them inside to safety. If any place in the town could be called that.

Penny returned and scowled at Tiarnach. "You have a real way with children. A god should know better."

He shrugged. "What am I supposed to say? Wee ones are barely smarter than dogs, 'cept far stickier. They don't even do good tricks."

She rolled her eyes and was about to scold him further when she spotted Jerak Hyden approaching the militia volunteers.

His eyes were tired and red and he had taken to wearing a thick travelling cloak sewn with many pockets, leather gloves and a wide-brimmed hat that cast his face into shade. He carried a heavy basket filled with small jars.

"Ah shit," Tiarnach muttered.

"Hello everyone," the alchemist said. "Are you ready to partake of my genius?"

Eight men and four women milled around uncertainly.

"Be certain," Penny said. "There will be side effects."

"What of it?" Jerak Hyden said. "Power always comes with a price." He held up a jar. "Drink this and it will make you swift and strong and you will feel no pain."

"It might kill you," Penny added.

The alchemist's eye twitched. "You are all likely to die anyway. You may as well take more of the enemy with you."

"Man makes a good point," Tiarnach added. "For once."

"I'll take it," a farmer said, reaching for a jar.

Penny grabbed his arm. "Are you sure, Daved?"

He shook her off. "I just want to kill the bastards. My town, my decision."

"That's the spirit, my good man!" Jerak Hyden said. "Drink it down five minutes before battle is joined." With that, the others took their own jars and the deed was done.

"What of your other weapons?" Tiarnach asked.

The alchemist carelessly tossed his empty basket aside. "Already on the wall and ready for deployment. Lorimer Felle's manservant and some young fellow with a fine moustache collected those earlier."

"Right then," Tiarnach said, herding the special militia towards the southern wall. "Are we all ready to kick the Lucent Empire in the stones and hack off some heads?"

Jerak Hyden watched the mindless brutes scurry off on their menial tasks. He calculated there was little chance he would see any of them ever again. Black Herran had requested his skills for the coming battle, but he had taken the liberty of doubling the dosage. It would result in almost certain death for those who imbibed it, but the ferocious effects would suit his own purposes far better. In times long past, she would not have cared what he did as long as it proved effective, but this tame demonologist was most unpalatable. Her newfound qualms were beyond his ken or his caring.

He scurried back to his workshop, now emptied of all useful supplies, powders and assistants, with only his newest creation sitting under a canvas in the corner. On a worktable, his captive vampire mewled and bubbled beneath its bloodstained sheet. The noise irritated him. Nobody in this accursed place understood the joy of quiet study and contemplation, or his pressing need for it. His belly rumbled at the smell of blood, and it occurred to him that he had forgotten to eat again. His tastes had changed somewhat over the last few days: he craved meat, the fresher the better.

He lit candles and lanterns, wincing at the increase in light, then took a knife and bowl and whipped back the sheet. The vampire's arms and legs were regrowing, nubs of new limbs sprouting like plant shoots. It piqued Jerak's interest, but with armies to the north and south he was forced to prioritise survival. If only he had more supplies to craft a truly magnificent alchemical weapon... but even the resourceful Black Herran could not be expected to provide all he needed on such short notice. He sighed and slit open the test subject's torso, collecting the thick blood that dribbled out. He set it down and then removed the canvas from his new war machine in the corner of the workshop.

Brass and steel rods had been arranged like a crude human skeleton, all gleaming blades and spikes. Gently glowing smoky quartz eyes followed his every movement. He flipped open a metal flask inside steel ribs and poured in the vampire blood, topping up its power supply. Red veins flushed through the quartz as its eyes brightened. He cackled and stepped back, taking in the exquisite sight of the very first artificial human.

All these years of thought experiments while locked away in Hive, trying to solve the power problem of converting intangible magic to physical mobility, and Lorimer Felle had unwittingly provided the answer – the body of the vampire served as a crucible, and its magic-rich blood became a potent source of power. If he could replicate that process in a more methodical manner then a new age of progress would dawn. Mankind would be as the gods: immortal, no longer a slave to the needs and fleeting desires of the flesh.

He had no time to attempt to graft a human consciousness into this initial body, or to create an exquisitely crafted artificial mind patterned on his own, but it was far more durable than flesh and bone. He hoped it would be strong enough to aid his escape from this doomed town.

His hands were shaking. His jaw ached and his eyes burned. The alchemist made a tiny cut in his forearm and poured the dregs of vampire blood remaining in the bowl over the wound. He shivered in pleasure as hot magic surged through his veins. He had been taking tiny doses ever since he had acquired the test subject, and was confident that his powerful mind would hold strong and stable if the change was less sudden. He needed to survive and escape Tarnbrooke intact, for the mind of Jerak Hyden, genius and master alchemist, was far too important to the world.

CHAPTER 36

It was eerily quiet on the walls, despite so many townsfolk packed onto them. Deathly silent and despairing, they watched the Lucent army formations advance on them from the south, a dread beast of white tabards and shining steel. They looked glorious and terrible in the sunlight, a far cry from the mud and blood splattered defenders of Tarnbrooke. They made the Lucent soldiers they had already defeated seem like amateurs. The heavy infantry was organised into ten precise squares marching in step, each led by an inquisitor in full plate harness with a half dozen robed acolytes bringing up the rear, providing magical protection and healing. At the head of this army, escorted by more holy knights, marched the Falcon Prince himself, radiating wrath. His sheer presence demanded the townsfolk fall to their knees and beg for forgiveness.

One of the townsfolk did just that. Amogg seized him by the throat and tossed him back into town, uncaring if the fall broke his neck. Nobody else dared repeat his mistake.

The Falcon Prince had arrived at Tarnbrooke with two thousand elite killers at his back, veterans of his many conquests and purges. All mercy had been scoured from them long ago.

Verena Awildan turned away from the sight and her loyal pirates helped her down from the wall, her little slynx curled tight around her shoulders. She cradled her bandaged stump as she approached Lorimer Felle and his manservant. The vampire lord was washed and neatly dressed and standing in quiet contemplation. Estevan was uncharacteristically unkempt, his hat battered and stained, tired eyes peering from beneath the rim. Messengers rushed to and from him as he organised the logistics of the defence.

She ignored the vampire and instead caught Estevan's attention. "You must remove the defenders from the palisade," she said. "I have told you of my battle on the sea. The men and women lining these walls only invite their own death: golden flame will sweep across the top and scour all life from it."

Estevan considered the rough defensive wall they had thrown up around the town in only a few weeks. "I am aware that a simple ditch and log palisade will not hold for long against such an army, but one might pray green wood will prove more durable than the seasoned planks of Awildan ships. I have discussed this with Tiarnach and Amogg and we are agreed that their likely course of action will be to breach it with fire and storm the gaps instead of making any attempt to scale it all. I assure you, those stationed on the top will mostly be for show."

Verena nodded and adjusted her bandages. "Your mind has always been wasted serving that big lump of a vampire."

Lorimer Felle didn't object, and instead a small smile played across his lips. "Amogg, Tiarnach and myself shall hold them at the breaches," he said, "if, of course, Black Herran and Maeven can ward off the worst of that golden flame. If they cannot, then it will likely prove a disappointingly short battle."

"What of Jerak Hyden and his creations?" Verena asked, mouth twisting with distaste as if she'd bitten into a sour lemon. "I don't see the little rat scurrying about."

Estevan pointed out small groups of masked townsfolk, carrying sacks and large storage pots into position on the wall near the hulking form of Amogg. Each also wore thick leather gloves and aprons. "The last of his weapons are being moved into position as we speak." He paused and frowned. "That's odd. I could have sworn he made more than that... something caustic stored in large clay pots..." He shook his head and continued. "In any case, Amogg Hadakk's arms will serve in place of a catapult. By now, Jerak should have finished his meeting with Tiarnach and the militia."

Verena spotted the red-haired warrior sauntering towards them, a spear in one hand and a buckler strapped to the other. A dozen grim-faced militia trailed after him, but of the alchemist there was no sign.

"Your salty Highness," Tiarnach said, sketching a bow. "Need a hand?"

The slynx around Verena's neck hissed at him, and he hissed right back. The little white creature looked affronted.

The pirate queen glowered at him. "As funny as finding a shit in my soup, you stinking savage. Please tell me you haven't left that mass-murderer to his own devices?"

The warrior scratched his beard with a filthy fingernail. "Not my sodding job to babysit him."

She rested her hand on the knife at her belt. "Then I'll deal with him myself."

Tiarnach shrugged. "You go do that. I've got all I need from the wee prick. His head can adorn a rusty spike for all I care."

Estevan looked to his lord, who sniffed the air. "The enemy draw close," Lorimer said. "It is time to put the final preparations in place." With that the vampire strode off towards Black Herran and Amogg, standing on the defences looking south.

"I am an old woman with one hand," Verena said to Estevan. "I will be useless in a battle; instead I will go and take care of our other little problem." She turned to her pirates. "Aleeva, you and three others come with me. The rest of you, make yourselves useful – most of these land pigs have no idea how to fight; be sure to steady them."

"Aye, My Crown," they said, and moved off towards the wall. Aleeva and the other three followed their queen, hands never straying from the hilts of their weapons.

"I have heard tell of this man they call the mad alchemist," Aleeva said as they turned left down the road leading past the temple towards Jerak Hyden's workshop. "How dangerous is he truly? What weapon does he fight with?"

"He'll probably be unarmed," Verena said. "But don't let your guard down. In his own way he is as dangerous as the Falcon Prince. He thought nothing of poisoning entire towns so he could study the effects on their bodies. Men, women, children, and even livestock, all are of no concern beyond furthering his lust for knowledge. Of all who served under Black Herran during her conquest of Essoran, he was the only one I would call an irredeemable monster. Worse even than Maeven."

Black Herran nodded to Lorimer Felle and Tiarnach as they joined her and Amogg on the creaking walkway atop the log palisade. They watched the bulk of the Lucent army cresting the rise just south of town, fur-clad scouts in the lead. A bannerman in pristine white tabard and silver chain climbed into view, the golden sunburst of the Bright One on a white flag flapped at the end of a bronze-capped pole he planted in the earth, not so far away from Black Herran's demonic sigil. Behind the bannerman came the Falcon Prince armoured in shining silver, his golden falcon visor lowered.

Maeven shoved past the sweating, shaking militia on the narrow walkway. The necromancer took up position beside her old general and stared at the distant form of the Falcon Prince. Her fingernails gouged bloody furrows into her palms.

"Are you sure these pricks won't just wait us out?" Tiarnach asked, pulling on scavenged mail, cinching the belt tight and donning a helmet. "Lots more o' them fuckers up north only a day's march away."

"I doubt they will stop to talk," Maeven said. "In their arrogance they will come in hard and fast. The Falcon Prince's wrath is brutally direct in nature. He thinks himself and his damned goddess invincible. It will not occur to him that he can fail."

"Pretty fire make it easy to kill," the big orc added. "Amogg say little humans scared to fight axe to axe."

"We face many inquisitors this time," Lorimer said. "How do you intend to counter them?"

"I don't," Black Herran said. "Thanks to Verena's experience of fighting at sea we have their range now, and most of them will be dead before they ever get within bowshot of Tarnbrooke."

Black Herran stared hard at the man who had come here to destroy her home of forty years. The Falcon Prince paused. His helmet turned towards Black Herran and Maeven. He seemed to shudder at the sight of them, but then he drew his sword and held it aloft. It burst into flames and then he pointed it at Tarnbrooke. His men advanced at a jog.

Black Herran gasped and her leg gave way, forcing her to grab Maeven's arm for support. "The bastards are right where I want them to be." Her mouth twisted into a rictus of pain as her entire body spasmed. The earth shuddered beneath the entire town's feet. Boulders crashed down from the cliff walls on either side of the valley.

Blood drooled from the demonologist's lips, eyes and nose as she sagged against the necromancer. Her spasms intensified, every muscle straining. Then all tension left her. She groaned and wiped her face with a handkerchief. "The great demon comes. Duke Shemharai's general, Malifer, rises from the burning pits of Hellrath."

The tremors intensified. Yelps of surprise and fear among the townsfolk caused Amogg to bellow: "This on our side! Big demon comes to eat up little humans."

The militia shifted nervously from foot to foot, not entirely sure if Amogg was reassuring or not.

"It is time to remove most of our melee force from the walls," Lorimer said to Estevan. "This place reeks of fear. The less the townsfolk see of this the better."

Three quarters of the Tarnbrooke militia and armed civilians were assembled into separate groups stationed a short distance from the palisade, ready to charge into any breaches that appeared. Those left on the wall bent bows and readied weapons for when the enemy came within spitting distance.

"It begins," Black Herran said, pointing to the peak of the hill where Lucent soldiers lurched to and fro, dropping weapons as they fell. She laughed, spraying flecks of blood as their formations were broken and scattered. The earth heaved up from underneath her demonic sigil, slabs of rock rising and splitting as something massive punched up from the depths.

Jets of steam and clouds of yellow gas billowed from the broken earth, scalding and choking. Men fell screaming, faces red and blistered; others flopped like landed fish gasping for breath. An inquisitor and a dozen of his soldiers dropped screaming into the depths as a chasm opened beneath their feet. Sheets of flame roared into the sky and the rotten egg stench of brimstone afflicted every nose.

A gaggle of bald acolytes raised their voices in prayer to the Bright One, an abjuration against all manner of evil. Rough, red-scaled hands the size of houses ripped free from the chasm in a torrent of stone. The earth juddered as they slammed down on either side, squashing the acolytes to paste and burying black claws deep into the hillside. A long, dreadfully fanged crocodile head rose into the air as the great demon general Malifer pulled itself from the gaping wound in the mortal world. It rose on two legs, and flexed two hands, but there the resemblance to humanity ended. It reared tall as the spire of the Tarnbrooke temple and thrice as long, a titanic demon armoured in pit-forged spiked steel wielding a heavy maul the size of a tree, the metal hammer head as heavy as a battering ram. Flame and smoke seeped from its fanged maw, and sizzling drool began to drip as it surveyed the feast of human morsels surrounding it. A long-ridged tail lashed the hillside, crushing a handful of men.

Scattered and terrified fragments of the Lucent army fell back in disarray, tiny ants scurrying for safety before the boot of this malevolent giant crushed all life from them. The Tarnbrooke militia on the wall paled and gripped their weapons tight. Steel clinked and leather creaked as the defenders shivered in terror and prayed to the Elder Gods that this hellish monster would destroy only their enemies.

The demon general's long, flat, inhuman head turned unerringly to locate Black Herran, its vibrant green eyes unblinking as it stared deep into her soul.

"This realm now belongs to Duke Shemharai," it roared, the inhuman voice somehow understood in every mind when such a mouth and throat could never utter human words.

"Not yet it doesn't!" Black Herran shouted, her voice hoarse and cracking. "Behind you stands the army of a goddess. By my blood and by my will, destroy it."

As if to reinforce the point, a lanky inquisitor in dusty plate pulled himself from some rubble, drew his sword and pointed it towards the towering demon. He yelled a prayer to the Bright One and unleashed her power.

A torrent of golden fire capable of reducing humans to ash slammed into Malifer's steel-clad chest. The huge demon was forced to take a step back. A patch of its armour glowed cherry-red. Then the demon lowered its fanged maw, one eye studying the insect that dared sting it.

It loosed a roar that shook shingles from roofs and set birds to flight for leagues around. Pots cracked, cats yowled and dogs fled. Black clouds boiled into being in clear skies, casting the town into gloom and lashing it with hail.

A clawed hand blocked the holy fire and the demon swung its huge maul down in the other. The head of the weapon hit like a thunderclap, crushing the inquisitor and a chunk of hillside with it. Dirt and pebbles rained down across the battlefield, and as the maul lifted it left a crater deeper than Amogg was tall.

Malifer examined its hand, noting the charred scales the same way a human would an unpleasant rash. "Know your place, vermin," it boomed. "Your bodies and souls are my sustenance." It stamped a few straggling soldiers to mush and bent low to scoop up another two, dropping the screaming men into its mouth and swallowing them whole.

The panicked enemy began to rally around the Falcon Prince as he drew his sword and advanced on the demon. His Goddess's power wrapped around him, glowing brighter and taller with every step as he assumed the titanic flaming form of the Bright One he had worn during the battle with the Kraken. His sword extended into an incandescent blade of a size to match the demon general's huge maul. His voice rang out, rich and clear and loud as a city bell: "I shall destroy you, servant of evil! This world bows to the will of the Bright One, and all that is impure shall be burned from existence. To the walls, chosen of the Goddess! This foe is mine alone."

Malifer laughed, a rumble like two colliding mountains, and swung its maul at the Falcon Prince's head. The champion of the Bright One dodged and struck back with his sword, quick as lightning. The burning blade pierced pit-forged steel with a shower of sparks.

The demon general hissed as its black blood sprayed the hillside, bursting into black and greasy flames wherever it landed. It turned and lashed out with its tail, swiping the Falcon Prince's leg and sending him crashing down atop his own soldiers, his huge body of golden fire obliterating twenty men in an instant.

As the two colossal powers fought on the hill south of Tarnbrooke, the remaining Lucent soldiers streamed towards the town, their precise and orderly formations abandoned in favour of savage bloodlust and naked terror.

"Here come the fanatics," Tiarnach shouted, hailstones rattling off his helmet. "Take your places, chug the alchemist's bloody potions and get ready to loose your arrows. I'll gut any man or woman who survives this fight without taking a pair of Lucent heads to sit on spikes. Make me a forest of Lucent skulls, you mad bastards!"

The final battle to decide the fate of every soul in Tarnbrooke had begun.

CHAPTER 37

The Tarnbrooke bowmen were hunters, not cold-hearted killers of men, and their shaking, hail-stung hands caused their aim to go awry. Arrows rained down on the Lucent charge, missing more often than not, or hitting raised shields and deflecting off helms. Only a few found exposed flesh, but every hit was one more ruthless fanatic that the farmers, butchers, spinners and innocent craftsfolk of Tarnbrooke would never have to face.

Lucent skirmishers held back from the front lines, picking off defenders atop the wall with their powerful war bows.

Arrows sped back and forth. People fell on both sides. The enemy were at the muddy ditch surrounding the town, slowed, making them better targets for the bowmen. Some slipped in the mud, falling onto sharpened wooden stakes while others got their clothing snagged, slowing them down. The charge did not falter.

Amogg acted as a living catapult, hurling Jerak Hyden's alchemical weapons out into the mass. Iron balls with fizzing fuses exploded into razor shards, shredding all nearby. Pots shattered, releasing powders to the wind. Men screamed and clutched their melting eyes, others fell clutching their throats or staggered about swiping at hallucinated enemies. Dozens of soldiers tore at helms and mail, scratching at skin rapidly blistering and breaking. The rest continued on, grim-faced and furious.

The wind shifted, carrying green and yellow clouds back

across a section of the palisade, then up and off to the west away from town. A dozen men and women of Tarnbrooke guarding that section dropped and fell frothing at the mouth, screaming with hysterical laughter even as they died.

Golden fire exploded against the western side of the palisade, blinding bright in the demonic gloom. It consumed logs and the bowmen atop them. An inquisitor sprinted into the billowing smoke of the breach, sword and eyes blazing. His men roared and charged after him, sensing victory.

A screech of steel, a thunk of flesh, and the inquisitor's severed head bounced back the way he'd come. A huge shadow stepped into the breach, axe cutting through the first rank of soldiers.

Amogg laughed as she wreaked bloody ruin, tossing hard men away like broken children's toys. "Fight good, little humans. Make Amogg Hadakk happy."

The Lucent charge slowed but still came on, more cautious now with shields at the fore, weapons probing and wary of the huge orc's superior reach. They all wore fine mail and sturdy helms, but even if their armour warded off the cutting edge, any blow from her heavy axe crushed bones.

Red Penny and a unit of female militia rushed to reinforce the orc warchief before she was overwhelmed by numbers. A wall of spears plunged into the enemy: thrust, withdraw, thrust, just like they had been taught.

Big as the elder orc was, she could not block the entire breach alone, and soldiers slipped through on either side. They tried to use their armour and strength to push through the forest of spears. Some hesitated on realising they faced women – a fatal mistake. Red Penny's spear-sisters did not hesitate. Thrust, withdraw, thrust…

Golden titan and towering demon general fought on the hillside above the town, flaming sword against heavy maul, every hit an impact that shook and cracked the earth. Burning black blood and golden fire rained down as they cut and hammered at each other's unfathomably powerful bodies, armour cracking under the pressure. Malifer's fanged maw snapped shut just shy of the Falcon Prince's golden nose, and the champion of the Bright One countered with a punch to its crocodile jaw. His fist hit like a fiery battering ram, the staggering impact a thunderclap booming through the valley.

Malifer recovered instantly, and both fought with deepening fury.

On the east side, more logs exploded into flame and ash. Two inquisitors, both slender and quick on their feet, advanced at a cautious jog with their followers arranged in a line behind them. They had learned from their holy brother's fatal overconfidence.

Tiarnach stepped forward through billowing ash and embers to block their way, red hair blazing in the firelight, a sword in each hand and a sneer on his face. He laughed at them and screamed: "Come and get gutted, ya goddess-fuckers!" His heart pounded with a mix of mortal fear and that old savage joy of combat he had missed so very much. For the first time in decades, he felt truly alive.

"Slay the corrupt heathens!" one of the holy knights yelled, waving his army onwards.

Nicholas and a group of the other male militia roared, "For Tarnbrooke!" and charged in to meet them, two rows deep, spears lowered. The two sides slammed together in vicious melee. Men screamed as steel pierced flesh and bone.

Tiarnach fought his way towards the inquisitors. He sliced a soldier's throat and kicked another in the side of the knee, shattering it. The man went down, trampled under the boots of his own side. Nicholas and another militiaman pushed forward beside their leader, spears thrusting for vulnerable eyes, necks and groin, desperately keeping the Lucent soldiers at bay. For now. Tiarnach knew the stalemate wouldn't last facing veteran soldiers in heavy armour.

He couldn't give the enemy the chance to push hard into the spear wall from behind the safety of their shields. He advanced, blades screeching off his helmet and mail as he waded through the enemy in a flurry of death. Something slicked his cheek, a burning line right along his jaw. A hasty parry left his knuckles skinned and bleeding. The pain was a badge of honour, a rejection of his previous cowardice.

A shield slammed into Nicholas's face and he reeled back dazed, moustache drenched in blood. One of the townsfolk pulled him back from the line before he was slaughtered and took his place at the front.

The inquisitors both came for Tiarnach, quick and slippery as fish, one hand holding burning sword, the other empty but outstretched. "Be consumed by the fury of the Bright One!" they cried. Incandescent fire roared from their hands, enveloping Tiarnach and the militiaman next to him. The stench of burning flesh filled the air.

A holy knight grunted, his fires dying. His sword dropped to the mud as he stared down in shock at the sword thrust through his armpit, avoiding steel plate to punch through weaker mail and linen gambeson.

Tiarnach twisted the weapon and blood vomited from the knight's mouth. He went down in a heap and Tiarnach yanked the blade free just in time to block a savage blow from the other inquisitor. Steel grated on steel as they shoved against each other. Glimpsed through the faceplate of his helmet, the knight's grey eyes crinkled in fury as his sword ignited and began cutting right through Tiarnach's.

A muddy boot to the groin sent the other knight reeling backwards, sword flailing and accidently cutting an arm off one of his own soldiers. The blood-drenched warrior came after him, roaring in savage joy: "Tiarnach of the Cahal'gilroy!"

He tossed aside the damaged blade and picked up the dead

knight's finely balanced war sword, then flung himself at the enemy, the Tarnbrooke militia at his back. He hacked off a soldier's hand and stabbed somebody else in the throat. Power roared through his muscles: the power of belief. This was the power of a god of war. The thrill of battle sang through him and he knew the battlefield was where he truly belonged, not drowning regret and sorrow in scummy alehouses.

An inquisitor at the back of the battle raised his sword and disappeared in a flash of lightning. It flashed again, stabbing down from a still sky to fry three nervous women with kitchen knives held in reserve closer to the centre of town. The holy knight reappeared and beheaded a young man in wooden armour, but not before the man loosed a blood-curdling scream that alerted Black Herran. The inquisitor staggered and leaned against the wall for a moment, apparently wearied by his magical exertion.

Another lightning strike followed, blasting two more reserve militia from their feet, then another. Three inquisitors had bypassed the town's defences, but appeared temporarily weakened.

Black Herran cursed. "Maeven! Lorimer! Kill them before they do too much damage."

The vampire charged the closest, fangs and fury, diverting the inquisitor's attention away from the dazed and blinded townsfolk. He dodged a masterful series of cuts from the man's burning sword and, quicksilver-swift, darted past with claws extended, his bestial strength rending steel and flesh like it was cloth. He took the knight's left arm off at the elbow.

The inquisitor screamed and lashed out with his blade, scoring a shallow hit on Lorimer's bone-plated shoulder. As the man reeled back, blood rhythmically spurting from a ragged stump, the vampire paused to examine his own wound.

The sword had sliced through flesh into the bone, and again

the wound refused to heal. Blood gushed down his chest and arm against his will. Armour was useless against their goddess-given magic. Bone and sharp spines submerged below his human skin, the wound remaining a vivid red slash. He reached up and tore off that chunk of his shoulder to expose bare bone, and tossed the charred meat away. New flesh and muscle flowed back in to fill the gap, leaving him with pristine skin once again.

Lorimer grinned at the white-faced inquisitor, fangs extending. "You had the misfortune to face Lorimer Felle, Lord of Fade's Reach."

The knight hissed in pain and attacked, ignoring his increasing weakness.

Lorimer admired the man's courage as he sidestepped the knight's next blow and punched a hole through his breastplate. But he admired the taste of a human heart even more, he thought as he ripped it free and sank his fangs into the steaming organ.

Maeven's dark power gathered around the next closest inquisitor, who laughed at her, even as serpents of black mist wrapped around him. "The Bright One protects!" he screamed, cutting down two townsfolk as he raced towards her.

"Not anymore," Maeven said as her mist seeped through the breathing holes in his helm and into his lungs. "Thanks to previous encounters with your fellows, and my exploration of Tiarnach's divine nature."

The inquisitor slowed, staggered and began coughing up blood as his face burst out in yellow pustules. He raised his sword sunward and disappeared in a flash of lightning.

Maeven blinked. "Well, well. That one had enough sense to flee."

Black Herran noted an accompanying flash behind enemy lines, and a silver figure falling to his knees, vomiting blood. "I suppose they had to have some still able to think for themselves. Will he die?"

Maeven considered that, then shrugged. "Expect the worst and you shall not be disappointed."

The third inquisitor nearest the town gutted two townsfolk and then fled down an alleyway leading to the centre, murdering all he came across, armed or not.

Black Herran had no time to dwell on it as a tremor knocked her from her feet. The fiery giant figure of the Falcon Prince had been knocked onto his back and Malifer's huge maul fell like a mountain to pound his chest. The earth shuddered as the Falcon Prince screamed, golden fire and blood seeping from cracks in his armour. For a moment, Black Herran dared to hope it would be that easy.

The next blow hit only earth as the Falcon Prince rolled aside, his own incandescent blade sizzling through a chunk of the demon's leg. He staggered upright and then forced Malifer back with a flurry of cuts, drawing blood from a dozen shallow wounds.

Smoke belched from the demon's maw, a roar of fury followed by a clumsy swing. The Falcon Prince ducked and ran the demon through, burning blade piercing pit-forged chest plate and out the back.

Malifer hissed in agony and shoved him away, sliding off the blade and taking several cautious steps back, maul held up defensively. A burning river of demon blood flowed downhill, and Black Herran knew then that the demon general was overmatched by the power of the Lucent Goddess that wrapped around her champion. It was only a matter of time before it was slain. The only question was how much more damage the demon could inflict before it died. Would it weaken the Falcon Prince enough?

Tiarnach and Amogg fought on, wreaking bloody ruin as the militia fell like flies around them. The enemy's superior equipment and training took a dreadful toll, and they ruthlessly exploited every mistake: every overextended thrust and clumsy attack led to gaping wounds and blood spilled. The defensive lines wavered and the townsfolk were pushed back. One step. A second, carrying them back into the breach in the wall. A third, the Lucent forces battering and breaking spear shafts as steel-shod boots trampled dying men and women into the mud.

Some of the Tarnbrooke militia began foaming at the mouth, their eyes red and bulging, veins prominent and pulsing on necks and faces. The effect of Jerak Hyden's potions welled up inside the twelve volunteers, turning fear to fury. Hellish screams ripped from their throats as they flung themselves at the enemy like mad beasts, hacking and slashing, biting and clawing, immune to fear and pain. The retreat flipped to a feral assault.

An old shepherd, white-bearded and weathered, tossed his broken spear shaft at a soldier's face and then darted past Amogg like he was a callow youth. He dodged two sword swings, then leaped over the shield of a scarred northerner and tackled him to the ground. He punched the soldier in the face, denting nose guard and breaking the man's jaw along with his own wrist. He didn't show any sign of pain as he shrieked in rage, pounding down again and again. A sword plunged through his chest. He ignored it, hammering down until his prey was dead and his own arm ended in a splintered mess of bone. Then he slid up the blade through his chest and sank his teeth into the throat of the horrified man holding it. Even as another sword split his skull, his teeth ripped out that soldier's throat.

A lumberjack's infected chest wound from the first battle lost its heat and the pain faded from his mind. Despite the healer's words of hope, he knew he was already dead, and the potion gave him one last chance to fell more Lucent bastards. His dead brother's axe was in his hand as he launched himself forward, hewing at a shield. Inhuman strength shattered the shield and the arm behind it, then caved in the man's head. A sword took his eye and half his face, another severed his left hand, but it didn't concern him. He split another skull before falling.

The remaining Tarnbrooke volunteers under the influence of Jerak Hyden's potions attacked the Lucent army in a frenzy. The militia took heart and steadied their lines, fighting with renewed vigour.

Then Black Herran watched the thirteenth fly into a blind frenzy. Fourteen... fifteen... twenty... screams from the town as frothing red-faced figures of children, the aged and infirm, raced from safety and towards the enemy with knives and clubs in hand.

"What is happening?" Maeven demanded.

"That bastard Jerak Hyden," Black Herran spat. "A dozen volunteers was not enough for him. He must have dosed whatever water, wine and food he could find with more accursed potion than he admitted to making. He does not care who he kills."

The necromancer snorted, "I would not expect anything less of that creature. Verena went to find the little wretch, but she is wounded and unreliable." She rested a hand on the hilt of her necromantic blade and began walking towards the town. "I will kill that last inquisitor loose behind our defences and then I will deal with the madman myself."

CHAPTER 38

Verena hated to turn her back on a battle. The clash of steel and the screams and shouts called to her. There was organising to be done, idiots to be led, and cowards to be threatened into compliance. But Jerak Hyden could not be allowed to run free, and her missing hand and burning wound urged her to take that pain out on his disgusting hide. At the moment it was about all she was good for.

Besides, she wanted to get as far away as she could from those two monsters duelling on the hillside above Tarnbrooke. The demon general was being driven back, blackened and bleeding from a dozen wounds. Every blow caused the ground to shake, and the clashing of magical weaponry rolled down the valley like peals of thunder. They might as well be warring gods, and for Verena, being up close and personal to the Kraken had been more than enough of that sort of thing to last her a lifetime. Around her shoulders, Irusen trembled and hid its pretty little head in Verena's hair. The little slynx hated magic more than the hail, and Verena wholeheartedly agreed.

With Aleeva and three of her crew surrounding her, she marched towards the building where Jerak had set up his workshop. Townsfolk raced up and down the streets, carrying arrows and spare weapons to the defenders, or helping the wounded to safety. A growing number of people were cursing and growing red in the face, punching walls and gnashing teeth. Verena could only think that fear and anger had driven them all mad.

She spotted the little rat of a man poking his head out the doorway of his workshop and shiftily looking left and right, ready to escape. He squinted through dusty spectacles at her and then fled back inside. The sound of a heavy wooden bar being dropped into place followed as he barricaded himself in his hole.

She smiled grimly and kept her good hand on her belt knife. She was going to enjoy slitting the madman's throat once they winkled him from his shell.

As they approached the doorway Verena began to realise that something was very wrong with some of the townsfolk. People were wailing and tearing out their hair, clutching weapons and howling like enraged animals.

An old man with bloodshot eyes and a matted beard clapped eyes on Verena and her crew. He grabbed a nearby stool and limped towards them, raising it like a weapon. Aleeva raised an eyebrow and waved a pirate forward to take it off him before he did himself an injury.

The salt-scoured crewman grabbed hold of the stool and ripped it from the old man's grip – or he tried to. He might as well have been trying to take Amogg's axe right out of her fist. The old man snarled, revealing snaggly brown teeth, and then slammed the stool into the pirate's face. Shattered splinters of wood and teeth flew as her man was launched backwards to sprawl motionless in the dirt.

"Cut him down," Verena ordered. Aleeva and the other two pirates drew blades and hacked the old man to pieces. He took a surprisingly long time to die.

Verena studied other townsfolk similarly afflicted, most of them loping towards the south, drawn by the sounds of bloodshed and seemingly unconcerned by the two massive figures pounding away at each other. Sounds of fighting and dying echoed down a nearby alley, the din attracting more deranged and feral townsfolk. "Accursed Jerak Hyden," she growled. "I warned them this would happen. Get that door open, you salty dogs."

Aleeva propped her unconscious crewman against the wall and began kicking in the door to the workshop. The old door splintered after the third strike, ready to give way.

"Leave me be!" Jerak squeaked from inside. "Go rob some peasants. I have too much important work to be bothered by ignoramuses."

"You've poisoned the townsfolk," Verena yelled.

"So?" he shouted, confusion evident in his tone. "They will be far more useful this way. Would you object to a few trees cut from a forest in order to craft a ship? There are always more peasants should you need them."

"You are a mad dog that needs to be disposed of," Verena snarled.

Aleeva gave the door one last mighty kick and it slammed fully open, the wooden bar behind it broken in two. Fragments of wood exploded across the room, cracking bottles, shattering vials, knocking over metal bowls and scattering powders all over the floor.

On a bench in the middle of the room, something moaned and twitched beneath a stained sheet. Verena assumed it was yet another of the mad alchemist's victims.

Jerak hissed in rage and slapped his palm to the back of a bizarre statue of a man worked in crude brass and iron, with blades instead of hands. The eye sockets of the brass skull flared blood-red.

Aleeva rubbed a dark hand over a stubbly, sweating scalp. "What you want done with this one, My Crown?"

"Put him on his knees before me," Verena said.

Jerak Hyden rolled his eyes. "You are little better than grunting cattle, dull of mind and entirely lacking in imagination."

Verena smiled thinly. "Oh, my imagination is far from lacking. As you are about to find out."

He muttered and slipped the iron control circlet onto his head. "Kill them, my golem."

The metal man shuddered and came to life, its insides whirring and clicking, cogs turning, sparks crackling like a miniature thunderstorm. It raised its arms, blades poised for combat.

The mad alchemist giggled, licked his lips and then grinned. "You are all dirty vermin. To the worms with you."

The pirate queen drew her belt knife. "Destroy that thing."

Her two crewmen leapt to obey, swords clanging ineffectively off metal ribs. The golem lashed out, blade-arms whirling, opening a crewman's arm from wrist to elbow. Aleeva picked up a wooden crate and flung it. The golem staggered under the impact, then righted itself.

"What is this thing?" Aleeva demanded, picking up another crate.

"The future of humanity," Jerak Hyden said, breathless with excitement. "An end to disease and death. Immortality is now within my grasp!"

One of the pirates backed away from the golem and bumped into the bench in the middle of the room, a steadying hand pressing down on the sheet covering it. He howled as fangs pierced the sheet and bit into his wrist. He staggered away and took the sheet with him, revealing the dissected but still-living torso of one of Lorimer Felle's vampire spawn.

Aleeva gagged at the sight of the pulsing, exposed pink and grey organs. She opened her mouth to utter a curse but didn't have the opportunity.

The side of the room exploded inwards, hurling Verena's first mate into the opposite wall as an armoured knight ploughed through, desperately trying to dislodge a portly middle-aged woman who was headbutting him, her face already a bloody ruin as it repeatedly rammed into his helmet. He wrenched her off and shoved her away. She staggered back and bumped into the gleaming man of brass and iron.

The golem beheaded her.

Verena, Jerak, and the Lucent inquisitor all paused for a moment, staring at each other in shock. Then the room burst into action.

The holy knight's sword came up and golden flames burst forth to envelop the golem.

Aleeva flung herself to one side as holy magic incinerated the vampire spawn and the two other pirates next to it, torching most of Jerak Hyden's tools and supplies. The alchemist himself sprinted for the doorway, a single step ahead of fiery death.

Verena remained untouched by the holy fire, the slynx curled around her neck hissing and warding off the magic. She blocked the doorway and the alchemist slammed into her, propelling both outside in a tangle of limbs. The slynx yowled as it was ripped from her mistress's shoulders to tumble down the street.

The inquisitor gasped as the golem advanced through his flames, metal bones glowing red and running, its insides steaming. A brass blade lashed out, and he blocked it with ease. The golem's hand snapped, burning metal spattering the knight's cuirass. It lifted the broken arm and then cricked its metal head, rods in its neck softening and wilting. Then it enveloped the knight in a bear hug.

The knight struggled but couldn't escape its metal embrace. The steaming body of the golem sagged over his armour, heating it. The knight screamed as his gambeson charred and his mail began to burn through to the skin beneath. He staggered back and forth, howling as he cooked inside his own armour.

Lightning flashed down through the roof and he vanished in a swirl of steam and smoke, the half-molten golem taken with him.

Jerak Hyden scrabbled to escape the pirate queen's clutches. He had two good hands but she was tough as old leather. A knee slammed into his belly and her teeth ripped a chunk of meat from his arm. He fell on top of her, screaming and slapping at her face.

His fist cracked into the old woman's jaw, splitting her lip open. He rose over her, triumphant. Which is when he noticed the hilt of a knife jutting from his chest, and with that came a wave of agony.

He staggered backwards, hands hovering over the knife, unsure if he should leave it in or not – the blood loss would be considerable. "What have you done, you imbecile?" he gasped. "You dare destroy so much wealth of knowledge and progress?"

Verena blinked away the tears and got up onto her knees. "Stuck like a pig," she cackled. "Finally, the fate you deserve. Whatever you think you know, the world wants it not." Jerak Hyden fell to his knees staring at the mortal wound. She rose to place her mewling pet back around her shoulders and then walked over to finish the bastard off...

Unseen by the two combatants outside the burning workshop, Aleeva rose from the rubble with help from another pair of hands. She looked up at the necromancer's scarred face and smiled. "Thank... oh."

Maeven's obsidian blade plunged into the pirate's chest. She shivered with pleasure as the woman's soul was sucked into the black blade. "Mm, soon you will awaken," the necromancer whispered to the weapon as she let the corpse drop. With all the deaths in this town she was so close to having the living weapon she needed to free her sister. It just required one or two last great and powerful souls.

For the first time in her life, she found herself agreeing with Jerak Hyden: if a few small eggs needed to be broken for her grander purpose then so be it. Once she had his and Verena's souls, her weapon would wake and then she would have the power of life and death in her hands: the power to kill gods, to kill anything.

She smiled and walked around the corner to witness Jerak Hyden dying with a knife buried in his chest. Verena ripped it out and plunged it back into his heart again and again, shrieking, "Die, you monstrosity!" as he begged for mercy that was never going to come.

"No!" Maeven screamed, rushing forward, slipping and sliding over rubble. Her magic reached out to stop the pirate queen, but was blocked by the slynx's strange power. She could not even leech off part of Jerak Hyden's soul due to its influence.

Blood gushed from the little man's mouth and the holes in his heart. He pitched face first to the dirt.

Verena turned to face this new threat. "And what do you want?" she snarled.

"I would be very much pleased to take your soul," Maeven said.

Verena grinned and advanced with her bloody weapon in hand. "Two monsters ended with one knife, what a bountiful harvest this is."

The necromancer was no cut-throat brawler, so she fled back around the corner and rested a hand on Aleeva's corpse. She knew she could not directly affect the pirate queen with magic, so she needed to improvise. She was husbanding her power to waken her blade but with all this death she had some to spare.

Aleeva's corpse rose and grabbed hold of Maeven's cloak as if trying to restrain a fleeing foe.

Verena turned the corner, grinned and broke into a jog. "Keep a hold of her, Aleeva!"

The slynx screeched, panicking as Verena closed in on the struggling, powerless necromancer. "It is time to end you," she gloated.

"I could not agree more," Maeven said as the corpse of Aleeva released her cloak to wrap both hands around Verena's throat instead. It squeezed. The power of the slynx dispersed Maeven's power, but the hands remained locked in place, the tissues swollen and solid in rigor mortis.

The slynx went mad, tiny claws shredding the corpse's face and eyes. Futile.

Verena choked and stabbed at the arms, trying to cut them off her. As the blood flow to her brain dwindled, she passed out.

The necromancer switched her attention to the pirate queen's vile pet. She grabbed hold of the slynx's squirming little head, shuddering at the sudden disruption to her magic. A twist and a snap and it was all over. She tossed the limp rag of fur into the burning workshop and sighed with relief. She made the corpse let go of Verena's throat and climb on top to hold her down.

When Verena stirred she looked up in horror at her first mate; Aleeva's face was an eyeless, horrific ruin. Verena hoarsely screamed for help, but none was coming.

"A bargain," the pirate queen said. "I know who your brother is, and where he is. My life for that knowledge!"

Maeven paused, her obsidian knife poised to plunge into Verena's heart. She wiped blood from Verena's chin with a finger, licking it and chuckling. "Oh, that? I knew all along. I just didn't have the means to reach him and kill him in the heart of his empire. I've been playing all of you like a harp to enable me to obtain enough power to end his existence. Black Herran has conveniently gathered everything I need all in one place."

Verena snarled and tried to kick her, defiant to the end. "You have tasted Awildan queen's blood, Maeven. You are accursed! May everything you touch slip from your grasp and turn to ash."

Maeven rolled her eyes. "Terrifying." Verena spat in her face even as the obsidian blade slid between the old woman's ribs. Hot fury and iron will flowed into the knife.

The necromancer looked down on the small corpse that had contained such a mighty soul. All personal animosity aside, Verena Awildan had been worthy of admiration. She had ruled more by force of will than force of arms, and had somehow managed to earn her people's loyalty – something far beyond Maeven's understanding.

The necromancer turned and walked back the way she had come, past the body of the mad alchemist, regretting the missed chance to obtain his soul.

Her grandfather's dry rasping voice echoed in her mind, trembling with excitement and yearning: *You will need another strong one to replace it, and quickly. One last victim: the orc warlord, or perhaps Tiarnach, if the knife is now able to absorb the substance of gods. Inquisitors, too, may serve if you can reach any. Please let me die.*

She considered his words. The ghost of her grandfather had the right of it, but she measured it would take a handful of the strongest inquisitors' souls to equal any one of her old comrades in arms.

"I will take what I can reach," she replied. "No matter who it is." It seemed to mollify him for now.

Then she would slaughter her little brother, murder Black Herran and end anybody else who dared to interfere with her goal. She hurried back towards the battle before some idiot with a spear got lucky and took any more valuable material from her grasp.

CHAPTER 39

The giant demon's maul slammed into the Falcon Prince's face, knocking the avatar of the Bright One onto his back for the second time. He fell, shedding golden fire as he struck and levelled the hillside. His fury was greater than his pain and he was back on his feet in an instant, leaking magic and red blood both. He lashed out, sword slicing a trench through the thick hide of Malifer's arm. They slammed into each other, struggling back and forth, carelessly trampling men beneath them, biting and punching, clawing and kicking like maddened beasts.

Black Herran clutched her section of palisade as it swayed alarmingly from the force of the impact. The Tarnbrooke bowmen's aim was thrown off but the press of Lucent soldiers forcing their way through the breaches in the wall was so tight it didn't matter. They loosed shaft after shaft, but it was not enough to slow down the enemy.

She hurt all over, ripped inside and out, and was in no condition to take any further part in the battle: summoning and then restraining the great demon had been akin to birthing a boulder. The power of all that pain and torment and spilled blood was still feeding her shadow demons, but little of it was usable in her current state.

Lorimer Felle joined her on the wall, a haggard Estevan accompanying his lord.

She watched the golden titan battling one of Hellrath's

greatest warriors, and noted a change in the fiery female form he wore. "Does the Falcon Prince look smaller to you?"

Estevan raised the brim of his hat and squinted. "Indeed. Every blow he suffers now seems to reduce his size." He cleared his throat and cast a worried look towards the Lucent battle lines as their reserve force of archers shifted location. "It would seem that the Lucent Empire are about to assault the western flank. I suspect our lightly armoured militia will not long withstand their bows. Even Amogg Hadakk might soon fall."

Lorimer nodded in agreement. "They thought to storm our wall, break our morale, and crush all resistance with a single charge. Now they will take us more seriously."

"Can you help Amogg hold the west?" Black Herran asked.

Lorimer considered the odds. "The number of inquisitors remaining is unknown. The chances of us holding are—"

A rock-splitting screech of agony drew every eye to the warring giants. The Falcon Prince had managed to shove Malifer's heavy maul to one side and stab the demon general through the belly. He grunted and sawed the burning blade higher, black blood and guts slopping out of a chasm in the beast's stomach. Its crocodile jaw snapped shut on the Lucent commander's arm, enormous fangs savaging it.

The Falcon Prince ignored the pain and shoved his blade higher, cutting through thick slabs of steel, muscle, organ and bone. Malifer was weakening. Dying. Spewing blood and bile and venomous hatred. One last heave and it was opened from belly to throat like a butchered beast, a hillock of black and burning offal forming at its feet as the malevolent light faded from its eyes.

The Falcon Prince roared a victory hymn. Sunlight broke through black clouds and the hail ceased drumming down.

"The chances," Lorimer said, continuing where he left off, "have just become none." He tucked Black Herran under his arm, abandoned the defences and ran for the greater safety of narrow streets and stone buildings.

The Falcon Prince's staggering form was cracked and broken,

his arm a limp mess of human blood and golden fire – a fire swiftly abating, his size decreasing with every heartbeat. He glared at the town that dared defy his will and divine purpose, then kicked the demon's enormous corpse towards it.

Tiarnach gave a soldier's throat a new, red mouth, wiped the sweat from his brow, and then looked up as a shadow fell over them. It was too late for any of them to avoid the falling giant. Lightning flashed as three holy knights buggered off to safety. He sighed heavily and muttered, "Butchered balls."

The corpse of Malifer landed on the eastern flank, crushing the palisade, several out buildings, and fifty people from both sides. The gatehouse collapsed. Tiarnach and dozens of others were blasted through the air by the shockwave.

The war god bounced and tumbled across rooftops, shattered wood and stone scouring his flesh. He crashed through the stone wall of the temple. His ribs snapped from the impact, then he rammed headfirst into a statue, splitting his helmet in two. He collapsed in a bloody heap, breath wheezing from burst lips and broken nose. The statue of Herlan, Lord of the Hunt, fell in pieces beside him, no match for his thick skull. Tiarnach had never liked that pompous prick anyway.

The militia that had stood beside him were now only bloody and unidentifiable rags hanging from broken beams and collapsed buildings. Some of the Lucent soldiers had suffered a similar fate, but their heavily armoured corpses were mostly in one piece. Nothing wholly mortal could have survived that.

A gaggle of children swarmed Tiarnach, escaping their yelling elders' grasps. They were all armed with eating knives. He recognised the brave little girl and boy from earlier as they helped him to his feet.

"We fight with you," the girl said, shaking in fear.

Courage. Loyalty. Comradeship. Only a few weeks ago he had imagined such things were all in his past...

Outside, the remnants of his dazed and battered militia began to scream as Lucent forces swarmed into the outskirts of town and butchered anything that moved. Tiarnach could sense three inquisitors had come in with them, burning balls of divine might itching his mind. They were coming to enslave and indoctrinate these brave children and "purify" the rest of the populace.

Tiarnach of the Cahal'gilroy was many things: a bloody-handed reiver, a murderer, a laughing killer who enjoyed his work, and lately, a coward. But he'd be damned to eternal torment if he let those Lucent bastards have their way with these brave folk. He spat blood and teeth and searched for a sword.

"Get back in there," he snarled at the children. "Don't get between a war god and his foes."

The old people cast terrified, but hopeful eyes his way as he heaved his battered body up to block the hole he'd made in the side of the temple. Here he would stand and here he would fall, and he'd take more of those bastards down with him.

Amogg knew the battle was lost. She had butchered brittle human males left and right in exchange for a few shallow cuts, but now the eastern flank had collapsed. Lucent soldiers streamed through towards the town, while others began methodically working their way down the palisade towards her, slaughtering the outnumbered defenders. Nicholas the tile maker and a dozen other militia were surrounded but put up a spirited defence, slowing the enemy down long enough for survivors to retreat to the narrow streets of the town and regroup behind barricades. Amogg thought there was much glory in their deaths.

What was left of Verena Awildan's pirates and the reserve militia had pulled back into the town under Lorimer Felle's command and began a vicious close-quarters street battle. Their knowledge of the terrain might give them a brief advantage. Of Black Herran there was no sign, and the orc did not much care.

The humans' battle was almost over but Amogg's fight remained. A glorious death awaited her. The giant of golden fire staggered towards her, its eyes a lightning storm and its sword an inferno of godly magic. The Falcon Prince's real body was visible, a shadowy shape glimpsed in the heart of the blaze. What she could see, she could kill.

Beside the huge orc, Red Penny and the remnants of her female militia fought on, many drenched in blood as the better trained and better equipped soldiers pushed them hard. Only a quarter of the original group remained and not one without a wound.

Amogg Hadakk punched a soldier, snapping his neck and spinning his helmet around, then swung her axe wide, knocking three men onto their backs. She eyed up the Falcon Prince, trailed her eyes from him to the palisade and down the crude steps leading to the dirt. She hefted the axe of her ancestors and fancied her chances.

"Retreat to town," she said to Red Penny. "Find vampire. He fight good and be your war leader now. Maybe you survive."

Red Penny's battered spear thrust out, clanging into a shield. A sword came down and the spear head snapped, dangling on a shred of wood. She dropped it and snatched up an abandoned Lucent sword. "Nah, I fight with you."

Amogg shook her head and kicked a man to death. "Go, Red Penny, orc-friend. Fight later or die quick here. I give order."

Penny grimaced and pulled back as a blade nicked her thigh. "What will you do?"

Amogg grinned, ringed tusks exposed and skin flushed shades of angry red. "I prove Amogg the strongest. Make prince of birds and big burny goddess regret they kill Wundak without glory. The axe of my ancestors thirsts."

Amogg lifted her weapon and roared. The Lucent soldiers flinched and paused in their advance, too afraid to face the elder orc's mighty axe. The Tarnbrooke militia seized their chance to turn and flee for safety. She didn't think badly of them – they were only human. One brave and swift enemy soldier tried to slip past her, but she grabbed his head in one hand. His helmet and skull crumpled in her grip and she flung his corpse back at the rest of his clan.

The Falcon Prince's golden form stomped towards Amogg, no longer the terrifying and mountainous avatar of his Goddess but still a giant figure of holy wrath. It stamped the defensive ditch and stakes flat, then ploughed through part of the palisade that had taken weeks to build.

She had seen that fire burn up humans like dry straw but that race were all made of brittle sticks and squish. Amogg Hadakk was the blood of Gardram, bred for battle and glory. With their footmen hesitating and only inching forward, the Lucent archers shot at her. Amogg stood and did nothing, giving them this one last chance to kill her. Arrows fell all around. One tinged off her axe. Another tickled her belly. She plucked it out like a human would a thorn and tossed it aside.

"You are mine now, vile beast," the champion of the Bright One boomed as the giant figure closed on Amogg.

Amogg laughed. "No, you mine!" She raced up the steps to the walkway at the top of the palisade and then jumped, the strong muscles of an elder orc launching her up and at the Falcon Prince. Axe raised and ready, she hurtled towards his real body encased in holy flame.

The burning giant's lighting storm eyes widened in shock.

"Amogg Hadakk is strongest!" she roared as she slammed into it axe-first. The body of holy fire resisted that first impact of metal, but she was chieftain of the Hadakk and she knew the great god Gardram would be watching this fight. Her massive body hit the axe and her weight pushed it through.

Fire enveloped her and ate into the elder orc's flesh, burning up skin, fat and muscle. It was agony, but her glory was exquisite. Before her eyes boiled, she witnessed her mighty axe strike true. Gardram was with her! The Falcon Prince's helm and forehead split open and her axe buried itself in his brain. The tales of gods and magic humans defeated by Amogg of the Hadakk would spread far.

She *was* the mightiest warrior of all…

The militia climbed over barricades made of carts, tables and barrels filled with dirt and took up positions. Red Penny turned back to witness the last battle of Amogg Hadakk, her heart pounding with savage joy as she witnessed the axe strike home. She shaded her eyes as the fiery form of the Bright One exploded, incinerating what was left of Amogg and everything else for fifty paces all around.

She sagged against the wall, filled with a mix of awe, sadness and desperate hope.

The Falcon Prince fell to earth among the ashes of his own men, his armour blackened and broken and his skull in two pieces, pulsing grey and pink oozing from the hideous wound.

Red Penny ducked as something slammed into the wall by her head: a cherry-red sizzling axe embedded in stone. The huge weapon of Amogg Hadakk had been flung free of the blast.

The axe quickly cooled, and she reached up and tugged it free, staring at the blackened but still-sharp steel that felt strangely light, and so very right in her hands. An inhuman presence touched her mind then, and found her… acceptable. Savage drums and war horns sounded inside her head for a moment and a blood-mad fury filled her as she took an experimental swing with the huge weapon.

"Let's kill the fuckers!" she roared as she took up position, ignoring the stares of the militia as she easily wielded the mighty orcish war axe with her scrawny human arms.

Shock rippled through the remaining Lucent forces. Holy knights and soldiers stopped and stared at an impossible sight:

the champion of the Bright One felled by a brute of an orc. An orc. A lesser race. They could not comprehend it. An inquisitor approached the ruined figure of their fallen lord, hesitant gauntlet reaching out to pull a shard of metal free of his skull with a sucking sound as bits of bone and brain came loose with it.

The Falcon Prince's eyes snapped open. Golden light bled from the mortal wound in his head. "I... I cannot be killed. Yes... impossible. Impossible. She is with me always. Always... we made sure of that." He rose on shaky feet. All across the battlefield his men fell to their knees in worship. They had witnessed a miracle!

"Worship us not with words but with swords!" he shouted, casting about for his own blade, resorting to lifting a humble unadorned footman's weapon from the smoking mud. "For the Goddess!"

His men rose filled with righteous zeal and surged towards the town, a mass of steel and fury baying for blood. Lightning flashed as holy knights used their divine power to carry them past the hasty barricades manned by desperate locals.

"Here they come!" Red Penny shouted, a snarl on her face as she hefted the orcish axe. Her shoulders and legs ached from the strain of combat and her hands were slick with her own blood, a gaping wound running up her forearm. She didn't care. "Amogg split that bastard's skull open for us, so let's finish the job."

Cooper Street was blocked by a ragged bunch of pirates and female militia, but they stood steady as the steel tide rumbled towards them. They had nowhere to run – another army was coming down from the north, one they were desperately trying not to think about.

She knew inquisitors were now behind their line somewhere in the centre of town, but didn't have time to think about it before soldiers crashed into the barricade, climbing it and hauling parts away from the other side. All thought dissolved into the madness of cut and kill.

Red Penny hacked and butchered, the axe of Amogg shedding hands and heads as she held the line. None of the enemy could withstand her, but she was only one woman.

A seamstress to her right went down screaming with a belly wound. To her left a militiawoman's face was laid open by a sword cut and she fell back trying to hold half of it on. Wooden armour, leather, rusted mail and pot-helms were insufficient to the task of protecting them. The militia and townsfolk were insufficient. They were farmers and shepherds, spinners and craftsfolk, not warriors. The remaining Awildan pirates were harder men and women but they were pitifully few. All of them were about to die.

A Lucent soldier scrambled up the barricade, leapt and landed in the space vacated right next to Red Penny. She turned – too slow – and his lips twisted into a savage grin.

The barricade exploded upwards, barrels and broken carts flying as a wall of solid stone rose from the bones of the earth to block off Cooper Street.

The single Lucent soldier gasped, his eyes widening as an old woman with white hair and a walking stick clacked towards him. He recognised her. The blood drained from his face.

"I have rested enough," Black Herran said, examining her blood-smeared enchanted ring.

The air turned black, thick with shadows that clawed at the soldier, stripping the sword and armour from his flailing limbs. Liquid darkness swallowed him and sank back into the earth below her feet.

Black Herran gasped and clutched her chest, breath hissing. She formed a fist and pounded it until the spasm passed. "Assist me," she demanded. Red Penny and two others leapt to it.

She was able to block three more streets with walls of stone before succumbing to a blood-flecked coughing fit. "Enough. I am done."

"Indeed you are," Maeven said as she approached down a side street, glistening black blade in hand. Blood dripped from it, and it seemed to squirm and throb in her hand. "It is time for you to honour our bargain. Where is my sister?"

Her tattooed, scarred face turned to the terrified militia. "Leave us."

They hesitated. The necromancer pointed to a bearded pirate and he fell dead as a rock, untouched by any weapon. The rest got the idea and fled, leaving the two magic users alone to finish whatever vile business they had begun.

Red Penny refused to look back: she had far more pressing concerns, and axe or not, she had no intention of facing down demons or the dead.

CHAPTER 40

Tiarnach groaned and shifted weight off his left leg. Something in his knee was broken, two shards of bone grinding together like quern stones. Not much else of him was intact or working as intended. He stood in the gaping hole he'd made in the temple, a sword in each hand, and got ready for his last battle.

Many of the townsfolk who couldn't fight had unwisely chosen to barricade themselves in the cellars of their own homes instead of hiding in the temple. Flames roared up from nearby buildings, hungry tongues spreading from roof to roof. Screams and the clash of steel closed in on the temple. A screaming cart horse galloped past, its mane on fire.

A helmetless inquisitor with shaved scalp dashed through a nearby alley and cut down a couple fleeing their burning home. He spotted the temple and the mass of people huddled inside its heathen walls and noted its single battered guardian. A grin spread across his face.

Tiarnach glanced back at the children. "Clear a space behind me, these pretty boys like spurting fire."

"Do any of you worship the Bright One?" the knight demanded as he approached their refuge.

Tiarnach noisily hawked up a blob of congealing blood and snot. "Nah. Her tits are no' big enough for me."

The inquisitor gasped and his sword ignited with the

power of his Goddess. "You will burn for that blasphemy."

Golden fire splashed against Tiarnach's chest. It was devoid of any actual divine will – just a sluice gate opened. All that power and all it did was make Tiarnach stronger. He yawned and limped right through the torrent, sword out and ready.

"Oh aye?" he mocked. "And when does the burning start? Tell a man, does your goddess suck your wee cock? Or were her lips open just for me?"

The inquisitor screamed and abandoned his holy power for good old-fashioned bloody murder. He came at Tiarnach swinging furiously. Tiarnach deflected the cut in exchange for a length of steel shaved off his own blade. His bad knee came up to ram into the knight's groin with the power of a small god. Bone cracked further but steel gave way and bent inwards.

His leg was broken anyway, Tiarnach had figured, so a little bit more wouldn't hurt – except it really fucking did.

The knight dropped, clutching his mangled groin, a strangled whine emerging from his mouth. Bright blood pissed down his greaves.

Tiarnach hissed in pain and hopped to him. He plunged his sword through the knight's neck, sawing the point back and forth until the man lay still.

"Aye, aye, all big and brave with power fit to burn a man to ash," he said. "Piss-poor fighter without it." Then he needed a piss, so he yanked his tunic up and sprayed it all over the dead inquisitor.

He limped back to the hole in the wall as terrified faces peered out at him. He nodded to the children and resumed his position. The adults seemed as terrified of him as they were of the Lucent Empire, but the children waved and held up their forks and eating knives. They loved him for being a bold bastard with a dirty tongue. They believed he was a god, and their small but pure belief filled him up like a starving man handed a jack of ale and a hunk of buttered bread.

Two more inquisitors with gore-crusted swords emerged from

a line of burning buildings with their visors up. One was tall and slender, and the other short but wide as an orc with an ugly face shiny with sweat. They noticed their dead friend and instead of charging immediately they lowered visors and moved to flank him, Tall Boy to the left and Orc Man to the right.

Tiarnach sighed. This fight was going to be a bitch.

Lorimer Felle fought the enemy in the middle of the street. He stood steadfast in the centre of a storm of swords. They pierced and cut his flesh in a dozen places as the Lucent Empire overran the Tarnbrooke positions, pushing the desperate militia led by Estevan and Red Penny back towards the market square and the vulnerable families sheltering inside the temple. The enemy were superbly trained veterans, vicious and determined, well-armed and armoured… and utterly unable to kill the vampire lord.

He found it all terribly boring.

His claws raked through a soldier's helmet, piercing steel, face and skull. He tossed the man aside and sank his fangs into the throat of the next, steel squealing as his teeth punched through armour to feast on hot pulsing blood. It proved a bitter meal. He ripped a chunk out and painted the man's fellows red, chewing thoughtfully while an enemy sword slid through his ribs and another opened up his belly.

Lorimer did not allow his intestines to fall to the filthy ground; instead they slurped and wriggled back into place, the wound sealing up behind them.

Try as they might, their blades could not destroy him. From behind the enemy battle line, a dozen archers took aim and loosed. He could not dodge them all and wooden shafts pierced his heart and lungs.

He yawned as his body ejected the offending arrows. He ripped the shield arm off a screaming soldier and beat the next man to death with it. "Do not believe all those old tales of wooden stakes through the heart killing my kind. It is merely a muscle like any other."

He blurred into action, claws ripping men open left and right, punches and kicks crushing skulls and shattering ribcages. He was bored, but he was also buying time for Estevan to retreat to safety and throw up more defences. That mortal was the only thing important to Lorimer in this entire dreary town. Well, that and Maeven's promise to help retake his homeland.

"Where are your god-touched knights and your vaunted holy powers?" he shouted, grabbing a soldier's hand and squeezing until it popped. He snatched the falling sword and danced among them, too swift and skilful to stop, and too strong to resist. They quailed before him. The vampire snarled as they whimpered and fell back stinking of terror. "Fight me!"

"I will fight you, creature of darkness," a voice cried. The Lucent soldiers peeled back to form a corridor. A dishevelled, golden-eyed knight with a haggard face covered in blood limped forward, flanked by four inquisitors bearing deadly burning blades. The Falcon Prince had come, his skull split down the middle of the forehead and held together only by magic and willpower.

A shiver of unaccustomed weakness ripped through Lorimer. He spied six robed acolytes murmuring prayers against him, and had to concentrate to shrug off their power. "Hello, Amadden," he said. "It has been a long time since last we talked. And time, it seems, has not been kind to your looks. Still, you have risen far since the days when you were one of Black Herran's captains."

Shocked faces turned to the Falcon Prince, whose lips thinned to bloodless lines. "Speak not of that treacherous whore," he yelled. "Once I have taken your head, I will have hers too."

Lorimer sighed and shook his head sadly. "Come, come. There is no need for vulgarity between two gentlemen, especially from one who bears the title of prince. I can fix your

face before we begin, if you would like? It would be the work
of moments, and the least I can do for an old ally. Your chosen
weapon is the longsword, is it not? I am eager to see how your
skills have grown."

"We were never allies," the Falcon Prince snarled, golden
light burning in his eyes. "And this is no duel, monster, this
is an extermination of vermin." He bellowed in rage and
unleashed a torrent of golden fire down the street towards the
vampire. All four holy knights accompanying him added their
magical might to his own. The buildings on either side erupted
into flames, stone walls and metal fixings running like water.
The muddy ground baked hard and brittle.

The fire dwindled and the Falcon Prince fell to one knee,
panting. Fresh blood poured down his face – he had used the
power of the Bright One to attack instead of keeping his broken
form together. Worried footmen helped him back up.

Smoke belched from the ruined homes on either side of the
street. "Check for any sign of a body," he demanded. "That was
Lorimer Felle, the last and most dreadful of the vampires."

Two holy knights strode down the street, eyes straining
through smoke and drifting ash.

The ground exploded beneath them, claws screeching
through steel and bone as an unholy burned beast rose from the
earth. Lorimer's smoking and sizzling hand speared through an
inquisitor's breastplate and ripped the heart free in a shower of
gore. He was on the other in a heartbeat, the vampire's head
shifting into that of a vicious wolf. His jaws clamped either
side of the knight's helmet. The knight screamed – briefly – as
helmet and skull both crumpled under the pressure.

The vampire turned to face his foes, a nightmarish amalgam
of man and wolf that gave them pause. "That was unsporting,"
he growled. "One might even consider it the height of rudeness."

He leapt into action, charging at the Falcon Prince five times
faster than any man. His jaws opened wide, bloody fangs ready
to rip and tear.

The Falcon Prince opened his arms wide in welcome and his head faced skywards, eyes closed in prayer.

A hand's-breadth from tearing off his face, the Lucent Goddess' power stopped Lorimer's charge. Massive weight slammed down on him. He growled and fought against it, claws inching towards vulnerable flesh, so close he could smell the blood of his prey. "Duel me like a man, Amadden," he said. "If you dare, without hiding behind your cruel god."

The force pressing down on Lorimer doubled. Trebled. Irresistible force slammed him to the ground, bones cracking and grinding as if stamped on by a giant boot. He tried to rise and failed to lift so much as a finger.

"Men do not duel dangerous animals," the Falcon Prince said, teeth clenched and blood running down his face. "They hunt them down and dispose of them."

Lorimer managed a chuckle. "The sheer arrogance of assuming that everything you believe to be just and true happens to be so. And that the many who disagree with you are evil, or somehow lesser. You are deluded to declare your many murders righteous by painting white over the blackest of deeds. You have made a murdering tyrant of yourself."

"You are naught but a beast given life by dark magic," the Falcon Prince said. "All life must die, and all darkness must be purified by Her light." He looked to his men. "Burn this thing to ash."

His remaining two holy knights stepped forward and extended their swords. Fire poured over the motionless vampire at their feet. Acolytes stepped forward to add their prayers to the assault.

Lorimer Felle was no stranger to pain, but even he screamed as his flesh was burned away layer by layer. He bit back the agony and resolved to die with pride. "You may have defeated me," he snarled, "but the good and the free will always rise to thwart you, tyrant." He grinned, his lips burning away to expose nightmarish fangs. "My people will be free. This is not over."

The Falcon Prince did not deign to answer. He watched the vampire burn until it fell silent, the legend that was Lorimer Felle reduced to nothing but macabre bones crumbling to ash in the centre of that magical inferno.

Of the many things the lying beast had said to him, it was not his words but that last grin that got under the Falcon Prince's skin. For a moment he felt a heavy doom upon his back. He prayed to his Goddess and in her light shook it off. Then he marched onwards into the town in search of Black Herran and his depraved sister.

Predictably, the two inquisitors tried their fire on Tiarnach first. They were nothing if not dull-witted pricks.

"Argh," the war god cried, writhing in the centre of the blaze. "Aw naw, you got me, you mighty bastards! I'm burning to death. Burning, I say!"

Tall Boy and Orc Man intensified the blaze, gritting their teeth against the pain such effort caused them. Mortal bodies were not sturdy enough to channel a god's power for long, and they had already done so several times during the assault on the town. Tiarnach, on the other hand, was able to steal a little of that unfocused divine power for his own, the worst of his wounds steaming as they slowly closed up. Sadly, his body remained a wreck and his knee was still in bits.

He reckoned it might have been his sniggering that gave the game away.

On seeing him healing, they cut off their fire. After a moment's consideration their burning blades also extinguished. They intended to use mortal steel to end him.

"Aw," he said with a sad face. "And here I thought you were going to heal me all up."

Tall Boy scowled. "I do not know what manner of dark creature you are to withstand the Bright One's touch, but your reign of terror ends here."

Tiarnach nodded back to the people cowering inside the temple. "Aye, right. Reign o' terror, is it? I'm not the arseholes burning towns and villages and ripping wee babes from their mother's breasts."

That got their attention focused solely on him, with nothing left over for the civilians inside the temple behind him. His body was hurting, but he was a hard bastard through and through, and he'd be damned if he'd let runts like these put him in the mud; he still had the Falcon Prince to face.

Tall Boy attacked from the left and the squat Orc Man from the right, identical opening moves to every one of the Lucent knights he'd fought so far – diagonal cuts meant to open him up from shoulder to opposite hip. These knights were drilled to perfection, which made them all too easy to predict. If he'd fought one, he'd fought them all.

Tiarnach's knee was done for, so his movement was limited. He couldn't parry one and dodge the other so instead he attacked Tall Boy, who boasted the greater reach. The other knight's sword cut only air as he moved, and Tall Boy's sword was still descending as Tiarnach dashed forward into the blow, with an explosion of pain from his knee.

The inquisitor's eyes widened in panic as Tiarnach's sword point came up, scraping along his chest plate and up through the soft tissue under the chin, cleaving through the roof of Tall Boy's mouth and into the brain.

Tiarnach abandoned that sword in its holy skull and tried to spin to take the next attack head on, but his leg betrayed him and buckled, pitching him to the dirt.

A steel boot slammed onto his left hand, crushing the bone around the sword hilt. He screamed and rolled, the knight kicking his sword away. He was unarmed. He was fucked. Through the slit in the knight's helmet, Tiarnach glimpsed Orc Man's teeth bared in glee, his eyes bulging.

"Time to die, monster," the knight roared. He lifted his sword.

A wooden stool crashed into the man's helmet, staggering him. A pot of piss shattered on his cuirass, followed by a rock.

Tiarnach gaped as the townsfolk streamed out of the hole he'd made in the side of the temple, makeshift weapons in hand.

Dozens of old folk and children screamed and rained down mugs and pottery. It was an impressive assault, but their enemy wore full harness of fine steel, making it almost impossible to harm him. Almost. One lucky throw got a shard through the eye slit to catch Orc Man in the eyebrow, drawing blood.

"What is wrong with you heathens?" the knight yelled. "You serve monsters. Turn towards the light!"

An old woman spat on him, spittle sliding down his shiny steel. "Ain't no monsters here but you."

The inquisitor's eyes hardened, mad with zeal. He was moments away from slaughtering the young and the old.

Tiarnach frantically searched the muddy ground next to him for a weapon – any weapon. He knew that golden fire was coming. His fingers buried themselves in a warm pile of horse manure. It would have to do. He howled and threw the steaming pile at the holy knight.

Praise me! Tiarnach thought as the mess hit the helmet, clogging up eye slits and breathing holes. Horse shit in the man's eyes and mouth!

The knight reeled back, pawing at his helmet. The townsfolk swarmed him. His flailing sword slit a woman's shoulder open but he was only one man, however skilled and powerful. The horde of peasants knocked him to the ground and laid into him with makeshift clubs and rocks. Steel pounded like a drum. The children were there too, knives and forks digging into vulnerable armpits, groin and neck. Spinsters fell on him, knitting needles stabbing in through the visor.

The holy knight, one of the elite of the Bright One, died like a rat in a sack.

The townsfolk stood over the battered corpse, breathing

heavily and shaking with terror. A little girl with a bloodied fork turned wide eyes to Tiarnach and raised her weapon in salute.

"Get me back up," he ordered as the sounds of battle nearby eased off. Most of the militia had been slaughtered. "More will be coming."

One broken leg and a mangled hand. He could still fight as long as he didn't have to move.

Lucent soldiers appeared in ones and twos, done cleansing nearby buildings of their cowering occupants. They eyed the dead inquisitors and wisely waited for more men to arrive.

Tiarnach ushered the townsfolk back inside the safety of the temple walls and took up position at the hole. He would not move. He would protect his people or die trying.

Tiarnach blinked.

His people.

He knew it for the truth. They had given him new courage, and a kind of peace came with it. He had failed the Cahal'gilroy, but he refused to fail the people of Tarnbrooke.

It was a strange sort of feeling, this desire to protect. The Cahal'gilroy had been bloody-handed reivers, exulting in their martial prowess and taking whatever they wanted from those weaker than them. He had revelled in it... but what was this well of newfound strength inside him? The belief of the people of Tarnbrooke flowed into him, not enough to heal much of anything quickly, but enough to enable him to stand and fight.

"Well, fuck me," he muttered as self-realisation washed over him. He felt better about butchering reivers than he ever had being one.

Well then, the war god thought, his task was simple: he would just stand here and kill all the enemy until their bloody Falcon Prince dared show his face.

CHAPTER 41

"Where is my sister?" Maeven demanded. "Tell me now and this town can still be saved. Your own family might not be here, but I will find them, and I will gift them eternal torment if you do not."

Black Herran cackled. "You cannot reach my family. That is not within your power, only mine."

The tattoo writhed angrily across Maeven's face. "Ah, then you must have sent them to Hellrath," she said through gritted teeth. "Always plans within plans. If they are safe, then why all the mummery of protecting this town?"

"Why indeed," Black Herran said. "Tarnbrooke has been my home for decades, and its people are good and decent folk. That is reason enough. One last good act among all the bad."

The demonologist leaned heavily on her walking stick. "A deal is a deal, however. Grace is in the temple of the Bright One in the Lucent capital of Brightwater. Not that garish great temple they built in the city, but a small private chapel deep below the old queen's palace out on the lake. Amadden has kept her locked away there for decades, safe from all harm, and all independence. I have never lied to you; this is the truth."

Maeven knew it was. "Thank you," she said, fingers gripping her black blade tight.

"I suppose you will kill me now?" Black Herran said. "I am too old and exhausted to resist, but I have all that I need from this life."

"Burn in Hellrath," Maeven said. "May your family join you in torment." She plunged the blade into her old general's chest and pierced what remained of the heart.

Black Herran gasped, magic sucking at her stubborn soul. She pulled the necromancer in close and kissed her on her scarred cheek face. "I will be seeing you. Soon."

Maeven flinched as Black Herran laughed, cruel and mocking. She shoved the knife in deeper. Harder. Twisting it in the hag's heart.

The old woman shuddered, then sagged in her arms.

The dread demonologist, the legendary general who could have ruled all Essoran if not the world, died with a soft exhalation and a smile on her lips. Maeven dropped her onto the ground, a small and fragile corpse that had housed burning soul and iron will enough to rival the very gods themselves. She scrubbed at her cheek, fearing some sort of last trick, but found only her own paranoia.

Maeven stared at the knife. No soul had flowed into it. Black Herran had been correct; that corrupt thing was long since claimed by something else. But her death had released just enough potent energy to fully awaken the weapon.

It pulsed in her hand, a heartbeat flush with warmth, with immeasurable power. A shard of the void beyond life: death incarnate. A weapon that could kill anything.

After all these years of building up the enchantments, we have finally completed our great work, her grandfather said, his voice dry as parchment and old bone. *Use that power wisely.*

She shrugged off her backpack and let it drop, taking out his finger bones and tossing them to the cobbles. "Thank you for all your tuition, grandfather. I no longer have any need of you." She ground his bones to dust beneath her heel.

She felt the ghost's shudder of relief as his soul was freed from its necromantic bindings. Her grandfather embraced his long-delayed death, and she allowed his soul to blow away on the wind.

She prodded Black Herran's corpse, just in case. She was really gone. Maeven ripped the enchanted rings off her old general's hands, breaking the fingers in the process. Whatever she couldn't use, she would be able to sell for a king's ransom.

She headed for the town's temple. Amadden would undoubtedly head there to tear down every sign of heathen worship. Her brother had never been imaginative.

She followed the sounds of battle and came to the temple, now with a gaping hole in one side. Corpses were piled up outside, three in the heavy armour of holy knights, and a dozen more in the garb of common foot soldiers.

Two soldiers lay gasping and clutching mortal wounds. As she walked past, she willed their hearts to stop, a death too good for them.

Tiarnach sat with his back propped up against the wall by the entrance of the temple, the earth beneath him stained dark. He was covered in dreadful wounds and his long red hair on one side was shorn to stubble, bone visible through a wide gash. Blood poured down his face and beard. Terrified faces of townsfolk peered out at the necromancer from the entrance he guarded.

"Maeven," he gasped, lips twisting in pain. "Not seeing me at my best."

She studied him for a moment. "That's arguable. I had expected you to be dead by now. Or fled."

"So sorry to disappoint," he said. "How do you fare?"

"Black Herran is dead."

He glanced at the obsidian knife in her hand. "Killed the cow yourself, did you? I can smell her sorcery on you. Ach well. Not unexpected, I have to say. What o' the others?"

"All dead."

"Bunch of weaklings," he snarled. "Just us hard bastards left standing at the end, eh?"

She snorted. "You do not seem to be standing right now."

"An old man needs a wee rest now and again," he snapped.

"Still got your fucking brother to behead, don't I? Where is the whelp?"

She looked to the south, where the last few defenders were fleeing for their lives through narrow streets and alleys, Red Penny leading a valiant but futile rear guard. "He shall be along presently."

She looked to her knife, and then at the ruined war god.

"You'll no' get much out of me," he said. "I'm wrung dry."

Her gaze moved to the townsfolk cowering in the temple behind him.

His eyes went cold and hard. "I wouldn't if I were you, wench. I've just enough left in me to deal with one corpse-botherer."

"I very much doubt it, you old drunkard," she said, but did not act on her impulse.

"I would murder for a cold ale," he muttered.

Lucent soldiers began arriving in force, heralding the Falcon Prince's entrance. They formed up in a line facing the temple, shields up and bloodied swords ready.

"Perhaps later," she said. "He's here."

Tiarnach heaved himself up onto one good leg, swaying dangerously, sword dangling from his one working arm.

The Falcon Prince limped towards them, his split skull leaking golden fire in spurts and hisses. His armour was a tattered ruin and his eyes dark and haunted. Somehow, he still managed to exude an aura of confidence and command.

His gaze met Maeven's and he stopped dead. His expression fell blank. "This slaughter is your doing, necromancer."

"Ah, my dear brother," she replied. "As always, you fail to take ownership of your dark deeds and selfish desires. The perverse thing you call a religion is all your own doing, Amadden. This invasion and slaughter are by your will."

The Falcon Prince's face turned to Tiarnach, standing amidst the corpses of his beloved righteous army. "The savage that calls himself a god. I thought I had ended you years ago. No matter."

Tiarnach spat a congealed lump of blood towards him. "I am a fucking god, you thief."

"Thief?" the Falcon Prince exclaimed. "In what way?"

"That holy fire is not yours," Tiarnach said. "There is no divine will behind what you do with it. You steal her lifeblood and make a weapon of it."

The Falcon Prince bared his teeth in a bloody snarl. "You know nothing. Vile monsters. You will be purged from Her world. Kill the witch." He limped towards Tiarnach with his burning sword out while his men surged towards Maeven.

Tiarnach knew he couldn't win. He could feel the divine power filling the Falcon Prince up like a man's bladder after a full day of downing ale. All he could do was slow him down and give that wretched necromancer more time to deal with his army. She hated her brother even more than Tiarnach did.

The Falcon Prince's mobility was hampered by wounds, less so than Tiarnach but the war god used it to draw the fight out and lead him away from the temple and the occupants he was protecting. He hopped away as the Falcon Prince gave clumsy chase.

Holy fire rolled over him. "That tickles!" Tiarnach shouted, feeling the blood flow from his scalp cease as he absorbed a little of that divine power. His knee felt like it might even bear a little weight.

"Impossible!" came the reply.

"Ach well," Tiarnach yelled. "The Bright One wouldn't want to burn her lover up now, would she? She loves my big hard cock." He put on a woman's voice and began to moan in ecstasy. "Oh, Tiarnach!"

Veins bulged in the Falcon Prince's neck and forehead. He screamed and broke into a lumbering charge. Both swung swords, but with different purposes. The Falcon Prince brought his round in a vicious but entirely predictable diagonal slash.

Tiarnach's cut came later, aiming for hand and sword rather than a mortal wound.

Tiarnach turned as the slash came in, sacrificing his mangled left arm and a few ribs to the burning blade. There was no resistance as it sliced through flesh and bone and took off his arm, and that was exactly what the war god had been counting on. The Falcon Prince overbalanced, his sword hand extended and vulnerable. A sword that cut through anything could also be a dangerous liability.

He hammered his sword down on the Falcon Prince's wrist. Plate armour was marvellous for stopping cuts, but his wasn't intact and there was little padding left to cushion such a heavy blow. Sword and wrist both broke with a loud crack.

Tiarnach fell atop him as both swords dropped to the dirt. The Falcon Prince rolled him over and slammed a knee into already severed ribs, crushing them inwards to pierce his lungs.

He aimed his spurting stump of an arm and jetted his blood into the Falcon Prince's eyes. Even blinded, he had the war god on his back and at his mercy. Steel-clad elbows, feet and knees were driven into the war god's torso again and again and again until Tiarnach lay still and broken underneath him, blood frothing his red beard.

The Falcon Prince stood, and clumsily wiped the blood from his eyes. He cleared his vision to see his foe grinning even as death approached.

Tiarnach managed one last wheezing chuckle as the Falcon Prince spun to witness the last of his men fall dead at his hateful sister's feet.

He might not have taken the bastard's head, but Tiarnach had ensured Maeven would. He died content, if death it could be called when you were a god.

Maeven enjoyed murdering the soldiers, her necrotic power stopping hearts and decaying brains. Two archers at the back died choking on swollen black tongues. The remaining inquisitors came at her head on, but now she had her awakened blade. She held it up and called to their souls. She snuffed out their lives like candles caught in a storm, and sucked their souls into it. Armoured forms fell like dead flies.

She walked among them sowing death and reaping souls to grant her ever more power, savouring the death of hope in the acolytes' eyes as they realised all their faith in their goddess could not save them.

Tiarnach had kept her brother occupied long enough for her to eradicate the little pests and ensure there would be no more distractions. She appreciated his consideration, which was not something she could have thought possible when this all began. He had proven surprisingly durable.

Her brother howled in rage as he beheld all of his followers dead at her feet. She exulted in his pain, anger and frustration.

They walked towards each other – their first meeting in forty years. It would also be their last.

"Sister," he hissed.

"Brother." She smiled at the hideous axe wound splitting his skull, the scars he had inflicted on her own face pulling tight. "It seems fate has decided to repay you for your betrayal. How delicious. If only Amogg Hadakk had cut a little deeper."

Golden fire spat from his head wound, angry tongues of devouring magic reaching towards her. She lifted her deathly void blade and divine fire flinched back.

"What have you done to Grace?" she demanded. Maeven cared nothing for empires, religion or conquest. All she cared about was finding her long-lost sister, the one person in the world she had ever loved.

"I have kept my sister safe from all the corruptions and evils of this world," he said. "Including you. You will never lay a hand on my pure and perfect sister."

"She is my sister too," Maeven replied. "And you keep her locked away like a pet."

He scowled. "You are no kin of ours. You are a vile worshipper of death and decay, not fit to set foot upon the righteous world I am building for her."

"You build this cruel world only for yourself, you self-obsessed fanatic," Maeven spat. "You never once asked Grace what she wanted, did you? Of course not. So, I am no sister of yours, am I?"

She struck first, talons of darkness striking at his heart. They shattered on his breastplate, his torn flesh still protected by the power of the Lucent Goddess. Maeven hadn't expected it to be so easy but it allowed her to gauge his remaining strength. Even after the damage inflicted by the giant demon, by Amogg's axe and Tiarnach's sword, it seemed he still overmatched her in raw physical and magical might. If he fought with careful calculation there was a chance he might even win, but she would never allow that to pass.

"I will kill you," she said. "And then I will bury my blade in the heart of your beloved Bright One and eat her soul."

Any sanity Amadden had left snapped. His eyes lost all semblance of control and humanity. He screamed. Golden flames boiled out of his wounds until fire sheathed him like a second skin. He loomed large above Maeven, four times the size he had been moments before. No artful sword technique for him now, just burning hands and feet filled with the primal urge to crush and kill. He swiped a hand through a building and she was forced to dodge the flaming debris.

She backed away, one hand lifted high and filled with necromantic magic. "Rise!"

The corpses of footmen and holy knights climbed to their feet, weapons clutched in hands that still remembered what to do with them. Only one corpse refused to obey her will. Tiarnach lay where he had fallen, stubbornly disobedient even after death, his eyes staring at her, filled with warning.

She moved away from the temple and its huddle of dirty peasants, and watched her corpse army swarm the burning figure of her god-touched brother. His terrible rage and golden fists incinerated them with every swing. Powerful as he still was, he had been greatly weakened by his battles and the occasional sword managed to pierce his body before he burned its wielder to ash. Red blood flowed along with the gold.

A squad of battered Lucent soldiers emerged from a side street, looking from her to their lord and back again. She reached into their chests and rotted their organs, then sent their corpses into battle on her behalf. It was far safer to kill her brother's men and send them to slow him down than it was to fight him directly. It was a death by a hundred pinpricks, his blood shed by the hands of his own men. How galling for him, she thought.

She fled south, reanimating the fallen as she went. A goodly number of Lucent soldiers had spread out through the town, kicking in doors and killing all those who resisted. And all the townsfolk resisted, whether they wanted to or not. She came upon several small groups and ripped the life from them on the spot. Any dazed survivors from Tarnbrooke she left alive, not because of any altruism but because they were weak and she had better prospects elsewhere.

Amadden roared as his burning body crashed through a house. He stumbled after her, swatting at the stinging corpses that plagued him.

She reached the tumbled, blackened remnants of the palisade and the piles of dead militia tangled up with Lucent soldiers. She recognised one she had spoken to before, a moustachioed man by the name of Nicholas. He rose with his fellows, picked up a spear, and they formed up into a wall of dead men blocking her brother's exit from the street. They lowered spears and marched. Lucent footmen crowded behind them, broken shields and bent swords at the ready. All this to weaken her brother enough to finally kill him. Her knife could have ended him in a moment, but getting close enough to use it was an unacceptable risk.

She looked to the huge demonic corpse of Malifer, but her power found no purchase in the demon's inhuman flesh.

Maeven awaited him in that place of death as he rampaged through her corpse army. The spears and swords took their toll on him, and his flaming armour flickered and dwindled as he left a trail of blood through the streets.

Finally, he stood before her, mere wisps of divine power leaking from him. His armour was shredded and his chest heaved for breath. He held a broken sword in his hand, devoid of holy flame.

She gripped her blade tight and lifted her hands high and wide, inviting him in as he closed on her. "If you really feel nothing for me then come, run your sword through my heart. I will not resist my brother's blade."

He snarled, and obliged. His sword split her heart and burst from her back. "Die, filth."

She wrapped her hands around him, pulling her brother into an embrace, her mouth at his ear. "I'm also heartless, or so Lorimer said."

Her black blade stabbed into his neck.

Death.

The golden fire winked out and his skull yawned open, brain fluids oozing out.

He sagged instantly, heavy in her arms. She dropped her brother like the garbage he was and frowned at the obsidian blade in her hand, watching as bright drips of red ran down the black.

There was no soul in that body to eat. But there had been something... A hint of power ripping him away just as she struck, something carrying his soul away to the far north. Brightwater.

His damned goddess had cheated her.

CHAPTER 42

Lucent Empire soldiers arrived, took one look at the corpse of their leader on the ground and fled for their lives. For most, the battle was now over.

As the town burned and the few remaining Lucent soldiers fought the ragged remnants of the town militia, Maeven sat on a bench and sewed up her chest wound with a needle and thread, the stitches neat as any seamstress. She willed the healing of her body to begin, slow and steady and directed. She was not quite a dead thing, half-alive at best and happy to keep it that way. Necromancy was such a useful skill.

A woman screamed nearby, shrill and annoying. It disturbed her sewing. She reanimated a dozen or so Lucent soldiers and set them hunting down their living brothers – anything for a little peace and quiet.

She finished up, tied off the threads and looked to the north, to where another Lucent army was marching through the Mhorran Valley towards Tarnbrooke, now only a few hours away. She got to her feet, cricked her neck from side to side and walked towards them. They were only mortal, and she was death incarnate. All they could do to her now was make her stronger.

Weeks later the necromancer arrived at the northern city of Brightwater at the head of an army of thousands of corpses that obeyed her every command. She sat on a padded shield held aloft on the shoulders of four dead soldiers, seeing no need to tire herself out when the relentless dead felt no pain or fatigue. They were by now, for want of a better word, ripe, and rotting.

It was a sunny morning and the lake glistened around the high towers of the castle on Lake Ellsmere, where the Bright One's chapel and her sister waited. The city itself appeared clean and organised, with the Bright One's sunburst emblem flying from whitewashed towers and brass spires across the urban sprawl. A newly built cathedral loomed large over the city, a glorious edifice furnished with stained glass and gold. It was a beautiful and peaceful scene, one she was about to ruin.

The knife thrummed in her hand as she waved her army forward, bodies empowered by their own stolen souls. To animate and control so many at once had been far beyond her abilities until the knife had fully awakened; Laurant Daryn and his hundreds had been such a strain, even though their old commander had operated as a secondary nexus of control. Now, commanding thousands of armed dead proved a simple thing.

After all these years of searching and preparing to free her sister, it was finally time. She had the power of countless souls, deadly arcane skill, and with her brother and most of his holy knights dead, and their main army destroyed, she finally had the opportunity.

For the first time in many years, Maeven felt afraid. What would Grace be like after being hidden so long away and "protected" by Amadden? Would he have forced her to join his twisted religion?

The guards on the city gates were confused at first, only seeing the Lucent army returned home unannounced. They were slow to close the gates and lower the portcullis. Slower still when she reached out and stilled their hearts. Her army poured through the gate and slaughtered anything that moved: men, women, children, animals, she didn't much care. Her attention was focused solely on reaching the castle at the centre of the lake.

She willed a hundred of her dead towards the cathedral with orders to kill everything and burn the place down. It was an abomination to her eyes. The rest poured ahead of her, a screaming tide of peasants, merchants and priests fleeing or falling before them. What few soldiers remained in the capital of the Lucent Empire were old or still in training. They put up only feeble resistance to her army of the dead, shrieking in horror as mortal wounds did little more than slow the corpses down.

The palace of the old queen lay ahead, the sunburst emblem of the Lucent Empire adorning every high wall and flying from every tower. The drawbridge was up, and an expanse of shimmering water cut it off from the city. Mailed bowmen and men in the battle plate of inquisitors lined the walls. It was a formidable force, but Maeven was beyond them all now.

She willed her shield-bearers to lower her down and she walked forward to the edge of the water, well within bowshot of the highest towers. She lifted her hands and summoned the power of the void. Black and green necrotic energies writhed into the air from her outstretched fingers and a dark mist boiled from her mouth, swiftly rising in a cloud above her.

Arrows flew from the towers. Wooden shafts rotted to nothingness and corroded steel crumbled into the lake. Her cloud of death billowed up and out across the walls of the fortress. Men bled from the eyes, ears and nose, coughing up streams of blood and bile as they died in agony. The holy knights survived only a little longer, divine radiance flickering around them as they staggered to and fro atop the walls clutching at their throats.

Then the dead rose inside the fortress and lowered the drawbridge to welcome their master.

She entered the courtyard and admired what was once

beautiful scenery, the dead flowers and brown ivy, the wormy wooden benches and mouldering wall hangings. If only it was easier to target only living humans.

She took a deep breath and delved into the minds of the recent Lucent dead. It was one aspect of necromancy she did not relish. They had only been dead for a matter of minutes but already the corpses' brains were decaying, all thought breaking down to a shattered mirror of memory fragments. She found what she sought and wrenched herself free from the sucking grasp of that greediest of mistresses, death.

The thick oak door of the keep crumbled before her. She entered the great hall where her wretched brother once sat at court surrounded by his boot-lickers, and turned down a narrow spiral staircase.

At the landing below, desperate priests and acolytes tried and failed to stop her. Those howling fanatics flung themselves into the very face of death. One last stand to save their goddess, over in an instant. It was admirable in its own stupid way.

She paused before the white doors leading to the most sacred chapel of the Bright One. Ornate carvings of vines and leaves covered them, picked out in gold and silver, inlaid with emerald and ruby and mother of pearl. Maeven took a deep breath and then pushed them open.

Inside was a plain chamber of pink marble that reflected the light of dozens of brass lanterns. It lacked the ostentatious artwork found in the rest of the capital, and boasted nothing grand like the great cathedral raised in the Bright One's honour. Fresh flowers sat in sconces all along the walls, a riot of rich yellows, creamy whites and pale pinks.

A door lay wide open to one side, revealing a glimpse of a four-posted bed covered in luxurious silk, soft fur and an army of stitched children's toys, some old and worn, others bright and new and arranged into neat lines. Maeven's wounded heart pounded painfully in her breast – one of those toys, a much-patched brown sackcloth horse with one eye, belonged to her sister. Her wonderful, gentle, simple sister. Racks of fine dresses lined the far wall, all of a size for Grace as she remembered her. The chambers were neat and orderly, and not lived in; more like a shrine of sorts.

Further ahead, a slender woman in a green silk gown knelt before a marble statue of the Bright One, depicted in a long flowing dress with flowers in her hair. The woman's ankle-length blonde hair spilled around her bare feet like a halo of light.

Maeven swallowed and looked around, but the chambers were empty. No holy knights or priests. Just her little sister waiting to be freed. Every dark deed, disgusting path of research, and betrayal Maeven had undertaken over the last forty years had all been leading up to this moment.

"Grace?"

Her sister's face turned only slightly, her chin and nose profile exactly as Maeven remembered it in her dreams. She had aged only a little; the benefit of living in a holy chapel perhaps. Grace said nothing in reply.

Maeven approached slowly, careful not to scare her. It had been so, so long. "Grace, it's me. It's your sister Maeven." She placed a hesitant hand on a narrow shoulder.

Grace turned. A knife in her sister's hand plunged between the necromancer's ribs. Those once-innocent blue eyes were feral and furious. "Grace is mine and we shall never be separated." Her sister's voice with her brother's venom.

Maeven lurched back, horrified. She looked into her sister using her arcane arts, and found only Amadden's soul squatting inside.

Grace began to glow, the light bright and white and blazing with divinity.

"This world must be purified for the Bright One," her brother said, using her sister's lips. "She must be protected from all that is evil and corrupt. You think you stopped me at Tarnbrooke, but I have other armies of the faithful ready to march."

Her beloved, innocent sister was gone, human soul scoured away by the torrent of belief flowing into her body. Amadden had always worshiped their sister, and he had turned her into his perfect ideal of a god, a hollow shell of a person that carried out his will.

"You destroyed her," Maeven said, choking back sobs. "You know it, and that has driven you mad."

The Bright One's head violently shook from side to side in denial. "Lies! She has ascended to a higher plane of existence to eternally watch over me."

The necromancer's horror turned to cold fury. Grace had always been unfailingly kind, often to her own detriment. She had been a good girl with humble wants and needs, and Amadden was everything that their sister never was. His possession of her body made a mockery of her entire life, and Maeven could not abide it.

Fire and lightning roared around her, but died the moment it touched Maeven's obsidian blade. Amadden's eyes – she refused to think of them as Grace's – widened as she plunged the knife into the Bright One's chest.

The might of a goddess worshipped by half of a continent was beyond mortal comprehension. Even Maeven's deadly weapon could not handle it. The blade shattered inside the deity's flesh. Although the divine power and mass of belief fought to resist, in the end, nothing could stop death incarnate. Everything died. Even gods.

The Bright One... Amadden, or whatever abomination he had become in their sister's body, was utterly destroyed. The empty corpse slumped at Maeven's feet, the last breath escaping its lips as a quiet sigh. The necromancer knelt in her sister's blood and wept.

A god died at her feet that day, and so did what was left of the necromancer's heart. She picked up the body of her sister and carried her up the stairs, out of the castle and back into the sunshine. Grace deserved to rest among trees and flowers and the open skies of the countryside, the things she had loved best. Behind her Maeven left a city burning like a pyre, its cathedral crumbling down to ruin. There was no mercy left in her now.

Maeven dug the grave beside a cherry tree that she knew Grace would have loved to watch come into bloom, then piled stones on top to deter scavengers. She sat on the grass, crying and cradling a shard of obsidian, all that was left of her knife. It no longer held a powerful enchantment, but the volcanic glass was still razor sharp, and she had nothing to live for now. She examined the veins in her wrists and set the edge of the stone to her skin.

Her hand refused to move, and the stone refused to cut. She tried again and again to no avail. And then she realised.

She was still bound by her blood oath to Lorimer Felle and his people. Until that oath was fulfilled she would never be free. She screamed and threw the shard into the distance.

Brightwater had been cleansed but there were many more Lucent soldiers and acolytes remaining in the northern towns and villages. Even though Lorimer was gone, she had sworn the people of Fade's Reach would be freed, and she had no choice but to see it done. That had been a price she happily paid to see her sister freed, and it had all been for nothing thanks to Amadden.

If she couldn't kill herself, then slaughtering every single one of those who had served her brother and oppressed Lorimer's people would have to do. If it was the last thing she ever did, she would scour her brother's great work from every nook and cranny of Essoran. She would ensure the bastard would only ever be remembered as a deluded tyrant, if at all.

EPILOGUE I

The night was bright with flickering fires and the ember-glow of smouldering buildings abandoned and left to collapse, their owners dead or missing. A cacophony of wails and sobs echoed through the streets accompanied by hysterical, relieved laughter. Tarnbrooke reeked of fire, burnt meat and loosed bowels. And blood. Delicious, fortifying blood.

After two days buried under a layer of mud and ash, dead, or close to it, Jerak Hyden slowly rose and stared at the knife holes in his clothes. The wounds in his chest had closed over into puckered red dimples, and he somehow knew his butchered heart had healed up better than before Verena's knife cut into it. His experiment with vampire blood had proven successful. He had felt the changes happening within his body while he lay there half-conscious and immobile. He would need to make more of his kind and take them apart to study the process of biological repair in greater detail.

His mind had returned to its usual state. For the most part – the scent of blood now aroused a deep hunger he had never felt in life. Almost like... Was this what lesser beings called lust? He searched the ground for his spectacles, then it occurred that his eyesight was already perfect. Every sense had been heightened, so much so he found it distracting and confusing. Not conducive to methodical research at all.

"Ow," he muttered. On probing his mouth, he discovered

his bodily desires had induced his mouth to form lengthened incisors designed to rip flesh. They were most painful and pricking his lower lip.

Interesting, he thought. Lorimer Felle had never mentioned the impracticalities of his condition. He made a further mental note and filed it away for future investigation.

"Thith will not do," he lisped. "Noth do at all." His mind ruled this body, and he willed it into submission, smiling as the fangs slowly retreated back into standard human teeth, bone cracking and resetting around them. He worked his jaw, marvelling at the pain such changes inflicted, and how irrelevant such a thing seemed now. Increased pain tolerance. Noted.

As an immortal being he now had no fear of age and disability and had all the time in the world to research and experiment. "So much to do, so much to do." All the time in the world and yet it would never be enough. There was more to existence than this mortal realm had to offer, and his very being burned with the need to study and experiment, to know everything about everything.

This new body he inhabited was far superior to a frail mortal man, but it was still dependant on blood and meat, and probably sleep, for survival. The artificial body he had created had proven to be an abject failure, but a good alchemist learned from failure, and he was certain with enough time and proper materials he could craft a far superior and more stable form for his consciousness.

"Jerak Hyden, the man-made god!" He liked the sound of his own words.

All he needed now were a few dozen subjects to begin perfecting the process. He would turn them into vampires, remove their limbs and hang them from hooks, draining their blood to power his new creations.

"That will not be happening."

He stopped and spun, but nobody was near.

"Behind you."

He spun again. Nothing.

His back vibrated with laughter. He peered back to see an inhuman mouth had formed on the rear of his shoulder. He screamed and reached back with clawed hands, ripped his own flesh free and tossed it onto the embers of a ruined building.

He stared after it, panting, one arm hanging limp.

"Pointless."

It was on the other shoulder now – another mouth, the skin darkening around open lips. "You willingly took my blood into your veins, Jerak Hyden. You ate the flesh of my spawn, my own flesh and blood. Like calls to like, and a body is naught but clothes to me."

"No, no, please, Lorimer," the alchemist begged as his body began to change, to grow tall and strong, dark-skinned and supple. "I am so very close to perfection."

"There is only room for one perfect being in this body," Lorimer Felle said. "However, I shall let you live for all the good work you have done here."

Jerak Hyden sobbed in relief even as his flesh was stolen from him and altered, flowing like water. "Thank you. Thank you. My great work to advance humanity is everything to me."

The vampire lord's mocking laughter answered him, his new body looming large over the alchemist's dwindling bag of flesh and bone.

Lorimer Felle took possession of the body and excreted all that was left of Jerak Hyden into a mewling bag of skin dangling in his hand. He used his vampiric flesh crafting arts on what was left of the alchemist to strip away muscle and bone, and to craft a loathsome new body to house the alchemist's consciousness: a limbless slug the size of a small dog, one with horrified human eyes.

"You will live, but you will never speak with a human tongue. You will read no book and write no journals. You will craft nothing. You will learn nothing. You are nothing."

Jerak Hyden screamed, a wet bubbling escaping soft sluggish mouthparts.

"You are loathsome vermin in my sight," Lorimer said as he dropped the creature that had been Jerak Hyden into a muddy puddle filled with refuse. "Sup on rot and decay as you deserve."

The vampire lord wrapped himself in a blanket and walked barefoot towards the northern edge of town where he could sense his manservant already awaited him. Estevan bowed in greeting, his wide-brimmed hat with its red feather bobbing in the crown, now somewhat foxed. He was accompanied by a scruffy donkey bearing heavy saddlebags already packed for travel. Red Penny was with him, bound in stained bandages and covered in bruises but carrying Amogg Hadakk's massive axe over one shoulder like it weighed nothing. She offered a respectful nod in greeting. A small girl at her side watched him with oddly fierce eyes.

"Thank you for fighting with us," Red Penny said, a strangely abashed expression on her face. "We are alive only thanks to you and the others."

Lorimer studied the girl and the heavy axe. "That," he said, "is not normal."

She snorted. "What is normal now? My new god charges me to build a cairn for Amogg and then return the axe of her ancestors to the Hadakk and tell them of her glory. He owes her that... uh, speaking of which..."

The little girl stepped forward and handed Lorimer a bucket and a filthy old rag.

"What is this for, child?" he demanded.

The girl steepled her fingers in prayer and grinned. "For toileting. The god of courage says you are full of shit."

Before Lorimer could fully process, Red Penny flushed, scooped the girl up under an arm and set off at a brisk pace back towards the centre of town with a hearty, "Safe travels!"

"What just happened?" Lorimer asked, staring at the bucket and rag.

Estevan unsuccessfully tried to stifle his mirth. "It would

seem that Tiarnach, too, has survived the death of his body. The townsfolk seem to have adopted him as their god of courage, so I imagine their belief somehow sustained his spirit."

Lorimer shot Estevan a betrayed look and flung Tiarnach's gifts to the mud. He pulled on his clean clothing and then turned to look over the town one last time.

"I suppose there are worse people to meet again," he said. "So long as it is not more than once a century. Never leave me alone with these fools, Estevan."

The old man smiled and looked away, embarrassed. "I shall endeavour to survive, my lord."

"Are you sure you do not wish to become a vampire?" Lorimer asked, again.

"Thank you for your kind offer, my lord," Estevan replied. "But I fear I am too soft-hearted for such a life."

The vampire patted his shoulder. "So be it, my loyal friend." He looked to the north. "Now to collect on the debt that Maeven owes me. Fade's Reach must be liberated, and the remnants of the Lucent Empire will not willingly loosen its grip on our lands."

He knew Maeven would betray him all over again given half a chance, but he was more than her match. Once his people were free, he would prove that.

EPILOGUE II

Black Herran found that dying was much like getting rid of a bellyful of bad wind, except this time her soul was the stink. It was a relief to be rid of that creaky old aching body and become a being of pure spirit.

The shadow demons she called her sisters held tight to her soul, dragging her through razor forests of volcanic glass and rivers of magma towards the black spires of Duke Shemharai's castle.

It was hardly an unexpected fate; she had made her dark bargain for power long ago, and now that debt had come due. Her family would be safe, and whatever became of her, that was by far the most important thing she would ever do. Forty years ago she could never have imagined thinking such a thing.

The jagged towers of Duke Shemharai's castle loomed ahead, walls of black glass wreathed in fire. Flickering faces appeared inside the flames, screaming in torment. Shemharai decorated his home with many such tortured souls, a display of enormous power and wealth, given souls were the currency of Hellrath. Their howls of pain were music to his ears but Black Herran found it all very gauche.

The road to his towering keep was lined with rusty, swaying gibbets. Human souls and condemned demons hung there to be gnawed on by imps and all the lesser things of this infernal realm. Some of the prisoners reached out to her through the bars, pleading, begging and cursing as the guards escorted her past.

A handful of tattered souls recognised her. These were some of the old nobility of Essoran she had plucked with her own hands and sent down to the Duke as gifts. Those souls began to laugh and jeer. Whatever forty years of torture had done to their minds, they had not forgotten who had condemned them to this hell. The scavenging demons scattered, put off by their victim's sudden and unexpected mirth.

The door to the keep had been fashioned from the skull of an ancient dragon. The jaw lowered to admit them, yellowed fangs the size of Black Herran welcoming them into Shemharai's lair.

The path to the great hall was lined with the nobility of Hellrath, those few who didn't want Shemharai's head stuffed and mounted on their walls. Hellknights in spiked black steel wielding baroque blades watched silently as she passed, their eyes leaking eldritch flame. Barons in twisted forms of human-headed beasts capered and jeered. Robed and antlered presidents surrounded by their scribes and minions sized her up and found her wanting. Hawk-headed counts and marquises draped in jewellery forged from human souls trailed their taloned fingers across her, causing agony as they tasted but did not harm her soul.

Black Herran did not shudder or cry out. She looked them in the eye. "I will remember this," she said. More than one looked away before she was dragged onwards by her shadowy guards.

The doors yawned open with an ominous creak, revealing a smoky hall dimly lit by soul-braziers, the wails of those being consumed inside echoing through the hall's rafters. Great stained-glass windows looked out over lakes of fire and smoke.

On a dais sat a throne of bones bound in stretched human skin. Perched atop a cushion of living, moaning flesh, sat the great Duke Shemharai – a bloated toad the size of a war horse with eyes and tongue of flame. Two hellknights with bodies of black iron and razor-edged claws flanked him.

Her guards dragged her forward, and the assembled demon nobility filtered into the hall after her. The shadow demons let go of her and grovelled low before flowing away into the corners of the gloomy hall.

"Black Herran," Shemharai said, purple lips smacking and spraying spittle. "I gave you power in exchange for many promises, not all of which came to pass. Your debt has come due, and for your failures you will service me from now until the time your pathetic little human soul wears out."

Black Herran did not much care to spend her afterlife wasting time on pleasantries and pretty talk. She got right down to business.

"You really are a jumped-up little toad, Shem. The very last thing I will be doing is listening to an incompetent like you."

Silence. Absolute shocked silence filled the great hall. Even the tortured souls burning in the braziers ceased their screaming for a moment.

Shemharai laughed, a wet squelching of slick skin folds and flaps. "Your human arrogance always did amuse me, wretch. It will be a great pleasure to train you to grovel at my feet. Your screams will be delicious music to my ears." His eyes burned bright and his flaming tongue licked drooling fat lips.

Black Herran looked at the assembled nobles of Hellrath and smirked, then scoured her gaze all the way round the rest. Some few who had intimate, sorcerous dealings with her in the past quickly slipped back into the crowd and made for the door. How wise of them.

Black Herran's gaze settled on the Duke's iron guards. "Alas, poor little Shem, left so vulnerable without dead Malifer's protection. You always relied on his might far too much."

The great Duke flopped forward on his throne, mottled flesh bulging grotesquely. "The problem with mortals is that they think so very much of themselves when they are naught but food and entertainment. You have no power here, wretch. No magical rings on withered flesh and bone.

No allies, no hope. Your arrogance earns you only more imaginative agony."

Black Herran snorted. "I have earned my arrogance by being prepared, and you have never been imaginative. Did you think I sat on my arse for forty years patiently waiting for you to claim my soul? What a fool. The problem with you, Shem, is that you treat your underlings like property, and that does not earn loyalty, only fear. I, on the other hand, earn both. Now, my sisters."

The world outside the great windows turned black. Then the screaming began, wails of panic and pain swiftly working their way deeper inside the castle.

Shemharai loosed a great belch and his two guards launched themselves at her, iron fangs and claws seeking to rend her soul. She stood her ground, and the smoky hall exploded as hundreds of her shadowy sisters slipped through the cracks in the stonework and sank their fangs and claws deep into the assembled nobility. Alone, shadow demons were considered weaklings, but nobody had ever seen so many working together. They had never suspected she had bred and fed so many of them.

Some of Shemharai's own guards turned and slew their brethren, closed the door to the hall and turned their blades upon any of the exalted guests trying to escape. Howls and hisses filled the air as burning black blood slicked the floor. The iron guards' claws dug into the shadow demons, shredding her sisters with ease while their own hardened bodies only bore shallow furrows from the weaker demons. But the numbers flooding the great hall began to tell, and the guards were worn down, carved up and cracked open for her sisters to feast on their hearts.

Some of the greatest demons present to witness her humiliation were already down, a handful of counts and presidents were swarmed and torn apart before they even knew what was happening, some stabbed in the back by their own underlings. Knots of barons and hellknights desperately fought the shadowy tide swamping them, burning swords, sorcery and talons slaying dozens of her sisters. An unstoppable torrent flowed in from outside to fill in the gaps.

In front of Black Herran, three of the oldest and greatest of her shadow demons rose up, great hulking black things with obsidian claws and fangs far larger than their kind normally produced.

"How did you breed this army?" Shemharai demanded. "You have not the personal power to sustain them. Which of the other dukes aids you? Tell me and I will devour you quickly."

"I prepared for this day alone," she said, "right from that moment we made our tawdry little deal. I took a weak little shadow demon you only used for spying and made a binding pact with it and all the progeny of its future bloodline. Mortal souls are the currency of Hellrath, Shem, and those I had in plenty. While I was conquering Essoran, I sent untold thousands of souls down to birth and feed this army of mine, and for the last forty years my sisters have feasted and grown strong. Every enemy I encountered and disposed of in the years of peace since then only added to their strength. And then came the Lucent Empire and the Falcon Prince – the perfect way to amass power far in excess of your own. I admit, I may have meddled a little in that whole debacle. Somebody had to give that dolt the idea to forge an empire. While you demons made your little deals and picked off souls here and there I reaped the souls of my enemies like fields of wheat."

"I own you," Shemharai screamed as his allies died all around him. "My name has been carved into your very soul."

Black Herran cackled and held up her hand. "You may own my soul, Shemharai, but Hellrath's greatest law is might makes for right: you can only keep what you can take and hold – and when I kill you that claim is void. With Malifer destroyed, you are doomed."

The air surrounding Shemharai ignited, cloaking his mottled flesh in eldritch fire. His tongue lashed out and garrotted one of the oldest of her minions, burning right through its shadowy neck. Whatever else Shemharai was, he was still a

Duke of Hellrath, grown fat and powerful after feasting on human souls for thousands of years. The shadows swamped him, nipping and tearing at his fiery flesh. Many of her sisters perished, burnt to ash with a single touch.

Black Herran looked back at the entrance to the great hall. The path out had been cleared, and those surviving nobles still trapped were pressed up against the wall, using sorcery and skill to ward off the dark tide of fangs and claws seeking to devour their hearts.

Shemharai laughed, his webbed hands taking a dreadful toll of the lesser demons swarming around him. "I am a duke! This pitiful collection of rejects cannot bring me down." Black Herran's demons hissed and leapt on him in a fury, and for a moment drove him to his knees, but their attempts to actually hurt him only succeeded in inflicting scratches.

Two of Shemharai's turncoat guards opened the doors to admit a group of her demons laden down with heavy clay pots, the lids carefully sealed with thick wax.

Black Herran waved them onwards. "That may be true, Shem, but who said I was only relying on the weapons of your kind? I had my shadow demons steal one of the mad alchemist's little creations. I enhanced it especially for you."

The demons leapt into the melee wielding the heavy pots like rocks, shattering them against the Duke's hard hide. Dirty green liquid slopped all over Shemharai, extinguishing his flames. He turned and ripped his attackers' heads from their bodies, and as the rest of the pack backed away from him he waited, confused as to what her plan entailed. His dread armies would already be on their way to the castle and any delay could only benefit him. Or so he imagined.

Black Herran thought that Jerak Hyden would have loved to take notes as the acid ate into the Duke's demonic flesh. Large patches of his outer hide blistered and sloughed off. He howled, dived and rolled as if it was some kind of fire he could extinguish. Then his burning hate-filled eyes fixed on her.

She backpedalled, her demonic sisters sacrificing themselves to slow the Duke down. His eyes never left her as his inner hide bubbled and crisped, flaking and falling away to reveal soft pulsing pink patches.

He almost caught her, his tongue curling around her ankle. One of her demons brought a slain hellknight's barbed blade down to sever his tongue just in time. The Duke reeled back, squealing and spraying blood everywhere.

The Duke was wounded and panicking as claws dug into the acid-burned holes in his thick hide. He rolled and flailed, threatened, raged and ate lesser demons whole. But eventually, he fell, one leg ripped free and gnawed on as the pack flayed him alive. The demon wielding the sword rammed it through his bloated belly, pinning the Duke to the floor of his own castle.

Black Herran picked up a fallen knife and approached. She plunged it into his bloated body and tried to slit him open from neck to groin, but found his demonic flesh still too tough. Her suborned hellknights did the butchery for her, cracking open bone and sinew to reveal the mewling Duke's pulsing black heart.

She cut it free and held it aloft in victory, then she sank her teeth into it.

Duke Shemharai shuddered and lifted a flayed hand towards her. "Please... I will..."

She tore a chunk of tough muscle free and began to chew. Thick black liquid gushed down her throat. His heart-blood burned like fine whisky as it slid down the gullet of her soul. When it hit her stomach that heat began building to a furnace. She bit and tore and endured the searing agony. With every bite she took a portion of Shemharai's power for her own, but her will was equal to the task. She didn't even notice when he perished.

She dropped to her knees as the changes began: skin turning dark and hard, fingers and nails growing into vicious claws, her short white hair growing out into a night-dark silken veil. Her human soul was becoming demonic, something only one of supreme willpower and arcane might could endure. She had finally succeeded in forcing her way into the great game of realms, gods and greater powers. Conquering Essoran had been such a petty ambition.

The newest Duke of Hellrath rose to her taloned feet and swept black hair back into hard spikes. Her burning eyes swept across all assembled in her throne room. All cowered before her.

She turned to her shadow demons, her dark sisters. "Bring me my mortal family. Be swift about it." She waited in silence for their return, and none dared raise their voice or lift so much as a finger as the hours passed.

Eventually, her demons returned from the caverns beneath Hellrath's Shadowlands, seeping through the walls to pool in front of her. A human hand poked through, followed by her daughter Heline's head. She peered around the still throne room and then focused on what had been her mother. She stared until recognition dawned. Then she sighed and clambered out, lowering a hand to pull out her sons. Tristan and Edmond stood beside her, gawping at their grandmother and the assembled host of demons.

"Mother," Heline said, arms crossed. "I assume this means you won. Don't go thinking we will be prostrating ourselves before you though." Demons shifted, nervous about her tone when talking to their Duke.

"Shemharai is dead," Black Herran said, rising from her throne and flowing towards her family. "There will be no prostration. We are family." She reached out a taloned hand and Tristan flinched back.

She stifled a sudden rage and carefully lowered her arm – it seemed she had some adjusting to do in this new body of hers. "The Lucent Empire is no more," she said. "The threat is ended and you can go home. Hellrath is no fit place to raise children."

Heline shook her head sadly. "Return to Tarnbrooke is impossible. We are the blood of Black Herran, and that will never be forgotten."

"Then we shall prepare you a new home in the mortal lands,"

Black Herran replied. "One far away from fanatics, demons, and disaster. There you can live a long and happy life."

"We were happy before," Heline said. "When you were just Dalia."

For once, Black Herran had no answer to something.

Her daughter took a deep breath, stepped forward and wrapped her arms around her demonic mother, heedless of spikes pricking her flesh. "I love you."

Duke Herran trembled. She cleared her throat and blinked away hot tears of black blood. "Yes, well. I think perhaps you should learn some rudimentary demonology before we send you back to Essoran. I wouldn't want you to be a stranger."

Heline's eyes narrowed. "No demonic deals."

"No deals."

Her daughter nodded, then stepped back and took her sons' hands. She looked around the throne room at all the dreadful demons and sniffed, unimpressed. "It's a decent start, I'll give you that. As for you lot, I wager my mother will be running this whole place soon enough. Best not to get in her way if you know what's good for you."

Duke Herran of Hellrath liked the sound of ruling this place. That would come in time, as would her vengeance on Maeven. She flexed her taloned fingers and smiled. Nobody could be allowed to stab her in the heart and get away with it – it would be bad for her reputation. Maeven deserved an eternity of agony for her own actions. Sooner or later, somebody would kill her, especially if given the right nudges. Then she would be there to collect her old captain's wicked soul – and what a weapon she would forge from it.

Duke Herran sat on her throne and vowed to make this the beginning of a reign that would make mortals, demons and even Elder Gods tremble at the very mention of her name.

ACKNOWLEDGEMENTS

Finishing this book off during the Covid-19 pandemic has been… interesting. On the one hand, creativity had nosedived under the relentless assault of horrible news, local lockdowns and the general awfulness of 2020. On the other, it's been great having the distractions of editing and polishing up the manuscript and the hope of good things coming in the future. Somehow I've managed to muddle through it all more or less intact…

As always, thanks go to Natasha, my family, friends, and my fellow writers who have all been incredibly supportive – something much needed and very much appreciated over the last two years! I hope to see you all again sometime soon once this dastardly pandemic is over.

Special thanks go to Ed Wilson, agent extraordinaire, and the ever-wonderful team at Angry Robot.

ANGRY ROBOT

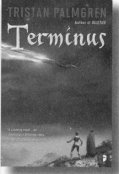

We are Angry Robot

angryrobotbooks.com

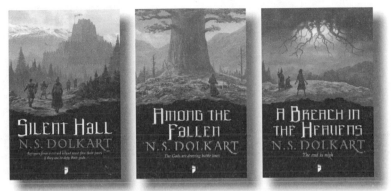

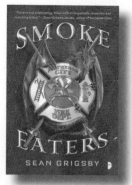

We are Angry Robot

angryrobotbooks.com

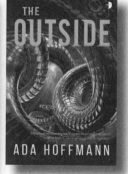